THE LITTLE BOOKSHOP BY THE HARBOR

JEAN STONE

kensingtonbooks.com

KENSINGTON BOOKS are published by

Kensington Publishing Corp.
900 Third Avenue
New York, NY 10022

ISBN: 978-1-4967-4302-2
ISBN: 978-1-4967-4303-9 (ebook)

First Kensington Trade Paperback Printing: May 2026

10 9 8 7 6 5 4 3 2 1

Printed in the United States of America

The authorized representative in the EU for product safety and compliance
is eucomply OU, Parnu mnt 139b-14, Apt 123
Tallinn, Berlin 11317, hello@eucompliancepartner.com

For Liliana

PRAISE FOR JEAN STONE'S VINEYARD NOVELS

"Filled with heart. . . . Perfect for long summer days. For fans of Debbie Macomber or Elin Hilderbrand." —*Booklist*

"Lie down on the couch, put a pillow under your head and enjoy the ride." —*The Vineyard Gazette*

"Annie Sutton is finally realizing her dream of living on Martha's Vineyard, when a surprise package is left outside her cottage door . . . a baby in a basket. The diverse characters, strong setting, and clever mystery surrounding baby Bella brims with holiday cheer readers will relish." —*Library Journal*

"Stone herself lives on the Island, and we can feel her love for it throughout." —*Martha's Vineyard Times*

PRAISE FOR JEAN STONE'S PREVIOUS NOVELS

"Stone's graceful prose, vivid imagery and compassionately drawn characters make this one a standout."
—*Publishers Weekly*

"A very smart and well-written book." —*Fresh Fiction*

"Stone is a talented novelist whose elegant prose brings the Martha's Vineyard setting vividly to life. . . . A very good read." —*Milwaukee Journal Sentinel*

"A wrenching and emotionally complex story. Sometimes, if you are very lucky, you can build a bridge across all obstacles. A very touching read." —*RT Book Reviews*

Books by Jean Stone

The Up-Island Series
Up-Island Harbor
The Little Bookshop by the Harbor

The Martha's Vineyard Series
A Vineyard Christmas
A Vineyard Summer
A Vineyard Morning
A Vineyard Crossing
A Vineyard Wedding
A Vineyard Season

Second Chances Series
Once Upon a Bride
Twice Upon a Wedding
Three Times a Charm
Four Steps to the Altar

Also . . .
Sins of Innocence
First Loves
Ivy Secrets
Places by the Sea
Birthday Girls
Tides of the Heart
The Summer House
Off Season
Trust Fund Babies
Beach Roses
Vineyard Magic

Books by Jean Stone writing as Abby Drake
The Secrets Sisters Keep
Perfect Little Ladies
Good Little Wives

Prologue

Amped. Pulsating. Ready for fun. The sun was warmer; the sky, clearer; the water, bluer. It was the day before Memorial Day weekend; the place was Martha's Vineyard.

Scanning the tiny harbor of Menemsha, Maddie surveyed the cluster of pleasure boats bobbing in their moorings, the perfectly sculpted dunes sprinkled with tall, waving seagrass, the *Rosa rugosa* bushes thick with fragrant pink blossoms—all prepped for the new season, all awaiting the onrush of tourists that would start the next day.

She winced.

It was supposed to be her first full, beautiful summer on the island, though after returning nearly a year ago, she often felt as if she'd never lived anywhere else. Her Wampanoag heritage whispered that her soul had never left.

But as she sat at the café table on the deck of her brand-spanking-new bookshop, Maddie feared if she clenched the handle of her teacup any more tightly, razor-sharp porcelain splinters would slice up her palm.

Closing her eyes, she inhaled a shallow breath of sea air, wishing she knew what to do, now that her hopes and dreams and every risk that she'd taken to reboot her future had exploded in a single, vicious, gut-wrenching twist.

And she wondered if, dear God, she should tell Grandma.

Chapter 1

October
Seven months earlier

"*Wake up!*" Grandma Nancy bellowed, jostling Maddie from sleep.

Maddie, however, was done grading students' papers and had earmarked a few days for taking a break to have fun. She hadn't expected it would start so soon after dawn.

"I hear a car out on the road!" Grandma prattled as she stood in the bedroom doorway, her frail, wiry frame lightly bouncing in her ancient slippers that might have been as old as she was. Her dark eyes were wide with joy, her chestnut-shaded skin multiwrinkled yet radiant, her stubborn white hair only partly corralled by a beaded headband.

The dirt road wasn't often used off-season; the vehicle on it most likely was a taxi, with Maddie's son, Rafe, in the passenger seat. To have caught the first boat, he must have left Amherst in the middle of the night; he'd planned to get a cab at the ferry terminal because, as a college senior, he'd said he did not need his mother to trek down to Vineyard Haven on a Sunday morning simply to greet him.

Oh, how Maddie loved her kid.

"I bet he's excited about Cranberry Day!" Grandma's ninety-year-old body seemed exhilarated, as if, like Maddie and Rafe, this would be her first time taking part in the centuries-old tradition.

Maddie rubbed her eyes. "I'm excited, too, Grandma. I never expected I'd be part of a cranberry harvest." Her voice was still filled with sleep; she hadn't intended to sound snide.

"You have much to learn, Granddaughter." The old woman pretended to huff as she spun around and probably smiled as she faced the front door where Rafe would enter. After all, Nancy Clieg's great-grandson was a gift that had resurrected her gusto for life. Maddie was grateful for that.

And though she was looking forward to the festivities, she was even more thrilled to have time with her son, a luxury that had been scarce since she'd come to the island last summer and stayed to look after her grandmother.

Pulling herself from beneath the quilt, she grabbed her clothes and headed for the bathroom to perform her ablutions—a favorite old British expression for grooming that her father once said was appropriate since they lived on the second floor of a nineteenth-century Victorian mansion in Green Hills, as far west in Massachusetts as one could get before falling into Upstate New York. Maddie had been born and raised in that house; it also was where she'd returned after her divorce, toting her then three-year-old son, and where she'd become determined to reinvent herself as a single mom and career woman. So she and Rafe had lived in the house with her father, Stephen Clarke, a retired professor at the local college where Maddie wound up teaching, too, though she now did it remotely. Life in Green Hills had been quiet, predictable, safe; their home hadn't burned down the way that Grandma's almost had two months ago.

Maddie sighed, then quickly bundled into an alpaca

sweater and yesterday's jeans. The cabin, where she and Grandma were staying until renovations to the cottage were done, was cozy and well heated. One drawback, however, was the persistent autumn wind that often swept up from Vineyard Sound and circled around and around the compact but somewhat drafty two-bed, one-bath structure that had been built fifty years earlier and was mostly used in summers.

Bang, bang, bang. A fist hammered on the bathroom door.

"Hurry up!" Grandma barked. "They're pulling into the driveway!"

"Yes, ma'am!" Maddie saluted because Grandma couldn't see her.

Dabbing light blush on her coppery-burnished cheeks (a shade lighter than Grandma's) and a touch of gloss to her lips, she heard Grandma open the front door and shout: "You're here!" which was followed by Rafe's jubilant laugh.

Maddie slipped into the living room as her six-foot-one, or maybe -two now, one-and-only child stepped inside and nearly swallowed her grandmother into his long arms. Though Grandma was, indeed, spunkier since they'd reconnected last summer, sometimes she looked tinier by the day.

"Hi, honey," Maddie said after waiting her turn, then hugging Rafe, who, though seven or eight inches taller than his mom, did not swallow her. "How was the trip?"

"Long."

He looked even more handsome than when she'd last seen him. If nothing else, Maddie's ex-husband, Owen, had given their son a few decent genes, though she was proudly accountable for Rafe's shining charcoal hair (identical to hers) and his perfect, coppery skin (lighter than Maddie's)—testaments to their Indigenous ancestors. But though she'd also like to lay claim to Rafe's clear blue eyes (a shade of the island sky), Owen's eyes also were blue, so she supposed it was a draw. At least Rafe had Maddie's father's sharp mind and her sensitivity, the latter of which was why, when Rafe had come to the Vineyard for the first time in August and learned of his true heritage, he'd wanted to stay. Thankfully, Maddie convinced him to return to college and finish his degree. With his academic focus on economics and environmental studies, she knew he'd be able to contribute a lot to the island and the Wampanoag tribe—now that he knew he was one of them.

"Never mind the hugging," Grandma Nancy interrupted. "I want to know if Rafe has a girlfriend. I want a great-great-grandkid before I croak."

"I'm waiting to find a nice Wampanoag girl," he said. "So I can carry on our Indigenous line."

"Well . . ." Grandma replied, unexpectedly flustered, "stop dilly-dallying, okay? I'm not getting any younger."

"Yeah," a familiar voice mocked from the porch. "Stop dilly-dallying. I've got berries to pick."

Maddie laughed with surprise as Rex Winsted (the gentle giant, as she liked to think of him) entered the cabin, which he owned. He also owned—and was the chef at—the fabulous Lord James restaurant on the water in downtown Edgartown. He was the same height as Rafe but broader, and unlike Rafe's full head of hair, Rex was totally bald. "By nature and Norelco," the fifty-something man once told her.

"Don't tell me you were Rafe's taxi driver." Maddie's gaze darted between Rex and her son.

"A coincidence, Mom. He called late last night and said he had to come up-island early this morning, so he offered to pick me up at the boat."

"You 'had to' make a trip up here at this hour?" Grandma asked Rex.

"I did," he said, his bright, cinnamon eyes twinkling impishly, as they sometimes did. "In case you didn't know, it's not only Indigenous Peoples' weekend. It's also the last long weekend for leaf peepers and tour busses, so we non-Indigenous folks have to work. Which includes picking the last of my berry crop so I can make today's special—blueberry buckle—always a hit with visitors." He held out an empty tin pail as proof of his mission. "But have a great day Tuesday. I've heard it's a memorable event."

"Easy for you to say," Grandma grumbled. "I haven't foraged for anything, let alone cranberries, since I was eighty-nine. We'll see how long I last."

"Right," Rex said. "My bet is you'll survive."

Rafe thanked him for the ride, then Rex waved his pail in good-bye, and jogged back down the porch steps and around to the backyard—his backyard—where Maddie hoped she'd left enough blueberries for his buckle, whatever that was.

After whipping up pancakes and adding the berries she'd looted the previous day, Maddie joined Grandma and Rafe at the small table that abutted the kitchen counter. Tucking into his breakfast, Rafe shared stories about college life, his studies, and his favorite thing, the rowing team. Two important regattas, one in Cambridge, the other in Saratoga Springs, New York, were still on the horizon before the fall season ended. Grandma nodded, mesmerized by all he said. Watching her watching Rafe made Maddie think about her father, alone in the Victorian back in Green Hills: He would love to be with them.

"I'm here until Wednesday morning," Rafe continued, "so can I camp out on the couch 'til then? I promised to help Joe set up tables and stuff tomorrow for the potluck dinner on Tuesday. Which leaves today and cranberry-picking day for us to be together. Okay?"

Joe was Grandma Nancy's much younger half brother, who'd helped Maddie in many ways since she'd showed up in July. Surprisingly, she'd remembered his lanky frame, his soft mahogany complexion, and the trademark ponytail he'd had even when she was a little girl. Rafe had developed a special bond with Joe, who was close to Maddie's father in age, yet worlds apart in spirit, style, and outlook on life. Where Stephen—like those of his 100 percent White, British heritage—was pensive and reserved in manner and dress, Joe was casual and open, and exuded innate calm. He'd introduced Rafe to their Wampanoag culture, and Rafe gobbled every morsel.

"The sofa's yours if you want it," Maddie said, sipping her strong coffee. "And I'm glad you'll be helping Joe."

"My brother isn't getting any younger," Grandma butted in. "Despite that he tries to act like he's still twenty-five when his half great-grandson is around." Nancy and Joe were born nearly two decades apart, yet they were close. Unlike Grandma, Joe hadn't married or had children, and he seemed to like having a family—especially with Rafe now part of it.

Rafe flashed a white-toothed smile. "Thanks. And Grandma? Not to change the subject, but I've been wondering if you'll help me with something." He leaned closer. "Will you teach me how to weave your baskets?"

Grandma Nancy's eyebrows shot up, their spikey white and black hairs springing out in every direction. "What?"

Her handmade baskets were legendary. Maddie had learned about them when Rex and his friend Francine showed up at Grandma's cottage in July, wanting to buy one for a friend's baby. It turned out that for carting pies and cakes to potlucks, keeping knitting and embroidery essentials together, and even safely toting babies, Grandma Nancy's handwoven Wampanoag baskets had been in demand for decades.

"Joe says nobody makes them like you do," Rafe continued. "I saw some in your storage unit at the airport when I was here before. They're so cool. And traditional, right?"

"Y-y-yes," Grandma stammered, as if she'd suddenly become confused, an occasional occurrence. "But I never taught anyone how to make them. I-I-I don't think I know how to do that."

"Sure you do," he said. "I'm a fast learner. Besides, somebody taught you, right? Was it your mother?"

She shook her head. "No. My grandmother Gladys. Gladys Nightingale."

Spotted Fawn. Maddie remembered finding the names of their ancestors in an old family Bible. Spotted Fawn had been Nancy's grandmother's Wampanoag name—Maddie's maternal great-great-grandmother, and Rafe's great-great-great. *Wow,* she thought. *How wonderful that Rafe wants to revive a tribal art.*

"How about if we start over Christmas break?" he was asking. "I'll be here a couple of weeks, so maybe you'll have time to teach me then?"

Maddie didn't ask what he thought Grandma did that could possibly keep her too busy to be with him. Nor did she ask how he would spend the rest of his winter break beyond the "couple of weeks" he'd be there. Chances were, Rafe's father had booked what had become an annual New Year's cruise-ship Caribbean vacation for him, his second wife, their twin daughters, and Rafe. Owen didn't know that his son hated the crowds, the ridiculous games (as Rafe called them), and the midnight buffets. Or that Rafe mostly occupied himself by babysitting his now nine-year-old half sisters because, as he'd told Maddie, it was more fun. Every year, he read *Treasure Island* to them, showed them magic tricks, and helped them master swimming, though the pool was jam-packed and the water too warm. He also said he counted the hours until each cruise would be over.

Grandma lowered her voice and said, "I stopped making baskets because of my arthritis. I'm not sure I can do it anymore."

"Maybe you can if we work together?" Rafe asked. "I bet there's still a good market for them. And the project might help keep both of us out of trouble."

Maddie stifled a giggle; Grandma, however, let out a big laugh, and, of course, would not say no to him. So she spit out a string of questions about what size baskets he wanted to make, and if he'd like to use ash or hickory, wide planks or thin strips. As they exchanged ideas, Grandma stuttered less and became more animated, and Maddie's heart swelled with love for them both. Then, as Maddie finished her breakfast, she spotted a figure outside passing by the window. Rex. She quickly stood, then scooted out the front door and down the steps.

"Did I leave you enough?" she asked, prepared to apologize for having raided the last of his blueberry crop.

"Got plenty." He tipped his pail to show a hefty mound of luscious-looking blue orbs. "I know where they hide."

"Great. Well, happy cooking. Or baking. Whatever it entails." She brushed back a runaway shock of her not-quite-shoulder-length hair, shoved her hands in the pockets of her jeans, and rocked back and forth a little. "And thanks again for picking up Rafe."

"Happy to help. Like I said, I had to come up-island anyway." He gestured to the pail again.

"Well, my son has asked Nancy to teach him how to weave her baskets. He feels like he fits in here, so thanks for all you've done to help make that happen. But I'll be sure he doesn't designate you as his personal chauffeur."

"Ha ha. I don't mind. And he does fit in, Maddie. The same way you do." The big man shifted onto one foot, and the other. Then he paused and looked at the ground. For a second, it seemed like he wanted to say something more. But instead of speaking, he lifted his chin, gave her a nice smile, and walked away toting his berries. He hopped in his truck and, as the ignition hummed, he raised his hand in a short wave. Then he deftly backed out of the bumpy, narrow dirt driveway as if he owned the place. Which, of course, he did.

As Maddie watched him go, she wondered why she felt disappointed that he hadn't said more. Trying to shrug it off, she fixed her eyes on her footing and climbed the few steps back onto the porch.

Which was where Grandma now stood at the screen door, hands on her hips.

"He left awfully fast," she groused, speaking her piece, as Grandma liked to do.

Maddie tried to act unaffected. "The Lord James will be busy today."

"Well, while you two were jabbering, Rafe and I decided we'll take a poll at the potluck about which style of baskets we should make."

"Great idea." Maddie offered half a grin and hoped that cleaning up the kitchen would dissolve her frustration. But as she maneuvered around her grandmother and went back inside, she saw Rafe standing at the sink, rinsing the dishes, and humming, so she refused to spend another second thinking about Rex. After all, life was beautiful, and friends didn't always need to know what was going on in each other's head.

And Rex was, indeed, just a friend.

Which was good, because Maddie had too much going on in her life to have room for anything more.

Chapter 2

Grandma announced she needed a nap, that she'd been up too dad-blasted early and had eaten too darned many pancakes. She teetered off to the bedroom; Maddie pitched in and she and Rafe had the kitchen spotless in no time. When they were done, she asked if he wanted to go with her to Morning Glory Farm to buy fresh ingredients for her potluck contribution.

"Corn, squash, beans," she said as they donned zippered fleeces and went outside to her old Volvo. "The Wampanoags call them the Three Sisters; they've been tribal staples for hundreds, if not thousands of years. When I was cleaning out Grandma's closet, I found her well-worn recipe for 'Three Sisters Stew.'"

"Cool," Rafe said. "But isn't it late for corn?"

She shook her head and tossed him the car keys. "No. But I have no idea why." In the Berkshires, fresh corn was gone by mid-September, but supposedly, the Vineyard often got an extra month out of its crop. She'd also heard a rumor that it didn't get as cold there or have as much snow as her hometown in the hills. As a runner, not a skier, Maddie hoped that part was true.

From his brief stay in August, Rafe remembered the way to State Road and how to get down-island to Edgartown. They rode in silence a while, each glancing outside now and then to take in the October vistas of ocean, ponds, and rolling green land decorated with red- and gold-leafed trees and white clusters of grazing sheep. "Calendar pictures," she suddenly remembered her mother calling the island views.

"This place is neat." Rafe interrupted her thoughts as he wheeled the car through Chilmark and into West Tisbury.

She agreed. A moment later she asked, "Have you thought any more about grad school?"

He paused, cleared his throat, and nodded. "Yup. And I've decided to hold off for a year."

Unlike Owen, Maddie rarely challenged Rafe's point of view. Instead, she gave him space, the way her father had given—and still gave—her. Rafe's father, however, was going to be livid. "Are you still thinking about moving here in May?"

"No," he replied.

Her heart sank a little. As badly as she'd like to see him go to grad school, she also pictured him at home here on the island, even more than she pictured herself.

Keeping a steady focus on the road, he said, "I don't have to think about it anymore, Mom. I made my decision to live here the day you told me we're Wampanoag. Maybe even before then. Like when I stepped off the ferry the first time."

Reaching across the console, she gave his shoulder a light squeeze. Then she sighed. "But if we're both living here, what will we do about your grandfather?" Though she hoped to stay with her grandmother until, well, until Nancy died, Maddie wasn't sure she could abandon Green Hills—or her father—forever. She liked it there. The upper floor—their floor—of the house was spacious and comfortable; each room was filled with shelves packed with volumes of books—eclectic titles of fiction, biographies, history, science, politics, art, and more.

When Stephen had still been teaching, he often said his dream for his "later years" had been to have a part-time job in a bookstore. Instead, since he'd retired, he'd become hooked on TV soap operas and game shows.

She shook off that last thought.

"You don't think Grandpa will want to live here if we do?" Rafe asked.

For years, Rafe and Maddie had been Stephen's only family. Other than a few distant cousins scattered in other states who communicated solely through tedious holiday letters, Stephen had no other relatives. And though he'd reconciled—sort of—with his mother-in-law, Grandma Nancy, last summer, he'd made no overture toward visiting again.

Maddie sighed. "Not counting a few long-ago memories, I'm afraid your grandfather has no reason to move here."

"But he'd have us."

"True. But let's take it a step at a time, honey." She looked out the side window as the up-island countryside glided past. She wasn't sure how to tell her son that she couldn't picture her reserved, white-shirted father—in his dress pants and leather slip-ons—relaxing on the Vineyard for more than a few days at a stretch. The closest he'd come to softening his sports-jacket-and-tie image that he'd had in the classroom was to dismiss the tie. Even now, he remained a long way from collarless, casual, denimed.

Rather than elaborating, she added, "It's hard to imagine him being happy here, Rafe. The same way I can't picture Grandma Nancy being happy in Green Hills." She didn't add that, as hopeful as she was that she'd remain there as long as Grandma was alive, Maddie also knew that one day her father might need looking after, too. With luck, the situations would not overlap one another.

Rafe laughed. "I get it. But you raised me to 'never say never' if I really want something."

"That I did," she said.

After they passed Alley's General Store, she directed him to go right; they soon reached Morning Glory and bought more things than they needed, including a cranberry-apple pie and a jug of cider. Once on the road again, Rafe asked if they could stop at Grandma's cottage so he could see how the restoration and renovations were progressing.

"Only if you tell me you meant it when you said you want a girlfriend who can carry our Indigenous line."

"I meant it. If you think it would be good."

"I think it would be wonderful. As long as you don't base your decision on that alone. Make sure you're a good match, and that you're totally, head-over-heels, crazy in love." She hoped he wouldn't ask if that's how she'd felt about Owen on her wedding day. Rafe did not need to know that her answer would have been no, that she'd mostly been trying to please her father by having his only child be married-with-children and living a life that might help him, a single dad, feel as if he'd done right by his little girl. Not that he'd ever said it.

"Mom!" Rafe cried. "This might shock you, but I've learned a few things about girls. And I do have a pretty good brain."

She laughed. "Yes, you do." But Maddie also knew when it came to relationships, bookish brains didn't always equate to being smart. At fifteen, Rafe had been in love with Kiera, a sweet girl who attended public high school and whose parents owned a luncheonette in town where Kiera worked on weekends. Maddie once thought one of the good things about the small town was that kids were protected. True, Green Hills was a college town, but other than an occasional uproar during finals week, it was peaceful. Scholarly. Secure.

Kiera O'Neill had seemed like a perfect first girlfriend for Rafe. He often came home on weekends from Deerfield, where Owen had ensconced him at the noted academy. On

Saturdays, after the luncheonette closed at three o'clock, the young couple walked down Main Street, holding hands, as if they were in a G-rated film. They stayed together throughout high school until Kiera's graduation, when she told Rafe she was pregnant. Or rather, that she *had* been pregnant, but her mother had taken her to have an abortion because Rafe "would leave for Amherst soon," "would rarely be home," and "would most likely find another girl, a college girl." With Kiera pegged for the local community college, her mother had predicted that her daughter would end up "being heart-broken, anyway."

Rafe was the one who'd been heartbroken. He left for college and, other than Christmas break, avoided going home. One night he told Maddie he kept hoping to hear from Kiera, saying she was sorry, that they'd get back together. There would be plenty of time for them to marry and have many kids, maybe even adopt one to make up for the one she hadn't had.

That was what he'd hoped.

Knowing her son was sensitive, yet strong, Maddie knew Rafe would weather the storm. And he did, though not until the end of his college freshman year when he came home and found out Kiera was married to a young man from North Adams who worked in the IT department at the art museum.

Rafe said he hadn't known that she even liked art.

Maddie refrained from pointing out that one thing had nothing to do with the other.

After that, he claimed to date "now and then." In his junior year he was with a sophomore girl (whose name Maddie couldn't remember) for a few months, but she dropped out of Amherst because she said she wanted to travel (though he later learned she'd flunked out). Rafe weathered that, too, but Maddie knew it was more like a rainy day than the Arctic blast of a Kiera-storm.

Tipping her head against the headrest now, she closed her eyes to the hum of the engine with her son adeptly at the helm. She decided that because he'd pronounced his brain as "pretty good," she'd let him find the way back to Menemsha.

And that's what he did, without assistance from his mother or GPS. Or from a girl from Green Hills or Amherst or anywhere else.

It wasn't long before they reached the cottage.

Once inside, Rafe let out a whistle. "Wow. It looks different."

Though severe fire damage had been confined to the kitchen and living room, Maddie—with Grandma's blessing—had decided to update much of the 1940s-era abode. New windows were in place; Sheetrocking would start in a few days. It would be a while before painting, light fixtures, and the grand finale, new furniture, would wrap up the goal of creating an old-but-brand-new home. For now, they had to dodge a sea of tarps and scaffolding and use their imaginations to envision the finished product.

"It won't be dark and gloomy anymore," Maddie said.

"Grandma's gonna love it," Rafe added.

Though, technically, Nancy was Rafe's great-grandmother, he, too, simply called her "Grandma," because it was easier. Besides, he'd never known his real maternal grandmother—Maddie's mother, Hannah—who'd been killed by a hit-and-run driver when Maddie was only five. As for Owen's mother, Rafe called her by her first name, Suzanne, because that was what the self-proclaimed socialite preferred.

"Grandma told me to pick out whatever I wanted for paint and furniture and anything else I thought needed replacing," Maddie said. "She said it will be mine 'one of these days,' so I might as well have it how I want. Meanwhile, I hope you're right by thinking that she'll love it."

"Are you kidding? Look how the sun's coming in," Rafe said, moving into the living room that offered a big view of the water—and would, as a bonus, showcase every acclaimed Menemsha Beach sunset.

The original cottage had two small windows along the front wall; Maddie had them replaced with nearly all glass from the corner to the front door, and from the ceiling down to thirty inches up from the new oak plank floor. In addition, the contractor had raised the roof, so the rafters were nine feet from the floor instead of seven, which meant Rafe no longer had to duck around the old beams which, like the small windows, were long gone.

Thankfully, after the fire, the insurance company had been generous. In addition, Maddie added money she'd been saving for future traveling; she'd since decided she could not think of a nicer destination than Martha's Vineyard.

"It's awesome, Mom."

She followed his gaze down the hill, outside to where Vineyard Sound curved into the harbor. Once the cottage was finished and furnished, painted and primped, Maddie knew she might want to keep it forever.

The crown jewel of the tour was the newly constructed bedroom en suite at the back. They went down the hall and stepped in.

"Wow," Rafe said again as his jaw dropped.

"My childhood playroom was once here," she said. "We called it my hobbit house, and it was a lot smaller." As in the living room, the windows were wide and tall and looked west.

The adjoining bath with its walk-in shower and spa-like soaking tub was also a big hit with Rafe. Overall, the interior would be spectacular and updated, while the exterior retained the look of an historic island cottage, albeit with larger windows and new, tan cedar shingles replacing the weathered gray ones. In a year they, too, would have adopted the silver-gray Vineyard look thanks to the sunshine and salt air.

"What about the sheds that were out back?" Rafe asked. "Are they staying or going?"

"They're already gone. They were close to collapsing before the fire."

When they were done oohing and aahing, they drove back to the cabin and allocated the afternoon to prepping for Cranberry Day.

Grandma was up from her nap, and made it her job to supervise Maddie assembling the Three Sisters Stew. Nancy explained that the seeds of the squash, beans, and corn had been planted together and flourished—the way people did—because they had grown up as a family. Maddie smiled and added garlic, onions, greens, and cornmeal.

"There will be other stews there," Grandma said, "but they'll all taste different." Then she insisted that Maddie add a secret ingredient—a splash of maple syrup. Thankfully, Rex, the chef, kept a bottle in the cabinet.

Maddie peeled the squash and chopped it into chunks with Grandma close at hand, not unlike how Stephen enjoyed watching his daughter make dinner. She missed him now; a soft edge of homesickness nudged her.

Thankfully, Rafe interrupted. "How disappointed will my father be if I don't go into the investment business with him and don't want my life to revolve around a country club like his does?" It was an unexpected question, though maybe it wasn't.

Maddie blinked. "I think you know the answer." There was no point in saying Owen would be crushed and probably angry. He also would be embarrassed when his business and golf partners asked what had happened to his only son.

She tried not to consider it a victory for her. She really did.

Then Grandma fiddled with the salt and pepper mills on the slate countertop. "You're serious about wanting to live here, Rafe?"

"Totally, Grandma."

"Well, it isn't all beach roses and daydreams. If you don't believe me, ask your mother."

As Maddie hadn't yet spent a winter on the island, she wondered if Grandma had mixed her up with Hannah, Maddie's mother.

"Why don't you tell me what it's really like, Grandma?" Rafe asked sweetly, as if he, too, had picked up on the flaw but had the grace not to correct her.

So while Grandma spewed a monologue about the harsh winds at the cliffs in January and how the cold air and gray sky sometimes made folks ornery, Maddie realized she could not cut her father out of their lives. She also knew he would not want to join them; Green Hills was where the memories of his beloved wife were set, and, though Hannah had died on the Vineyard, she was buried in Green Hills. *No*, Maddie thought. *He would not want to leave.*

Stripping the husk from another ear of corn, she scraped the kernels into a bowl, wondering why life had to be so complicated when so much of it now seemed so right.

Monday morning, Rafe left for Aquinnah to help Joe set up for Tuesday's celebration. With Grandma content to park in the overstuffed chair by the fireplace in Rex's cabin and browse through the rest of her recipes that were unearthed from the ashes at the cottage, Maddie decided to go for a run on the beach.

Clad in her Nikes, yoga pants, and a thick sweatshirt, she jogged down the driveway. But as she reached the road, a taxi pulled over and stopped. To her surprise, her father got out.

She froze. "Dad?"

He was dressed in the gray wool coat he'd bought last year because he said his hair was getting whiter by the day and that flyaway strands didn't show as much when they landed on a similar shade. He also wore the gray and light blue, Scotch plaid scarf Maddie gave him one Christmas. Though it was only two months since she'd seen him, somehow, he looked older and a bit shorter than his former five foot ten.

"Yes, I'm the old man you call Dad," he replied with a comical grin. He handed the cabbie cash, then hoisted his overnight bag onto his shoulder. As the taxi made a U-turn, Stephen gave his daughter a quick hug. "I decided if Rafe wouldn't come to Green Hills, Green Hills would come to him." He was a kind man, but his sense of humor often missed a beat. "He said he'd be here for Cranberry Day."

"Seriously?" She wished she hadn't sounded startled. Rafe, after all, was his grandson, and they'd always been close. Maybe her father had sensed that the island was stealing Rafe from him. "I mean, yes, he arrived. Tomorrow's the big day."

He gestured toward her shoes. "You out for a run?"

She swallowed. She supposed he wasn't there only to see Rafe. Most likely, he missed her, too.

"Just a short run to the beach. I can go later." She said "later" as if "later" he'd be gone, as if she expected he'd reserved a round-trip cab ride to and from the ferry, that he'd drive the journey of multiple hours back to Green Hills in the same day he'd arrived. "How long can you stay?" she swiftly added.

"Actually," he replied, "I'd like to join you for tomorrow's festivities. I've never been to Cranberry Day, though your mother told me stories about it every fall."

Pressing her lips together, Maddie tried to look happy. It wasn't often that he mentioned her mother, as if the mere word was too painful. "Well, you're certainly in time to taste-test my Three Sisters Stew," she said.

Then she took his arm and led him up to the cabin. And wondered how she was going to tell him that, except for the potluck tomorrow night, Cranberry Day was only for tribal members. Which did not include him.

So Rafe is serious about living here. Which means Maddie will want to live here, too. I never expected, or particularly wanted, her to stay. Why would I? I got to be ninety years old without needing to dig up the past like a load of clams, only to find out they were rotted, pecked to death by the gulls.

No. I never wanted my granddaughter to become an island girl. The risk is—always has been—too great.

All I wanted was to see her. After forty years I deserved that much. I thought if I saw her from afar that would be enough. But before I knew it, I was forced into sharing Rex's cabin with her, talking to her, getting to know grown-up Madelyn. Doing things like trying to decipher these old recipes for her. But I'm glad I showed her some things from the past. And told her good things about her heritage. Because Stephen wouldn't have known what to tell her.

And Maddie was entitled to know the good things.

Not the other stuff.

No. Not that.

She's been here a few months now. Long enough to know that reality isn't always the fluffy lies in the tourist guides.

So it might be okay if she stays a while.

As long as she never finds out.

Lucky for me, few people knew the truth.

And now they're dead.

Except one or two. And I never did know how much they knew.

Chapter 3

Stephen set his overnight bag under what Rex had told Maddie was an oval-leafed, thick-barked sassafras tree that sat at the end of the driveway and emitted a soft aroma of root beer.

"Let's walk to the beach," he said. "I don't remember ever being on this side of the harbor."

Together, father and daughter ambled down the dusty road, their footsteps barely making a sound.

Stephen smiled as they walked. "I was never here at this time of year," he said. "It's quiet, isn't it?"

Of course he hadn't been there in the fall. He'd been busy teaching, providing for his small family, then for the second child—a brother or a sister for Maddie—that he and Hannah had hoped to have, something Maddie only recently learned.

"Grandma says fall is nature's way of easing us into winter," she said. "That it's the bridge between chaos and solitude." A couple of shorebirds chirped as if they agreed.

Stephen didn't reply.

"Rafe's with Grandma's brother, Joe, right now," Maddie said. "They're at tribal headquarters, setting up tables and chairs for tomorrow." The tall trees gave way to sand dunes and clusters of beach roses, their leaves having already turned amber and golden. "And I don't know how to tell you this, Dad," she finally added, "but Cranberry Day is only for tribal members. Except the potluck. Grandma said they've been inviting their neighbors and friends in recent years."

"Oh," he said. "I didn't know."

"As you said, you've never been here in the fall. I'm sorry you came all this way."

He nodded. "There's a lot I need to learn if you wind up living here for a while."

"Me, too." She didn't say she already was living there, had been for "a while," and would be for a while longer.

"So, should I leave today?"

She scowled. "No! Come to the dinner tomorrow night. And why not stay a few days after that? Rafe goes back to school Wednesday, but I'd love to have you stick around." Not only hadn't she seen her son since August, but she also hadn't seen her dad.

He squinted up at the sky.

"As long as you don't mind sleeping on the couch," she quickly added. Surely, Rafe wouldn't bat an eye at roughing it on the floor. He'd done that before. "It would be nice, having the three of us here."

Stephen thought for a moment. "Will he be back later today?"

"Yes."

"Okay, then. How about if I stay tonight, but leave in the morning?" His tone was flat, no doubt muted by disappointment.

"But, Dad, you can come to the potluck . . ."

"It's fine, Madelyn. I should have let you know I was coming. But I'll be here for Christmas. If that's still okay."

"Of course it is! By then we'll be back in the cottage and have more space." Though Grandma's cottage would now have three bedrooms, Maddie didn't elaborate; she wasn't sure if having her grandmother and her father in the same house for more than two or three nights would be wise.

They reached the beach; it was low tide, when the sand was wet yet firm, perfect for running.

"The water's darker now than in summer," Stephen said. He moved down to the shoreline; Maddie followed. "You're happy here, aren't you, Madelyn?"

"I am, Dad. I like helping Grandma." She bent her knees, trying to shake off the urge to break into a run. She wondered if he was going to say he was lonely in Green Hills, that he missed having Rafe and her there.

As their footsteps grazed the water, their conversation was sparse and not entirely comfortable. Then Stephen said he'd recently seen Don Jarvis, Maddie's department chair. Jarvis had asked after Maddie, and he'd prodded Stephen about whether he thought she'd ever come back to the college, teach in person, and be interested in sliding back onto the tenure track that she'd abandoned.

Managing a small smile, Maddie didn't respond. She couldn't explain that her life had changed, that her world was now focused on different things—like wondering how it was that the October sun could warm her face while, at the same time, the light breeze made her wish that she'd worn gloves. There was no way to explain that her life was now a dichotomy of a career path and the path of an ancient way. Or that on a morning like this, she preferred the contradictions of autumn weather to the predictable stale air of a classroom. She didn't say those things, because she truly was trying to take one day, one week, one month at a time.

They reached the opening into Menemsha Harbor where, on the opposite side, the slips that once moored summer yachts and pleasure boats were silent, save for gentle waves lapping the wooden docks, waiting for the putt-putt of fishing trawlers to return from their day's work.

"I don't know about you," Maddie said, "but I could use coffee."

"Good idea," Stephen replied. He looped his arm through hers, the gesture feeling oddly like a reversal of the roles between parent and child, as if the child now needed to bear the weight of another elder besides Grandma.

Early in the morning, Maddie packed a thermos of coffee for her father, along with two blueberry scones—Rex's creations and frequent contributions to his nonpaying tenants. Then she and Rafe bid Stephen good-bye. They'd had a pleasant time the night before, with Grandma and Stephen being polite to each other, and Rafe livening things up with tidbits he'd learned that day from Joe—things like how the tribe often referred to the Vineyard as "Turtle Island," an Indigenous Peoples' name for the earth, and that near the cliffs in Aquinnah, a large rock, shaped like a giant toad, once served as a Wampanoag post office where tribal members left messages for each other. Joe admitted that some people, including him, still did on occasion.

Stephen seemed to enjoy the evening, which made his departure bittersweet. Maddie told him she would have invited him for Thanksgiving, but Grandma already said she did not believe in celebrating that "mythical" day. Maddie understood. (It also didn't matter to her because Rafe would be with Owen and the "steppeople" that day.) Stephen said he'd planned to wait until Christmas, anyway, that he'd been invited to share Thanksgiving dinner with fellow retired professors. Then, nearly as quickly as he'd arrived, he was gone.

And Cranberry Day began.

The events passed in a blur of emotion, commotion, and, best of all, community. Grandma and Joe taught Rafe and Maddie the centuries-old art of harvesting the berries that grew wild in the bogs. The land was tribal, so the crop had never been fertilized or sprayed—the Wampanoags were, and had always been, respectful of Mother Earth, who, since ancient times, had been tending to the bounty; that year, the berries were a healthy bright red thanks to the ideal balance of rain and sun.

At lunchtime, dozens of families gathered at Lobsterville Beach and lit a bonfire; the elders—Grandma Nancy and Joe included—then shared stories of their ancestors. Children had the day off from school; they played quahog games, and raced cranberries down the dunes. As the day waned, people moved to and from their homes to rest; back at the cabin, Grandma napped, while Maddie cleaned the berries they'd picked, and Rafe and Joe yakked about dozens of things.

When they started to get ready to rejoin the others, Grandma pulled out the tribal skirt she'd worn seven decades earlier on her wedding day—the same skirt Maddie donned last summer when they'd celebrated Grandma at sunset on the beach. Now, she asked Maddie to put it on for the potluck. Wearing a white, long-sleeved woven top and Grandma's wampum beads, Maddie again felt as if she truly belonged. Rafe further honored their heritage by donning—again—his great-great-grandfather's rawhide necklace with the wampum pendant carved into the shape of an arrow.

Before heading out the door, Grandma asked them to stand next to each other; while she clapped her hands, making them laugh, Joe snapped a photograph. Then the four of them were off to the big hall, where, among their people, they dined on fish and venison, clam fritters and chowder, and seaweed pudding, which Maddie and Rafe agreed tasted better than it sounded, especially since it was served with sharp cheddar cheese. In addition to cranberry-inspired desserts, they had blueberry "slump," which was sort of like a cobbler. Maddie didn't ask how—or if—it differed from a buckle.

Through it all, snippets of conversation landed on her ears, tales of this and that, of past and present. Soon the drumming started, and the diners were treated to traditional chants and dancers whose costumes flashed arcs of vibrant colors as they twirled and swayed around the room.

"I want to learn to do that, Joe," Rafe said, his eyes fixed on the drummers.

"First, you must know the stories," Joe replied. "Our stories are behind every beat of every drum."

"Then I'll listen. And I will learn."

Which was when Grandma tugged Maddie's sleeve. "This was your mother's favorite part. Not the drumming, but the dancing. By the time she was ten, she knew every step."

Sometimes, when Maddie least suspected it, the mention of her mother—no matter how brief—caused a groundswell of emotion in her. Like now, when she fixed her eyes on the dancers and willed her sorrow to quiet. But it was hard not to try and picture her mother at ten, twice as old as Maddie had been when Hannah died in the horrible accident, too long ago for Maddie to have a clear memory not only of it but, sadly, also of her mother.

"You look so much like Hannah," many people had commented when Maddie came back to the island in July.

It might be true. The only photo Maddie had seen of them together was of her mother *Holding baby Madelyn*, as someone had scrawled on the back. But in the picture, Hannah's head was bent, looking at her precious bundle, so the camera hadn't captured her face. If there were other photos—on the island or in Green Hills—neither her father nor Grandma knew where they were.

"Cameras were a luxury we couldn't afford," Grandma once explained.

"It was too hard for me to keep them," her father had said. "Every time I saw one . . ." He'd returned to the newspaper he was reading, his sentence trailing into oblivion.

There was no reason for Maddie to disbelieve either of them.

But now, out of the blue, as she sat on a folding chair in the headquarters of the Wampanoag Tribe of Gay Head (Aquinnah), above the singing and the drumming, she almost heard her mother's soft voice: "My little pumpkin." Suddenly, Maddie remembered that Hannah had often called her that. All these years, she hadn't recalled it until now. In addition to the groundswell inside her, a film of moisture now coated her eyes.

Do not cry, she admonished herself, biting her lip. *Not here. Not now.*

But, longing to hear the voice again, she closed her eyes. And forced herself not to whisper: "Mommy." The word was, after all, how she still thought of her mother. Having been so young when Hannah died, Maddie hadn't grown past the "Mommy" stage into the "Mom" or the "Mother" ones. Four decades later, it remained the same.

"Hey!" Rafe gave his mom a playful elbow in her side. "Are you sleeping, or what?"

Quickly, she opened her eyes and rallied a smile. "I'm listening," she claimed. "Everything is fabulous."

"Yeah," he said above the noise. "Too bad Grandpa didn't stay. He would have loved this."

She nodded in reply, but she honestly didn't know how Stephen Clarke would have felt. Maybe his stomach would have been roiling. They'd both lost so much—he, his wife, and Maddie, her mother—though she'd also lost the connection to her roots, these roots. Scanning the room, the flashing colors, the enraptured faces singing in rhythmic chants, the audience absorbed, pensive, happy, she let herself meld into the wonders of her community, her people, her *now*.

In this place, in this world, her loss slowly eased.

After the festivities, Maddie was determined to become one with the group, the way Rafe was doing. She began by helping to clean up. Weaving around the tables, stacking a large tray with plates and utensils, she said hello and nice-to-meet you to everyone she encountered, young and old, some of whom she recognized from Grandma's summer celebration. It was much easier to socialize there than at the "must attend" faculty events at Green Hills College.

She moved to a table where two elderly men were musing over olden days, one a clear-eyed, patient Wampanoag; the other, a weathered, grumpy, fair-skinned man—perhaps a non-tribal guest.

"Too bad about Arnie's bait shop in Menemsha," the Wampanoag man said to his companion.

"Decades of hard work down the drain," grumpy guy answered. "Where's everybody going to get their stuff?"

"Wholesalers, I expect."

"Or stop fishin'. Ain't there nobody to take it over?"

"Changing times, my friend."

Both men shook their heads.

"I hope no one scoops up the place for a T-shirt shop," said the Wampanoag man. "There are already too many of those down-island."

Grumpy guy scratched his beard and harrumphed. "Might depend on what the town can get for the lease. Most likely, they'll get more from a washashore."

Maddie continued collecting the used dinnerware, trying not to reveal that she was eavesdropping.

"Not necessarily. I expect they'll be fussy about who gets in there."

"But when times change, stuff like this changes, too. If that happens, it'll screw up the whole harbor." Grumpy guy pronounced *harbor* as if it had an "ah" at the end. Then he harrumphed again.

As Maddie moved to the table next to the men, grumpy guy then said, "Hey, you. Girl. You're not from here, are you? You wanna take over a bait shop?"

She smiled. "No, thank you." She continued on her mission, musing about what she'd heard. She'd seen the sign ARNIE'S BAIT & TACKLE since she could remember; it was down the road from Mr. Fuller's ice cream shack. As a kid, she'd always sprinted past by the gray-shingled bait shop, afraid that worms would crawl outside and "get" her.

Juggling the heavy tray that she felt was indicative of a successful event, Maddie was appalled to know that the bait shop—and its worms that she'd never seen—would be among her few, clear memories of the island. But her mouth curved into another smile as she walked toward the kitchen, knowing that her mother would be pleased that Maddie was growing at ease among their people.

After deducing that the memories Cranberry Day evoked had been too emotional for Grandma, Maddie decided to leave her alone. It had been a long day; they all were tired. With Rafe settled on the sofa, Maddie, too, went to bed. She slept straight through the night, then woke up with no time to waste: Rafe needed to catch the eight-fifteen boat in order to make his afternoon classes.

"What a cool trip this was," he said once they were in the car, traveling down State Road toward Vineyard Haven.

Maddie sipped on the coffee he'd handed her as they'd walked out the door; she still wasn't fully awake. Thank goodness Rafe was driving.

"I wouldn't have traded the last three days for anything," he added. "We should have the picture of us that Joe took blown up and framed." Then he gestured to the outfit she had on.

Maddie's gaze moved down: in her need to dress fast, she'd jumped into the hand-beaded skirt and the white top she'd worn the night before. The only difference was that she'd tossed on a jacket. "Well, this is embarrassing."

He laughed. "No! It's cool, Mom. You had lots of compliments last night. And Grandma loved every minute of it."

Maddie sipped the coffee again. "I think the whole day was too much for her. She might sleep for days."

"Yeah," he said happily. "But she's amazing."

He was, of course, right. Nancy Clieg was amazing; there was no need for Maddie to worry about her.

So she grinned and nodded along with Rafe, the two of them looking like bobbleheads crafted by the same artist.

"Speaking of Grandma," he said, "did she tell you the results of our poll about which baskets to make?"

"No. She was too eager to climb into her bed."

"The tribe recommended three sizes—small, medium, large. They think more people will buy them if they use them for different purposes. And they thought we should offer a variety of wood slats. At least in the beginning. Then later we can focus our work down to the ones that sell the most."

"Brilliant," Maddie said. "Do you agree?"

"I'm excited. Mostly because it's fun to see Grandma so happy."

Maddie was glad Rafe hadn't noticed that Grandma had been on the verge of an emotional meltdown.

They made it to the boat as the walk-on passengers were boarding.

"Thanks, Mom," Rafe said, snatching his backpack, opening the car door, then leaning over and planting a fast kiss on her cheek. "For absolutely everything. I can't wait 'til Christmas. When I'll learn to make baskets. And hear more of Joe's stories, cuz I really, really want to drum."

"Great. Now shoo, before they wheel the ramp away."

She moved into the driver's seat as Rafe laughed and raced across the pavement toward his passage to the mainland, which was often called "America," which Maddie now felt was an insult. If America implied a workable community with responsible, respectable, and respectful people who cared for and about one another, who shared what they had, and who treated Mother Earth as a root of life, then up-island—not the mainland—should be considered the stronghold of America.

With a long sigh, she wondered where in heaven's name that mental monologue came from. Then she remembered she'd had a dream before she'd woken up. It was about Arnie's Bait & Tackle. But instead of an old fisherman behind the register, her father had stood there, chatting with customers.

"Very funny," she said aloud.

Then she tapped her fingers on the steering wheel, waiting to watch the big boat back out of its berth because it's what one often did.

And then a spark of intuition sparked: *Could I take over the bait and tackle?* Could she turn it into something else—anything but a place that sold T-shirts or . . . worms? Maybe she could sell her grandmother's—and Rafe's—handwoven baskets. Maybe even the herbal teas Grandma made. And what about . . . books? Books about the island, its past, its present, its people. Books with photographs and memoirs. She could also sell fiction and nonfiction, whatever was perfect for beach reading. And maybe, just maybe, Maddie could get her father to be with them after all . . . standing behind the counter where he'd been in her dream.

Clearly, Maddie had either been given a gift of inspiration, or she'd been struck by lightning on her head.

Chapter 4

The only way Maddie knew she'd be able to shake the idea of owning a bookshop would be if she talked to someone she could trust, someone who was an entrepreneur and would be honest and tell her if the concept was harebrained—or not. Someone to talk sense into her. Without hesitation, one such person quickly came to mind. So, after Rafe and the ferry departed, she drove to Edgartown.

She parked at Memorial Wharf near the Chappaquiddick Ferry, a couple of blocks from the Lord James restaurant. She could have found a space closer, but she wanted to be able to escape unseen if she changed her mind at the last second. Turning off the car, she took one more breath to convince herself she shouldn't be shy. Or embarrassed. Or worried that she'd sound foolish.

Then she texted Rex.

CAN I STOP BY FOR A MINUTE? She had no idea if eight forty-five was too early to rouse him from sleep. I'D LIKE YOUR OPINION ABOUT SOMETHING.

Within seconds, her alert dinged.

SURE. WHAT TIME?

WELL . . . I'M SORT OF OUTSIDE THE RESTAURANT.

He didn't respond. She hoped she wasn't interrupting anything—or that anyone might be with him. Anyone like a . . . woman? Why had Maddie assumed he'd be alone? The thought triggered a memory of a boy named Bobby who she'd quietly adored in high school. One day, he'd asked her to go to Jan's, a local diner, for a Coke. Maddie's cheeks had flushed, her palms grew damp, her whole insides got jittery with excitement. But once settled in a red vinyl booth, Bobby asked if her friend Tracy had a boyfriend. How could Maddie have known that Bobby liked Tracy? And what the heck did that have to do with where she was right now? "You're forty-five," she muttered. "Not fifteen." And Rex was a friend she wanted to consult on a business matter. Not a man she was lusting after.

Ding, ding, her phone dinged.

GIVE ME 5 MINS, he'd typed. DOWNSTAIRS DOOR IS UNLOCKED. COME UPSTAIRS TO MY APT.

She waited ten minutes, tapping her fingers on the steering wheel the whole time. Then she got out of the car, smoothed the front of her grandmother's skirt, and walked to the Lord James, where Rex lived "above the shop," as he'd once referred to his apartment. She took another breath, went in, and climbed the steps. But as she raised her hand to knock, the door opened. She almost rapped him on the chest.

"Oh! Sorry!"

"Happens all the time." He smiled, stepped away, and welcomed her in. Despite his weathered jeans and navy blue T-shirt, he didn't look like he'd just rolled out of bed. And being bald saved him from having to comb his hair before greeting a visitor.

"Coffee?" he asked.

"Sure." Suddenly, she felt ridiculous, as if her idea for a

bookshop was unrealistic. A fantasy. After all, Maddie was a teacher, not a businessperson, and she knew beans about the island compared with the people who'd grown up there. Her thoughts scrambled as she tried to come up with a different topic she could ask him about that would not make her sound as if she'd come unplugged.

Willing herself not to stammer the way Grandma did when she was confused, Maddie said, "I'm sorry, Rex." Her voice was steady but squeaky. "I shouldn't have come. Not to mention so early. But Rafe needed the early boat . . ."

He reached for her hand, which she knew must be god-awful damp. "Please don't apologize," he said with a smile. "Just tell me if you want a blueberry or cranberry scone for breakfast. Something tells me you haven't eaten yet." He let go of her hand and glanced down at her skirt. "Nice outfit," he said.

In spite of her teeter-tottering emotions, Maddie laughed. "You're very observant, for it being so early and all." At least he hadn't mentioned her wet palm.

"I'm no Sherlock Holmes, but it stands to reason if Rafe needed the early boat, you jumped out of bed and into the first available clothes. Assuming you wore that to the potluck last night."

She had no recourse. "So you also deduced that I'd draped it across the chair in your guest room last night, which made a perfect option when I was in a hurry."

"Correct." He backed up and ushered her inside.

"You win," she said, then dutifully obeyed and followed him into a sunny, gleaming kitchen. Leaning against what looked like a tall freezer, she watched him dump half the contents of a French press container down the drain and start making a fresh one. A lone mug sat in the sink, so perhaps there was not a woman lurking in the bedroom. As in Rex's up-island cabin where she and Grandma currently lived, this place was tidy, but unlike the cabin, it appeared newly decorated in black and white with bright red accents here and there, and a wide window overlooking Edgartown Harbor. And as at Menemsha in October, the pleasure boats that clogged the harbor in season were gone, having either been put into storage or navigated to somewhere south of here.

"I hope I didn't take you from something important," she said, praying that if she stalled long enough she could concoct another reason for her presence, instead of sharing the ridiculous pipe dream that she'd suddenly felt compelled to ditch her career and sell books. And baskets. And Grandma's teas that were definitely not USDA inspected, as they might need to be.

Oh, she thought. *I need help all right, but perhaps not quite the kind I'd thought.*

"I was doing paperwork," he said. "Ordering food. Paying bills. Exciting stuff. Thanks for showing up and saving me from it." He put the kettle on and cranked up the burner to high. "How did yesterday go?"

She forced herself to stay focused, the way a professional adult person would. The way her father would. "Cranberry Day was incredible." She wished she wasn't so nervous in his company.

"Did Rafe have fun?"

"That's an understatement." As always, Rex was nice. Even-tempered. Kind and generous, yet strong. But other than knowing he'd grown up on Chappy, and then lived in Boston many years, where he'd become a chef, Maddie knew little about him. "Have you been to the potluck since it opened to the public?" She was stalling, and she knew it.

He reached into an upper cabinet, took down two plates, then plucked two scones from beneath a small glass dome. "Nope. Like I said, things are crazy here with the long weekend and the busloads of fall tourists. But I've heard it's great."

"It was." She knitted and purled her fingers together. Maybe she should just tell him what she'd overheard about Arnie's and her harebrained idea and get it over with. If he laughed, so what? Once the post-fire renovations to Grandma's cottage were done, it's not as if Maddie would ever need to see Rex again. But as she opened her mouth to speak, he interrupted.

"Maddie? Before you ask me what you wanted to ask, I have a question."

She blinked. "Okay?" It was odd that she'd posed her response as a question, but that's what she did.

He folded his arms across his broad chest. "Are you seeing anyone?"

She blinked again; her breath seemed to have left her. "Like, am I dating someone?" Standing so close to him, her legs quickly turned to, well, jelly, she supposed. Like beach-plum jelly, the kind Grandma Nancy used to make.

He rubbed his hand over the top of his bald head. "Well . . . yes. Are you dating anyone?" He might have blushed. She wondered if his palms now were damp like hers.

Then she had another thought: *Is this what he'd wanted to ask the other day before he'd winked, climbed into his truck, and driven away?* Right now, however, he was waiting for an answer. "The last date I had was our picnic on the beach," she said.

"That was a while ago."

"August."

"It's the last time we were alone." He shoved his hands into the pockets of his jeans and moved a step closer. "Until now."

"I guess so. Yes." The heat in the kitchen seemed to rise. She wanted to fan her face or tuck her hair behind her ears. She wanted to feel like something other than a teenager.

Where the heck had this come from? And why am I so . . . excited?

He took another step. Then he leaned down and kissed her on the lips. She pressed her back against the freezer; her eyelids fluttered; her pulse sped up. He looked into her eyes. And kissed her again. Softer, warmer, melting the lot of her.

He stepped back. "I hope I didn't misread anything. I only know I've wanted to do that since the first day we met."

She swallowed air. "Since you broke into my grandmother's shed?"

He laughed. And kissed her again.

She didn't know whether the warmth coursing through her was from his kisses or because she was too close to the stove. Then she remembered she was leaning against the freezer.

"Rex?" she whispered. "Maybe I've wanted you to kiss me since that first day, too." Her response was so spontaneous she realized it was true. That first time they'd met, there was something about him . . . something different. Something special. And, after she'd broken her foot, when they had their first (and only) date, he'd brought a wheelchair. He'd taken her to a beach that had a wood boardwalk that led down to the sand, where he gently lifted her up and set her on a folding chair, and then presented her with a gourmet lunch. When Rafe intruded on the date by calling to say he was on the boat, en route to the island, Rex speedily gathered everything and chauffeured Maddie to the Vineyard Haven pier so she could be there to greet her son.

Since that magical afternoon, she and Rex had seen each other often, but he was right, they had not been alone, what with the fire and the commotion and the rest. And now, the only thing that felt strange about being alone with him was that it wasn't like her to share her feelings with anyone, let alone a man. But Rex was different from others she'd dated since her divorce—none of them had made her cheeks—and the rest of her—so warm.

Then he turned off the burner on the stove, and tucked

her hair behind her ears the way she would have done. The next thing she knew, he was leading her from the kitchen, through his living room, and down the hall toward what she thought—what she hoped—was the bedroom. She went with him willingly, eagerly, her senses fully lit, her heart swelling with anticipation, ignoring the ghost of her upbringing that cautioned: *It's too soon, Madelyn. It's too soon.*

Her clothes, including her white top and her grandmother's skirt with the beads and the embroidery, wound up on the floor in a corner of the bedroom. Maddie had pulled her clothes off more hurriedly than the previous night when the bed she'd climbed into had been empty. It was far nicer this morning when Rex had crawled under the covers next to her. No matter if her conscience thought it was too soon.

What it had been was wonderful. Startlingly wonderful.

"This is the confusing part," he said once their bodies separated and they both caught their breath. He turned onto his back, stretched his arms over his shoulders, and clasped his hands behind his head. "It was our first time together. So now for the big questions. Who gets up first? Me? Am I expected to stand up, wrap a sheet around my lower parts, and disappear into the bathroom so I can give you privacy to get dressed? Or do you wrap said sheet around yourself and go first?" He scrunched his eyes closed. "I don't do this very often. To be truthful, it's been a long time. So I could use some direction. Please."

Maddie watched him. She wanted to laugh, but her belly had started to ache and her head had started to hurt with a singular, disturbing thought: *What if someone finds out?* She was new to the Vineyard. For all she knew, Rex had done this sort of thing many, many times. He might even have a reputation for it. Not to mention that his early years had been tough, having spent more than a night or two in the jail in Edgartown, thanks to a few teenage antics. On their first date and only real date, he'd started to explain another "situation" to her, but there hadn't been time for him to share the details because they'd rushed off to get Rafe.

Still, why had she never asked him about it?

Because, she reasoned, *one picnic on one afternoon did not mean you were dating the guy or ever would. Or should.*

As for now, if the news escaped that she'd slept with him, she might become a laughingstock washashore, with little chance of holding her head high, let alone of starting a business she had no business starting in the first place.

"Hello?" he quietly asked from beside her.

Reaching to the floor from the side of the bed, she retrieved a comforter that one of them had kicked off. She quickly pulled it up and managed to cloak her body with it. Then she looked at him.

"You're wonderful, Rex," she said, feigning a smile. "But believe it or not, this is highly irregular for me." *Highly irregular?* Had she actually said such a snooty thing? She hauled herself up, collected her clothes, and headed for a doorway that looked like it led to the bathroom. "I'm sorry," she muttered, her back toward him now as she stepped into what, indeed, was a bathroom.

And that was the end of that.

It wasn't until Maddie was outside in the fresh air, pulling her phone from her purse and heading toward the parking lot, that she realized Rex hadn't said a word, hadn't tried to convince her to stay, hadn't apologized if he'd upset her. But she didn't have time to dwell on that now. Three new voicemails were waiting, all from Grandma.

"Where in blazes are you, Madelyn?" the woman snarled in all of them. "Are you lost?"

Fast-walking toward her car, Maddie quickly returned the

calls, assuring her grandmother that all was well, that she'd simply forgotten to turn her phone on after waking up late and hurrying to get Rafe to Vineyard Haven. For good measure, she added that she'd stopped for coffee and to do a little shopping. After the part about Rafe, the rest were lies; she hadn't even had the coffee Rex had offered.

Then she said she wanted to make one more stop, which she did not. What Maddie wanted was more time to process what she had done before facing the woman who she'd taken into her charge. Which perhaps should have been vice versa.

It wasn't until Maddie was halfway back to the cabin that she remembered she hadn't told Rex about Arnie's Bait & Tackle. So at least that was a good thing. It would be better for her to investigate the possibilities for a business on her own rather than risk following the advice of a man she barely knew.

Driving the long way, she finally came to State Road, where she went left, drove a bit farther, then steered into the overlook that offered a commanding view of the still waters of Tashmoo Pond. She sat for half an hour, struggling to figure out how to open a bookshop, but her thoughts kept getting entangled with images of Rex, the warmth of his smile, the sense of his touch. After a while, she realized her absurd state-of-the-moment was perfectly normal and boiled down to something she'd always hated admitting: "Madelyn Clarke," she said aloud, "you are human after all."

With that, she pulled out of the overlook and headed up-island, amused by herself, which felt rather good.

But when Maddie arrived at the cabin, Grandma Nancy wasn't amused.

"I almost called our local constable," she said when she greeted her granddaughter at the front door.

Ken Lawrence was Chilmark's police chief, who Grandma

liked calling the local constable for some quirky reason, probably because since he'd grown up on the island, she still viewed him as a kid. Maddie supposed that Ken could have put out an all-points bulletin for the missing granddaughter. At least Maddie had dodged that wave of humiliation.

"Where were you?" Grandma persisted. "Were you in Menemsha at the cottage? At my house that you won't let me see yet?"

"No, Grandma," Maddie said, brushing past her and walking into Rex's cabin on tenterhooks, as if he might have gone there ahead of her and would be standing, leaning against the kitchen counter, arms folded, a smug look on his face warning her he was seeking reprisal since she'd dismissed his company as well as his prowess.

Grandma was definitely not amused. Her face was pinched, her eyes suspicious. "You obviously weren't doing errands," she said, both hands planted on her hips. "You don't have any packages."

Maybe Rex had phoned and spilled the bag of embarrassing beans.

Maddie sighed. She set her purse on the end of the sofa and took off her jacket. "I didn't say I was buying things. I was looking for things like new dishes and linens for when we move back to the cottage." It was another lie, but seemed harmless compared to confessing what she'd really been doing.

"What's wrong with my old dishes?" Grandma barked. She'd obviously forgotten they'd been ruined in the fire. Melted. Because they'd been plastic.

"They were destroyed in the fire."

Grandma scowled. "The firemen should have been more careful."

Maddie hung her jacket.

"So where are they?" Grandma barked. "The new ones?"

"I was *window* shopping, Grandma," she repeated. "I had hoped I'd be able to surprise you. But I couldn't find anything you'd like." She went into the kitchen, wishing she'd grabbed one of Rex's scones on her way out, then berating herself for thinking about him again. She'd have to stop that.

Staring into the refrigerator that looked almost as empty as her heart suddenly felt, she wasn't in the mood for the Three Sisters Stew that she'd saved for dinner tonight. She wondered why she was ashamed of her behavior—not only of what she had done, but also of how she'd left, as if what *they'd* done hadn't mattered. As if *he* hadn't mattered.

Stop it! her smart self screeched at her not-so-smart one.

On top of everything else, she now felt guilty that she might have been surly to Grandma. She softened her tone. "Someone told me that beyond what they show, LeRoux has other samples, but the dishes would have to be ordered. Maybe we can go to the store together?" LeRoux was a nice home goods store up the hill from the ferry terminal, where Maddie had not window-shopped that day or any other as yet. She shut the refrigerator door and turned back to Grandma, who was gnawing on her lower lip. Which made Maddie feel even more guilty, especially since Grandma had been so upset the night before.

"Right now, however," Maddie continued, "I need to shower and get into clean clothes. Then I'm going to take you to lunch because I love you, and I'm sorry if I worried you. And I'm sorry if I seemed angry with you. I'm not. And I promise that from now on, I'll be sure my phone is always turned on."

They went to the casual family restaurant—Plane View—at the airport because Grandma said she liked to watch the planes take off and land and because she loved the burgers. She also wanted to visit her nearby storage unit. At least she seemed in better spirits.

All through lunch Maddie tried not to think about Rex; twice Grandma asked why she wasn't listening. Then she wanted to know what she thought of her idea about Orson.

"Whatever you want, Grandma," Maddie replied. The name "Orson" sounded familiar, but she couldn't place him. It wasn't until they were done eating and heading toward the storage unit that she remembered Orson was the name of Grandma's 1950 F-1 Ford pickup truck that had been sitting idle in the storage unit for God only knew how long.

"Ta-da!" Grandma called out when the garage-like door rolled up, revealing the truck and the nests of cartons stacked in its bed. Grandma must have wanted to rescue her stash of baskets to help her teach Rafe how to make them.

But Grandma neither mentioned the baskets nor walked to the cartons in the back of the pickup. Instead, she squeezed around the side and climbed in on the driver's side. Maddie opened the passenger door.

"Are you planning to drive us somewhere?" she asked.

Grandma laughed. At least she was laughing and no longer scowling.

"I turned my license in when I turned eighty, and I'm too old to be interested in breaking the law." Then she added that Joe sometimes brought her there so she could sit behind Orson's wheel and remember the good times they'd had. Which might have been her real reason for wanting to be there now.

"What do you think?" Grandma asked. "Will he like him?"

Again, Maddie didn't know what the woman meant. She closed her eyes, wishing they could leave so she could go back to the cabin, sequester herself in the guest room, and resume wallowing until she was done once and for all.

Then her text alert sounded. Stepping out of Orson, away from Grandma, she dug her phone from her purse. Part of her wished it was from Rex.

Hi. I made it to Amherst in one piece.

It was, of course, from Rafe. Her wonderful son.

She tried not to ungratefully feel disappointed, and responded with a hugging emoji.

"Madelyn!" Grandma called. "Put down the phone and answer me!"

"Sorry. What did you want?"

Grandma let out a loud sigh. "I want to know if you think Rafe would like to have Orson. A combination present for Christmas and his college graduation. Joe can get the engine spruced up and a new set of tires. Maybe even a fresh coat of paint. And new seat covers. What d'ya think?" She patted the dashboard as if she were expecting Orson, not Maddie, to reply.

Maddie's anxiety started to slide away. Thinking about Rafe's happiness had a way of doing that.

"I think your great-grandson would be honored to take custody of Orson," she heard herself say and knew it was true.

"Took you long enough to decide," Grandma sputtered.

Climbing onto the passenger seat, Maddie glanced around the interior that was closer in age to Grandma Nancy than to Maddie. "It's a wonderful idea, Grandma. Really. He'll never expect it. And sometimes the best gifts are the ones we don't expect."

Right then, she wondered if Rex was one of those gifts. And, if so, how—or when—she would ever know.

Chapter 5

Maddie knew that, sooner or later, she'd see Rex again. After all, he was their temporary landlord of sorts. What she hadn't anticipated was that when she and Grandma returned from their outing, his pickup would be parked at the cabin. The sight of it alone made her palms sweat.

"I would have told you Rex would be here if you'd answered your phone this morning," Grandma said when Maddie stopped the car. "He called right after you and Rafe left. He said that since the tourists have fled, he has leftover scallops that need cooking. He wants to make us a casserole in a white wine cream sauce. I told him to bring it on!" Grandma hated leaving messages; if she absolutely needed to, she kept them short, though not typically sweet: "Where in blazes are you, Madelyn?" was an example.

As soon as Maddie turned off the ignition, Grandma bolted from the car and trotted up to the cabin at her maximum speed, which wasn't fast but showed enthusiasm.

Trying to gather an ounce of confidence, Maddie remained glued to the frayed fabric of the seat of her car. She knew she'd be fine. After all, she was in charge of her own life, her own happiness.

This morning simply had been a harmless misstep.

She would put up her guard and be fine. After all, she was a confident, career-minded woman, though her colleagues and friends back in Green Hills would question that if they saw her right now. Especially if they saw the haphazard creases in the skirt she'd worn earlier, thanks to her having yanked it off and tossed it onto the floor, not caring that it landed in a heap. An act of passion, if ever there was one.

She took a deep breath for what could have been the hundredth time that day, and marched into the cabin as if it was hers, not his.

"Hey," she said. "I didn't expect to see you here."

Grandma paid no attention; instead, she was busy twittering around the tiny kitchen like a child who'd consumed too much sugar, pulling plates from the cabinet and silverware from the drawer, despite that they'd finished lunch less than two hours earlier.

"Sorry to let myself in," he said, as he focused on scrubbing the pan he must have sautéed the scallops in because hints of garlic and butter scented the air. "But I don't have much time 'til I have to get back and start prepping for the dinner crowd, slim though it will be."

Maddie remained standing, her gaze fixed on his muscular back that looked even more muscular thanks to the black T-shirt he had on.

"No problem," she finally said, recalling that at some point in recent days, he'd mentioned that despite the drop in tourism, the Lord James would open daily until Christmas Eve, then shut down until Valentine's Day. He said he liked to use those weeks for deep cleaning the restaurant and taking care of whatever fixing and freshening up was needed. She blinked and looked at her bustling grandmother. "So I guess it will be the two of us tonight, Grandma. And I'm afraid I won't be hungry for quite a while."

Grandma frowned, then nodded. "Right. Then I'll go take my nap." She abruptly stopped futzing, thanked Rex for the scallops, then vanished into the front bedroom, leaving the plates and the silver on the table, slightly askew.

So, Rex and Maddie were suddenly alone, standing in silence, not exactly a postcoital kind, what with Maddie still in her jacket, and Rex with his hands in suds.

He spoke first. "You okay?"

She shrugged as if he could see her, as if his back wasn't still toward her. "Sure."

His head moved up and down in a semblance of a nod. "Good." He turned on the faucet and rinsed out the pan.

Maddie knew the uncomfortable silence was absurd. Especially since they were two reasonably intelligent, middle-aged adults who, mere hours earlier, had not been awkward together even though they had been naked.

"Rex."

"Maddie."

They spoke each other's names simultaneously. Maddie laughed. Then Rex did, too. He turned off the water, and Maddie took off her jacket. Then they faced each other, the only things between them the small table, the counter, and a whole bunch of jumbled feelings, at least on her part, and maybe on his, too.

"I was worried about you," he said softly, so Grandma wouldn't hear.

"I'm fine," she whispered. "Sorry I dashed out like I did. I guess I was startled."

"By me?" He dried his hands and walked around the counter and the table so they were closer.

She laughed again. "No! I was startled by me! I was totally out of my realm. I'm only a girl from the hills."

His cinnamon eyes sparkled like sugar on a ginger cookie. He smiled a crooked smile.

She wished he hadn't done that; it caused a ribbon of warmth to swell inside her.

"I told you," he added, "it's not an everyday thing for me, either. But neither of us seemed to have wanted to be somewhere else, doing something else. And it wasn't like it was planned."

Of course it hadn't been planned, she wanted to say. He hadn't even known she'd show up at his door. She moved to the opposite side of the living room, in case Grandma had her oyster-shaped ear pressed to the door.

He followed her. "I kind of thought that you liked . . . it."

"I did. It was nice. But it's not a good time for me, Rex. I'm not looking for a relationship. My life is beginning to start over—so I don't think it's fair to either of us for me to get involved right now." She sounded like a damn textbook therapist. Or the confident woman she pretended to be.

"I get it," he said. "Can we at least be friends?" The sparkle in his eyes faded a little.

"We *are* friends, Rex. I don't know what Grandma and I would do without you."

He gestured toward the oven. "For starters, you might not be having scallops tonight."

She laughed a faint laugh. "See? We are definitely friends."

"Good friends?" The half smile widened. "Because I'd like that, Maddie."

She knew what he meant. She could not say no. But she could not say yes. "Maybe in time?"

"It's a deal." He glanced at his watch. "But right now, it really is time for me to earn a living." He grabbed his plaid flannel shirt from the back of the sofa, started to button it, then stopped. "Wait. Before we got distracted this morning, you said you wanted to ask me something. Was it important? Or can it wait?"

She pressed her lips together, then shook her head. "It was nothing major. I figured it out after I . . . left." Her words sounded awkward. Maybe he hadn't noticed. But as much as Maddie knew it was too soon for a relationship, she was grateful she was still levelheaded enough to make her own decisions.

If the aftermath of her morning with Rex had taught her that, it had been worth a few awkward moments.

"Arnie's Bait and Tackle is closing," Maddie told Grandma.

It was long past dark. They were wrapped in toasty shawls, sitting on the front porch of the cabin, an LED lantern on the end table between them.

"How'd you hear that?"

"Last night at the potluck. Two men were talking about it. I didn't ask their names."

Grandma snickered. "Old men, I suppose. When it comes to gossip, they're worse than old ladies."

"They said something about Arnie leaving the island to live with his nephew in New Hampshire."

"Yup, that's what's floatin' around. I heard it from Lisa when she stopped by to say hello this morning."

Lisa was Grandma's petite, thirtyish neighbor, who had a penchant for wearing jumpers no matter the season, and tying back her long hair in a bandanna. She lived halfway down the short hill from the front of the cottage along with her husband, a fisherman, and their two young kids; she worked at the Chilmark Town Hall, where she heard almost everything that went on up-island and with whom. Luckily for Maddie, Edgartown was far enough away that the young woman might not have heard the latest about Maddie and Rex. Not yet, anyway.

Then Grandma chuckled. "You know you've lived here too long when things like bait and tackle start a conversation."

Returning the chuckle, Maddie asked, "I suppose you've known Arnie a long time."

"Long enough."

"You're not sorry to see him go?"

"Don't care one way or t'other. I suppose his customers will miss him. Unless another bait shop takes its place."

Maddie carefully formed her question. "What if the closing is a chance for me?"

Pausing only a beat, Grandma laughed. "You want to run a bait shop?"

This wasn't starting off as Maddie had hoped. "No. I'm thinking about turning it into a bookshop. Not as big as the ones down-island, but something to serve up-island residents and seasonal people, too. I'm thinking I could also sell your baskets and serve your herbal teas along with a few tasty treats."

Grandma raised a curious eyebrow. "You came up with all that since last night?"

"I did. I think the idea gelled after you said you want to fix up Orson for Rafe . . . He'll be so excited, Grandma. He really wants to live here. As much as I hope he still goes to graduate school, he has time for that. For now it might be nice to have a project we can all have fun with. And a good way for me to get to know the island better."

"In that case, our young man had better learn how to make my baskets fast. My days for doing that are numbered, especially if it requires speed. I used to be a racehorse. Now I'm more like a tortoise." She chuckled again.

"I'm sure we can make it work, Grandma. Hey, if we have them to sell, we'll sell them. And if we don't, we can ask people to check back."

"Okay. But you want a bookshop? Aren't you a teacher?"

Maddie didn't want to say she'd chosen that career mostly to please her father. Not unlike why she'd married Rafe's father. But that it now felt as if, like Owen, Green Hills College—and teaching—had run its course. Rather than belaboring all that, she simply said, "I'm ready for a change, Grandma, and this feels like something worth looking into. And I do love books."

As much as she would not do this intending to try and please Stephen again, the shop might give him a reason to come to the island and be with them in the summer, though she did not mention that to Grandma now.

"What do you think, Grandma? Should I find out more?"

The old woman fidgeted on the Adirondack chair, then stood up. "Actually, what I think is it's October and I'm freezing my behind off. As for opening a bookshop, I think you're off your rocker."

Before Maddie digested Grandma Nancy's comment, the woman tottered off into the cabin, her toasty shawl dragging behind her.

The next day, Joe took Grandma to visit her friend, Winnie Lathrop. Maddie was relieved; she'd be tied up teaching an online class, which was easier to accomplish when her grandmother wasn't installed in the living room, four feet from where Maddie sat at the table with her laptop. As comfortable as Rex's cabin was for two, the space didn't work well when one of them had to Zoom. On top of that, the class that day was boring, the students seemingly as disinterested in talking about methods of journalism as Maddie was in sharing them.

When class was over, she decided that, off her rocker or not, she wanted more information before ditching the bookshop idea. And the best place to get it might be from Arnie himself. So she put on a sweater and drove to Menemsha Harbor.

A sign taped to the window of the bait shop read: CLOSING FOR GOOD. LAST DAY SUNDAY OCT. 26. So, he really wouldn't be reopening. And another business could move in.

Noticing that the interior lights were on, Maddie tried the door handle; the door swung open. A strong fishy smell greeted her; she didn't want to imagine what it would cost to make it go away. Instead, she scrutinized the interior layout; it looked bigger than she'd expected, though picturing it as a charming little bookshop was difficult, what with rippled pegboards on the walls, rows of rusted metal shelving, and old refrigerated coolers lining the perimeter.

"Help you?" The voice wasn't enthusiastic; it came from between the shelving that was mostly empty.

As Maddie moved toward the sound, an elderly man appeared. He wore a long rubber apron, knee-high boots, and a faded baseball cap bearing the shop's logo above the brim. If she'd ever seen him, she didn't recognize him now.

"You're closing on the twenty-sixth?" she asked.

"I am. But if you're looking for deals, you're too late. Yesterday one of my competitors scooped up my tackle inventory—rods and reels, hooks and lures—the whole kit and caboodle. Got plenty of bait, though. If you're planning on fishin'."

She thought of the worms and quickly shook her head. "Not for me, thanks. But I've been thinking about buying a tackle box for my son for Christmas." She told herself she'd lied for a greater good.

"Sorry, they're gone. Check Nate's place down-island in a couple of weeks."

"Thanks. I'll do that. It's too bad you're leaving, though." She looked out the windows across the back wall and saw what appeared to be a deck between the shop and a walkway that edged the water in the harbor. Several more coolers cluttered the space out there, but a cheerful paint job and a few café tables could create a nice area for summer customers to sip Grandma's teas and snack on treats.

The man frowned. "I'm eighty-three. It's time to retire."

"My goodness. You don't look eighty-three." That, too, was a lie, as his face had more lines than a 1960s Rand McNally road map. Perhaps he'd spent too many years in sunshine winking off sea water.

Arnie laughed as if he knew she was being kind.

"Are you moving off-island?" she asked. "Somewhere south?"

"Like Florida? Could you picture a guy like me living there?"

"Well. It's warmer than here." Of course, she knew that Florida was nowhere near New Hampshire, where Arnie's nephew supposedly lived.

He shook his head. "Nope. But I am moving off. Going to my nephew's in New Hampshire." Again, the "ah" sound of Boston rolled off the last syllable of Hampshire. "My lease isn't up 'til the end of the year," he continued, "but I want to be outta here by Halloween. Seems appropriate, seeing as how change can be scary." He snorted at his joke.

Maddie nodded. "Well, good luck to you then."

"And good luck finding a tackle box."

With what she hoped would be seen as a pleasant wave, she let herself out of the bait shop and walked down Basin Road toward the driveway that led up to Grandma's cottage. If she was going to be serious about this, she'd need to gather as much information as possible. Rex's brother-in-law, Kevin, had been a building contractor in Boston before relocating to the Vineyard; he should know what it would take for the transformation. Once he was done with the restoration and renovations to Grandma's cottage.

Chapter 6

As Maddie hiked up the hill to the top of the driveway, she bypassed Lisa's place and took the narrow dirt path up to the cottage. Because it was a weekday, she was happy to hear the sounds of hammering, buzzsawing, and voices coming from within.

"Kevin?" she called out as she carefully stepped into the living room and spotted him in the kitchen, hammering.

The hammering stopped, but the buzzsawing that seemed to be coming from one of the bedrooms continued.

Rex's brother-in-law looked up from his work.

"Hey, Maddie. How's it going?" He set down the hammer and walked over to her.

For an instant she wondered if Rex had told him about her, about them. She had no idea if mature adult males ever outgrew that teenage stage. Then she reminded herself she was paying Kevin's invoices, so chances were, if he knew, he would not bring it up.

"Things are good," she said, looking around. Two walls of Sheetrock now were in place. "How's it going here?"

"Great. You want a tour?"

Since the work had begun, Maddie had only stopped by a few times; she didn't want Kevin and his crew to think she was planning to hover, watching their every move, or worse, that she'd pressure them into rushing. "No need for a tour, thanks. I brought my son over on Sunday. He's impressed. So am I."

Kevin pushed a handful of light brown hair off his forehead and nodded.

"I want to ask you about something else," she said.

He glanced down the hall where the saws were buzzing. "Let's go outside where we can hear."

Once they were in the front yard, she gave him the rundown on what little she knew about the bait shop. "If it works out that I can get it, a good revamp will be important. Of course, I'd prefer to have you and your crew do the work if you're not too busy."

He smiled. "First of all, I'll be glad to help however I can. We're on schedule to finish here with your grandmother's Christmas deadline, and I'd love to have a winter job lined up. Would that work for you?"

"Honestly, all I know is that Arnie is closing later this month. As for the rest, I have no idea where to start. But you're in construction, so I thought you might be able to steer me in the right direction."

He held up a finger. "Hold on a second." He pulled his phone from his pocket, turned his back to Maddie, and moved several steps away. So she looked back at the cottage and waited.

The difference that the new front windows made was astonishing. When the work was done, the house would be pleasantly welcoming, the way a Vineyard cottage should be. It would be perfect for her grandmother and her. And for Rafe, if he wanted to be with them. And if Maddie had a bookshop right down the hill . . . *Wow*, she thought, turning again, facing the harbor, *I really will have a whole new life.* It was surprising . . . and exhilarating.

After a couple of minutes, Kevin walked toward her again, tucking his phone back in his pocket.

"You're in luck," he said. "I've only been on the Vineyard a few years and don't have many connections yet, but there's one guy I know who knows pretty much everyone. Even better, he's agreed to help."

Maddie would have been elated if not for a small pang of intuition that twisted in her stomach.

"Give Rex a call," he continued. "You have his number?"

Yes, she had his number.

Forcing a smile, she thanked Kevin and told him she'd keep him posted. Then she headed toward the sandy path that led down past Lisa's house and out to the road. Once safely in her car, she rested her forehead against the steering wheel. If she wanted to pursue the idea of a bookshop, she supposed there was no getting around it. She had to call Rex. Or, later, try to explain why she had not.

The following morning, they met for a late breakfast at Waterside Restaurant in Vineyard Haven.

"You could have called me first," Rex said, once a server delivered their order: a breakfast burrito for him, toast and jam for Maddie.

She was a foolish, nervous wreck. At least he was polite enough not to ask if this was why she'd showed up at his door two days ago.

She took a sip of Earl Grey.

"Ask anyone on the island," he continued. "I don't bite." He cocked that enticing smile of his.

She took another sip.

Rex set down his fork. "Okay. I get it. But it's okay for friends to help each other, Maddie. Like it or not, I already have. I called one of the Chilmark Select Board members last night, only to flush out some facts. The shops on the harbor are leased from the town, and Arnie is definitely leaving. So, technically, the space will be available as of January first."

She blinked, set down her mug, and looked at him. "Seriously?"

He held up a hand that stalled her enthusiasm. "I used the word 'technically,' because I know these things don't usually happen fast. The Select Board won't—*can't*—negotiate anything until they and members of the Planning Board have assessed the place. The guy I spoke with said that can take a week or a month . . . or a year. The timing depends on lots of things, including priorities on their calendar."

"Oh," she said, "well, that's understandable." She didn't know if it was true, but it seemed like the right thing to say.

"It also depends on how many interested parties there are. And they'll need to see a plan from a potential lessee."

"A plan? That sounds discouraging. I was hoping to rent the place, maybe for a year." It was bad enough that her initial idea was probably far-flung and unrealistic, but now, what with possible red tape, competition, and no doubt other hoops she'd have to jump through, she'd most likely be biting off more than she possibly could chew.

Rex didn't roll his eyes at her comment. He was, after all, a nice man.

"There is some good news, though," he went on. "No one else has come forward yet to say they're interested in the space. So if you're the first to submit a letter of intent—tell them your background, your ties to the island, and what you intend to do with the shop—you might score a few extra points. Oh, and in the letter you'll need to say you'll have a blueprint to them before Thanksgiving. That's pretty quick, but it's officially off-season now, and Kevin has worked with an architect who might be able to make it happen. And give you a deal in the process." He paused. "My two cents, however, is that the town's property assessment will reveal some issues of structural deterioration and safety. The building is old. Part of it was replaced after the coast guard fire in 2010, but that's a long time ago now."

The phrase "far-flung and unrealistic" now felt like a certainty. She sighed. "The truth is, Rex, it might not work no matter what. Let's face it, I'm a college professor, not an entrepreneur. I love reading books, but, honestly, I have no clue how to sell them." Then she remembered she hadn't known if she was capable of earning a PhD, either, or that Owen (who wasn't her ex at the time) had thought the idea was "cockamamie"—which he not-so-kindly shared with her after she'd enrolled in her first class.

"Not so fast, Maddie." Rex reached across the table and grabbed her hand. "You're smart and energetic. I, for one, think it's worth pursuing. In case you were wondering."

She forged a smile. "Okay. That's good to know." After a brief moment of more contemplation, she added, "So Kevin could contact the architect and set up an appointment for me?"

Rex grinned and slowly removed his hand from hers; she tried not to let on that she'd liked it there. "I could go with you, if you want," he said, then glanced down at his untouched burrito. "With Kevin, too, of course."

Of course, she thought. *Safety in numbers.*

They finished eating, then said their good-byes, and Maddie headed back to the cabin to get to work on a letter of intent. It might not get her the shop, but if Rex said it was worth pursuing, maybe it was. And maybe he was, too, sometime down the road.

Back to the cabin, Grandma was still out. So Maddie sat cross-legged on the sofa, opened her computer, and drafted a letter for the Select Board, touting her background, education, and commitment to the island, not having a clue if the last item would prove correct. But she could hardly say she might only live there until her grandmother died, after which her son might stick around for a while, not that he'd want to run a bookshop.

She did confirm that a formal blueprint would be ready before Thanksgiving, then drew a loose sketch of a floor plan based on what she remembered about the shop. As she worked, she reminded herself that her world would not come crashing down if the bookshop didn't materialize; it wasn't as if owning one was her lifelong dream.

All she needed was the courage to go through with this first step. Despite that the rest was starting to feel overwhelming.

Closing her eyes, she tried to relax. Then her mind drifted to money.

Simply to get things up and running would be expensive. The town might pay for necessary structural reinforcements, but Kevin and his crew would have to be paid, starting with the architect. Then, with furnishings, fixtures, a computer system, and the upfront cost to stock an initial inventory, the dollars would cha-ching, cha-ching.

With luck, Rafe could build a website and a social media platform and maintain them. But would he want to spend his time on that? And how would she pay for everything else? Did she dare withdraw from her meager retirement fund?

Yes, it was overwhelming. Writing her dissertation had been easier.

Closing her laptop, she realized she should probably give up the idea before it dragged her—and the people she loved—underwater.

And then, her phone rang. She sighed.

It was Rex again.

"We can do it," he said, as if he'd been reading her mind from Edgartown. "If you let me help you."

He sounded so upbeat she did not have the courage to say, "Thanks, but never mind."

"Best of all, I know an investor who loves to support small, up-island businesses . . . and who's willing to kick in whatever you need for start-up costs."

For a moment, she thought she must be asleep.

"Maddie? Did you hear me?"

She cleared her throat. "I'm listening." She blinked. "But how indebted would I be to this investor? Like, how much interest will it cost me? And what if things don't pan out?"

"Don't worry about that now. An investor always knows there are risks."

"Oh, Rex, I don't know . . ."

"It's aboveboard, Maddie. Will you trust me? As your friend?"

She hesitated, then said, "Of course I trust you." She waited for her intuition to provide an answer. When it didn't, she calmly said, "And thank you. But I'd rather try and do this on my own."

He laughed. "Okay, but the offer's there if you change your mind. As for now, Kevin said the architect can meet you at the bait shop, ten o'clock Friday morning if that works for you. Unfortunately, I'll be prepping food at the restaurant, but Kevin can go with you. Everything will fall into place, Maddie. Let's talk again tomorrow." He rang off without saying good-bye, as if he was in a hurry to help put things in motion. Cockamamie as this plan of hers might be.

Later that night, after Grandma Nancy had, once again, padded off to bed, Maddie stepped outside onto the front porch, smiled up at the stars, and let her enthusiasm bloom.

Yes, she thought, everything about the bookshop could fall into place. To be safe, however, she would not tell Rafe or her father—and she wouldn't tell Grandma that things were underway—until a deal was sealed. Then, if it did not pan out, she wouldn't let anyone down except Rex and Kevin. And herself.

With another breath of the cool, clear air, Maddie turned to go back inside. Which was when she saw a white envelope sticking out from under a rock that someone must have left on the porch. Reaching down, she moved the rock aside and picked up the envelope. Bold, black letters on the front simply read: **MADDIE.** Unsealing the flap, she took out a single sheet of paper. Even in the dim light spilling out from the cabin, she could see the message:

GET OFF THE ISLAND. AND DON'T COME BACK.

Chapter 7

Mid-December

Maddie had not left the island. Nor had she told anyone what she'd found.

After several days, when no other notes appeared, she'd dismissed the note as harmless, a joke planted by someone with too much time on their hands. Occasionally, when coming or going, she glanced under the rock. But weeks ago she'd tucked the note in her suitcase and forgotten about it.

Kevin's architect had pulled together everything required for her lease application. She'd presented the blueprint and proposal to the Board before the deadline; they'd hinted that a decision might be made "in January." Rex reminded her that the anonymous "investor" was still available if need be, but Maddie said so far, she really wanted to try to work out the financial part on her own.

Meanwhile, she became immersed in buying new and replacement things for Grandma's cottage and in learning whatever she could find online about running a bookshop. With Christmas growing close, and as engaged as Maddie was, she could not remember being happier. She'd had lunch with

Rex three times (Kevin was there, too), and the outings went smoothly, with the conversation confined to the inner politics of Vineyard life, and how they might or might not affect her plans.

As for Rex, she was content with them being friends, and pleased that he was, to some degree, involved in her project, especially because of his island know-how and connections.

And then Kevin suggested that the three of them visit a few independent bookstores on Cape Cod.

"A day trip," he said at their most recent lunch. "I want to check out their shelving and fixtures, and I thought you might be able to find a few merchandising approaches that are different from the Vineyard bookstores. And Rex . . ."

"Don't tell me," Rex said. "I can check out the in-store cafés because I don't have a clue how one should look or be run." He looked at Maddie and rolled his eyes lightheartedly.

"Well, if Maddie wants to offer tea and snacks . . ." Kevin said.

Rex patted his shoulder. "I'm kidding, man. The truth is, I could use a day off the rock. And there's a new restaurant in Falmouth I wouldn't mind looking in on. Sample a few things off the menu. My treat."

They picked Tuesday, a week and a half before Christmas.

Which was why Maddie was sitting on a bench on the boat now, half listening to Rex talking with an old friend instead of Kevin, because Kevin wasn't with them after all; his wife, Taylor, had "come down" with something during the night, and he didn't want to leave her alone. "Life on Chappy is great," he said. "Unless one of us gets sick." And though, in addition to being a caretaker of several properties on Chappy, Taylor was an EMT with a penchant for diagnosing people, Kevin wouldn't allow it when she was the one who was ill.

Rex had called Maddie at six thirty in the morning, told her the situation, and gave her the chance to bail.

She only took a second. "No, I'd still like to go, if you're up for it. I've been looking forward to it."

"Well, the weather looks decent. Maybe flurries this afternoon, but otherwise good." Snow flurries in December in New England were hardly a showstopper.

As had been planned, they met at the terminal in Vineyard Haven, where Maddie parked her vehicle and got into Rex's, and they boarded the eight-fifteen to Woods Hole. By then Maddie knew that "eight-fifteen" was the proper way to say it, as no one who lived on the island referred to it as "the eight-fifteen *boat*." Slowly, she was learning how things ticked.

Since the day they'd been "together," and their breakfast soon after, Maddie and Rex had not been alone. Which might have been why, when he saw the "old friend," he'd asked if she minded if he sat behind her and talked with him.

Finally they pulled into port on the Cape side in Woods Hole (known for its Oceanographic Institution, famous for amassing the team who discovered the remains of the RMS *Titanic* back in 1985), and began their expedition.

Rex suggested they start in East Sandwich, because it was about forty minutes away, and by then the bookstore there would be open. They then planned to circle down to the store in Mashpee, then back to one in Falmouth—the town next to Woods Hole—where the restaurant was, too. He'd made reservations on the six-fifteen back to the Vineyard. If they finished earlier, they might be able to catch the three-forty-five, if there was vehicle space.

It seemed like a perfect plan.

And it was. At the three independent bookstores, Maddie took lots of photos and notes; instead of feeling overwhelmed, she was now downright enthusiastic. By the time they were seated in the restaurant for their late lunch, she reminded herself—again—not to get too excited until she had a final answer in January, which seemed like a century away.

"Hungry?" Rex asked, picking up the menu.

"Starving." She ordered flounder meunière seared in olive oil, salted butter, and thyme; Rex chose the monkfish because he said he rarely sees it on a menu, despite that it's known as "the poor man's lobster." He explained that most of it's exported to places like Europe and East Asia.

Their conversation was easy; for dessert, they shared a dark chocolate torte with whipped cream and a raspberry sauce. And though it had been a "business trip," Maddie thought it felt a lot like a date—except that the man did not seem interested in her beyond the whole business thing.

She knew that should please her, and yet . . .

Rex checked his watch; it was five forty. They'd dawdled too long at the restaurant, and needed to hurry.

After gathering their things, they rushed up to the desk where he quickly paid the check, and told Maddie they should be okay to make it back to the island. Until they stepped out of the restaurant and were greeted by snow that was swirling in the wind. Blustery, high wind; the kind that caused the big boats to be cancelled.

And so it happened: The six-fifteen (as well as the seven-thirty) would not be running. Even if winds died down in time for the eight-thirty and nine-forty-five, the freight deck—for the vehicles—was already booked.

"I can get a room and stay here tonight," Rex said, as they sat in the parking lot, watching as the Island Home bobbed in its mooring. "We can at least get you a ticket to walk on one of the later ones."

"If they run," Maddie replied.

"Well, yeah."

In another life, in another world, Maddie might have thought Rex had bargained with Kevin to bail on them today, and also had arranged the cancellations. But as charming as Rex was to her, Maddie doubted he had such powers.

"I have an idea," she said. "If the earliest I can get on is the eight-fifteen, we should try and find a room for you now before everything's booked."

"Good point," he said. He pulled his black knit beanie over his bald head and drove back to the main road.

All the rooms in Woods Hole hotels and inns were booked. So they trekked back to Falmouth, where Rex grabbed the last available room at the Inn on the Square. The desk clerk showed them to the room and left them alone; Rex quickly suggested that they brave the outdoor elements and go get a beer at the Quarterdeck. If he was trying to avoid the awkward minute of the two of them standing so close to a bed, she was grateful.

The Quarterdeck was a few short blocks down Main Street; the town green was decorated for the holidays, with twinkling lights and carolers doing their best to bring joy to the world. The cozy pub also was decked out in festive greens with big red bows, and was shimmering with tiny white lights. After they brushed the snow off their coats, a hostess sat them at a table in the front window, which offered a great view of people darting along the sidewalk, laughing merry laughs as they attempted to buffer themselves against the blustery snow while toting bulging shopping bags.

Rex ordered a beer; Maddie, a glass of chardonnay. In spite of the circumstances, she was aware of how relaxed she was, which she knew was because she was with him.

"So," he said, "do you want something to eat?"

She laughed. "Didn't we just stuff ourselves?"

"Well, yes. I guess we did." He looked down at his hands and busied himself by removing his gloves. Then he started shaking his foot, making the table shiver as if it were outside in the wind.

Without hesitation, Maddie reached across the table and put her hand on his. "Rex. Please tell me you're not nervous about us being here alone." Though the thought was kind of sweet, it also made her a bit sad.

He raised his eyes to hers and smiled. "It's that obvious?"

She laughed. "You remind me of Jeff Carson at my eighth-grade dance."

"Who?"

"Jeff Carson. He sat at the table next to me in the junior high school gym. Every time he looked at me, he wrung his hands. He never did ask me to dance."

Rex sat back in his chair. "Can't blame him. I hate dancing. I never did get the hang of it."

"Maybe Jeff hated it, too. We'll never know."

The drinks arrived. Maddie took her hand off of Rex's and wondered if he felt the same sense of loss she'd felt when he'd done that with her weeks earlier.

She tasted the wine; Rex lifted his tall mug of beer, but his eyes remained steady on her.

She wasn't sure if that was the moment she knew she was in love with him, but it was the first time she was sure that she was right.

Later, as they walked back to the inn, Maddie looped her arm through his. The wind had quieted; the boats no doubt would be back up and running. Neither of them bothered to check. Instead, once in the room, they crawled under the bed covers together, warmed each other against the chill, and made love until dawn.

Grandma survived the night in Rex's cabin. Before Maddie had called to say she was stranded on the Cape, she'd contacted Joe, who said he'd be happy to stay with his sister, whether "the ornery old girl liked it or not."

After falling asleep at dawn, Rex and Maddie finally arrived back on the island early the next afternoon. She couldn't believe how happy she felt—not crazy, giggly, hyper-happy, but a mellow, happy-all-over contentment that radiated from her head to her toes.

And, this time, it hadn't been too soon.

As an added dose of happiness, she was looking forward to spending the holidays with her family.

The next day, Joe picked Rafe up in Vineyard Haven and brought him to the cabin; Maddie's father would arrive on the weekend. She wasn't sure when to tell them about the bookshop, and if she should try to enlist their participation before she knew if the former bait shop could be hers for sure. For now, she only wanted to enjoy having all of them together.

After lunch, her heart filled with only good things, Maddie cleaned up the kitchen while Rafe and Joe set out in search of a tree. Then she helped Grandma into the car; they headed first for the airport storage place in Oak Bluffs to locate the tinsel and tree ornaments among Grandma's stockpile; after that, and more important, they would move back into the cottage. Grandma would finally get to see the inside of her newly restored home. Hopefully, she would love it.

Of course she would! The place was too gorgeous not to. Still, Maddie placed her hand over her stomach to try and ward off what felt like a few thousand unwanted butterflies suddenly infringing on her peaceful mood. If Grandma hated the way the cottage looked, Maddie had no idea what she should do.

"When we get home we'll decorate the whole house," Grandma said, as if they hadn't already discussed it. She admitted she'd "given up on the holidays" years earlier, which was why she'd boxed up her holiday spirit along with the decorations, and stowed all of it away. After all, she'd thought she'd lost everyone in her family except Joe, and her interest in celebrating anything had vanished.

Maddie understood that. When she'd been a little girl, Christmas seasons with her mother were magical. She remembered making pretty cookies with her, saving two for Santa, then filling snowmen-shaped covered tins for neighbors. She helped her mother wrap presents in shiny red foil paper, and she wore a green velvet dress with a white crocheted collar to the faculty family party at the college. After her mother died, the magic did, too.

But now, it was back—until they reached the storage unit.

Walking several paces ahead of Grandma, Maddie opened the door.

She stopped. And stared.

Orson was gone.

The classic 1950 F-1 Ford pickup had disappeared.

With it had gone Rafe's surprise Christmas/graduation gift.

Maddie closed her eyes and felt her joy being snuffed out like a holiday candle.

With the butterflies now flocking busily inside her, she quickly steadied herself and turned to her grandmother. "Wait there," she said quietly. "Something's happened, but we'll figure it out . . ." Her words tumbled out, pointless, like unfurling a sail in a blizzard.

But Grandma kept approaching.

"Please," Maddie begged, "I don't want to upset you."

"What's wrong?" Grandma was only a few feet away now. "Did someone break in and steal Orson?"

Maddie sucked in a breath.

Grandma squealed. "Gotcha!" Then she broke into a string of cackles. "Orson is fine. I wanted him fixed up before I give him to Rafe. The guys at Deke's Auto Body in West Tis' have the old boy. They promised to have it ready for Christmas. The original Deke—grandfather to Deke-the-third who runs it now—was a good friend of Rex's father, Stan, but, like Stan, he died decades ago." Like a child on Christmas morning, her eyes danced while she jibber-jabbered.

"Joe and I put our heads together," she continued, her words clicking like reindeer hooves flitting across rooftops. "Orson will be red, because Rafe told me it's his favorite color. And he'll have black bumpers—Orson, not Rafe—matching running boards, and a shiny chrome grill." She rubbed her hands together and moved next to Maddie, who stared into the empty space.

"The bench seat will be reupholstered," Grandma continued, "and vintage controls will replace the old ones. The only visible upgrade will be shoulder seat belts so the old boy can pass state inspection." She beamed. "Even the original AM radio will look the same, but it's going to have a hidden Bluetooth connection, which was Joe's idea. I don't know what that means, but Joe promised Rafe will love it." Finally, she stopped talking.

It was another minute before Maddie's breath steadied again and her butterflies retreated. Pushing down tears, she gave Grandma Nancy a hug. "He is absolutely going to love it. But it must be costing a fortune."

"What should I do, save my money for my old age? I hate to tell you, girl, but that *mishoon* paddled off into the sunset a long time ago."

Maddie remembered one night over dinner when Grandma told Rafe that *mishoon* was the Wampanoag word that meant canoe.

Putting an arm around her grandmother's shoulders now, Maddie said, "Come on, let's get to work. We have decorating to do."

Butchie and I, oh, we were great lovers, the meant-to-be kind. When folks asked how we met, we made up different times and stories for fun, like: "We met in third grade at the little red schoolhouse," or

"We met when we were twelve, fishing for stripers at Dogfish Bar," or, my personal favorite, "We met at the Gay Head Light during the war, when we were both scouting for U-boats." In reality, the boats would have attacked the island on the opposite shore. I guess folks believed us because who doesn't like a good love story? Besides, the truth was pretty boring: We had no idea when we'd actually met, we were both just always there.

We were young when we married—only sixteen. But things were different then. We were tribal kids; when we approached the elders about marriage, they encouraged us. After all, they already knew us. We were too young, but nobody cared because, like I said, we were meant to be together. Besides, we wanted to have a "pod of kids," as Butchie called it, as if kids were whales. He loved everything about the sea; like his father and grandfather, he was a fisherman since he was old enough to hold on to a pole.

We did not have a pod, we only had Hannah, who was born less than two years into our marriage, the same year Butchie and his pals built us the cottage in Menemsha on land he bought and paid for from working hard and with a little extra from his father and grandfather. We never did figure out why we didn't have more kids (God and Moshup know we tried plenty hard), and by the time our girl was ten, Butchie was dead at age twenty-eight when the great ocean took him.

All this blabbering is because folks oughta know I blame Butchie for everything that happened after that. Right up 'til, and including, now. If he hadn't gone out that day like I warned him, he wouldn't'a drowned. And I wouldn't'a made such a mess out of everything.

Chapter 8

They wedged a dozen cartons marked XMAS STUFF into the back of Maddie's Volvo next to the suitcases she and Grandma had been living out of for the past four months since the fire. At last, they were on the road, heading to the cottage for "the big reveal." Traffic was light, so the trip to Menemsha did not take long.

Parking next to Joe's truck in the small lot abutting the backyard, Maddie was glad Joe and Rafe were back—hopefully, they'd found a nice tree. As soon as Maddie stopped the car, Grandma shot out of it and started riffling around the back seat.

"Rafe can bring everything in," Maddie said.

"Hold your horses," came the reply. "I'll be right there." After more riffling, Grandma pulled a paper bag out of a suitcase and announced she was ready. But as they made their way toward the back door, with the cottage in view, her footsteps became slower.

Then Rafe came outside and Grandma picked up her pace and let him escort her in. They were greeted by the sight of a perfect fir that Joe was setting up in the living room. It was full and lush and fit nicely in the corner by the wall-to-wall front windows where the swivel rocker (for Grandma) was going to go; though Maddie ordered it weeks ago, it wouldn't get there until January. Which did not matter now, as a soft aroma of Christmas balsam filled the room.

"Very nice," Grandma said, nodding at the tree, the living room, and the kitchen.

So far, so good, Maddie thought.

Then Grandma turned and scurried down the hall, still clutching the bag she'd dug out of the car. Maddie and Rafe trailed behind her, while Joe secured the tree upright in its stand.

They stopped by the renovated bathroom first. Grandma made no comment, but didn't seem to hate it. Then she checked her old bedroom, with its freshly painted powder-blue walls and new furnishings, including a queen-size bed that replaced the old double one with the squeaky-spring mattress. The woman still didn't speak, but wasn't complaining.

When they reached the second bedroom, Joe caught up to them. The room had been Hannah's, where she'd slept, where she'd dreamed, where she'd grown up. A full wall now stood where the closet once was; across from that a new bed was flanked by white ash armoires. Maddie planned to keep this room for herself and let Rafe use the front room when he was on-island, or when he simply was "on," as Maddie heard some islanders say.

Then her thoughts were interrupted: She realized Grandma was scrutinizing every inch, pressing down on the mattress, poking through the armoires—both of which had been custom-made by a craftsman on Chappaquiddick and a friend of Rex's. She even stooped—the paper bag rattling but not escaping from her hand—and peered cautiously under the bed, as if something would lunge out at her. And still, she didn't speak.

Which was when Maddie's butterflies were reborn with gusto, as if they were converging, preparing to fly, en masse, from Aquinnah to South America the way the monarchs did in autumn.

Without warning, Grandma stopped inspecting. She stood up as straight as her osteoporosis would allow, her nostrils flaring. Then she growled, "Where in tarnation is your hobbit house?"

Maddie swallowed. Hard. Her special place, her secret hideout, her playroom filled with dolls and toys, a cot, and an old seamen's chest was now gone. The only access had been through a tiny door inside her mother's bedroom closet; the only light had leaked through a single round porthole.

Slowly, Maddie looked to Joe, hoping he would answer Grandma's question.

After gathering his thoughts, Joe tactfully said, "Sorry, Nancy. But with the tiny door through the closet being so small, and the porthole not big enough to use as an egress, the hobbit house wasn't up to today's safety codes. The town made us take it down. When we came up with the design for a safer, beautiful addition, they were thrilled." He smiled broadly and held out his hand. "Come with me and see for yourself."

Poor Joe, Maddie thought. He'd had nothing to do with the changes (they'd been her decision alone), but he was willing to take Nancy's heat over the outcome.

Another moment elapsed before Grandma decided to let her brother lead her down the new hallway, created out of what had been her mother's closet, where passage into the hobbit house once was. Now, however, the hall led to the big, sunny new bedroom.

Grandma stood in the doorway and didn't move, her body as rigid as the statue of the swordfish harpooner that stood high on the dunes down by the beach. She stared at the wrought iron, queen-size bed Maddie had bought and the white down comforter that was certain to keep Grandma warm in winter, no matter how hard the coastal winds blew.

But as Joe edged Grandma into the room, her face crinkled into what looked like balled-up waxed paper, her eyes pitching from one side to the other.

In addition to a long, double dresser—also of white ash, also custom-crafted on Chappy—matching nightstands stood on either side of the bed. Extra storage space came with a walk-in closet. And a peaceful rocking chair upholstered in a print of blue hydrangea blossoms sat in the corner by the picture window that looked out to the backyard toward Menemsha Beach and the tranquil water of Vineyard Sound. Next to the chair Maddie had set one of Nancy's original, hand-woven baskets, complete with recent editions of print magazines her grandmother favored.

"It's for you, Grandma," she said tenderly. "And look, you have your own bathroom with a walk-in shower." Maddie walked to the bathroom and motioned toward the space for which she'd spent days and then weeks choosing perfect combinations of white and burnished silver, accented by sea-glass-green painted walls and thick, pale blue towels. A small pot of almond-scented, cream-colored blossoms of meadowsweet sat on the vanity because she'd read that the herb thrived in moist areas. In small doses, it also made a wonderful tea for settling stomachs—which Maddie could have used right then.

"Very pretty," Grandma said at last. "It looks like a picture in one of my magazines." She said it as if she were the owner of several magazine publishing firms, much the way Maddie's father referred to "his game shows" as if he were the producer.

In any event, hope sparked that Grandma loved her new space.

But as Maddie moved to hug her, Nancy shook her head.

"But I want my old room back," she said matter-of-factly. "And I hope my bed with the squeaky-springs mattress met with the town's approval, because there's no way I'll sleep on one of these fancy things." With that, she did an about-face and called to Rafe, who'd been standing by the door. "Be a good boy and tell Joe you need to borrow his truck to take me back to Rex's cabin. I don't belong here anymore."

She stalked off.

Rafe looked at Maddie, then at Joe.

"Take the truck," Joe said to Rafe. "Your mother can bring me home."

Rafe left to catch up to Grandma.

And Maddie pressed both hands to her stomach, closed her eyes, and tried to breathe. "She hates it," she told Joe.

"Yup," was all he said.

She could have begun a back-and-forth conversation about how-can-she-possibly-hate-it and what-on-earth-are-we-going-to-do. Instead, Maddie wandered around the room, straightened the pillows, the comforter, and other things that did not need straightening, while Joe sat in the rocker.

It wasn't until she heard the back door close that Maddie made a decision.

"Okay," she said. "No matter what Grandma chooses to do, I'm moving back here. If she hates this room, I'll use it. As for her old room, if she hates the new bed, too, she can sleep on the sofa. Or, if she wants to stay at the cabin by herself, I can't stop her. In the meantime, how about if we decorate the tree?" She was proud of herself for not crumbling.

But as they made their way back to the living room, her gaze was drawn not to the tree standing idle in the corner, but to the fireplace mantel. Carved decades earlier from a thick piece of aged oak which, according to Joe, his and Grandma's father—Isaac Thurston—had found in Menemsha Hills, and had sawed and chiseled, sanded and coated with something called intumescent paint that was fire resistant. After the fire, it had needed some reconditioning, but, thanks to Kevin, it was back in its proper place, and now served to showcase three items that hadn't been there when they'd arrived that afternoon: Hannah's painting of a Menemsha sunset, the small clay pot with the daisy that Maddie painted when she was a child, and the slightly bruised, somewhat battered quahog shell.

On the floor in front of the fireplace was the paper bag Grandma Nancy had been toting. It was empty now; the mementoes—unlike Grandma—were rightfully home.

Chapter 9

When Rex called Maddie later in the evening, he said he'd love to head up-island and see how they were settling back into the cottage.

Maddie sighed. "Don't bother." She gave him the rundown of how she and Joe had trimmed the tree, though her heart had barely been in it. "I just dropped Joe off," she continued, "and I'm driving back to the place Grandma hates."

"And Rafe?"

She smiled as if he could see her. "He elected to stay at the cabin so she won't be alone."

"But you'll be alone? Is that an invitation?"

Maddie laughed. "Well . . ." She wasn't sure if she was ready for anyone to walk in on them. "If I went to Edgartown there'd be less chance of Grandma showing up at midnight if she has a change of heart."

"How soon can you get here?"

"That depends on if you have a spare toothbrush."

"I'll find one. Or I'll use a vegetable brush from the kitchen, and you can use mine."

"Sounds like something I wouldn't want to miss."

After hanging up, Maddie steered onto the shoulder of the

road and texted Rafe: I'M GOING TO SPEND THE NIGHT WITH FRIENDS IN EDGARTOWN.

He quickly responded: COOL. SEE YOU TOMORROW—JOE AND I ARE GOING SCALLOPING AT DAWN!

All of which was why, the next morning, Maddie was not sitting alone at the new marble-topped, walnut-based table in Grandma's cottage enjoying a late breakfast while admiring the dressed-up Christmas tree. Instead, she was under the covers of Rex's king-size bed down-island, where she'd happily been all night.

Nicest of all, was that last night Rex admitted that until they'd gone to the Cape, he'd been keeping his distance from her because he did not want to just be friends.

Maddie no longer wanted distance, either, so she moved closer now, tucking her head onto his shoulder. "Have I told you I like being here?"

"That depends. Do you mean 'here' as on the Vineyard or 'here' in bed with me?"

"Both."

"Huh," he said, toying with her hair. "Imagine that. So . . . will you be okay if I go away for a few days?"

A warning of intuition pinched her heart. She stopped herself from saying, "No, I won't be okay if you go away." Right then, she did not even want him to get out of bed. So she chewed her lower lip and reminded herself not to have expectations. Wasn't that what she wanted? So she squared her jaw and, trying to sound playful, said, "It depends. How long is a few days?"

"Six."

"Hmm. How far?" Maybe there was a restaurant convention in Boston, or even better, on the Cape. Maybe he'd want her to join him . . .

"California," she heard him say while she was musing. "We're leaving New Year's Day."

She winced. She wanted things to keep blossoming between them—as they finally were. But why . . . *California*? And who were the "we"? At this stage of their relationship, were questions like that appropriate . . . or too intrusive?

"I'm going with Kevin," he added before she could ask. "And Francine and Jonas and their kids."

Francine managed the Vineyard Inn over on Chappaquiddick; she and her husband, Jonas, were Rex's friends, family by choice if not by blood. They were young, with two small kids, and Maddie loved their company.

She relaxed. "Should I feel left out?" she quietly asked.

"Nope. I'm only going because Taylor backed out." Taylor was Rex's sister and Kevin's wife, who seemed to cancel a lot of things, or maybe never wanted to do them in the first place. "She hates flying," he continued, "so I'm taking her place. The restaurant will be closed until Valentine's Day—hooray—so I won't have to worry about that."

"Well," Maddie said, "at least you'll be somewhere warm. I'm sure you'll have fun." Despite a pang of envy, she didn't pry into why the heck they were going all the way across the country.

"We're going to see Kevin's sister, Annie," he added, as if he'd read her mind again. "She's the writer who owns part of the Vineyard Inn on Chappy. She's also the one who backed me so I could buy the Lord James. I told you she lives out there now, right?"

"Yes, you did." She wondered if Annie was the mystery investor he'd mentioned that possibly could help fund the bookshop. Lucky for Maddie, he'd also told her there was no romance—never had been—between Annie and him.

"Anyway, I'll be back before you know it. Meanwhile, I hope you'll forgive me when I tell you why I was so eager to see you last night. Not counting the sleeping part." He turned onto his side, their eyes inches apart. "But it's something that might change your life."

She tensed. "What could possibly be better than what we're doing right here, right now?"

"Well, okay. Nothing could be better than this." He toyed with her hair again. "But how about something else? A friend of a friend swore me to secrecy. But Arnie's is moving closer to being yours. If you still want it."

Maddie blinked. "You're joking."

He gently stroked her cheek. "I don't joke about stuff like this. You have a couple more hurdles. There's competition—only one is in the running, an art gallery, I think, but the guy who wants to do it is pretty young—and the Planning Board is waiting for the results of the structural study, which they should have any day. Otherwise, it looks hopeful."

She turned onto her back and stared at the ceiling. "Wow. I'm stunned. I didn't really dream that the town fathers would want a washashore to be in such a great location."

"Not every washashore has a couple of non-washashores in their corner."

"You mean you," she said. "They don't have you."

"And Joe."

Maddie slid up from the covers, pulling the sheet around her. "Joe?"

Rex nodded. "He called a while back and said Nancy told him about your idea, which, unlike her, he thinks is great. So I asked him to go with me when I brought a batch of scones to the town hall. But before you think I tried bribing them with pastry, it's something I like to do now and again. I do own property up-island, if you recall. Anyway, Joe told the Board president—who happened to be there and who I've happened to know for years—that you're more than capable of putting together a successful business for up-island. He also mentioned that you're Wampanoag."

Before she could respond, Rex reached up and rubbed her back. "So what do you think? Are you prepared to invest your time and money—it will take lots of both—and your future on this island? Can we start spreading the news? And can I tell your grandmother it's okay with you that she moved back into her old bedroom?"

Maddie winced. "What?"

"She called this morning while you were still asleep. She said she was freezing in the cabin and wanted to go home. Personally, I think your son had something to do with her change of heart."

Maddie laughed. "Please say you didn't tell her I was here."

"Let's put it this way. This morning, while it was still dark, Rafe moved her stuff—and her—back into the cottage. She noticed you weren't there. Rafe said you were at a friend's in Edgartown, but, as you know, our Nancy's pretty sharp. So when she called she asked me if you'd been with me all night. I didn't reply. Which was when she said you'd better not do anything stupid like get married and then change your mind." He grinned.

"Argh!" Maddie cried. "You drive me crazy, Rex Winsted." At least when she'd texted Rafe last night, he hadn't pried. In truth, he'd seemed more excited to tell her that he and Joe were going scalloping at dawn.

"I'm supposed to drive you crazy," Rex said with a chuckle. Then he leaned over and kissed her.

In spite of her stomach tumbling again, Maddie kissed him back. Then she realized, this time the sensation inside her likely wasn't butterflies at all, but premenstrual cramps. "Hold that thought until I return," she said, grabbing her purse and making her way to the bathroom.

* * *

After closing the door behind her, Maddie leaned against the sink. The bookshop might happen, it really might. Her father would soon be there for Christmas and, apparently, Grandma would, too. She would hug Grandma. And yes, she would tell her father and Rafe about her plans. Her father would be happy; Rafe would be ecstatic; and Grandma would get over her snit as long as Rafe was there. Best of all, the family would be together again in the beautiful "new" cottage Grandma would come to love, if it was the last thing Maddie did.

Removing a tampon from her purse, Maddie quickly checked herself. She fully expected she was bleeding. But she was not.

Steadying herself on the marble counter of the vanity, she knew she'd been so busy she hadn't been paying attention to her body. Except to know that in the past year, the timing of her periods wasn't always predictable.

Then she realized what the godawful problem was.

And that it wasn't fair.

She'd finally found a man who was special and seemed to care about her—and her interests—and who looked like he might stick around. On top of that, they had wonderful sex. But now, dear God, her hormones, along with her uterus, were drying up. Her time had come for the dreaded *menopause.* Which meant her physical desires were on the verge of shutting down. Soon they would be done. Over. *Finito.*

Oh, sure, she might have her little bookshop. She'd have her family and a new life. But without the ability to have a real relationship—including the physical part—would she be able to love completely?

With the kind of self-pity Maddie detested, she grasped her stomach, hung her head, and thought, *Sometimes life really sucks.*

Standing in Rex's bathroom, staring into the mirror, Maddie reminded herself that next year she'd be forty-six. But wasn't that too young for menopause? Or for perimenopause—its precursor?

She leaned closer to the glass, searching but not seeing any wrinkles, sags, or other vicious signs of getting old. She missed her friends back in Green Hills. If only she had an island friend, a woman her age who might be going through the same thing. But the only females she knew either were too old or not old enough.

Then another horrid thought surfaced: *hot flashes.* When she'd still been teaching full time at the college, she'd shared an office with a professor named Gwen. A decade older than Maddie, Gwen had worn short-sleeved shirts for two long winters and opened the windows, welcoming the icy air. Other than a rare negative comment about her students, the cost of living, or life in general, Gwen never shared personal issues. But the reason behind the flush that often laced her cheeks, and the fact that she often fanned herself with whatever textbook was within reach, clearly announced her condition.

Lifting her chin now, Maddie wondered how long it would be before she developed puckery skin, and if her neck would be the first to go. Rex was older than she was, but so far, his skin was fine. Of course, he was a man, and from what she'd also witnessed at the college, men tended to escape a major downturn at middle age, often becoming more handsome, until later when they nosedived into old age all at once.

And how would Rex react? Would he still want to be with her if she couldn't match his bedroom enthusiasm? He was attentive, but had he been around a woman during what Grandma once distastefully referred to as "the change"?

Maddie puffed her cheeks and pushed out a burst of air.

Then—*yay!*—her senses kicked in: Rex's sister, Taylor! If she was older than Maddie, it wasn't by much. They'd met a few times; Taylor was, after all, married to Kevin, the genius contractor. Could Maddie foster a friendship with her and find out if she'd already experienced the inevitable? As a bonus, since Maddie hadn't yet seen an island gynecologist, maybe Taylor could steer her to one. It might be awkward to ask Rex how she could befriend his sister, so maybe they could get together with Taylor and Kevin during the holidays. Would that seem contrived? Then Maddie remembered that the holidays included New Year's Eve. She could have a party and show off the cottage restoration. It would be only natural for the contractor—and his wife—to be invited. Unless Taylor backed out of that, too.

"Hey!"

Maddie flinched as Rex called to her from the other side of the bathroom door. "Are you okay in there?"

"Great!" she said. "Never better!" After all, Maddie always found it easier to tackle any problem once she had a plan.

Splashing water on her face, and then running her fingers through her hair, it occurred to her that what she'd thought were cramps were gone now. Which was good. Because she now had a bookshop to think about . . . and a party to organize. And maybe menopause wouldn't turn out to be so bad.

Chapter 10

"No," Grandma Nancy declared later that day after Maddie returned to the cottage and broached the subject of a party. The woman was sitting at the new table, a cup of tea and a cookie set in front of her, her head bent as she perused a print edition of the *MV Times*. She made no reference to her hissy fit the day before. "I've never much cared for Taylor Winsted. I don't want her in my home."

Joe and Rafe had been and gone from scalloping and were out somewhere in search of lunch. So they weren't there to plead Maddie's case.

"But you like Rex, don't you?" Maddie already knew that Grandma had adored him since he'd been a kid.

"Rex's sister isn't one whit like him." With that, she set down the paper, deserted her refreshments, and went into the living room. After dropping onto the sofa, she clicked on the remote, neither acknowledging the new 55-inch plasma Maddie had bought, nor admitting that Rafe had showed her how to turn it on—because surely he had.

Obviously, the discussion was over, so Maddie retreated down the hall. As she reached Grandma's old bedroom, she peeked in and saw suitcases open on Grandma's old bed that

Joe and Rafe must have dragged out of somewhere and returned to its rightful place. All of which confirmed that the woman had refused to claim the lovely en suite. So, praying for patience, Maddie tromped off to the lavish new room that apparently was now hers.

Dropping onto the hydrangea-covered rocker, Maddie wondered if Taylor also would prefer not to be in Grandma's house. Hadn't Joe once said Nancy could be cantankerous? Maddie hadn't remembered her that way, but, yes, sometimes she was snarly now. Maybe she'd changed after Hannah was killed. Surely such heartache could do that to a person.

As Maddie sat, quietly rocking, her eyes were drawn to a corner of the room where Joe had stacked what he'd called the "boxes of junk that were stashed in Orson." Maddie had hoped Grandma would go through them—especially the one that held memories of Hannah that Maddie had loved browsing through when she'd been a little girl. In truth, she, too, hadn't been ready to look again.

Until now.

Slowly standing up, Maddie inched toward the cartons; the one with her mother's things was on top, as if Joe had set it there on purpose. She reached down and lifted it; it didn't weigh much, it never had. "It's nice to keep old things," Hannah once told Maddie. "But it's more important to hold your memories in your heart."

It was one of those comments that came as a surprise when Maddie remembered it.

Moving the box onto the bed, she ran a thumbnail through the packing tape that was yellowed and crinkled, as if Grandma had sealed the box right after the accident and did not open it again. Perhaps she'd thought it was better to hold her memories of Hannah in her heart, too.

Peering inside, Maddie started by lifting out old ticket stubs, a pressed flower, a pink ribbon. Then she found the high school yearbook. Maddie remembered how she'd loved looking through it because her mother's drawings appeared on many pages. Opening the book now, she thumbed through it, smiling at Hannah's recreations of island venues: the Flying Horses Carousel, the Capawok movie theater, the redbrick lighthouse up-island at the cliffs that had since been moved back from what had become a ledge due to erosion. And then, there was her mother's graduation picture, her high cheekbones, her gleaming dark eyes, her shining black hair. Island people often told Maddie how much she resembled Hannah, but Maddie knew that her mother was more beautiful.

Her eyes now damp, she closed the book and set it aside.

Next were handmade tribal ceremonial clothes: a beaded, fringed skirt, similar to Grandma's; two colorful shawls, neatly folded; traditional deer hide moccasins; and a small box. She lifted the lid: inside were a pair of oval drop earrings, each with a polished purple-and-white piece of wampum framed in silver. They were the earrings her mother wore every day in the summer when they were visiting Grandma.

Without wavering, Maddie removed her pearl stud earrings she'd bought to celebrate receiving her PhD. Then she put on the wampum ones. Like her newfound heritage, she would honor the earrings and wear them proudly.

She thought she'd reached the bottom of the box when she noticed a large piece of cardboard on the bottom that seemed to be protecting another layer. She took it out, unveiling two rectangular parcels—each wrapped in tissue paper—that had rested beneath. Carefully, she unwrapped one: Inside was a double picture frame, each side holding an eight-by-ten-inch photo. On the left was a black-and-white image of a young woman holding a baby swaddled in a fringed blanket. On the right was a color photo, a different young woman also holding a baby. Maddie deduced that the image on the left was her grandmother holding newborn Hannah. And that the one on the right was Hannah—holding her. Unlike the similar photo, in this one, Hannah's face was visible.

Maddie squeezed her eyes closed, tears welling again. She clasped the open frame to her chest. After a few minutes, Maddie dried her eyes and carried the frame to the nightstand where she stood it, open, on top. She hoped Grandma wouldn't mind.

Returning to the box, she sat and opened the other tissue-wrapped rectangle. It, too, was a photo, but only one. It was in color, and showed a young man in a suit, standing tall, next to a young woman in a simple white dress; she was holding a pretty nosegay of lily of the valley. It wasn't hard to tell that her skin was a couple of shades darker than the man's. On either side of them was a pedestal, each holding a floral bouquet that looked freshly picked. The backdrop was a plain wall; an American flag stood on one side and the Massachusetts flag was on the other. Maddie undid the clips that held the backing of the frame in place. And then she saw an inscription. Not that she needed to read it; she had, after all, recognized the couple.

Mr. and Mrs. Stephen Clarke, someone—her mother?—had penned. Beneath that: *September 9, 1978. Our wedding day.* Nearly two years before Maddie was born.

The fact that Stephen and Hannah were not flanked by bridesmaids and ushers, not even a best man or maid of honor, implied that the wedding was simple; the presence of the flags indicated they'd had a civil ceremony, perhaps at a town hall. A civil ceremony, not a Wampanoag one, not a Congregational one, which she might have expected because her father once said he'd attended Sunday school in an old, white-steepled church when he was a boy.

Then she wondered if the reason behind the sparse setting

was the difference in the color of her parents' skin. She was still considering that when she sensed someone standing in the doorway.

"Have the party if you want, Madelyn," Grandma said, her eyes fixed on the box parked on the bed. "And, so you know, I changed my mind about the cottage because it does look pretty. Until it's all yours, I'm happy to live here the way you want it. As long as you sleep in this bedroom and let me sleep in mine. Lucky for me, Joe kept my bed at his house, cuz he figured I might want it back."

Maddie stood up. "Oh, Grandma . . ."

The old woman gazed around the room and shook her head. "No buts. This room will be your new hobbit house, grown up now, like you." She turned away and garnered a small chuckle. "And you have lots of space in there for Rex. Sooner or later, back and forth trips to Edgartown will get tiring for you both."

By the time Rafe picked up Maddie's father on the weekend, Maddie, Grandma, and Rafe were well-acclimated to the cottage. Grandma even had conceded that the upgrades to the kitchen and hall bathroom were pretty "handy." She was happy that Joe brought her old mattress back so she could squeak again. She was not, however, crazy about the bigger windows—"It'll be hard to walk around my own house in the buff," to which Rafe replied, "Go for it, Grandma. Maybe you'll teach the summer people a thing or two." "Don't get your hopes up," Grandma replied, swatting his arm. They seemed to enjoy teasing each other. And all in all, the readjustment was at last going smoothly.

On Christmas Eve, Joe joined them; he grabbed two blankets and a pillow and called dibs on the floor in front of the warm, radiant fire, not wanting to boot Rafe off the couch where he'd been sleeping since Stephen arrived and Rafe relinquished the third bedroom to him.

"Family shuffles show we care about each other," Grandma proclaimed, as if the message was a traditional tribal mantra.

In the morning, gifts were exchanged: a warm robe for Grandma, a gorgeous alpaca sweater for Maddie. For the men: new chest waders for Joe to wear in the cranberry bogs; a kayak for Rafe to explore the ponds and the creeks; and a top-of-the-line PFD ("Personal Flotation Device," Rafe explained) for Stephen, so he could accompany his grandson on salt water boating adventures. Santa had also left stockings filled with edible and non-edible carefully selected small gifts for everyone.

Then Rafe handed his mother a special package: the photo Joe had taken of Rafe and Maddie on their first Cranberry Day. It was framed and ready for a place of honor on the mantel.

With presents now shared, and the Christmas tree twinkling, they crowded around the table and savored Grandma's cranberry bread, roasted chestnuts, and hot cocoa. Which was what they were doing when a knock came on the front door.

"Get your coats," Joe said after he opened the door that Grandma still didn't like to lock. "It's time for a short walk."

Maddie knew what was coming next.

They donned their coats over their pajamas; it took Grandma a minute to zip hers over her new robe. At Maddie's suggestion, they changed out of their slippers into shoes, then went out the door. Whoever had done the knocking was no longer there.

They followed Joe around to the back of the cottage and up the slope toward the small pine grove that led to the parking area. Rex—the secret knocker—was there, arms folded, leaning against his vehicle. Next to him stood Orson, Grandma's 1950 F-1 Ford pickup that glistened bright red now, with gleaming black bumpers and running boards, and a shiny new chrome grill. A huge green bow adorned its roof.

"Oh!" Grandma squealed. "He's finished!"

Without a word, Rex handed Grandma the keys.

"Grandma?" Rafe exclaimed. "Is this your truck?"

She shook her head and moved next to him, her little frame looking tinier next to his tall, sturdy one. "No," she said, her voice cracking. "Orson is yours now. Merry Christmas, grandson. And Happy Early Graduation."

Rafe's blue eyes grew wide and quickly filled with tears. He raised a hand and pressed his fingers to his mouth—apparently, he couldn't speak. So he leaned down and wrapped Grandma in one of his hugs.

And Maddie's heart was full.

At that point, she figured everyone was crying or trying not to, but it was hard to tell through her own tears. The word *momentous* came to mind.

After a few minutes, Rafe insisted they go for a ride. He and Grandma settled inside the cab; Joe climbed into Orson's bed in case of mechanical failure, and Stephen joined him—not that the political science professor knew diddly about drive shafts or pistons.

"I guess Rafe is happy," Rex said after the others left and he and Maddie wandered down to the beach. The air was still and silent, except for the rhythmic lap of the gentle waves of Vineyard Sound against the shore. Rex slipped his hand around hers; the gesture felt as natural to her as waking up in the morning.

"That's an understatement," she replied with a quiet smile. Then she moved closer. "I have a gift for you back at the cottage." Because there had been little to do while she and Grandma Nancy had waited at Rex's cabin for the cottage renovations to be finished, Maddie had convinced Grandma to teach her to knit. The result was a chunky, soft, powder-blue throw made of alpaca yarn; she hinted that it was something they might enjoy together.

"Oh?" he asked. "Well, as it happens, I have your gift right here."

They stopped walking; he reached into his pocket and pulled out a small box. A strip of sparkling silver ribbon had been looped and twisted into a bow and tied around the wrapping of white coated paper. She looked up at him, bit her lip, and quickly opened the box. Inside, cocooned in shiny silver paper, sat a silver bangle bracelet that showcased a polished oval piece of wampum framed in sterling. Without thinking, Maddie touched one of her earrings.

"The earrings," she said. "The bracelet is almost the same."

"I noticed," he said, leaning toward her for a closer look. "I hope it doesn't mean that I have competition."

Maddie laughed. "They were my mother's."

"I confess," he said with a sly grin. "Your grandmother told me about them. She helped me pick out the bracelet so it would be a close match."

Slipping it around her wrist, Maddie then stood on her tiptoes and kissed him. "I love it. You are amazing, Rex Winsted."

He pulled her into a soft embrace and said, "As are you, Madelyn Clarke."

Chapter 11

A storm was due on New Year's Eve—snow or ice, maybe both, or so the weather folks predicted. Maddie reviewed the guest list: Joe (not that family should be considered a guest); Rex, of course; Kevin and Taylor; Maddie's mother's childhood friend Evelyn, along with Evelyn's son, Brandon (who was also Maddie's attorney), and Brandon's husband, Jeremy; Lisa and her husband, Mickey (from down the hill); and Francine and Jonas, who was Taylor's son and therefore Kevin's stepson and Rex's nephew. Luckily, Francine's assistant at the Inn, a girl named Lucy, whom Maddie hadn't met yet, was home from college for the holidays and said she'd stay on Chappy, cover for Francine at the Inn, and babysit Francine and Jonas's little kids. With Rafe and Stephen, Grandma and Maddie, the number totaled fifteen. Maddie wasn't sure if fifteen adults would fit into the cottage all at once. She'd asked Rex if he would bring a few folding chairs from somewhere (the restaurant? The Inn? It didn't matter). He said sure. Of course, he'd already offered to cater the party, but Maddie had declined.

"Bring one appetizer and maybe one dessert," she said. "Grandma and I will do the rest. I need to try my hand at entertaining for the first time in my life." When she and Owen were married, he insisted that their parties were catered; he said that way, if anything failed, their guests would have others to blame and not her. Later, social functions at the college always were on the campus and the food service folks provided an elaborate array of hors d'oeuvres that tended to taste the same. But Maddie had been off the entertaining hook there, too.

Still radiating with the happy buzz of Christmas, Grandma eagerly helped Maddie plan the menu and pick out music for party ambience—a "playlist," Rafe called it, and said he'd sync it to his laptop, which would be easier than pulling discs in and out of Grandma's CD player. Grandma didn't argue; after all, she'd been teaching him to make her traditional baskets, and he'd been chauffeuring her around in reborn Orson, and it was clear she was convinced that he could do no wrong.

Rafe also ran countless errands for party items, as did Joe and Stephen. Incredibly, everyone finished their tasks before the sun went down at four thirty on New Year's Eve. Even more incredible, the potential storm had traveled out to sea, so Maddie didn't have to wonder if she could freeze the cream cheese and shrimp dip, the baked brie with cranberries, and the pecan-stuffed mushrooms, or if the residents of the cottage would spend days surviving on nothing but.

Though her father had not originally intended to, Maddie was glad he'd stayed for the party. Even better, he and Nancy seemed to be getting along, though Maddie supposed they might never be best friends.

An hour before the party, Maddie was in her bedroom suite, dressing in a winter-white knit skirt and cowl-neck sweater she'd bought for the occasion because they would showcase her mother's wampum earrings and Rex's beautiful gift.

As she slid the bracelet on, her phone rang.

"I'm bringing one less chair," Rex said. "Taylor doesn't feel well, so she won't be coming."

So much for trying to befriend his sister and get the low-down on menopause. On the plus side, Grandma wouldn't have to deal with her.

After hanging up, Maddie finished dressing. Then, looking into the full-length mirror, she noticed that, yes, the purple of the wampum combined with the silver definitely complemented the skirt and sweater. She liked the way it looked; she liked the way *she* looked. Pretty, maybe. Happy, definitely. Both of which felt really nice.

The guests arrived and crowded into the cottage right on time. Kevin was in charge of showing off the renovations: oohs and aahs quickly echoed up and down the hall.

"I got to keep my old mattress," Maddie heard Grandma say when the tour group reached her room. "The fact that you can change something does not mean you have to." After a slight pause she added, "And I'm keeping my bedroom drapes open at night, so anyone who wants can look inside and see me in my altogether."

Laughter filled the air; Maddie groaned lovingly.

Once the tour was over and the eating and drinking were underway, Rex, in his "formal" attire of a light blue dress shirt and black jeans, moved to the fireplace, where he'd lit a fire. Then he turned off the music, raised his glass, and clinked it with a spoon.

"Okay, neighbors and friends. I have an announcement. Or rather, Maddie and I have an announcement."

The jam-packed room fell silent. Maddie's cheeks grew warm, not from the fire or a hot flash, but because she sensed that her coppery skin was blushing. She hoped he wasn't going to announce that they were . . . an item. As far as she knew, only Rafe, Joe, and Grandma had tracked that so far.

She bit her lip and waited.

"I expect we're all familiar with Arnie's Bait and Tackle?" Rex asked the group.

Maddie gulped. She took a breath and wanted to yell, "*STOP!*" Had he forgotten not to reveal the plan until, and if, it was certain to happen? She hadn't even told Rafe yet, nor her father. But as her heart raced and her brain searched for a way to shut him up, Rex kept talking.

"Some of you might know old Arnie has retired. But, as luck would have it, one of our favorite washashores—and one of tonight's hostesses—is going to convert his space into a bookshop."

Maddie stood frozen, her feet cemented to the new floorboards Kevin had installed. She had no idea how to stop the bald man at the mantel.

"Well," Rex went on, avoiding her eyes, "this afternoon I received word from our marvelous town fathers—and mothers—that the deal is official. All that's needed is for Maddie to sign on the dotted line."

She nearly dropped her glass. She set it on the table and pressed both palms to her cheeks, trying to quell the heat. She thought about retreating out the back door and praying for a menopausal cure-all blast of cold air, but didn't know how she could possibly thread her way around all the chairs and the people in the way.

"Seeing as how he did such a great job on this place," Rex kept talking—*God, why was he still talking?*—and gestured toward Kevin, "my talented brother-in-law will handle the renovations. And he'd better get a move on because Maddie plans to open the place at the start of the season."

Had they talked about that?

Evelyn interrupted. "A bookshop! How perfect. We've needed one up here." Her face glimmered with well-applied makeup; her white hair was perfectly coiffed, her white cashmere cardigan and white wool pants complemented a festive, red satin camisole. Evelyn was the epitome of an attractive, well-tailored woman of means.

"If you have kids' books," neighbor Lisa—who was dressed for the occasion with a string of multicolored flashing lights dangling from a black corduroy jumper—interjected, "Loren will spend her allowance there!" Loren was Lisa and Mickey's young daughter.

Maddie then realized that rather than stand mute, she needed to speak. So she cleared her throat and said, "The back deck will be a small café where customers can enjoy tea. And maybe scones." Then she glanced toward her grandmother. "I'm hoping you'll provide your herbal teas, Grandma?"

Grandma stared blankly at Maddie as if struggling to process the news. "I knew you and Rex were up to something," she scolded. "I guess no one told you it's not nice to keep an old lady in the dark."

"But Grandma—" Maddie began, then Rex interrupted.

"We didn't want anyone to be disappointed," he said. "In case it didn't work out."

Maddie, still bewildered, simply nodded agreement, though Rafe and her father surely were wondering why Maddie hadn't told them.

"Unfortunately," Rex addressed his attentive audience again, "Maddie must sign the papers at the town hall on January third at eleven in the morning. As someone who went through this kind of process a few years ago, I wanted to be with her. But unfortunately, I'll be on the other coast with Kevin and Francine and Jonas and their gang."

Kevin, Francine, and Jonas cheered and the others applauded.

Once the little crowd quieted again, Rex said, "So, Brandon, as Maddie's attorney of record—if there still is such a thing—I'm hoping you can attend the meeting with her, and look over the legal parts before she signs?"

"It will be my pleasure!" Brandon said, brushing back a shank of reddish-blond hair that now and then drooped onto his forehead.

More applause.

"Well," Grandma bellowed, apparently shedding her misconception this was the first time she'd heard about the idea of a bookshop, "at last we'll have something to liven up our little harbor. And, Maddie, if you run out of money, we can always sell my property across the creek!" She might have said it with sarcasm; it was hard to tell.

Maddie was speechless. Not only about the bookshop news, but also because everyone now knew that Grandma owned land in Aquinnah—the land they'd planned to give back to the tribe. Which meant that Maddie had to make a go of the shop so the tribe would have the land which once belonged to them. *No pressure*, Maddie thought. Which might have been Grandma's intention when she'd announced it.

"This calls for more music!" Rafe interrupted as he moved to his laptop. "My mom's going to be a shopkeeper on Martha's Vineyard! Yay!"

"Santa Baby" filled the airwaves and happy chatter resumed.

Scanning the room, Maddie noticed one person who did not seem thrilled: her father. He'd backed away from the group and was standing in the doorway by the hallway, watching Francine and Jonas, Evelyn and Brandon start to dance. And Lisa, who had persuaded Grandma to dance with her. The other partygoers were clapping to the beat. Stephen watched them all, but Maddie knew the smile he wore was fake. He obviously wasn't pleased with her impending career change. So chances were, he wouldn't want any part of it.

* * *

"Dad?" Maddie asked after they'd all been glued to the new TV, the ball had successfully dropped in Times Square, and Rex had sent Kevin, Francine, and Jonas across the creek to his cabin for the night (no sense driving on the dark roads back to Chappy). The other guests also were gone; Rex had finished cleaning the kitchen (because he couldn't help himself), kissed Maddie on the cheek, wished Rafe and Stephen a Happy New Year, and gone out the door, too, saying he hadn't packed yet, and they were leaving in the morning. As for Grandma, she'd retired to her squeaky springs an hour before midnight.

Stephen had turned off the music and was sitting across from the fireplace; he'd told Rafe to use the guest room, that he wanted to sleep where he could watch the embers die. So Rafe retreated, leaving Maddie and her father alone.

"Dad?" she repeated.

"Nice party," Stephen replied, his gaze fixed on the simmering logs. "Nice people."

She turned from him and went to the Christmas tree, its bulbs casting their soft rainbow of colors, which, with the radiance from the fireplace, provided the only light left in the room. The next day, their holiday time would end; as was their tradition, they'd take the tree down, leaving only a lingering aroma of balsam that would last a couple of days. By then Rafe would be back on the mainland (or wherever he'd go with Owen and "the stepfamily" this year). Her father also would be gone, and Maddie would be left to figure out how to open a bookshop without his interest or his help.

She sat beside him on the sofa and looked into the embers, too.

"You don't seem very excited about Rex's announcement." She saw no reason to ease into the topic.

Stephen paused, carefully choosing his words, as he always did. "I was surprised. That's all."

"Not in a good way?" she wanted to ask but instead waited for him to continue.

The logs crackled, the tree glimmered in silence.

"I'd hoped you'd come home," he finally said. "I'd hoped that after the renovations were done on this place, after you had your grandmother situated again, that you'd come back to Green Hills and get on with the life you'd worked so hard for. I hoped you'd check in on your grandmother and visit her sometimes, maybe in the summer like you used to do. But . . ." His words trailed off, drifting up the flue like a wisp of smoke.

She shifted on the cushion. "And I'd hoped if I had a bookshop it would encourage you to spend more time here," she replied, "that it might be something we could do together. I didn't expect you to move here, but . . ." Her words then followed his, disappearing into the night as unsettling words between them often did.

After another minute, he patted her knee. "All I want, Madelyn—all I've ever wanted—is for you to be happy."

She did not pull her gaze from the embers. "After Rafe graduates, he wants to live here, Dad. He wants to be part of the heritage he never knew. But I'll come back and spend time with you. Rafe and I both will. After Grandma's gone, well . . . I'm learning to take things as they come." She didn't mention if she thought Rex would be in her future, because she didn't know.

Stephen's eyes glided from the fireplace up to the mantel, to the painting of the Menemsha sunset Hannah had painted, the one with the silhouettes of young Maddie and Grandma Nancy strolling on the shoreline.

He sighed. "The only suggestion I have for you is to go to bed. You must be tired from all the work to make the party such a success. We'll talk more about your plans another time. Meanwhile, I'll leave tomorrow, after we take the tree down. I need to get my feet back on dry land." Stephen's "another time" often meant never. Especially when emotions were involved.

With that, Maddie gathered a comforter and a pillow for her father and planted a quick kiss on his cheek. Then she went down the hall toward her new bedroom, removed her winter-white clothes and beautiful wampum jewelry, climbed into her flannel pajamas, and did as she'd been told.

Maddie slept late. When she finally made her way into the living room, she was greeted by the aroma of fresh coffee. Rafe was standing at the tree, slowly removing one delicate ornament at a time, wrapping each in tissue and nestling it in its proper box. Grandma Nancy was in her new robe and standing near him, supervising. Through the window, Maddie saw winter-blue sky; the air looked peaceful, in post-holiday silence. Her father must have walked down to the beach, in spite of their family tradition to disassemble the tree together.

"Happy New Year!" Rafe said merrily. "Coffee's on the stove. And fresh cranberry muffins from Orange Peel Bakery."

"You already went out this morning?"

"Um, yup," Rafe said.

"He took your father to the boat," Grandma said. "He decided to leave early cuz there's a storm brewing in western New York that he wanted to beat."

Maddie glanced at the couch, where the pillow rested atop the comforter, which was folded neatly. Her first thought was that her father's reason might have been a white lie. Maybe he and Grandma sniped at each other this morning over something meaningless. Or maybe he simply was tired of the gnawing loss of Maddie's mother and her ghostly presence everywhere.

Then she remembered the bookshop. And his reaction.

She'd been annoyed that Rex spread the news as a done deal before her father had been told it was a possibility. Once

Rex was back from California, she'd mention that she wished he hadn't done that. But there was no reason to argue; he'd been excited and wanted to share the joy with people he cared about and who cared about Maddie.

She sighed, then raised a hand and pressed her fingers to her forehead.

"As long as you two have the tree under control," she said, "I think I'll go for a run." She lifted her chin and offered a weak smile. "Save me a muffin?" She retreated to her bedroom without waiting for an answer.

After changing into her running clothes and sneakers, she headed out, jogging up the slope to the parking place behind the cottage. She raced down Chowder Kettle Lane toward North Road, where she took a right, moving faster with each step, trying to escape the questions bouncing in her mind.

Should she really open the bookshop?

Or should she go back to Green Hills, where her father clearly thought that she belonged?

And . . . had she been fooling herself into thinking he'd want to be part of her adventure? Had it made her feel less guilty for abandoning him?

She reached Arnie's Bait & Tackle. She stopped. The wooden sign that once flapped back and forth in the breeze off the harbor had been removed; sheets of cardboard were duct-taped to the windows. Like summer traffic, Arnie had left, but the structure still stood, waiting for her to make up her mind, now that the town fathers and mothers had made up theirs. All she had to do was sign on the dotted line.

"*Arrrgh!*" she bellowed, stirring the still air.

Finally giving up, she pivoted toward the hill off Basin Road that led up to the front of the cottage. Then she walked, because running did not resolve a single thing; that day, it only made her calf muscles sore.

When the cottage came into view, she spotted Rafe

through the big, new windows, standing where the tree had been. Like Arnie—and her father, and their guests—the tree was gone now, too.

With a resigned sigh, she stepped onto the first granite slab at the front door. As always, she glanced down as she ascended, being careful not to trip. Which was when she saw an envelope sticking out from under the top step.

Her hand started to tremble as she reached to grab the envelope. Like before, bold printing on the outside read: **MADDIE**. She ripped the seal open. Again, a single sheet of paper was inside. It had large black felt-tip letters that read:

WHY ARE YOU STILL HERE?

Chapter 12

Her breath stopped.

Her first thought was she had to tell someone.

Her thoughts whirred, with names careening through her mind.

Rex?

Grandma?

Joe?

Definitely not Rafe. She refused to upset her son for what could be no good reason.

But would the others patronize her, try to calm her down by saying it must be a prank, the way Maddie had first thought?

Maybe they'd be right, because who would do this to her? The first note had arrived when she was staying at Rex's cabin across the harbor. Whoever sent the new one knew Maddie was back in Menemsha now, which felt more than creepy.

She wondered if someone might be trying to block her from taking over the bait and tackle, someone who might think that books and tea and scones were only for summer people, not for islanders trying to make a living. As if fishing itself wasn't hard enough without another wrinkle, now they'd have to travel down-island for bait and supplies. It wouldn't matter to them that no one had stepped forward claiming they wanted to run another bait shop. They could blame Maddie, because that would be easier.

But who had known about her bookshop plans?

Only Rex and Kevin knew before the first note arrived. And Grandma, but at the time, she hadn't taken Maddie's idea seriously. Besides, Grandma wouldn't try to stop her from staying on the Vineyard . . . would she?

As for Rex and Kevin, neither of them would have written either note. Maddie was sure of that.

She supposed it possible that whoever wrote the first one hadn't known about the bookshop idea but did now . . . and was using it to ramp up their agenda, whatever that might be. That prospect, however, seemed weak. The "investor" Rex might have spoken to would know now, too. And the town fathers and mothers would, and anyone else at the town hall who saw the forms, or possibly heard gossip. And there was the unknown competitor who wanted to open an art gallery . . . and all of Maddie's new friends who'd been at her party New Year's Eve.

But no matter what, the first note had arrived before she'd made her bookshop intention public—so only Grandma, Rex, and Kevin had known.

So the bigger question was: *Why would anyone want me to leave?*

For now, Maddie only knew she needed to talk to someone she trusted, someone who knew up-island, its people and its inner workings, which excluded the Chappy folks—Francine, Jonas, and Kevin. She didn't want to upset Joe or worry Grandma, but she could call Brandon. Or wait another couple of days when she'd see him at the meeting. Aside from them, Rex was the only one she could trust.

Had he already left? She didn't know, hadn't asked, if they were flying from the island to New York then to L.A., or if they were taking the boat then the bus to Logan Airport up in Boston.

She stood on the front steps, pondering the note, when Rafe opened the door.

"Mom? Any reason you're just standing here?"

"Not really," she said, stuffing the note into her pocket, wishing her brain would stop racing. She glanced down to the ground. "Except I need to ask Kevin to replace these granite slabs. They're . . . dangerous."

"I heard that!" Grandma called from the living room. "Those steps were put there by your great-grandfather, Madelyn. We will not replace them."

Rafe shrugged. "She's the boss."

Maddie nodded and went inside.

At lunchtime, Joe stopped by to haul the tree off to the goats at an island farm. But first, they shared party leftovers, and he stuck around a while, asking Maddie lots of questions about the bookshop that he, too, was excited about. She didn't need to wonder if he had sent the notes—he was far too kind for malice.

The little group—including Grandma, who'd done a one-eighty about the bookshop—then tossed around a number of ideas for the shop, some good, some not, but Maddie applauded them all. There would be time to cull them later; right now, the banter was fun and better than sharing what she'd found under the rock. Especially since in the morning Rafe would leave, and she didn't want him worrying that something bad might happen to her after he was gone.

Finally, the conversation was exhausted.

"I promise to keep everyone up-to-date," Maddie said. "Meanwhile, let me at least get the paperwork signed!"

Then Rafe coaxed Grandma into telling stories about the "olden days" on the Vineyard, which Grandma Nancy liked to share, though she embellished them a little more each time.

By five o'clock, Grandma said Joe had to leave because he was cutting into her nap time and he needed to get to the goat farm. Rafe said good-bye, told Joe that though he'd love to come back during spring break, that's when the rowing team had training camp; their first competitive spring regatta would be the week after that.

Joe grinned and said, "Spring is when things bloom again, and when we clean up our tribal land and ponds for the new season, which helps ensure a healthy environment for all our growing things. As much as I wish you could be here, you have many springs ahead."

The men hugged, Joe left, and Grandma went to bed. Rafe asked his mom if there was somewhere the two of them could go for a drink and a few munchies.

Tired as she was, Maddie never passed up an invitation for some alone time with her son.

They drove to Vineyard Haven before they found a place that was open. An abundance of empty parking spaces suggested most of the New Year's revelers had chosen to stay home and rest.

All the better, Maddie thought.

They parked on Main Street and ducked into the restaurant; they were seated at a long, comfortable bar. Maddie ordered a glass of white wine, and Rafe got a beer. He wasted no time broaching the bookshop topic again.

"It's a great idea, Mom," he said after taking his first sip and wiping a trace of foam from his upper lip. "And a cool surprise. But what was up with Grandpa? Like, doesn't he agree?"

Maddie sighed. She'd always tried to shield Rafe from the few spats she and her father had—especially those over Stephen's retirement addiction to television when she'd suggested that he find a more challenging hobby, not bingo or jigsaw puzzles, but maybe pre-Columbian art or climate change. Something that would encourage him to travel, meet other aficionados with brains as sharp as his, former academics who kept engaged with the world. It might have worked if Stephen had started when he'd still been teaching, before he'd holed up in the Victorian, nice as it was.

He'd countered by saying she was being judgmental. Which she knew she probably was.

Now, however, as she sipped her wine, she remembered that her son—sitting on a barstool next to her, legally drinking beer—was an adult now. And whatever "was up" with Stephen was definitely due to her.

She set down her glass. "It's my fault, Rafe. I was excited about the prospect of a bookshop. Part of the reason was I hoped it would also give Grandpa something to do that he'd enjoy, something where he could use his financial skills and manage that side of things. Most of all, because it looks like both you and I will be here a while, I hoped it would keep us together as a family."

"Makes sense."

"It did to me. But I should have asked his opinion before I went ahead with the plans. I meant to, but the Select Board accepted the proposal sooner than expected. And I sure didn't think I'd hear the news the same time everyone else did. But Rex was thrilled for me. Understandably, though, it shocked your grandfather—which was my fault, and mine alone."

Rafe toyed with his beer bottle, a Sam Adams, Maddie noted. She didn't mention he might want to check out the history of the beer that she'd heard had been named after one of the founding fathers of America, a second cousin to the second president of the United States, and might not have had a great relationship with their Wampanoag ancestors. It would make for an interesting conversation, but not today. So Maddie kept it to herself and waited for his reaction to the current situation.

"You're right," he said. "You screwed up, Mom."

Yikes. As with Rex's announcement, she hadn't expected that.

"It wasn't intentional," she said in her defense.

"Well, geez, I know that."

"I tried to apologize."

"What did he say?"

"First he said that all he ever wanted was for me to be happy. Then he said I must be tired, and that I should go to bed. This morning, of course, he said nothing because by the time I got up, he was gone."

Again, Rafe swigged from the bottle.

"Give him time, he'll come around." He sounded like the older generation advising the younger one. He set down the beer and looked into her eyes. "But you're excited, aren't you? You didn't want a bookshop only for Grandpa's sake, did you?"

"No. I want it for us, Rafe. So we can carve out a life on the island. Your grandfather is an important part of our family. So, naturally, I want him included."

"Okay, but if that doesn't happen, don't forget I majored in economics as well as environmentalism. I could help you with the books."

"Well, then, there is hope. Though I already have you pegged for the website and social media."

He laughed, then said, "Changing the subject, what's the deal with you and Rex? Anything you want to tell me?"

The question came from out of nowhere, sort of like Rex's announcement.

"Um . . . well . . . he's become a good friend."

"Huh. You two seemed a lot closer than when I was here in the summer."

"We'd just met last summer. Since then, he's been a big

help, not only by letting Grandma and I use his cabin, but with lots of other things."

He nodded again, smiled again. "By the way, nice bracelet. It looks like it matches the earrings you had on last night."

She elbowed his arm. "The earrings were my mother's. The bracelet was a Christmas gift. Before you ask, yes. Rex gave it to me." She felt her cheeks flush.

"He's a good guy," Rafe said, then ordered another beer.

Then her phone pinged in her purse. She pulled it out and glanced at the message.

ARRIVED AT LAX. GOOD FLIGHT. MY NAMESAKE SAT ON MY LAP MOST OF THE TIME. She knew he was referring to Francie's little boy called Reggie, whose formal name was "Reginald"—Rex's legal name—because Rex had delivered the baby during an emergency.

Maddie sighed. Rex really was gone. She checked her pocket; the note was there. She couldn't ask him what to do . . . he was in California to have fun, not to be interrupted by a drama queen. As soon as she got back to the cottage, she would put the note in the nightstand beside her bed, along with the first one she'd already stashed there.

With that decision, she turned back to Rafe and asked if he was looking forward to his last semester at Amherst College.

The next morning, Maddie drove Rafe to the boat, and Grandma went along for the ride. Rafe had wanted to go in Orson, but Maddie didn't do well driving a stick shift, so she couldn't guarantee that she and Grandma would get back to Menemsha with the ancient pickup in one piece.

"Joe will keep Orson in his garage until you come back," Grandma told him. "He'll take good care of the old boy."

Maddie was relieved that the truck wouldn't have to go

back to the storage unit at the airport. Now that they were living in the cottage, she and Grandma would have the space to go through the items that were still there, bring them home, keep what was wanted and donate or recycle the rest. One thing Maddie knew was that she was going to hang some of her mother's canvases in the bookshop. They would not be for sale.

"Let's stop at the Black Dog Café for lunch," Grandma said after they bid Rafe good-bye. He'd begged them not to wait until the boat pulled out of its berth; he said it made him feel like he was a kindergarten kid.

"The café it is," Maddie said, and guided her car from the parking area. She was not, however, hungry. With her father, Rex, and now Rafe off-island, her stomach was queasy. Probably because she felt alone. And extremely vulnerable, because whoever had left the notes knew where she lived, and might also know that the men she trusted most had left the island. She wished she was more at ease with being independent; maybe, as Rafe had said about her father, she needed time.

A few miles up the road from the center of town, the Black Dog's lot was crowded. Maddie squeezed the Volvo half into a space, half onto the grass, a maneuver she'd picked up from watching summer drivers.

With the holiday crunch now over, the restaurant was filled with islanders in off-season flannels and jeans. Luckily, two people were about to leave their table, so Maddie quickly claimed it. Grandma said the place had had a makeover, and that she liked the old way better, when the tables were often lopsided and the chairs uncomfortable, but you could order just a coffee and sit for hours reading a newspaper that someone before you left.

She ended by grumbling, "It's too nice in here now."

As they waited for their food (Grandma asked for a grilled

cheese sandwich off the kids' menu, and Maddie ordered a bowl of chowder), Grandma scanned the place.

"Dottie Granger's over by the window," she said too loudly. "I was in school with her mother, who the world hasn't missed since she dropped dead feeding her chickens."

"Grandma," Maddie shushed her, "people will hear you."

Grandma shrugged. "Nobody listens to an old lady." She scanned again. "Over there? The last seat at the bar? That's Gil Martin's son, Henry. Gets his personality from his mother."

Maddie had no idea who Gil Martin or his son, Henry, were, or if the mention of his mother's personality was a compliment, though knowing Grandma, that was doubtful.

Then a white-haired man dressed in tan canvas pants and a yellow slicker began to pass their table, then he stopped. "Nancy?"

Grandma blinked.

"It's me. George Landers."

Glancing at Maddie, Grandma said, "George Landers is the medical examiner who lives on the Cape in Sandwich now. We almost needed him last summer, didn't we?" She turned to George and laughed. "This is my daughter, Maddie."

Maddie wasn't sure if she should correct Grandma about their family tree, but opted to simply smile at George, who grinned as if he understood the error.

"Nice to meet you," he said.

"You, too," Maddie said. "And I'm glad we haven't needed you so far."

"Somebody must have," Grandma interrupted. "Otherwise, why are you on the island?"

"Happily, it's not for business. Stripers are still biting. Caught a couple yesterday at Dogfish. Off Ken's boat."

Nancy raised one eyebrow and looked back to Maddie. "Dogfish Bar is on the other side of our harbor, past Lobsterville Beach," she said, as if Maddie needed a lesson. "Ken Lawrence is our up-island constable."

Maddie felt a small tug in her stomach. She remembered Grandma had considered calling Ken last October when she thought Maddie had vanished, but was canoodling with Rex. She almost laughed that she thought of that word: *canoodling*. It must be as old as Grandma, which didn't seem much older than George-the-medical-examiner.

Tuning out Grandma's chatter, Maddie wondered if she should follow George to the table where Police Chief Ken, aka the constable, might be sitting. Maybe he wouldn't mind if she pulled up a chair and told him about the potentially threatening notes that she'd received. But Maddie could not be that forward, especially since the man was there for lunch with a friend. Still, she'd fuse the name Ken Lawrence to her brain, in case another note was waiting on the front steps at the cottage.

By the time their food arrived, she was tired of thinking.

Chapter 13

Maddie parked in the small space at the top of the hill in the backyard. She told herself it would be easier for Grandma to walk down the gradual slope to the back door, when, in fact, she'd decided to avoid the front steps.

As they made their way to the cottage, a sharp January wind spun up from the harbor, no doubt making the swordfish harpooner shiver in his sculpture, in spite of the red hat that a brave someone had dared to climb up and adorn him with for the holidays. Maddie put her arm around Grandma's shoulders, trying to keep her steady.

Once safely inside, Maddie quickly arranged new logs in the fireplace and lit them; Grandma stood near the flames, rubbing her palms together.

"So Rex is off to California?" she asked.

Maddie could have done without that reminder. "Yes." Attempting to avoid further conversation about Rex, she removed her jacket, hung it in the closet, and started to make tea.

"I wonder if that woman Annie Sutton will come back with them," Grandma continued. "I always thought the two of them had something going, if you catch my drift."

Maddie plunked the kettle on the stove, a wee bit harder

than necessary. She did not, however, take Grandma Nancy's bait.

"She was engaged to that Edgartown policeman," Grandma went on. "But I'm not sure if the wedding ever happened." Having seen people she knew at the café must have stimulated an underlying need for gossip.

"He only went because Taylor decided not to," Maddie heard herself say.

Grandma stood, stared into the fire for a moment, then said, "Huh." She took a step back. "Well, time for my nap." She shuffled off toward her old bedroom without removing her coat.

Maddie took a mug out of the cabinet and wondered why she felt uneasy. Was her intuition trying to tell her that something was going to go wrong? Then she realized it wasn't her intuition that had poked her. It was a slice of envy. *Because Annie Sutton apparently had enough money to risk so Rex could get the Lord James.*

But as she stood, waiting for the water to boil, she vowed she would not let Grandma's offhanded comment ruin the day. Rex would or would not return alone—Maddie couldn't control his movements or his intentions. Sure, they'd had fun together and he bought her a nice bracelet for Christmas and she knitted him a throw, but that didn't mean that he owed her. Unlike Grandma, Maddie would mind her own business. And, right then, that was to try and figure out how to run a bookshop. Because tomorrow she had to show up at the town hall and sign her life away, or rather five years, which was the length of the lease.

She'd created an attractive workspace for herself in the bedroom—a nook with a corner desk and a view of the water. Right then, however, sitting by the fire seemed more important. So Maddie trotted to the bedroom, grabbed her laptop, and returned. When the tea was ready, she set her mug on the end table and curled up on the sofa, wrapping her great-great-grandmother's warm blanket around her legs. Then she put her computer on her lap, opened it, and googled *How to open a bookstore.*

Every article started by listing costs: inventory, construction and fixtures, signage. Instead of becoming bogged down by money, she began skimming articles and extracting interesting points: how to choose the books, unload the cartons, and "receive" the inventory (a computer job); how to shelve the books and keep track of what was where (another computer job). And, hallelujah, there was software for everything except for how to open the cartons and take the books out, which she was fairly certain she could manage. She could also manage to learn new technology; she'd readapted many times, as the college often updated systems while upgrading methods to disseminate information, conduct online classes, and more.

She tried not to wonder what the heck she should do about teaching now. She'd only committed to conduct one online class in the coming spring semester; she now hoped it would be her last.

Opening a new file, Maddie organized her list while being grateful that Rafe wanted to be involved, especially by helping her learn an accounting program. Her father could have done it, but she couldn't count on him now. The reality of that was stinging, but she was determined to stay the course.

The flames in the fireplace crackled and popped while she cut-and-pasted countless tips and tricks. And though her back was aching and her neck was stiff from hunching over the keyboard, she wasn't discouraged by her "stuff to know" and "stuff to do" lists. When she started to waver, she closed her eyes and said, "I can do this. Yes, I can."

Then her phone rang. Unfortunately, it was still in her purse, which now hung from the doorknob of the coat closet in the hall. Hoping it was Rex, she untangled her legs, ran to the hallway, and dug it out. Caller ID said the caller was unknown, but that didn't stop her. There were lots of people on the island who weren't yet in her contacts list.

"Hello?" she asked, breathless from her dash.

At first there was no answer.

"Hello?" she said, more loudly.

There was breathing.

But no answer.

Then *click*, a hangup.

Maddie moved her phone from her ear and stared at the screen, as if doing that would tell her who the caller had been and what they'd wanted. Then a chill as cold as the January wind outside shot up her spine.

Which felt an awful lot like her intuition. And not the good kind.

Maddie wondered if she should call Ken Lawrence.

But she didn't—couldn't—know if the bullying notes and the anonymous call were even connected.

Nor was she sure if Ken was the right person. As a registered Wampanoag now, Maddie wondered if she should call tribal headquarters first. She could ask Joe if that was the protocol, but then she'd have to tell him everything. She'd have to tell Grandma, too, because she'd blow her stack if Maddie shared something with Joe that she hadn't told her first.

In that moment, all Maddie knew was that standing at the coat closet in the hallway, staring at the dark screen of her phone, would get her nowhere. So she retreated to the living room, sat back down on the sofa, and fixed her eyes on the dwindling fire. She supposed she should get up, go outside, and fetch more logs from the stack in the backyard so the room would be nice and warm when Grandma roused from her nap. But moving from the hall back to the couch had depleted her energy.

She wanted to believe the call was a mistake. That someone, somewhere, had plugged in a wrong number and, not recognizing the voice, had rudely hung up.

It was plausible.

Wasn't it?

There was, of course, the breathing. It wasn't the heavy stuff of an obscene call, though it had seemed deliberate. Not that she would know the difference. She struggled to assess the situation.

First the notes.

Now a call.

Was the same note-writer trying a new method to scare her? Unfortunately, Maddie did not believe in coincidences, though many times she wondered why not. Like when she'd wanted out of her marriage, and Owen *happened* to fall in love with his now society wife. Or when she'd been second-guessing getting a PhD as a middle-aged woman without teaching experience, and a position at Green Hills *happened* to become available, and she *happened* to become the leading candidate for their tenure track. Or, most recently, when she *happened* to overhear the conversation about Arnie's Bait & Tackle that *happened* to be down the hill from the cottage, and Rex *happened* to know people at the town hall . . .

She blinked. She wondered if the fire in the cottage that relocated Grandma and her across the harbor to Rex's cabin had also been a coincidence.

What was going on?

And why with her?

Shaking her head, Maddie groaned. "Stop it, stop it, stop it." She quickly stood up, her phone sliding to the floor. "*Nothing* is wrong!"

The notes had been a kid's prank.

The unknown call was a mistake.

With both hands planted on her hips, she moved into the

kitchen and poured a glass of wine, which she carried to the big windows, and looked out toward the harbor where the sun was beginning to set. Soon she'd hear from Rafe, a call or a text, saying he'd made it back to Amherst in one piece.

After that, she'd refocus on the bookshop and what she'd learned that afternoon, all while telling herself that Rex would be home in a few days, and wouldn't be toting Annie on his arm.

She took a short gulp; the wine somersaulted down her esophagus into her stomach, where it landed like a smoldering ember from the fireplace.

"Yuck!" She bolted back to the kitchen and dumped the remaining contents in her glass down the sink, hoping the seesaw of emotions—an up, a down, an up, a down—wasn't due to a couple of silly notes and a single breathing call. Maybe it was part of menopause. Which, weird as it seemed, was preferable to something sinister.

So maybe Maddie didn't need to worry that someone was out to get her. Maybe what she needed was a gynecologist. If there was one coincidence in her life, it might be that Rex had taken Taylor's place and gone to California, because he wouldn't have been any help with her current dilemma. But maybe his stay-at-home sister would.

"Taylor?" Maddie asked when the woman answered the phone. "It's Maddie. I hope I'm not bothering you." In truth, she didn't care if she was.

"You need something?" the husky female voice replied.

Rex once admitted that his sister, who had been a curious, fun kid, had turned into a tough adult, and he had no idea how Kevin had pulled her down off her high horse and got her to marry him. Or why he had. Though Maddie had only been in Taylor's company a few times, she knew that chitchat wasn't one of her strong suits.

"Actually, yes, I do need something," Maddie asked her

now. "It's time I got hooked into the medical services here. Can you recommend a good primary care, a dentist, and maybe a gynecologist?" She figured she might as well go for a trifecta.

"Dr. Gagnon for a primary; Dr. Naylor for a dentist. I have no idea about a gynecologist. I had a hysterectomy when I was thirty. And that was up in Boston, not here."

Maddie scribbled the names Taylor gave her, but stopped, pen in air, after the word *hysterectomy*. She didn't know if she should say she was sorry or if Taylor would rebuke her for trying to be kind.

She decided it would be safest to say, "Oh. Well, thanks for these. And how about a good hairdresser?"

"Patti in West Tisbury. I'll text you her number."

"Thanks."

"Anything else?"

"Only to say we missed you at the party the other night. It was a good time."

No response.

"Are you feeling better?"

"Yes."

"Okay. Good. And thanks again."

Taylor hung up without saying good-bye.

Maddie slipped her phone into her pocket and wondered which of the parents Taylor took after. Definitely it wasn't the one that Rex did, because the siblings' personalities were polar opposites—the Arctic and Antarctica of Chappaquiddick.

Returning to her laptop, Maddie googled *gynecologists, Martha's Vineyard*: four names popped up. Rather than picking one based on the number of stars after their names, she jotted them down. Maybe she should ask Grandma about someone from the tribe. The Wampanoags had lived on the island over ten thousand years; maybe the methods of the tribal women would be more to Maddie's liking—more natural, with herbal remedies instead of prescriptions.

Glancing at the clock, she noticed it was nearly five, long past sunset. She decided to wake up her grandmother, or the woman would not sleep well later. But first, Maddie put the kettle on again so they could have tea together.

Surveying the containers of Grandma's herbs, she selected lavender; when the water was ready, she poured two mugs. While the herbs steeped, their soft aroma filtering through the kitchen, Maddie smiled, thinking that the scent could gently waft throughout the bookshop. With that happy thought, she picked up both mugs and began to carry them down the hall toward Grandma's bedroom.

Until, back in the living room, her phone rang.

She stopped.

It rang again.

A million things sped through her mind: it was Rafe; it was Rex; it was . . .

To maintain her sanity, Maddie ignored it. "If it's important, they'll call back," her father always said when the phone rang during dinner.

With that reasoning, she continued on her wake-up mission. But when she arrived in the doorway of the bedroom, Grandma wasn't sleeping. Instead, still clad in her coat, she was sitting on the edge of the old bed, clutching a pen and a small book. Her eyebrows were pinched, the lines of her brow more crinkled than usual. She looked like she was thinking about something unpleasant. Or painful.

The longer you live, the more you have to put up with.

Some stuff, you have no choice. Like I didn't choose for Butchie to drown at sea, though if he'd had his druthers, he'd of preferred that to being stuck in a hospital bed, hooked up to tubes, or tied to a wheelchair, drooling from one corner of his mouth when he got to be old. I know for sure that he woulda begged not to have been forced to learn those nasty things like computers and the internet and the damn mobile phones. No, Butchie was a fisherman through and through. A full-blooded Wampanoag who lived by the land and the sea our Creator provided. He was a man who hadn't minded that his hometown of Aquinnah was the last town in the Commonwealth of Massachusetts to get electricity, which didn't happen until 1951, not long before Hannah was born.

The only thing he really missed out on was that he would have loved to watch her grow up.

I often wondered what he would have done the night Hannah was killed. But all the wondering in the world wouldn't change what happened, or so I've been telling myself these past forty years.

One thing I do know is that he wouldn't have let anyone bully him into living in a house he didn't like, especially if it was fancy, the way the cottage is now. No. Butchie would rather have lived under the sky and the sun and slept under the stars, his boat rocking gently beneath him.

Oh, how I loved that about him.

I wish I had the courage to write all this down in a notebook so my granddaughter, Madelyn, would know these things after I am gone. Sadly, I learned too late that our stories should be told. Or maybe I was too afraid of being judged.

After all, I had good reason for that.

Chapter 14

"Grandma? Are you okay?"

After a short pause, Grandma winced. "Did your phone ring?"

Maddie handed her one of the mugs. "I didn't get it. My hands were full." She gave her a mug. "Your lavender blend. One of my favorites."

The woman set down the small book and stared, stupefied, at the tea, as if she wasn't sure why she'd accepted it. "Who was on the phone?"

"I don't know." Had Grandma been napping while sitting up, gazing blankly into space? "It probably was Brandon, confirming our meeting at the town hall tomorrow." Maddie sat in the chair by the bed and sipped from her mug. "Do you think we'll be able to stock your teas in the bookshop?" she asked, hoping the thought of being included in the venture would bring Grandma's senses back.

The narrow shoulders slowly raised and lowered in a shrug. Then she promptly stood up. "I need to use the bathroom." She brushed past Maddie, handing her the mug as she went.

After sitting for several minutes, Maddie juggled the mugs,

got up, went back to the living room, and sat on the couch. She'd had odd conversations with her grandmother on occasion, so she wasn't shocked.

"I had a who-zie," Grandma said when she finally emerged.

"A what?"

"A who-zie-what-zie. When you came into the bedroom I'd just had one of those. It's what you get when somebody walks over your grave. A premonition thing. Intuition. Whatever you call it."

The chill Maddie felt earlier found her spine again.

"Your mother used to get them, too," Grandma added.

So do I, Maddie refrained from sharing.

With a tired sigh, Grandma flopped down next to Maddie. "That corner looks strange with nothing in it." She nodded in the direction of where the Christmas tree had stood.

"I've ordered a nice chair for there. But, Grandma? What do you think your who-zie-what-zie meant?"

Another narrow-shouldered shrug. "Dunno. Something dark, usually. Something bad. Maybe I'm finally going to keel over for good."

"Don't be ridiculous," Maddie said. She wondered if Grandma's premonition could have been about the bookshop, and if Maddie should start to take the family psychic tendencies more seriously.

"Okay, I probably won't keel. The who-zies usually turn out to be nothing, anyway. 'Much ado about nothing,' Hannah used to say. Then she'd make tea and we'd forget about it." She lifted her mug from the coffee table and raised it, as if toasting her long-deceased daughter.

"Not to change the subject," Maddie said, which was exactly what she intended, "but do you think I'm being foolish to open a bookshop?"

"No more foolish than I was to start weaving baskets for a

living. Course, we didn't need as much back then. Before Butchie died, we fished for food or grew our own; we chopped wood to heat this place, and packed seaweed around the foundation to keep the wind and the dampness out. I made most of our clothes. But there was gas to put in Orson, and an electric bill to pay, cuz in Menemsha, we had it thirty or more years before they had it in Aquinnah, who didn't get theirs until right before you were born."

Maddie wasn't sure—again—if she should correct Grandma, if she should tell her she wasn't her daughter but her granddaughter. There was little harm in the mistake, but maybe she should coerce Grandma to see a doctor, too.

"You mean it wasn't long before Hannah was born," she said, testing her.

Grandma squinted. "Well, yes."

Then Maddie's phone rang again; her neck tightened. She quickly picked it up, and saw that it was Rex.

Giving Grandma a quick wave, she headed to her bedroom, relieved to hear his voice.

"Hi," she said. "Are you having fun?"

"Hi yourself. Yup, it's great. Today we went to Malibu and watched them film a movie Annie wrote. It was fun. Her place is in the Hills—it's really nice, but cooler than we expected. When we got back from Malibu, Kevin went in the pool and nearly froze to death. Early tomorrow he and I are renting motorcycles and going on an adventure."

"What about Francine and Jonas?"

"They're taking the kids to Disney's Hollywood Studios."

She laughed. "I'd rather be with them than on a motorcycle."

"Nah, you'd love it here."

"How's Annie?"

"Good! But I think she misses the Vineyard. She says the traffic here makes summer in Edgartown feel deserted."

Again, Maddie wondered if Annie would be moving back.

"So, how're you?" Rex asked. "Ready for the big meeting tomorrow?"

They talked about the bookshop; Maddie gave him a rundown of the questions she planned to ask.

"You'll be fine," he said. "Just sign the lease and worry about the rest later."

He had faith in her. She still didn't know how that had happened. Or why, if there was a why.

"Yes, sir," she said with a small laugh. "By the time you return I'll be in debt up to my eyeballs."

"Great! You'll be like the rest of us! We'll celebrate. I'll take you to the diner for breakfast."

"Breakfast? But I don't live in Edgartown. How early will I have to wake up to make it there for breakfast?"

"Good point. Maybe you should come to my place the night before so we'll be on time."

She liked his suggestion.

Later, after they'd hung up, Maddie felt confident about the town hall meeting and pretty sure it was why he'd called: He'd wanted her to know he was supportive. Which made her feel confident about him and about *them*. Maybe it really was the start of a relationship. She wondered when, or how, she'd know for sure.

"Argh!" she moaned, wondering if anyone had created dos and don'ts for becoming a couple after forty, and if she should start googling that.

Refusing to give in to exasperation, she decided to find out if Grandma wanted dinner yet. But when she went into the living room, Grandma wasn't there. A quick check found that she'd retreated to her bedroom, and was now under the covers, snoring.

* * *

Chilmark Town Hall was, as Grandma described it, "within spittin' distance of the community center, the school, the library, the cop station, the fire guys, and the new ambulance building—all right there at Beetlebung Corner where State, Menemsha, Middle, and South roads collide."

Brandon's truck was already in the lot when Maddie arrived. Glancing in the mirror, she checked her lipstick, smoothed the skirt of her tailored navy suit, and hoped they didn't hold her attire against her.

"You look like a schoolmarm," Grandma had said, unsuccessfully stifling a laugh.

"I want to look professional."

"Why? You already have the go-ahead. All they want's your signature. And your check."

In the academic world, appearances mattered, which wasn't fair because not every woman could afford—or wanted—to shop at high-end clothing stores. Still, sometimes—like now—Maddie felt she made a better impression if she wore what she thought were respectful clothes.

By the time Grandma made the comment, it had been too late for Maddie to change.

With her laptop full of lists, a file folder in hand, and the check with the last of her readily available funds that had been earmarked for her retirement, she whispered to her mother to please be by her side. Then she made her way into the building.

She was directed to a small conference room that featured a table too big for the space. Brandon was there, standing, squeezed between the table and a window, looking out. He turned and greeted her.

"Hey, Maddie. They'll be here in a few minutes."

Maddie didn't ask who "they" were because she supposed that, as Grandma implied about her outfit, it wouldn't matter.

She nodded, and edged around the table so she and Brandon would be sitting on the same side, an act reminiscent of a college meeting, where the faculty tended to land on one side, administrators on the other.

They waited.

At twenty-five minutes after eleven, a man with shaggy hair entered the room. He wore baggy jeans and a flannel shirt buttoned up to his neck; his added bowtie gave him a few points. Maddie hadn't met him when they'd presented the proposal and the blueprints.

"Sid Akins," he said, extending a hand first to Maddie. "You must be Madelyn. Nice to meet you."

She said it was nice to meet him, too, because that's what one did. Then she asked him to please call her Maddie.

Clearly Brandon already knew him; they shook hands and said, "Hey, Sid" and "Hey, man, how are you?" as if they were frat brothers, though Sid looked like he had twenty years on Brandon's forty.

"I'm all you get today," Sid said as he sat across from them (of course) and set a folder on the table. "Bob and Sheila are wrestling with some problematic road variance papers." He snickered a friendly snicker, as if pleased that he'd wound up with them and not the problematic road variance.

Nonetheless, Maddie's palms began to perspire when Sid removed a thick stack of papers from his folder; her stomach coiled into what might rival an official U.S. Coast Guard knot.

Several minutes passed in a blur, as Brandon skimmed one of Sid's sheets after another, sliding each over to her for her perusal, not that she was capable of digesting the legal mumbo-jumbo. She was glad she trusted Brandon.

The next thing she knew, Maddie had signed in one, two, three places and handed over her check that the Green Hills College Credit Union had required three days to cut but waived the waiting period because it was for Maddie, daughter of Professor Stephen Clarke, professor in her own right. Perhaps they also knew how she'd be dressed that day.

Given the size of the commitment and the major life-changer it was for her, the fact that the entire procedure took less than thirty-five minutes (after Sid joined them) made it seem anticlimactic.

"That wasn't so bad, was it?" Brandon asked once Maddie had said, "Thank you," and "It was nice to meet you," and Sid had said, "Good luck with the bookshop. I'm sure it will be a winner," and they'd said good-bye, and she and Brandon left the building.

They stood on the dirt lot outside.

"Well, it didn't take long," she said.

"They did their work behind the scenes. It might be a small town, but they know what they're doing." He smiled. "How about if I treat you to lunch to celebrate?"

Maddie hadn't eaten; it was already noon, and the knot inside her had begun to loosen. "Sure. Where?"

Brandon looked around as if expecting to see a restaurant. Then he said, "Not much open up here at this time of year. How about the Black Dog Café in Vineyard Haven?"

It was where she'd gone with Grandma the day before, so at least she knew the way. "Sounds great," she said, and they got into their respective vehicles and started their ignitions.

But before Maddie drove away she tipped her head back against the headrest, closed her eyes, and tried to take in what had just happened: She was now officially the proprietor of a bookshop for the next five years. Whether she was ready or not.

Chapter 15

The restaurant was bustling again, but not like in summer. They found a table by the window that looked out to the outdoor patio and the landmark vintage rail car that Grandma said no one really knew how the heck it got there or why.

"So," Brandon said once they were settled and had ordered—a Reuben for him, a codfish sandwich for Maddie—"how does it feel to be an official islander?"

She pressed her fingers to her forehead. "Terrifying."

"Good! If you weren't terrified it wouldn't mean as much to you." He probably was right.

Maddie then sipped her coffee. "By the way, if I haven't already said it, thanks for your help, especially for your support today."

"Anything. Anytime. My mother adores you and she's happy to see your grandmother so 'energetic'—her word since you've been here. She's tried to look out for Nancy ever since your mom died."

"I know. And I appreciate it. I've also stopped trying to make up for the years I missed with Grandma. She's still pretty sharp for ninety, though she does have moments when she's challenging."

"The bookshop will be a godsend for her. Between that and you and Rafe, well, her life has had a huge turn for the better."

"I hope you're right." She lowered her eyes and toyed with her fork. "I'll be honest, though. She gives me mixed messages. Sometimes I think she would have preferred that I moved back to Green Hills and visited a few weeks in summer, like my mother and I used to do."

Brandon leaned back in his chair. "Nah. She's just getting used to not living alone. To not needing to fix her own food or dust her house."

"Ha! I'm not sure she ever did much of either."

Lunch arrived; they ate in silence for a few, congenial minutes. Maddie liked being with Brandon, and she liked that he and his husband, Jeremy, had become her friends. Beyond Brandon's legal expertise, she trusted him . . . and trusted that he could be rational, not emotional, if she told him about the new wrinkle in her life.

"Brandon? May I ask you something . . . strange?"

He set down the sandwich and took a gulp of coffee. "Ask away. It's probably nothing I haven't heard before." He was a pleasant man with no agenda and no strings.

But as Maddie opened her mouth to speak, a woman stopped beside their table.

"Brandon!" Her white hair was short; her skin was pale, allowing her red lipstick to take center stage. "How are you, dear? How's your mother?"

"Doris," he said, as he stood and gave her a small hug. "Nice to see you. Mom's fine."

Maddie shifted in her chair and smiled at the woman, who now looked at her suspiciously.

"Do you know Maddie Clarke?" Brandon asked. "Nancy Clieg's granddaughter?"

No, Doris said she did not.

"My mom and hers were childhood friends." It was a perfect thing to say because it made it clear that Maddie had deep island ties and hadn't come over on the boat just for lunch.

"How nice," Doris said as her face softened in acceptance.

"I'll tell my mother you asked after her." He smiled and sat back down, a clear indication that he did not intend to foster a conversation.

Maddie said it was nice to meet her.

Doris took the hint, told them to enjoy their meals, and moved to the dining bar. It occurred to Maddie that the café wasn't the place to go to if someone didn't want to be noticed.

"Sorry about that," Brandon said, and picked up his sandwich again. "You were saying?"

She wondered if she should forget it. What if he told her to go to the police? A dash of bad publicity might not bode well for her soon-to-be retail business. Even though she was a Wampanoag, which purveyed a message of respect, she also was a washashore. As Doris's first glance had underscored.

"Maddie? You look pensive. What is it?"

She smiled and rubbed her hands together. "Okay. You're probably the only one I'll tell this to because it's kind of weird and others might overreact." She wondered if she was referring to herself.

He set down his sandwich and fixed his green eyes on her. "And so . . . ?"

"And so, it's probably nothing, but . . ."

His eyebrows elevated.

"I received two anonymous notes."

He said nothing, but he listened.

So she told him. She recited the contents and the method of delivery under the rocks—first at Rex's cabin, then at the cottage. And she told him about the bizarre "breather call."

Brandon scowled. "Did you see the number?"

She shook her head and told him the screen simply read "Unknown."

"Did you tell Rex?"

Maybe Brandon had figured out that she and Rex were sort of a couple. After all, he was a smart man.

"No."

"Did you save the notes?"

She nodded.

"Okay. What do you want to do about it?"

She thought for a moment. "I have no idea. The first note came over two months ago; the second one on New Year's Day. The phone call was yesterday—and might not even be connected. Maybe I just needed to tell someone, and I knew you wouldn't overreact and make a big deal out of it."

He nodded slowly. "Let's hope there's no reason for that. But you haven't gone to the police?"

"No. And I don't want to if I can help it. My grandmother . . ."

Brandon nodded. "She doesn't need this kind of stress."

"Exactly. Besides, though it's disturbing, it seems as if there was any real threat, something would have happened by now."

They sat quietly, then he asked, "Will you do me one favor?"

She looked into his eyes. "Of course."

"I have to go back to Boston tomorrow." His primary practice was in the city, where he mostly worked until the summer. "I have a new client in Montreal, so I might be in Canada on and off. Even if I am, will you let me know if you get another note? Or another weird call?"

She agreed. And felt better already.

When they finished eating and Brandon walked her to her car, her phone rang in her purse. They stopped and glanced at one another; at least if it was another mystery call, Maddie knew at least she had support right there. So she quickly pulled out her phone and checked caller ID.

She blinked. "It's Kevin. All the way from sunny California."

Brandon nodded and waved. "Give him my best," he said, then waved, and started toward his car.

"Hi, Kevin," Maddie said into the phone. "How's it going out there? Is everyone having fun?"

There was dead air for a moment, then Kevin spoke. His voice sounded wavy, uneven. He sounded almost childlike, as if he'd been crying.

"Maddie," he whispered. "There's been an accident." He paused, then added, "It's Rex." He paused again. "And it's bad."

Her eyes blinked. Her breathing felt like it stopped. Then her phone slipped through her hand as her body toppled to the ground.

The next thing Maddie knew, Brandon was bent down beside her, helping her up. He snatched her phone out of the grass.

"Kevin?" he shouted as he opened Maddie's car door and nudged her to sit down, leaving the door ajar. "Are you there?"

Maddie didn't hear anything else. She sat, shaking, watching Brandon's every move, trying to interpret his expression as he listened to Kevin.

Later, she had no recollection of Brandon having driven her home. She remembered nothing until she and Brandon and Grandma were sitting in the living room at the cottage—the same room where, only three nights earlier, Maddie had kissed Rex good-bye.

"The strap of his helmet broke when he landed on the rocks," Brandon was telling Grandma now. "He and Kevin were riding motorcycles in the San Gabriel Mountains. Kevin's fine, but Rex . . . Rex broke his neck in two places. He's in surgery now."

Rex broke his neck but is alive?

Then Maddie remembered that Brandon already had told her that. She set both elbows on her lap and pressed her hands over her face.

"I told Kevin I'll go to Chappy and check on Taylor. He called her before he called Maddie. Taylor might not want company, but, still, he's the only family she's got. And Kevin, of course."

Maddie wondered if she should offer to go and sit with Taylor. She couldn't do that. She wasn't sure she could stand up, let alone drive to the *On Time* ferry, the little raft-like boat that provided the ninety-second link from Edgartown to Chappaquiddick. Besides, Maddie was not family. She wasn't even an official half-a-couple.

"I already contacted Joe," Brandon added. "He'll pick up Maddie's keys and have someone take him to the Black Dog. Then he'll drive her car back here."

See? she thought. *I can't go to Taylor's. I don't have my car.* She was ashamed she was glad to have a solid excuse.

Then Brandon said, "It's going to be a while until they know the extent of his injuries or his prognosis. Until then, the doctor said we'll need to be patient. For a while."

Grandma let out a sound, a kind of whimper.

Maddie found a way to stand up and make her way to the front door. Then she opened it, went out onto the hateful granite steps, leaned over, and threw up on the ground.

Chapter 16

January–February

When Maddie was a little girl her favorite toy was her mother's jack-in-the-box. Maddie loved sitting cross-legged in the middle of her small bed in her room in Green Hills and winding the crank over and over. "All around the mulberry bush"—her little shoulders tensing, tensing—"the monkey chased the weasel." Then, as if hypnotized, she slowed the pace of the cranking, slower, slower, her anticipation building with the lyrics until "pop!"—the lid snapped open and Jack shot up—"goes the weasel!" And Maddie burst into peals of laughter. Jack wasn't a weasel after all, but a funny clown in a polka-dot shirt.

She'd thought of that toy many times since Rex's accident, not the music or the verse or the laughter, but the way she'd been submerged in a dazed state. She also pretended to pay attention to conversations around her and to the responsibilities of starting a new business. But in truth, Maddie was lost in her own space, anticipating the next pop of surprise.

Her father came back to the Vineyard soon after Brandon called him. So did Rafe, who flew back from Barbados, where

Owen and the stepfamily were cruising. Joe came to the cottage every day; after all, Grandma had always thought of Rex as one of her own, and Joe had come to feel that way, too.

Maddie's relationship with Rex went unmentioned, though everyone's support suggested they knew about it. It was, after all, tough to hide the fact that she was upset, worried, afraid for Rex and sad for herself—a casserole of emotions that only Rex, the chef, could have created.

Joe set up a space at his house for Grandma and Rafe to work on their baskets during the day, away from the commotion at the cottage—the bookshop planning discussions, the updates on the building renovations, the weeding through piles of construction and decorating samples. And, of course, distanced from the stacks of books that would soon start to arrive. For the time being, Stephen was keeping them in Hannah's old bedroom—where, next to the bed he was using, he'd set up a small office for himself—so Maddie wouldn't have to be faced with them yet.

At first, she hadn't known if she should fly to California, if Rex would want her at his bedside. But she hadn't known if anyone would expect her to go, including him, if he wasn't in a medically induced coma and had a say in the matter. Then Kevin said Taylor was going. And that ended Maddie's dilemma, because, fear of flying aside, Taylor was Rex's next of kin.

Besides, Annie Sutton was there, however she fit into the mix.

All Maddie knew for certain was on the day they'd learned about the accident, she'd put on the wampum bracelet he'd given her and hadn't removed it.

Like Kevin, Francine and her family returned to the Vineyard. Maddie vaguely recalled that Francine stopped by one afternoon and said she was going to supervise Rex's restaurant staff for the annual deep cleaning and touch-ups inside the

Lord James, and to make sure all was shipshape for the reopening on Valentine's Day weekend. She said that Rex—in addition to wanting the place looking good—never wanted his workers to lose their paychecks, especially in winter. Because Francine ran the Vineyard Inn and its food service on Chappy, she'd already passed the exam for the food handlers' license needed to run a commercial kitchen, which would also allow her to step in and do that at the Lord James if needed.

Staying busy on Rex's behalf seemed important to everyone. Maddie, however, often woke up drenched in a sweaty, scared panic that she'd committed to opening a business she now struggled to care about. She considered asking Grandma to sell one of the land parcels in Aquinnah in order to pay off the lease. Once that was done, she could have her father take her home to Green Hills so she could climb into her familiar, comfortable bed—alone—the way she'd been most of her life. For weeks, the only positive step she'd taken was to phone Dan Jarvis at the college, and leave a message saying she couldn't teach this semester, and to please scrub her name from the roster for good. No matter what happened—or didn't—in the days and weeks ahead, she no longer cared about teaching, either.

People came and went from the cottage, some bringing meals and cookies or cakes, which Maddie mindlessly ate. Many of the kindhearted contributors hung out for a while and spoke in quiet voices as if someone had died, which no one had. As far as they knew.

On a not-too-cold last-week-of-January day, the day before Rafe had to go back to Amherst, Joe arranged for a Fireball ceremony, a traditional Wampanoag healing ritual. He and Rafe rolled up bedsheets, encased them in chicken wire, then shaped them to look like soccer balls. Next, they soaked the balls in kerosene. A group gathered on the beach at dusk;

they chanted and prayed and drummed a little, then Joe and Rafe lit the soccer ball shapes on fire and kicked them from one person to another. The traditional belief was that when the participants came in contact with the flames, the pain they felt would help heal Rex, their brother not by origin, but a White man who had helped the tribe in many ways for many years.

Maddie participated because she did not want to say no.

Two surgeries and a godsend of meds later, Rex was inched out of the coma. Taylor reported that he now knew his name, and that he recognized her. But he didn't seem to know what happened, where he was, or why Annie Sutton was there.

Another week passed, and another.

One cloudy afternoon, as Maddie was devouring half of the last slice of chocolate cake baked by neighbor Lisa, she was musing as to whether Rex would notice or care that her jeans had grown tight, thanks to bursts of sugar she'd come to depend on to give her body a quick charge and help take her mind off of him. Then she wondered why, no matter how benign her thoughts were, they always seemed to wind up on Rex.

She was thinking about that when the back door opened; she figured it was Kevin with the latest news. He'd been calling Taylor every day and reporting upbeat updates to Maddie:

"He's doing great."

"He's starting to talk."

"He took three steps today."

Each time, he added, "Rex survived, Maddie. And he's not paralyzed."

She had no way of knowing if all of it was true or simply words shared to boost her spirits and offer a spark of hope. Kevin wasn't chocolate or sugar, but she appreciated his effort.

"Maddie?"

The voice wasn't Kevin's but her father's. She shoved the second half of the chocolaty slice into her mouth.

"Kevin needs an okay on some improvements to the original layout before he takes the next step," Stephen said.

It had been over a month since Rex's accident, yet her father was still there, still watching out for her.

Glancing at the table, at the stack of papers he'd put there the night before, she remembered him saying he'd read a number of book reviews on summer releases that they could pre-order. He'd asked for her thoughts on them; she hadn't done that yet.

"Let's go see Kevin," she answered. "Then I promise to check the reviews." Maybe the sugar would have done its job by then. Besides, right then walking down the hill seemed easier than reading—and trying to absorb any written words. And maybe seeing the physical space would help reboot her enthusiasm again, even if she needed to pretend for her father's sake and Kevin's.

"You might want to change into your boots," Stephen said. "There's snow on the ground."

She didn't ask when it had snowed or how much there was. She simply bypassed her sneakers and laced up her boots. Then she went to the hall closet, put on her jacket, knit hat, and mittens, and followed him out the front door.

She wouldn't have been surprised if a note was sticking out from under one of the steps—unless the sender feared it would get lost under what looked like an inch of snow. Or maybe he or she had lost interest in everything, too.

The changes to the bait and tackle shop were jaw-dropping. Gone were the narrow aisles, the ancient coolers, and, most importantly, the acrid aroma of fish. Unclogged from Arnie's stinky bait and colorful tackle, the space seemed larger, brighter, more inviting. The back wall was a window that showcased what would become the deck, its railing peeking out over the water. A long counter was framed against a sidewall with lots of space to display extra merchandise like Grandma's baskets, herbal teas, and whatever else might come their way.

On the other side of the room, Maddie spotted a staircase; she mentioned that she didn't remember seeing it before.

"Pull-down stairs were there," Kevin said. "They led to an attic."

"An attic?" Her voice sounded weak, as if she hadn't been using it much. Probably because she hadn't.

Kevin shrugged. "It was more like a crawl space, but the town let me raise the roof three feet, which makes a huge difference."

"It's empty now," her father contributed. "We thought you could use it to expand the retail area. Or maybe use half the space for retail, and half for storage and a small office."

"But won't running up and down the stairs to replenish stock be exhausting for customers?" she asked.

"Got it covered," Kevin said. "We've made room for a small lift that's being designed to also work for wheelchair patrons or other people who might have trouble using stairs. Also, before you ask, I ordered a new HVAC system; it has a high-power dehumidifier that will mitigate dampness on both floors, because the books will need protecting from being practically on top of the water. I put in the same system at the Lord James, and it works great."

They fell silent for a moment, as if the mention of Rex's restaurant reminded them of where he was and why he wasn't there, chatting, laughing, adding his two helpful cents.

Maddie broke the silence and climbed the steps to the upstairs space, which was as welcoming as the first floor. Between new skylights set into a cathedral ceiling and full glass walls on the front and back, the reflection off the harbor created a sensation of being in a snow globe, with rays of sunlight whirling in the air instead of flecks of snow. Once the finish work was done, the effect would be awesome.

"We also reinforced the flooring to accommodate the weight of books," Kevin said. "I worked with the town engineer to determine the average weight of a dozen books, multiplied it by how many would comfortably fit in the room, then doubled it, and added the weight of a dozen well-fed customers."

"Does the town have to approve it?"

"Already done," Kevin replied.

She sighed. "How did you do this so . . . fast?"

"Pigheadedness," Kevin said. "I got that from knowing Rex." Now that his name had been said out loud, Maddie felt calmer.

It was true that Rex could be a pigheaded stickler about his work. So she laughed. It was the first time she'd laughed in weeks.

"But what do you think?" her father asked. "Do you like what we've done with the place?"

"It's incredible," she said, her voice now sounding almost real again. "I can't believe you did all this while I was . . ."

"While you were getting organized," her father said, and rested a hand on her shoulder.

She closed her eyes.

"Hey," Kevin said, "let's go back down, and I'll show you something else."

They moved toward the steps; Kevin kept talking while they made their descent.

"There was only room for one restroom," he said, "but we found a way to make it private by putting it at the end of the hall past the showroom, the lift, and a small storage closet for miscellaneous things."

"No offense, but I'm amazed that a man would have

thought about privacy," Maddie said. "I'm also surprised that both of you plowed ahead with all this. Did it ever occur to either of you that I might want to forget about doing this and leave the Vineyard?" She tried to sound cheerful, not that it worked.

They were back on the main floor by then. Her dad looked at Kevin. Kevin looked at him.

"No," Stephen said, "it did not occur to me that you'd change your mind." He shook his head. "Not once."

Which Maddie knew was his way of saying he'd be okay if she stayed there. Then it occurred to her that maybe the fall-out from Rex's accident wasn't the only reason her brain and body had been rocking—maybe it was also a kind of menopausal mania. Or a combination of both.

"So," Kevin said, his mischievous eyes dancing, "shall we talk about paint? Powder blue and pale green? Like the shades of sea glass we did in the new bedroom at the cottage?"

As their conversation continued, the haze slowly lifted, and Maddie felt herself begin to resurface at last.

Chapter 17

Valentine's Day would fall on a Saturday that year, which would be fun for many people, but not Maddie. Though she almost felt like herself again, the valentine she wanted remained in California, continuing to recuperate. Taylor had returned to the island; updates were less frequent and still didn't suggest when Rex might be able to head east. Maddie felt bad that, despite all she had to do, she hadn't even offered to take a day or two to help refresh the Lord James.

Now, however, it was Thursday, the day before the restaurant reopening, and Maddie decided it was time to "get over" herself, as her former students would have phrased it. So she called Francine.

"Don't you have a bookstore opening soon?" the young woman asked when Maddie offered to volunteer.

"My dad and Kevin have everything under control. And my dad probably would love to kick me out for a bit. Now that I'm functioning fairly well again, he knows I could easily micromanage every move they're making. I've never worked in a restaurant," she added, "but I'd love to do something. Anything. Please?"

"Truthfully, I could use your help," Francine replied. "I

can handle the kitchen—I think—but I don't know beans about waiting tables. Except how to use an iPad and take orders. But I think the rest is harder than it looks."

"Well, I've never waited tables, either, but I cleaned up the potluck tables on Cranberry Day, and my son once had a girlfriend whose family owned a luncheonette."

Francine hooted. "Then you're hired! We're going to do Friday dinner, Saturday lunch, Saturday dinner, and Sunday brunch and dinner. Too much for you?"

"Nope. I'll be there. What about clothes? Is there a uniform? Or a staff dress code?"

"Do you have anything black? Shirt? Pants? Skirt? Something washable?"

"I have a black dress." She didn't mention she'd bought it for her grandmother's funeral, which happily hadn't happened. Or that it was a summer dress, but she'd make it work.

"Perfect. The first reservations are for tomorrow night at six o'clock. Can you be here around three thirty, so we can go over the basics?"

"Sounds fine."

"Wonderful. Maddie, you've saved the day. I really didn't know how we were going to manage. And, hey, here's an idea. We don't close until after ten, and it's a long drive back to Menemsha in the dark. Why don't you sleep upstairs in Rex's apartment? I'm sure he won't mind . . . you've stayed there before, haven't you?"

Maddie blushed. As always, she was grateful that her light copper-colored complexion would have pretty much concealed it if Francine had been there in person. But the flash of shame remained the same. "I was there a couple of times, but I didn't think anyone knew."

Francine giggled. "This is an island, Maddie. And it's off-season, when not much gets past us. The good news is we don't get into gossip."

"Then I won't be embarrassed."

"Don't! Personally, I think it's cool. Rex is a good guy. And . . . oh, girl, no wonder you've been preoccupied . . ."

"And it's why, if I can lend a hand now, I'll feel like I'm helping him in a small way."

They fell silent, then Francine said, "I'm glad you called. And I'm so sorry I haven't been up to Menemsha since right after his accident."

"You have a family, Francine. This has been hard for you, too."

"I guess." She sighed into the phone. "But now that we've both felt sorry for ourselves and each other, I can't thank you enough for offering to help. It'll be an onslaught—we're booked absolutely solid."

"Great. A good onslaught ought to give me a final shake back to reality. So thanks back." They said good-bye, then Maddie realized she had no idea how her father would feel when she told him he'd be dining alone with Grandma all weekend.

Her father's response was a surprise.

"Don't worry about me," Stephen said when Maddie gave him the news that night after Grandma had gone to bed and Maddie stood by the refrigerator, trying to decide if she wanted a bowl of ice cream for dessert or an apple. "Your grandmother will be at Joe's all day. I was thinking about asking Evelyn out to lunch. She's been a good friend—she helped me set up the books for the shop. Did you know she and her late husband formed a charitable foundation for island services?"

Maddie knew about the foundation; the surprise was that her father wanted to take Evelyn out on Valentine's Day. It would be nice for her, as each day the woman soldiered through a heart condition that too often threw her active life an unwanted curve ball. Maddie also supposed that Stephen, like his daughter, deserved some fun—especially after spending so much time around his mopey daughter, not to mention Grandma, who'd taken up pacing as if it were an Olympic sport.

So she said it would be nice of him to treat Evelyn. Then she turned from the freezer, foregoing another snack, nutritious or not. Instead, she decided to pack. So she said good night to him and set out to hunt for proper waitress attire.

Several minutes later, as she stood in front of the lovely white ash armoire, Maddie discovered that her black dress was tight—the cakes and casseroles had definitely affected her dimensions. Racing around the Lord James all weekend would provide a good start for her commitment to scale back, even if her hormones didn't agree. Maddie promised herself that, after the weekend, no matter what, she'd get back to running every day; her only exceptions would be cold, snow, wind, or, worst, high tide.

Continuing to rummage through her meager wardrobe, she found an old black cardigan. It was sad and tired, but the lighting in the restaurant would be romantic, which, with luck, would help mask her outfit's cling and its age.

Next, she tossed clean undies into her suitcase, makeup, and other essentials, then she layered black jeans (also old, but they'd always felt too big) and a black turtleneck, so if she dumped food on the dress, she could wear those. Then she added her flannel pajamas. If Rex were there, she would have packed the sexy-ish nightie she'd bought on a whim after they'd slept together the second time.

But she wouldn't be sleeping with him that weekend.

Not wanting to sink back into a hollow of depression, she slipped on an old nightie, crawled into bed, and forced herself to get excited about the weekend.

* * *

Arriving in Edgartown earlier than planned, Maddie found Francine already hard at work.

"Got time for the tour now?" Maddie asked.

"Absolutely," Francine answered.

They headed to the kitchen to check it out; after all, Maddie had never seen it, having only been at the address three times: once as a restaurant customer, once as an unexpected upstairs visitor who had quickly followed Rex into his bedroom, and the last time—again, only upstairs—soon after they'd been stranded on the Cape.

Ahhh, she thought, then reluctantly pushed aside the memories as Francine introduced her to Rex's sous chef, who was busy prepping vegetables, and whose name Maddie promptly forgot.

Next, she had a quick lesson in kitchen basics, after which Francine presented her with a crisp white apron that she'd set out on a desktop next to a small stack of iPads.

"When you need another clean apron, they're over there in the bottom drawer," she said, pointing across the room, "in the chest next to the freezer."

The freezer, Maddie thought. It was bigger than the one upstairs in the apartment, where Rex had kissed her the first time and melted her heart and her body. She choked back a sneaky tear as Francine continued.

"Okay, grab an iPad and let's go into the dining room. I'll teach you how to take orders. You won't have to worry about taking phone reservations because we're booked—unless there are cancellations, but those are probably doubtful." She handed Maddie a menu, took one for herself, and they left the kitchen, thankfully away from the freezer, because Maddie had no time to dwell on the past, wonderful as it had been.

Friday night the Lord James was crowded with joyful couples, some with faces Maddie recognized from around the island, though she didn't know their names. The only diners she knew were Kevin and Taylor, who were there "to support my brother," Taylor said, her voice more gentle than somber, as if her time with him in California had softened her. Or scared her.

Maddie would have liked to have said something kind, but she didn't dare start a conversation about Rex, fearing she'd cave to her emotions. So she merely nodded and tapped in their orders.

When the last couple of the Friday night crowd paid for their bourbon-glazed salmon, pan-seared striper, and the chocolate torte that they'd shared that featured heart-shaped strawberries floating in thick, sweetened cream, they put on their coats, and Francine locked the door behind them. She leaned against it, and let out a huge sigh.

"And we'll do it again tomorrow," she said. "Twice."

Maddie was so tired she barely made it up the stairs to Rex's apartment, which was freezing—she'd never thought to turn the heat up a bit when she'd arrived. Quickly donning her nightclothes, she realized her feet were cold. Because surely Rex wouldn't mind if she grabbed a pair of socks, she tiptoed to his bureau, pulled out a pair, and slipped them on.

Ahhh, she thought. *Much better.*

Then she headed toward the bed and fell asleep before, burrowed under the covers, she could get caught in a web of worrying about him, for him, for her. When she finally woke up Saturday morning, the room was bright, the sun reflecting off Edgartown Harbor, spritzing sparkles across the ceiling much the way they appeared upstairs in her new bookshop. She allowed herself a peaceful smile, until she realized her feet were hot. And her phone was ringing. Loudly.

Fumbling her way out of bed, she grabbed the phone from the nightstand before it kicked over to voicemail. If she'd stopped to check caller ID, she would have known who was on the line.

"Maddie?"

She rubbed her eyes. "Yes?" The voice sounded vaguely familiar, as her still-groggy brain struggled to emerge from its fog of sleep.

"It's me," a male said hoarsely. "Rex."

She knew she must be dreaming again. "Rex?" she whispered, as if she spoke too loudly she'd be wide-awake and her dream bubble would burst.

The next sound was a cross between a rumble and a cough.

"Sorry. Can't talk well."

Which was when Maddie knew it was him, it really was. She sat down on the edge of the bed.

"Rex?" she said, more loudly that time, hoping it might somehow help him clear his throat.

"I was an accident." His voice sounded as if it was being filtered through gravel. His sentence didn't make sense, and yet, of course, it did.

"So I heard." Her eyes filled with tears. "How do you feel? Are you still in the hospital?" Kevin hadn't had an update for a few days, and Maddie hadn't had the courage to ask. Or to call Annie, not that she had her number.

"Annie's house," he replied. "Nurse."

Did he mean that Annie was nursing him?

"Is Annie there?" she asked. "Can I talk to her?"

"Nurse," he said.

She tried to form her words again, hoping if she enunciated differently he might better understand. But as she began, another voice came on the line. A female voice.

"Hello?"

Maddie swallowed. "Annie?"

"No. This is Beth. One of Rex's nurses."

"Are you at the hospital?"

"No. His doctors agreed he could leave as long as he has twenty-four-seven nursing care. I'm on seven-to-seven, morning to night. He's been at Ms. Sutton's house a couple of days now, and my shift just started. We also have an aide on duty. Anyway, he insisted I let him call you."

Maddie bit down on her lip that had started to quiver. "How . . . how is he?"

"He's coming along. He has physical therapy twice a day and occupational therapy once every afternoon. For all he's been through, he's doing well."

She closed her eyes. "He won't be coming home for a while though, right?"

"That's not for me to say. I only know the doctor won't release him to travel until he's well enough. But his daily progress is good."

"May I speak with Annie?"

"Sorry, she left for work already. We're here in her nice cabana, though. She had it set up like a hospital room for him, except it has a view of the ocean. Rex likes looking out at it."

Of course he does, he grew up on an island, Maddie wanted to say, but did not.

"Shall I put him on again to say good-bye? It's time for his medication and a little more sleep."

"Yes," Maddie said. "Please." There was a faint rustling sound, followed by words Maddie couldn't decipher.

"Maddie?" His voice sounded clearer that time, but tired.

"I miss you," she said, though she hadn't meant to because she didn't want to upset him.

"Be home soon," he said.

Swallowing and closing her eyes again, she simply answered, "Good. Because I can't wait to see you."

"Bye."

"Bye, Rex." Silence followed. Then she added, "I love you."

"Hello?" The voice came from the nurse again; Rex must not have heard Maddie's last words.

Which was probably just as well.

Exhausted as she still was from the night before, Maddie did not want to go back to sleep; she wanted to shower, run downstairs, and share the news with Francine. After all, she'd talked to Rex, she really had. And he'd sounded great. Sort of.

Her first stop was his upstairs kitchen to start brewing coffee. A small bag sat next to the fancy coffeemaker; Maddie picked it up and peeked inside. A bagel that wafted of "freshly made" was tucked inside. A note was included—a nice one, not scary. *See you downstairs at 11:00? Eat this first. Lox and cream cheese in fridge. You'll need the energy! F.*♥ Below that Francine had written*: P.S. Great job last night, Tks.*

Francine was a dear girl.

Then, checking her watch, Maddie saw it was ten fifteen.

Her long-lost adrenaline kicked in.

After wolfing down the bagel and chugging half a mug of coffee, she took the quickest shower she ever had, then dressed in the black pants and turtleneck and quickly rinsed her dress because the restaurant had been crowded the night before and, yes, a patron had bumped into her while she balanced a tray and two plates with bay scallops, fresh-caught in Vineyard waters that day, and potatoes *dauphinoise*, from an original eighteenth-century recipe from the South of France that somehow managed to splatter Maddie's apron and one side of her dress.

As she hung the dress on the shower rod, she wondered if other women had showered there—and, if so, how many. At this age, it was more a curiosity than a need to know, unless one of Rex's "formers" still had her sights on him.

She supposed it was possible.

But with no time left to lollygag, she swallowed her penchant for overthinking, put on her game face, and rushed downstairs where she donned a clean apron and prepared to serve the happy couples.

Somehow, she made it through the weekend, though by Sunday night, she felt sick. She wondered if she'd stressed herself out by working practically nonstop for so many hours, and if menopausal women shouldn't do that. But to be honest, Maddie knew that over these past weeks, her brain wasn't the only part of her that had been suffering: She hadn't felt terrific since she'd stood in the parking lot at the Black Dog Café on January 3rd, and Kevin had called with the news about Rex.

But she was too tired to think about feeling a bit off, as her father would have called it; her task for the weekend was complete, and she'd loved every second of it.

After Francine locked up, Maddie hugged her good-bye and decided to stay in Rex's apartment that night, too, rather than make the drive back to Menemsha.

She slept better than she thought she would have.

In the morning, she tidied up after herself and repacked her suitcase. On her way out of the bedroom, she saw the socks she'd borrowed sticking out from under the bed; they must have landed there when she'd peeled them off Saturday morning. She picked them up now, folded them, and opened the top drawer of Rex's bureau to put them back where she'd found them. But as she started to set them inside, she noticed a blank envelope. In her hurry, and in the darkness on Friday night, she hadn't noticed it before.

It didn't look like the same size as the one the notes were delivered to her in. And yet . . . she couldn't resist lifting it up to be sure. As she did, she saw a greeting card, not a note, under the flap; he hadn't yet tucked it in.

Maddie had no intention of looking at it, but the front of the card was staring up at her. It was white with black outlines of two stick figures, one of a boy, the other, a girl. The only color came from two red hearts, placed anatomically (sort of), and had red dotted lines connecting his heart to hers and hers back to him. Both of them wore a smile, and they were holding hands. More out of instinct than curiosity, Maddie opened the card; there was no printed text or sentimental poem, only a line of scrawly penmanship that read: I LOVE YOU SO DAMN MUCH. Beneath that, Rex had signed his name.

Maddie was stunned, then excited, then . . .

Wait, she thought. Her name wasn't there. Had the card been meant for her? Or for someone else?

Her pulse started to gallop; her stomach somersaulted. Quickly, guiltily, she shoved the card back where she'd found it, as if someone else was in the room, witnessing her intrusion. If the card wasn't for her, she didn't want Rex to think she'd been snooping.

Besides, there was nothing she could do about it.

Not a damn thing.

Except hyperventilate, which was what she started to do.

Sitting back down on the bed, she tried to ease her breathing. She wondered if she should see a doctor or call Taylor, the EMT. She decided to first go outside for fresh air.

Maybe this was what jealousy felt like. Maybe it was how Rafe had felt after the Kiera debacle. Maddie now felt guilty for not having tried harder to prop up her son.

But that didn't matter now, either. She needed to be able to breathe.

Grabbing her things, she hurried down the stairs and outside. She paused on the sidewalk and took several short breaths of cool, fresh morning air. As she closed her eyes and concentrated on breathing, she was finally able to slow her thoughts, which helped her breathe more deeply and then feel a little better, very little, but at least it was moving in the right direction.

Making her way to her car, she decided to head for the hospital anyway. If menopause was responsible for her overreaction, she needed to get some medication or simply advice, something to help keep her body under control, "nip it in the bud," as Grandma might say.

She wondered why first her father, now Grandma were kicking around in her current frazzled brain.

Maybe because they help calm you, she thought.

And they did. Until Maddie drove past the pharmacy at the Edgartown Triangle and she had a sudden, strong zap of intuition, followed by another flash of panic. After a quick gulp, she made an illegal U-turn and pulled into a parking lot, where she turned off the engine and, again, struggled to breathe normally.

Five minutes or more later, her strength regained, she got out of the car, walked into the store, and made a purchase. Then she swung a left out of the lot, and found her way to West Tisbury Road, heading back to Menemsha, not to the hospital. But when she was almost at the airport, she changed her plan again—because she could no longer pretend she was fine . . . without first losing her mind.

Pulling into the airport lot, she stopped the car, dashed into the terminal, and hurried into the restroom. Thankfully, the handicapped stall was vacant; there was more space in there, though she had no idea why she thought that should make a difference. Locking the stall door behind her, she sat on the toilet, ripped open the pharmacy package, and peed onto the wand of the pregnancy test.

Three minutes later, the result boldly announced: *positive*.

Chapter 18

Maddie had no idea how long she sat in the restroom stall at the airport, staring at the stripes on the wand. She kept thinking it must be a mistake. Surely these things weren't perfect. She was forty-five years old—time for menopause, not motherhood. Wasn't it? Maybe something got mixed up with her hormones and resulted in the wrong reading. Oh, sure, she'd read about "older" women getting pregnant, but those were tabloid stories, weren't they? Either exaggerated or simply made up?

Then again, it could be why her black dress was too tight.

She had no clue when her last period was, but it definitely had been a while. September? October? She and Rex first had sex the day after Cranberry Day—four months ago—and only twice since then, both times in mid-December. Maybe the mysterious symptoms she'd felt in the fall had been this. But what were the odds that she'd gotten pregnant the first time with him? The first time for her in a very long time? It wasn't as if she was a fertile Gen Z girl.

Rex, she thought. He was three thousand miles away, barely out of a coma, and might love someone else "so damn much."

How would he react?

Her hands flew to her cheeks as she thought: *My God, what should I do?*

When she and Owen were married, she hadn't needed a stick and a couple of blue lines to tell her she was pregnant: For nearly two years, they'd been trying to start a family. Maddie hadn't felt at all nauseous—and she waited more than three months before seeing the doctor. After her appointment, and the positive results, she told Owen.

His face had turned crimson. He'd slammed down his wineglass, nearly cracking the stem. They were having dinner—seared scallops on a bed of baby spinach with pomegranate glaze. Among other things, he was a food snob, though, as it often did, the meal had come from his favorite restaurant, not her.

"When the hell did you plan to tell me?" His tone was a tick shy of shouting.

Maddie was shocked. She took a sip of ice water; she'd thought he'd be happy. Or at least grateful that she would contribute to his family's privileged line.

"I . . . I wanted to be certain. Most miscarriages happen in the first trimester, so I . . ."

"So you were going to wait and tell me if you did? That you'd say, 'By the way, dearest husband, I was pregnant but didn't bother to tell you'?"

Too baffled to think of a comeback, she tossed her napkin onto the table, fled the dining room, grabbed her purse, and flew out the back door to her car. Though she knew Owen was self-centered, his reaction seemed over the top. Once out of the driveway, she drove to the Victorian, knowing that at least her father would be happy with the news.

"I'm so pleased," Stephen predictably said. His cheeks had brightened, partly due to the wee dram of scotch he held in one hand, the single pleasure he allowed himself every evening. "Your mother would have been thrilled." His eyes misted, and Maddie hugged him; she knew then that everything would be fine.

And it was. By the time she got home, Owen was in the living room, rubbing the back of his neck. He tripped over an apology, claiming he would have wanted to share in her excitement from the start. It was a watered-down excuse, but Maddie accepted it.

Rex, however, wasn't Owen. At least, it didn't seem like he was. Unless it was why her intuition in October had tried warning her it was *too soon* to sleep with him.

Suddenly, the words he'd written on the card in his drawer mattered more to her than a panic attack.

Then came a sharp *rap, rap* on the metal door of the stall.

"Are you okay in there?" a woman's voice called from the other side.

Maddie fought to compose herself. "I'm fine." The words squeaked out, false as they were. "I'll be out in a second."

"No problem. I work at the airline counter and saw you run in here a while ago. I got worried when you didn't come out. I'm not trying to pry—but there's not much action in the terminal this time of year, so it's easier to notice things."

Right, Maddie thought. And she doubted that many women raced into the restroom and then didn't come out for God only knew how long she'd been in there. She'd forgotten the part about living on an island where, like it or not, people paid attention to each other. Cared to ask if they were okay.

Which was nice.

"I'm fine," she repeated, feeling stronger that time. "But thank you for checking."

"Okay."

The restroom door opened, then quietly closed.

Maddie sighed. After another minute, she stuffed the test and its results back in the pharmacy bag, tossed it into the trash, and left the restroom. Out in the terminal check-in area, she noticed a young, redheaded woman behind a counter. The woman waved; Maddie smiled and gave a thumbs-up to her ministering angel.

She supposed if she didn't come up with a solution for this dilemma soon, she could always return to the airline counter and ask the redhead if she knew a good island ob-gyn—with the emphasis on the OB.

When Maddie got back to the cottage, her father wasn't there.

He'd left a message on the table that said he'd be back around two, that he'd driven Evelyn to one of her committee meetings, and he was going to putter around in some stores until she was done.

Maddie was glad he was gone; his absence meant there would be no need to try and mask her emotions—at least for a while.

She flopped onto the new sofa that Grandma pretended to like but probably didn't; would the old woman act the same way with a baby? How could Maddie raise a baby around her if that was the case? It was bad enough that Maddie would be over fifty when her child started kindergarten . . . and ready to retire when he or she was Rafe's current age, and ready to graduate college. And unlike Rafe, this baby would hardly get to know its grandfather before Stephen died, even if he lived to be as old as Grandma was now.

And there was Rex. She didn't know if he hadn't had children because he hadn't wanted them or because his relationships hadn't gone in that direction. But what about now? He seemed content with his life, with his restaurant, his friends, his Chappy family. And he was a little more than a decade older than Maddie, so . . .

She scrunched her eyes and let out a yelp.

"I can't do this!" she shouted to no one. Even discounting Rex's age, she did not have the courage to tell him. Nor could she bring herself to google *Pregnant over 40*, for fear of learning too much about potential complications.

One thing would be certain: Though Grandma and Rex had a special bond, this circumstance might complicate that—and might be perceived as Maddie's fault.

And there was Rafe. How would he feel about having another half-sibling? He was a wonderful, caring young man, but still . . . he was her son. He might be embarrassed. Enough to leave the island and return to predictable Green Hills?

Ugh. She dropped her face into her hands again.

The only things she did know were, first, she was pregnant, and second, she would not marry Rex. She barely knew him. He barely knew her! Besides, where would they live? She couldn't operate the bookshop from Edgartown, nor could he operate the Lord James from Menemsha, especially in summer when the commute either way would take forever.

And why was she worrying about all of this when she was not even sure if Rex could—or *would want to*—come back from California?

Above all else, however, the most important question was: Could she really go through with this—and, if so, should she?

As she took another shallow breath, a cry bubbled up in her toes, then swept up her legs, weakened her knees, and gripped her four-months-pregnant belly, where it paused for a moment until it continued its path to her shoulders, up to her face, and, finally, spilled from her eyes and ran down her cheeks.

She curled up in a ball as if she were the baby.

A short while later, she did not hear the back door open. Nor did she sense the footsteps coming closer. It wasn't until the intruder squatted beside her and took hold of her hands that she realized Rex was there.

He leaned forward, took her in his arms. She buried her face in his chest.

"Sssh," he whispered, rocking her gently. "Sssh. It's okay. I'm home now."

She raised her head, meeting his eyes. "I'm pregnant," she whispered.

He tipped his head and conjured a slight grin. "I know."

"But how . . ."

"You're not the only one with intuition."

Then he swooped her up off the couch and hugged her so tightly she feared she and the baby might break.

Laughing, she pushed him away. "When did you get back?"

He looked awfully good for someone who'd been in a coma for weeks. And his voice sounded normal, as if he had not swallowed gravel.

"I flew home as soon as I figured it out."

"Liar. You had no idea, did you?"

"Yes, I did. I talked to Taylor. She said you looked like crap."

Taylor? Was he joking? And yet she knew he must be right about her looking like crap. Especially now with her tear-streaked cheeks. "What if I look like crap for the next five months?"

"Then you'll look like happy, pregnant, glowing crap."

Together, they laughed. Then Rex tucked her hair behind her ears; she looked in his eyes and saw love looking back. And when he leaned down and kissed her, a soft, passionate kiss, she utterly melted.

Then he rubbed his hand over his bald head. "So, what do you think? Shall we get married?"

She gulped so loudly he must have heard it.

Then the front door opened. And Maddie woke up.

* * *

"Sorry. I didn't know you were sleeping."

"It's okay, Dad," Maddie said, gently rubbing her eyes, not yet wanting to erase her dream.

"How did the weekend go?" he asked.

"Fine. Great. Busy." At least that was true.

"You must be tired. Waiting tables is hard work."

She supposed he was comparing teaching to being a server. "It was fun, though."

Stephen took off his hat and gloves and unzipped his jacket, then set some papers on the table and moved toward the hall closet because he always picked up after himself.

"Shall I make tea?" Maddie asked because she didn't know what else to say. Or do. Other than not share her news. "Have you had lunch?"

"It's after three. And yes, I ate in town while Evelyn was at her meeting."

Maddie heard the rattle of clothes hangers; she checked her watch, surprised that it was so late. "How is she?"

"She's doing well. Busy. I think her new medication is helping."

"That's good." As Maddie started to stand, she noticed that her belly looked watermelon-swollen. Not that her father would recognize it for what it was. *But a woman would*, she thought. Other than the women who'd come and gone with cakes and casseroles these past weeks, she had only walked around when Grandma or Francine were there. Maybe Grandma's vision had faded enough, and Francine was too wrapped up in the hustle of the restaurant, for either of them to have noticed. Still, she quickly sat down again, in case Stephen was more aware than she gave him credit for.

"Your grandmother's not back from her appointment?"

Maddie scowled. Then she remembered Joe saying last week that he would take Grandma to the hospital today for her annual checkup. *Good thing you didn't go there after all*, she thought.

Bumping into her grandmother in the halls of Martha's Vineyard Hospital would have called for an explanation.

"No, she's not here yet," she said, then added, "On second thought, would you mind making the tea? You're right. Waiting tables is hard work."

"Coming up. Lavender?" Good dad that he was, he ambled into the kitchen, while Maddie tried hiding her belly with Grandma's hand-knit throw.

"Sounds great. Thanks, Dad." While his back was turned, she got up from the sofa and quickly moved to the kitchen chair. She knew her hide-and-seek behavior was ridiculous, but since checking that wand, she felt as if her belly was now a billboard. Painted in neon. With giant spotlights on it.

"Sandwich? Someone brought us ham."

"Okay. And a slice of cheese? Maybe a few chips?" She was hungry. She would, however, have to clean up her diet if she was going to go through with having the baby—a phrase that suddenly caught her off balance. Though Maddie never had a problem with others who made a different choice, she knew it wouldn't work for her. Instead, she would face whatever came with raising the child; after all, she was fortunate to be a well-educated, responsible woman. Somehow, she would manage to embrace the situation and be grateful for what lay ahead.

There, she thought. *Decision resolved.*

"Rex called yesterday," she managed to say.

Her father let out a whistle. "Really? Wow. How is he? How did he sound?"

"He was kind of groggy and hard to understand, but his nurse took the phone and said he's doing well considering what he's been through." They weren't nurse Beth's exact words, but close enough.

"Well, that's great news," Stephen said.

She nodded, determined not to cry. And then, as her father set the plate and the tea in front of her, she did.

"Madelyn . . . ?" he asked.

She briskly wiped her cheeks. "Sorry. I feel so bad for all he's been going through."

"We all do."

She nodded again.

He walked back to the kitchen. "Maybe he'll be home before we know it."

She wondered if he had a clue that she and Rex had become more than friends. Then she remembered the card in Rex's bureau drawer and cradled her belly again.

"In the meantime," Stephen said, "I have something that might cheer you up." He returned to the table and put several packets of coated cardboard next to her plate. "Paint chips from the hardware store. Kevin said there's no hurry, as long as he can order by April. You only need to pick the shades you want. I brought blues and greens and whites and ivories. I can get other colors, if you'd rather."

She wiped her cheeks and forced a smile. "These will be fine. Thanks, Dad."

"Oh, and there's this," Stephen added, pulling an envelope from his pocket and handing it to her. "I found it sticking out from under a rock at the front door."

One of the worst parts about being ninety is when you forget things you wish you could remember, and remember things you wish you could forget.

In my day, I was pretty smart for a girl. But even those who weren't like me had rough times, too, like back in the early '60s when codfish were abundant. As a fisherman, and a good one at that, Butchie got caught up in the glory and the greed; how was he to know he was contributing to the overfishing, making matters worse for those yet to come?

Not that he lived long enough to know.

He went out one day alone. His fishing and business partner, Evelyn Morgan's father (I forget his first name—the last one was Davis) warned him against it, said a storm was brewing at Georges Bank—their favorite spot. But Butchie saw big dollar signs, a chance to do some serious investing for our future.

Some future it turned out to be. The storm was worse than predicted. Butchie's boat capsized out there in the Bank, bringing Butchie down with it.

So that's one thing I remember I wish I could forget. Maybe the older somebody gets, more things like that come back to haunt them. If we could pick and choose our memories, we might not be afraid who might find out what, or the stuff that would fall to pieces after that.

Like what could happen now.

Chapter 19

She'd promised to call Brandon.

In order to do that, Maddie would have to stand up and navigate her way to the sofa, where she'd left her phone. And she'd have to go somewhere where her father could not overhear her conversation.

Moving right then, however, did not feel like an option. Though she was in a straight chair, she'd started to rock back and forth, the envelope clutched in her hand. It now seemed like, for months, she'd been targeted; mostly, she'd wondered *who?* Now the bigger question seemed to be *why?*

Was it to bully her? Scare her? Or was it only a harmless prank?

Three notes—and a single, stupid phone call that probably wasn't related—over a four-month span hardly suggested her life was in peril. If so, her intuition surely would have kicked in by now to warn her.

Wouldn't it have?

Brandon most likely would say it was time for her to go to the police. But with no signature or return address, no pattern to the timing of the notes, and nothing else that revealed a darn thing, notifying the police seemed pointless. Other than watching the cottage twenty-four-seven—which she couldn't expect them to do now with their smaller, off-season staff—she would be asking the impossible.

She couldn't tell Rex for obvious reasons.

Joe might know of an up-island mischief-maker inclined to try and run off a washashore for fun. But telling Joe might stir up discord within the tribe.

She supposed she could leave a note of her own under the rock, calling the perpetrator's bluff: *I'm sorry you don't want me here. Tough luck. I'm not leaving.* But that would be juvenile, as if she was tugging at her ear lobes while sticking out her tongue.

After pondering her options, Maddie made a decision: In light of Rex's condition, her pregnancy, and still having late-night doubts about moving forward with the bookshop, worrying about a few pathetic notes was petty and self-indulgent. The level of danger was low; she might make things worse if she—or the police—tried to flush out and confront the sender. The only sensible solution was to forget it.

With her tea and sandwich untouched and envelope still sealed, she stood up and walked down the hall, past the room where Stephen was perusing the internet. Once in her bedroom, she deposited the unread note in the nightstand on top of the others, changed into a nightgown, and lay down on her bed. Worn out from the weekend and all the worrying that had followed, she stared at the ceiling and tried to focus on being happy that Rex had called, that he was and would be okay, and that everything would come together as it would. Or would not.

By the time Maddie awoke, it was dark. And though she would have preferred to savor the quiet, she was hungry.

Getting up, she put on her robe and slippers and padded down the hall toward the kitchen. But as she approached her mother's old room, she heard her father say something in a low voice. Thinking he'd been speaking to her, she turned to go in but the door was closed. Then she heard him laugh.

She stopped.

His next words were clear. "I hope it's only a matter of time. How long can you wait?"

Was he talking to himself? Maddie wasn't sure if she should interrupt or keep walking and pretend that she hadn't heard. She waited a few seconds, but there was only silence. Maybe he'd had a talk-to-yourself moment; she was guilty of those—usually in the supermarket—which she followed by a short prayer that no one had heard her.

But as she started to step away, his voice resumed.

"There's another minor complication, but I think we can get around it."

He was on the phone. Her intuition pricked her like a thorn on a *Rosa rugosa*.

"Look, Dan," the lower tone said, "I don't know what else to say. She gets more entrenched in this place every day. But I can't believe it's too late."

She went rigid. Her father was talking about *her* . . . to . . . *Dan*? As in Dan Jarvis of Green Hills College? The same man who had practically handed her the tenure position that she'd since turned down in order to stay on the Vineyard and be with her grandmother and have a new life?

Maddie leaned her ear close to the crack in the old wood doorway that hadn't needed replacing after the fire.

Stephen had ceased talking; he must have been listening. Then he said, "I'll keep trying. Remember, I want her there as much as you do."

Maddie wasn't sure if she felt angry or afraid.

Creeping back to her bedroom, she closed the door and went back to bed. But even under the covers she couldn't get warm.

Had her father been trying to appease Dan? Or did he genuinely want her back in Green Hills? Had he been pretending to help set up the bookshop to indulge her . . . while, all this time, he'd been plotting against her?

Then she remembered the notes.

GET OFF THE ISLAND, the first one had read. She'd found it right after Cranberry Day, when she'd been sure it was from someone who'd heard she wanted the old bait and tackle shop. But her dad had left the Vineyard two days before the note arrived. Could he have put it on the front porch at Rex's cabin, where she—or Grandma, or Joe, or Rafe, all of whom had come and gone those couple of days—hadn't noticed? Or had someone delivered it for him? If so, who else would have agreed to the charade?

Grandma? Joe? Not a chance. At least she didn't think there was. But who else?

A single name came to mind: *Evelyn*?

No. Not Evelyn, either. Maddie scolded herself for being suspicious of people who'd done so much for her.

"Maddie? Are you awake?" His voice again. That time, at her closed bedroom door. "I see you didn't touch the sandwich. If you're hungry now, so am I. How about if I take you out to dinner?"

She didn't answer because she didn't know how she'd react. Maddie had never liked confrontation, had never been good at it, preferring to swallow her anger. She wasn't sure she could do that now. For the first time ever, she might erupt at her father. So, instead of risking a showdown, she squeezed her eyes shut, pulled the covers up to her neck, and willed herself to ignore the one man on the planet she always had trusted.

More than once, Owen had chided Maddie about being what he called obstinate. The following morning, she decided to use it to her advantage. Maybe obstinacy would help her sneak out of the cottage, away from her father. Otherwise, she'd be tempted to ask how long he planned to stay now that she was functioning again, her life heading in a new direction whether he liked it or not.

Her unspoken statement, however, went unnoticed; by the time she showered, dressed, and gathered her things, no one else was in the cottage. There was only a note on the kitchen table.

A note! she thought with acerbity. Stephen still hadn't mastered texting. Or hadn't wanted to master it. She picked up the scrap of paper and read: *Dropping Nancy at Joe's, then doing errands. See you later—D*

Her father had always signed messages to her with a simple "D," as in Dad. It was cute when she'd been six or seven. But if a note was how he chose to communicate, she could play his game.

Grabbing the pen he'd left on the table, below his message she wrote: *I'm out for most of the day.* She did not sign it with a "D" for daughter as she'd typically done. Instead, she grabbed the paint chips and stomped toward the door with what she recognized as adolescence at its finest.

Her father's car was not in the tiny lot behind the house. Nor was it by the bookshop at the harbor, which was Maddie's first stop. She'd hoped to find Kevin so they could resolve the shades of paint and decide what color should go where. But the shop was locked, the blinds were drawn, and no one answered when she knocked.

Behind the wheel again, she headed to North Road then onto State toward Alley's in West Tisbury, which was thankfully open year-round; she stopped and grabbed a coffee, yogurt, and a corn muffin because she and the baby were starving.

The baby! she thought with an equal mix of perplexity and terror.

Then she got out of the car, tossed the coffee, and went back inside for a decaf.

Once in the car again, she dove into her breakfast before continuing on her mission. She sat chewing, contemplating, struggling to corral her bouncing thoughts, wondering when she could tell Rex. She slid into fantasy: If Rex was home, she could text him.

I'M HEADING TO CHAPPY, she'd type. I'LL STOP IF YOU'RE AROUND? Just because she was pregnant did not mean she'd take it for granted that she could barge into his place without notice. Any more than she'd done last October. Maddie was good at not being clingy.

Rex would text back: YES, PLEASE! I'VE BEEN THINKING OF YOU. Maybe he'd sign off with three heart emojis, though she supposed he wasn't that corny. Still, it would be nice.

She would go to his place; he'd make coffee, she'd ask for herb tea; they'd linger at his table. Then she would tell him. And he'd be the one consumed by emotion.

"You've made me the happiest man on earth," he'd say.

Then she wondered if life had been easier when there were unspoken rules about couples being married before babies began to arrive, back when wedding vows were supposedly the key to a happy life.

Now who's being pathetic? she asked herself.

With a sigh, she swallowed the last crumbs of the muffin and what was left of the yogurt, remembering that none of her daydreams mattered. So she turned on the ignition and drove out of the lot, wondering why she was wasting gas driving to Chappy. Maybe because it was as far as she could get from her father without having to get on a boat.

After what took forever, she arrived at the *On Time*. By

then she was tired again, but perked up when she saw that the captain that morning was Kevin.

Following his guiding gestures, she rolled the Volvo onto the flatbed and turned off her engine. Hers was the only vehicle on board.

"You're exactly who I've been looking for," Maddie said with a smile. On the way, she'd decided to visit Francine. After all, the young woman had given birth to Reggie while living on the Vineyard, so no doubt she had an ob-gyn.

Kevin's smile was broad and genuine. "I'm filling in for Joel, who had to make a quick run to the Cape. I'm on duty 'til noon, after which I'll be up yonder at the bookshop. You need something important?"

Only some advice on what to do about my baby, my lover, my father—and, oh yes, the state of my life, she wanted to say. Maybe she'd have the courage to spill all of that to Francine.

"Actually," she said, "I was hoping you could help me choose the right shade of blue."

Kevin blinked. "For the baby's room?"

Maddie might have laughed if she hadn't been so startled.

"What?" she asked, as blood raced to her cheeks.

He swept his palm over his face. "Oh, man. You're talking about the paint chips, aren't you?"

She dropped her forehead onto the steering wheel, then forced a short laugh. He was joking, of course. There was no way Kevin could know . . .

"Oh, God," he said. "My wife will divorce me if she finds out I told you."

Maddie raised her head, her eyes shooting toward him with horror. "Taylor knows?" she blurted out. "But . . . but how . . . ?"

He blinked again. Then he cleared his throat and said, "Friday night. At the restaurant. She . . . well, she said she could tell by looking at you."

Maddie dropped her gaze to the small mound of her belly.

"Taylor's an EMT," he continued. "She spots all kinds of things."

Oh, God, Maddie thought. How many others had noticed? She wanted to gulp, but her throat had constricted.

"I haven't told anyone." He spoke fast. "Honest. I promised Taylor I wouldn't. And she won't tell anyone, either."

Kevin was such a good man. But right then he sounded like a ten-year-old caught stealing a cookie from Chilmark General Store.

"It's okay, Kevin. I only just found out myself."

"So . . . Rex doesn't know yet? He's the father, right?" His cheeks flamed with embarrassment, as if wishing he could snatch back each word as fast as he'd said it.

Maddie decided to save him further humiliation. "Yes, Rex is the father." It felt good to admit it, but also strange that Kevin was the first person she actually told. "And I sure can't tell him right now."

He lowered his eyes. "I'm so sorry, Maddie. Hopefully, he'll be home soon. And I bet he'll be wicked excited."

At least Kevin hadn't hinted that his sister, Annie-the-screenwriter-in-California, might get in the way of that.

"Meanwhile," he added with a slightly mortified grin, "you have big doings on Chappy today? Other than trying to find me?"

She decided not to share further details of her currently confusing life. "I thought I'd stop by the Inn to see if Francine has recuperated from the weekend."

"Sorry. She brought the kids to the library, then she was going to go shopping."

Maddie laughed. "You know everyone's comings and goings off Chappy?"

He shrugged. "Only when I'm driving the ferry. If you

want, you can back up. I won't have to charge you if we don't cross."

So Maddie put her car in reverse and headed back to Menemsha.

Though she was almost home, Maddie decided to ask Francine the name of her ob-gyn right then, before she forgot. Because her car was old and she hadn't updated the Bluetooth connection, communications weren't always reliable, so she pulled into a lot adjacent to the Chilmark Town Hall, fished her phone from her purse, and scrolled to Francine's number, hoping it would be one less thing to have to think about. But the call went straight to voicemail.

"Francine," Maddie said, "I keep meaning to ask the name of your ob-gyn. I'm overdue for a mammogram, and I need a good women's doc. Please call or text. Thanks!" She tried to sound cheerful, which was not always easy when she was trying to lie. She supposed it wasn't an honest-to-goodness, full-blown lie, as sooner or later she would need a mammogram.

As she pulled out onto the road, she dropped her phone back in her purse . . . and instantly heard the ear-splitting blast of a horn . . . followed by a sharp jolt, a crunch of metal-on-metal, and a loud crack of glass. A white pillow-like thing blew up in front of her, her face brushing its middle. A caustic odor of what smelled like jet fuel filled her nostrils and maybe her lungs.

Then . . . silence.

She might have blacked out for a minute.

The next thing Maddie heard was someone knocking on her side window.

"*Lady? Lady? Are you okay, okay?*" The words rushed at her like water from a burst pipe.

She shook her head to try and clear the blur, then turned

her face away from the pillow. Her neck swiveled toward the sound. She was greeted by a pair of dark, frightened eyes.

"I called an ambulance."

It was a young man, not much older than Rafe. Maddie was glad she'd figured that out. Maybe it meant her brain was still intact.

Pushing the air bag out of the way, she managed to yank the handle and jerk the door open.

"I'm okay," she said. "I think."

He stepped back while she hoisted herself off the seat and stood on the packed dirt of the lot . . . which was when she saw that the front of her car was jammed into the passenger side of a dusty, rusted-out pickup truck.

She wailed, "I did that to you?"

"Yeah. I guess you didn't see me." No harsh accusation, no litany of cuss words.

"I . . . I was putting my phone away . . . I'm so sorry . . . I must not have been looking." Her gaze traveled from the side of his vehicle to the long crack in her windshield.

"Yeah. Stuff happens. As long as you're okay."

She figured she was the same age as his mother. Or older. "I'm okay." She winced, as a small pain gripped her back. "And you?"

"I'm fine."

"Good." She rubbed the base of her spine. "Thank you for being so kind."

He shrugged. Something Rafe would have done.

Then an afterthought hit her with an impact as strong as the one when her car hit the truck. She put her hand on her stomach and started to tremble. *Will I lose the baby?*

The shriek of sirens interrupted.

EMTs. Police. A fire engine. They all arrived simultaneously.

She wobbled to the other side of her car, plucked her purse from the front seat, and extracted her license. She couldn't, however, get her registration out of the glove box, as it was wedged shut.

The EMTs—one, a middle-aged man with a ginger-haired buzz cut and beard, the other, a young woman who did not look old enough to drink in Massachusetts—cautiously helped Maddie into the back of the ambulance. The young woman left; seconds later she was in the driver's seat of the ambulance. The man started checking Maddie's vitals. She was embarrassed that she was shaking.

Then a young, sandy-brown-haired police officer asked how she was feeling. She said her head hurt and she was cold, but she thought she was more shocked than hurt. He nodded, then said a tow truck was on the way; he asked if she had a preference of auto body shops, as if this happened to her often. She mentioned Deke's, the place Joe had brought Orson to be spruced up for Rafe. She told the officer to say the car belonged to Nancy Clieg's granddaughter, the mother of the boy for whom he'd done such a nice job restoring Orson-the-red-pickup.

"Everything seems normal," ginger-beard EMT said once the officer was gone. "But it's usually a good idea to go to the hospital and get fully checked out."

The fact that Maddie still trembled might have prompted his recommendation.

Then, without warning, she said, "I'm pregnant."

He unpeeled the blood pressure cuff from her upper arm, smiled, and said, "Then that's a good reason to go, right?"

Chapter 20

"Can we call someone to get you home?" an emergency department admin person asked, once Maddie had been fully checked and was being discharged. The back of her neck hurt with what the doctor described as a "minor whiplash," her shoulders were sore, and her lower back felt trampled on, not by an elephant but perhaps a toddler, like Francine's son, Reggie, the one named after Rex. The name that was now ever-present in Maddie's mind.

"You most likely grabbed the wheel too tight," the doctor had assured her. "It's a common reaction." He'd added that everything seemed fine, most importantly, the baby, though he suggested she see her obstetrician—which was when she'd asked for a name.

"Dr. Mason is a year-round island resident," was the reply. "It might be a good time of year to get an appointment."

So, Dr. Mason it would be. *That was easy*, she thought.

As for a ride, she supposed she could ask them to call Taylor, who might be busy with her caretaking jobs, but Maddie couldn't think of anyone who wasn't busy. Or was there. On second thought, she decided she did not want to deal with

Taylor—the first person who'd recognized that Maddie was pregnant—a woman she barely knew. She could have asked them to call Joe, but Grandma was probably still at his place, and the call might scare her. Of course, the most likely person to pick Maddie up would be her father. *No*, she thought. The last person she wanted to see was him.

But she did want to get back to the cottage; she wanted a cup of hot tea and a good rest. At least she could hibernate in her room where she wouldn't have to talk to him.

So that left . . . no one.

She supposed it was against hospital regulations to ask to pay the admin woman to skip out for a while and drive her home.

After another moment of useless pondering, Maddie said, "I don't want to bother anyone at home; I'll call a taxi." She tried to look pleasant and not desperate. Later, she'd call Kevin, tell him what happened, and reassure him that she and the baby were fine, in case he'd somehow heard about the accident through the grapevine. Or from his EMT wife.

On the way to Menemsha, Maddie sat in the back of the cab, stared out the window, and thought—with reluctance—about her father. It was the first time Maddie had been in a car accident; it might be extra hard for him. After all, they were staying in the same cottage, right up the street from where her mother had lain in the road, instantly killed, the clams from her basket strewn around her.

Maddie considered the possibility that each time she left the cottage, Stephen worried that she, too, might not return.

As the car navigated the hills and curves toward up-island, the afternoon light wrestled to peek through gray clouds, while tall trees on either side stood winter-naked, framing the rolling farms. She wondered if she'd needed to have the accident so she could understand that even if her father had written the bizarre notes, even if he was in cahoots with Dan Jarvis, Maddie needed to forgive him because he was her father and she loved him very much.

With that in mind, she rested her head against the back of the seat, and thanked God the baby had been spared.

Stephen's car wasn't behind the cottage. A lump swelled in Maddie's throat. Had he packed his belongings and gone home? She went inside and checked Hannah's old bedroom; his backpack and valise were there; his clothes remained hanging tidily in the armoires.

She sighed, grateful that he hadn't left.

Grandma wasn't home yet, either.

As badly as she'd thought she wanted to be alone, instead she wished there was someone she could talk to. So Maddie decided to walk down to the bookshop and see if her father was there, or if Kevin had arrived. But as she opened the front door to step out, she nearly bumped into Taylor.

Taylor flinched; Maddie recoiled, unsure which one of them had been more startled.

Then Maddie laughed, to break the awkward ice.

"Are you looking for your husband?" Taylor, after all, was not a drop-by-for-a-cup-of-tea kind of person. And now that she knew Maddie was pregnant . . .

"Is he here?" the auburn-maned woman asked, responding to a question with a question.

Maddie shook her head. "I'm actually heading to the bookshop with paint samples. Have you checked there?" She supposed it was a stupid question; of course Taylor would have first looked for her husband where he was working, not where Maddie lived.

"He's not there."

"I saw him earlier at the Chappy ferry; he said he'd be up-island later. Would you like to come in for tea and wait?"

Since she'd assured Kevin she would not tell his wife that he'd spilled the pregnancy beans, she had to remember to be careful about what she said.

Taylor hoisted her woven bag higher on her shoulder. "Sure."

Hoping they might be able to become decent friends—as Rex's sister, Taylor would be the baby's aunt—Maddie stepped aside and Taylor came into the cottage and Maddie then hung up their coats. Taylor opted for black huckleberry tea, then sat at the table, and Maddie moved to the kitchen.

It was all somewhat awkward, but that wasn't a surprise.

"I was in a minor car accident today," she said as she filled the kettle. "At Beetlebung Corner. "

Taylor harrumphed, or something like that. "That can be a bad spot," she said.

"It was my fault. I pulled over to make a call. When I hung up, I didn't pay attention, and I drove straight into the side of a pickup."

"Anyone hurt?"

Ah, Maddie thought and wondered if the baby subject would—or should—arise after all, or if they both would smoothly circumvent it.

She shook her head. "The young man in the truck didn't have a scratch. My air bag went off in my face, which was good, but I do feel like I have a sunburn. The EMTs came, and took me to the hospital where I got the all-clear. So, no, no one was hurt." She took a breath of relief.

"My brother would have been a wreck if you were hurt." Then Taylor fiddled with a button on her cardigan, evading the unspoken subject. "I don't know if you know it, but I'm an EMT, too. In case you're ever in Edgartown and need one."

Indeed, she was evading.

"They're lucky to have you right there on Chappy."

"I try to do my part."

Maddie served the tea and sat down, wondering if she could just broach the baby subject and stop the nonsense. As an EMT, maybe Taylor was trained not to divulge information . . . except, apparently, to her husband. Then she had an idea.

"I still haven't seen a gynecologist. At the hospital they mentioned a Dr. Mason. Do you know anything about him?"

Taylor shifted in her seat. "He's a she. And yes, I know her. Helen Mason. She's an ob-gyn. Been here a long time. From what I've heard, she does a good job."

"Great. Thanks."

Taylor sipped her tea.

Maddie saw it as an opportunity to change the subject. "I'm also sorry I don't have cookies or anything to offer you."

"When my brother's around, we get enough baked goods from him. As if running his restaurant isn't enough, he thinks it's also his job to provide fresh muffins and scones to half of Chappy."

"You must miss him."

"Yes." She sipped again, then glanced at her watch. "I'd better go. If I see Kevin, I'll tell him you have the paint samples. Or I can deliver them." It was obvious she did not want to discuss Rex. For which Maddie was grateful.

"Thanks, but I need Kevin's advice. I've picked the colors, but I'm not sure which ones should go where."

Taylor stood up. "Okay. Thanks for the tea." She pulled her knit cap over her mass of hair and retrieved her jacket. "Good luck with Dr. Mason," she added as she walked toward the front door. "In addition to being a gynecologist, she's an obstetrician. But I don't suppose you'll need one of those." She went out the front door before Maddie could determine whether the last comment was meant to be funny or sarcastic.

But Maddie had more important things on her mind than to try to analyze Taylor or her motives.

She would start by calling Dr. Mason to schedule an appointment.

Then she'd rent a car so she wouldn't be stuck in the cottage until hers was fixed; she was told it could take a while because her insurance company was based on the other side of the state, and that Deke's couldn't start to work on it until they responded.

Next, she had to figure out the best time—and most effective way—to talk to her father about his phone call with Dan Jarvis.

Last, but certainly not least, she must call Rex and tell him about the baby. Before someone else did.

"Dr. Mason is off-island until the end of March," a woman who answered the phone said. "I can refer you to someone on the Cape, or I can book you here on, say, April second at one p.m.? You can start taking prenatal vitamins, if you haven't already. A pharmacist can help you with that."

April 2nd was six weeks away, later than Maddie had hoped. She did, however, want a Vineyard doctor, rather than be dependent on the ferry—and the weather—to get her back and forth to every appointment. So she quickly accepted, and prayed she and the baby would stay healthy until then, when she'd be a full five-and-a-half months pregnant. Between now and then, she'd have plenty to do. Starting with getting the vitamins, which prompted her to pick up her phone again and track down a rental car; she was told they could deliver one the next morning.

Sitting on the sofa, gazing out at the winter-still harbor, she wondered if she should call Rex before she talked to her father. If she could tell Rex the news, would that help Stephen understand? "I have to stay on the island now, Dad," she could rationalize. "Rex is excited. He's never had children; I can't take this one away from him."

But as she picked up her phone, Stephen opened the back door and walked in. He'd developed a way of doing that at inopportune times.

"I thought you were out," he said before *hello*. "Where's your car?"

"In the shop. I was in an accident."

"What?" His voice was knee-jerk sharp. He slipped off his gloves and moved briskly to the sofa before taking off his jacket. "Are you okay?"

"I am, yes. It was a minor thing." She waved it off, then gave him a condensed version of what happened. "Actually, Dad, I'm more upset about a conversation I overheard yesterday. The one you had with Dan Jarvis."

With his eyes moving to his hands, he jammed the gloves into his pockets. It was hard to tell if he had paled, because since he'd come back after New Year's, the once clean-shaven Stephen had grown a neat, salt-and-pepper beard that made his blue eyes stand out, but minimized any pink that might have come to his cheeks.

"Oh," he said, and stared at the floor.

Maddie riveted her eyes on him. "May I ask what it was about? Other than me?"

He made a small sound like a wounded bird. "It's complicated."

"Life's complicated, Dad. Especially for me right now."

He turned his face toward the window, away from her. "Dan's been a good friend for three decades." At least he didn't add that without that history, Maddie might not have procured her teaching position, or been chosen for the coveted tenure track.

"He's in trouble, Maddie. Enrollment has declined in the

department. Fewer students are choosing to major in English. They're more interested in IT, AI, and whatever other initials smell like cutting-edge technology. Which, of course, affects the school's pocketbook. Your classes were a big draw. But now that you're stepping aside . . ."

"I'm not *stepping* aside," she said. "I already stepped. And I'm not sure how the school's drop in enrollment is my problem. Or my responsibility to fix." Standing up, she went to the fireplace and picked up the small pottery bowl with the daisy on the front. "Do you know what this is, Dad? I painted it when I was four. I went to summer day camp here. And Evelyn was my teacher." She set down the bowl, then picked up her mother's painting of the sunset with two silhouettes walking on the beach, hand in hand.

"And this? You probably know my mother painted it. You might not know that the silhouettes are Grandma Nancy and me." She rested the canvas back on the mantel next to the little bowl, and decided not to show him the quahog shell, because that would be cruel.

"Anyway," she continued, "I don't expect Dan to understand how much the Vineyard means to me, or that I feel cheated out of not having been allowed to spend time here with my grandmother when I was growing up. I'm not blaming you; I'm sure it was a painful time—and subject—for you. And for Grandma. But the fact is, I am Wampanoag. And being on the island makes me feel I've come home."

Stephen remained quiet.

Now was the time for Maddie to tell him the other news. But the words were stuck in her throat like a large, uncoated pill.

He sighed deeply, then said, "I'm sorry, Madelyn." His voice was low and noncommittal.

Heat rose in her face, perhaps due to the emotional roller coaster of her physical condition. Or because she felt entitled to more than a limp "I'm sorry," as if she were one of his students disappointed by a grade.

"Well, *I'm* sorry to tell you that I have no intention of going back to the Berkshires. Shit happens, Dad." Maddie rarely swore. When she did, it was to make a clear point that she meant what she said. And in that moment, she felt affirmed about her decision. Finally. There would be a bookshop. There would be a baby. And she hoped Rex would be part of their lives however it worked for him. And her. But mostly for their child.

It wasn't until she huffed off to her room and sat in the lovely rocker with a view of the harbor that Maddie recognized that not only hadn't she told her father she was pregnant, she also hadn't asked if he'd written the notes. Or if he thought Dan had found—and paid—someone to deliver them.

For now, all she knew was that her father was angry and upset, and despite her own exasperation, there was no reason to make things worse. Besides, if he'd known about the notes, surely they would stop appearing now.

Chapter 21

March–April

The days and weeks passed quickly. Maddie made decisions about the bookshop, traveled around the island in the tiny rental car that was uncomfortable and costly but got her wherever she needed to go, as she shopped for furnishings for both inside the shop and out on the deck. She zoomed with Rafe, finessing the logo design for the Little Bookshop by the Harbor—as Maddie decided to call it; they determined the dimensions for a sign, which an Amherst friend of Rafe's offered to paint at no cost, if they let him include an image of it in his portfolio.

As for interacting with her father, Maddie kept it respectful, always aware that he was helping to launch her business. Also, she was fairly sure that whatever his missteps were, he'd done them with good intentions. Still, she needed time to rebuild her trust.

When she wasn't thinking about the bookshop, she browsed online for baby things. She'd tried not to spend time dwelling on Rex. She'd only spoken with him two more times; the conversations had been brief, each somewhat more coherent than the previous one. Unless that was her hopeful imagination.

Mostly, she kept focused on the tasks that needed doing, while half wondering if, between her father and Rex, someday she'd receive a gold medal for patience.

Suddenly, it was the middle of March. A little over two months until the grand opening. And four months until the baby would arrive.

Grandma came home from Joe's early one evening with a pot of his homemade fish chowder and a loaf of fresh-baked, 7-grain bread for their dinner.

"He's trying to make up for Rex not being here," Grandma said. "And though you kindly haven't asked, my basket count for the bookshop is up to eight—five large and three medium. Rafe's working on the small ones. Ten years ago, I'd have made twenty-eight in the same time."

"I'm sure what you've done is wonderful, Grandma. Don't forget that Rafe's contributions are only possible because of you. As an added bonus, Kevin found a perfect spot in the shop where the baskets will have center stage."

Grandma smiled an atypical, shy smile.

Then Stephen sauntered out from his office/bedroom, and announced that something smelled good and that he was hungry.

Thanks to Joe, the meal was tasty, but the atmosphere around the table was again subdued. Maddie picked at her food; her stomach was tentative. They had ice cream for dessert, then her father retreated to his room again, and Grandma wanted to watch more episodes of *Father Brown*, now that Maddie had set up streaming services. For three hours, she and Grandma sat mostly in silence, sharing bits of thoughts as to whodunit. Maddie couldn't wait to go to bed. Thankfully, Grandma finally said good night.

By the time Maddie cleaned the kitchen, turned off the lights, and got ready for bed, she was tired. But she couldn't sleep.

She needed to talk with someone.

After a while, she pulled herself up and leaned against the headboard. She glanced at the clock; it was after midnight. Closing her eyes, she rubbed her growing bump that she'd been artfully disguising in big winter clothes. Soon, however, it would be spring, and her condition would be obvious to everyone on the planet. It was ludicrous that the only people who still knew the situation were Kevin and Taylor. Then she remembered that the Tri-Town Ambulance crew knew, the doctor, and a few ER healthcare workers—none of whom she could call to have a chat.

She needed to tell someone she felt close to.

But she couldn't share it with Rafe over the phone.

And Grandma Nancy would be sound asleep by now.

She even considered calling Evelyn or Francine, but it was ridiculously late.

Nor was it the time—night or day—to tell her father since their conversations remained strained.

The only one she could call was Rex. Maybe he was well enough now to hear the news. Maybe it would provide him with added motivation to step up PT, OT, and whatever other kind of rehab he was getting. Maybe it would give him the perfect reason to get well and come home.

Sooner or later—sooner would be better—she'd have to take the chance.

She glanced at the clock again: twelve fifteen. Which meant it was only nine fifteen in Los Angeles—and maybe he'd still be awake. Before changing her mind, she got out of bed, put on her robe, and picked up her phone. Then she sat on the floor, huddled against the bed on the side where anyone with a yen to eavesdrop would not succeed. There had been enough eavesdropping lately.

Without second-guessing, she scrolled to Rex's number and hit send.

It rang once, twice, three times.

Her heart thumped faster as his phone kept ringing.

But just as she was ready to hang up, someone clicked on.

"Hello?"

It wasn't Rex.

It was a woman.

"Beth?" Maddie asked, pleased that she'd remembered the nurse's name.

"I think you have the wrong number. Who do you want?"

"Um . . . Rex?" She had no idea why she'd said his name as if it was a question. What she really wanted was to end the call.

"I'm sorry," came the reply, "but Rex is sleeping. Do you want to leave a message?" It must be one of his caregivers, clearly determined to protect her charge.

Oh, sure, Maddie thought. *Say Maddie called to tell him that she's pregnant with his baby.* That wasn't going to happen.

"Please tell him I'm thinking of him and wondering how he's doing."

"He's sleeping," the woman repeated. "But I'll pass on the message." After a quick pause, the woman said, "Wait. Is this Maddie?"

For half a second, Maddie was thrilled to think he'd told everyone in Southern California about her. About them.

"I didn't look when I grabbed his phone, but I now see 'Maddie' on caller ID," the woman added, and Maddie closed her eyes.

"Yes, I'm Maddie," she replied. "And you are . . . ?"

"It's Annie, Maddie. Annie Sutton, Rex's friend."

For all Maddie knew, she might have thrown up then or said something really stupid. Later she was only sure that she did not mention the baby. The rest was a stupid, jealous blur.

Somehow, Maddie slept straight through until eight the next morning, yet she woke up exhausted. Physically, emotionally, the whole ball of wax. On top of that, she was cold.

Hauling herself from bed, she headed for the steady warmth of the rainfall shower, where she scrubbed herself from head to toe, washed her hair, shaved her legs. She was determined to have a great day. Then the shower ran out of hot water.

After bundling up in a thick sweater and knit pants that stretched over her belly, she donned wool socks and slid her feet into fuzzy slippers.

First, she'd make a mug of steaming tea. Goldenrod, caffeine-free tea. Foraged up-island, cleaned and dried—all by Grandma Nancy. Then Maddie would walk down to the bookshop where Kevin might be, and together they could choose which paint colors should go where, and she'd be done with that.

But half trotting down the hallway, eager to get going, her grand plan quickly changed. Grandma was sitting at the table, a mug of tea in one hand, a pencil in the other, her shoulders bowed over a sudoku magazine that Rafe had given her for Christmas.

"About time you got up," the old woman said without lifting her eyes.

Maddie was taken aback. Joe typically picked Grandma up not long after dawn and took her to his place, where she spent the day crafting baskets—all eight of them in two-and-a-half months.

"Well, good morning," Maddie said. "Are you okay?"

"Never better," was the reply.

"You're not going to Joe's? Is he okay, too?"

Grandma set down the pencil and raised her eyes to Maddie. "Everyone's fine. Even your father. I sent him down-island to do errands so you and I could have a conversation."

"He's okay, too? My dad?"

"Like I said, everyone's fine. The only thing that's wrong is the tension in this house. I told your father it's high time the two of you made things right between you, and now I've said the same to you. I did, however, also tell him that your bad mood is probably due to your condition."

Maddie was standing half in the living/dining/kitchen space, the other half still in the hallway. Under the circumstances, her thoughts might have been racing, but they couldn't race or do much of anything because, like the water in the shower, they'd turned cold.

"Make your tea, then sit," Grandma added. "We need to talk. Because it's high time you admitted that you're pregnant."

Grandma tapped her fingers on the tabletop, while Maddie felt the blood drain from her face, if blood really did that sort of thing. She took four steps toward Grandma, then sat across from her, knowing she could not deny the allegation.

"Are you happy?" Grandma asked. "It's Rex's baby, isn't it?"

Maddie's shoulders relaxed. Then she laughed, but held her gaze on the table and not her grandmother. "Yes, Grandma, it's Rex's. Believe me, it couldn't be anyone else's."

Grandma didn't interrupt.

"Am I happy?" Maddie continued. "It's complicated. I do know I'm embarrassed. But yes, I'm happy about the baby." She raised her eyes to meet her grandmother's. It felt good to see the old woman's dark eyes start to twinkle. "But I'm worried about Rex. He doesn't know yet . . . he has so much to deal with now. I tried calling him last night to finally tell him, but he was asleep. As far as I know, the only one who's figured it out has been Taylor, who told Kevin. And now you know."

After a quick "Ahem," Grandma said, "And your father knows."

Maddie's jaw squared. Her spine stiffened. "What?"

Grandma sighed. "I explained what I meant by your 'condition.' He deserved to know, too, don't you think?"

Dropping her gaze back to the table, Maddie felt as humiliated as when she'd been thirteen, and her father caught her on the back porch kissing Tommy Jenkins.

"So now my dad's ashamed of me."

"Not at all. Though he does want to talk with you about your plans."

Maddie wrapped her arms around her middle. "Rex should have known before everyone else, Grandma. I was hoping the news might help him find extra strength to get well faster. But I don't suppose that's how it works." She struggled to hold back tears. "Plus, he could get better but want to stay in California. We haven't known each other very long—or very well. He's older than I am and"—she paused, wiping tears that leaked out again without permission—"what if he gets better but doesn't want a baby? Should I go through with it? I'm forty-five, Grandma. Being pregnant alone is a risk . . ."

Grandma let her ramble.

"And what will Rafe think?" Maddie added. "I don't want to lose my son's love. Or his respect."

Then Grandma held up both palms. "Stop. That's a lot of whats and what-ifs. Maybe you should listen to the advice of an ancestor. My grandmother, your great-great-grandmother, Spotted Fawn, said when our minds are troubled, our Creator will guide us. I believe that. I also believe maybe it was our

Creator who decided it was time for you and Rex to have a family of your own. Because these things aren't usually a coincidence."

"But . . ."

Grandma held an arthritic finger to her lips. "Hush." Then she smiled a rare smile. "A more important question now is do you want tea or don't you? Before your father went down-island, he made a quick trip to Orange Peel; there are fresh croissants with mozzarella, spinach, and roasted tomatoes on the counter."

Not wanting to ask if Stephen had gone to the bakery before or after Grandma told him the news, Maddie hesitated, until hunger overtook her emotions. She stood up, went into the kitchen, and put the kettle on. Then she took a plate and reached for the bakery bag . . . to which a large Post-it was attached. Her father's distinctive cursive read:

I was wrong, and I'm sorry. I called Dan and retracted what I'd said. Also, I'm elated about the baby. Rex is a good guy. He signed the note with his longstanding—*D.*

Maddie set down the plate and more tears started to well.

As if on cue, the back door opened, and her father stepped inside.

He looked at her. He waited.

"I read your note," she said.

He handed her a bag from Rainy Day, a gift shop in Vineyard Haven, and gave her a hug. "I'm so sorry, Maddie. Forgive me?" He sounded like he meant it.

"Oh, Dad, of course I forgive you. We've all been a little stressed."

"A *little* stressed?" Grandma called out. "Why do either of you think I spend all day, every day at Joe's? These crippled up hands of mine couldn't make baskets every day if my life depended on it. But the hubbub around here has been too much for this old girl. And the secrecy! I've known about the baby for the past two months at least! Good grief, *look* at the girl!"

All eyes floated down to the five months' of evidence; Maddie and her father laughed.

Then she reached into the bag from Rainy Day and pulled out a soft, stuffed bunny in pastel sea-glass green—a shade similar to one she'd chosen for the bookshop.

"The woman in the store said it's a perfect color for a baby who isn't here yet. And look"—he pointed to the eyes and mouth—"these are hand-embroidered so nothing will fall off."

Maddie pressed the bunny to her chest and whispered, "Thanks, Dad. It's wonderful."

He hugged her again.

After several seconds, Grandma interrupted. "Enough blubbering. I waited 'til we got all this out of the way before I had my breakfast. Now somebody please hand me a croissant before I starve to death." She chuckled, though from her, it came out more like a cackle.

Stephen chuckled, too. "Go sit," he told Maddie. "I'll get everything. Coffee?"

"Goldenrod tea this morning, thanks, Dad. No caffeine for me." She patted her belly, hoping Grandma was right, that their Creator had been guiding Maddie all along—no matter what Rex decided to do. If she ever got the chance to tell him what was going on.

Chapter 22

Breakfast turned into a small, but festive, party. Grandma, Stephen, and Maddie gorged on the flaky croissants while Grandma and Stephen took turns sharing tales of when Maddie was a baby: her first word (oddly, it had been *quahog*, which she'd spoken clearly one summer when she was about a year old, and they were at Grandma's); her favorite toy (a Cabbage Patch doll named Lorna that wasn't exactly a doll for a baby, but her father had bought it and her mother had propped it up on the bureau out of reach and Maddie loved staring at it); the time when the plumber (who was at the cottage fixing something or other) had tickled her under her chin right after she'd had a swallow of creamed turnip, and she instantly upchucked (Grandma's favorite word back then) all over him.

"A minor offense!" Maddie cried out now with a laugh.

To which Stephen replied: "Speaking of 'minor' incidents . . . and not to put a damper on the morning, but I must digress." Then his jovial mood tempered. "While I was out this morning, I checked in at Deke's. They heard back from your insurance company, Maddie—your accident was not minor. Your car is being totaled."

Under the circumstances, yes, her father's news put a damper on the party. Especially since Maddie hadn't told them about the cracked windshield or the air bag going off or the fact that she'd blacked out for a minute. And now Stephen was understandably upset because he'd seen the car's crumpled remains.

"Oh," she said, trying to sound nonchalant, not wanting to break their happy mood. "I guess I'll need to buy another car. I'd better do it fast, because I think the little box I've been driving around in is killing my back. Not to mention that keeping it any longer would be wasting money."

He set down his fork and got serious. "Whatever you get should be a brand-new model, with all the latest safety features—for the baby."

She smiled.

"And safe for you, too," he quickly added. "Maybe an SUV?" He stood up. "Wait here," he said, as if Maddie or Grandma would be going anywhere.

He disappeared down the hall and quickly came back with his laptop. Then he started typing. "How many miles were on the Volvo?"

"A hundred sixty thousand. Give or take."

"That's more than I have on me," Grandma commented, while Stephen's fingers flicked over the keyboard as if he'd been a techie all his life.

"The car is fifteen years old," her father continued. "Your insurance might still give you a few thousand dollars for it."

Maddie lowered her head, her happy mood headbutted by reality again. "Oh, great," she sneered, then jerked her chin up. "Hey! Maybe I can drive Orson. At least until Rafe's graduation." Then she remembered that Orson had a stick shift. "I can ask Joe to teach me to shift it. In fact, let's get rid of the rental tomorrow. I'd rather put the added cost toward buying a new car." When she saw Joe next, if he agreed, she'd set up a training time.

"Good idea," Stephen said, as his fingers kept searching. "Until I have to leave, we can share mine." Then he stopped typing, sat back in his chair, and groaned. "What with startup costs for the bookshop nearly maxed out, I think we can rule out you buying a new SUV. At least for a while."

A pall blanketed the room as if a Vineyard skunk had waddled in.

"I can help," Grandma said. "In fact, I can buy it. Will you let me do that for you, Maddie? And for the baby?"

She wanted to say *Thanks, but no thanks*. She wanted to be an independent woman who was going to take responsibility for herself and for her baby and would not need a handout from her ninety-year-old grandmother, most of whose money, Maddie knew, was tied up in island real estate. She'd rather buy something she could afford.

"Or . . ." Stephen said, "how about if Nancy and I split the cost? The baby will be joining our family, right? So why not let us buy the vehicle that she'll be traveling around in?"

Maddie smiled again because it was cute that he'd referred to the baby as "she" instead of "he." As much as Stephen treasured Rafe, Maddie always thought he'd been happy that he and Hannah had a daughter.

"Are you hoping it's a girl?" she asked.

He looked like a deer in the proverbial headlights. "Well, no. As long as it's a healthy baby."

"Liar," she teased, swatting his arm, and the mood instantly elevated. "You have a grandson. Now you want a granddaughter, don't you?"

He grinned and shrugged, and Maddie laughed.

"Girls are expensive," Grandma chimed in.

"Speaking of which," Maddie said, "can we go out for dinner later? I've been so busy I forgot to go shopping."

"Great idea," Grandma said. "Where to?"

"I've been secretly craving Asian food and pickles," the mother-to-be-for-the-second-time said. "Let's go to Vineyard Haven, but stop at the market first for pickles. They might not be on the menu, and no one should challenge a pregnant lady's appetite."

Her father looked stupefied, and Grandma rolled her eyes.

For a little while, it was almost as if they were an ordinary family.

Brunch was so filling, they skipped lunch. Late in the afternoon, they left the cottage in two cars: Maddie turned in the rental, then joined her father and Grandma. After stopping for pickles, they headed to Main Street in Vineyard Haven.

At the Asian restaurant, they joked and laughed and ate, and, at Stephen's suggestion, they shared sesame seed balls for dessert. Maddie was amused that her grandmother and her father were acting as if they'd always been pals and not reticent in-laws; she also was happy that she and her father were back to their "old selves," with no more tension poisoning the air between them.

Then Stephen said, "And now I have another announcement." He raised his teacup as if in a toast.

"Is it as impressive as having a baby?" Maddie teased.

"Hardly," Stephen said. "But it's overdue. As much as I hate to break up our team, I have to return to Green Hills by April second—I need to prepare a talk for a conference in Worcester the following week. They're calling it, 'The Future of Liberal Arts Colleges in New England.'" He gave Maddie a small grin. "Don't worry. I won't mention you."

She returned the grin while shaking her head. Sometimes, Stephen did have a sense of humor she could understand.

"Anyway," he went on, "I want you to know I've loved almost every minute of being here. And I especially hate to leave, what with the baby news. But before I go, I promise that things for the bookshop will be in good shape."

"Oh, Dad," she said, resting her hand on his arm. "I can't imagine what I—what *we*—would have done without you. But I'm happy that you'll speak at the conference. You have so much to give."

Grandma held her left arm out to her side and, with her right arm, pretended to play the violin.

They all laughed at the gesture.

Then Grandma leaned toward Stephen and said, "This is when you just say, 'Thanks, Madelyn.'"

So he did.

Then he said, "But I'll be back in time for the opening, and stay until after my granddaughter's born." The "granddaughter" sentiment didn't go unnoticed.

"Before then, however," he added, "I'll see you at Rafe's graduation."

"To Rafe's graduation," Grandma said, lifting her teacup and clinking with Stephen.

Maddie regretted that she'd been so preoccupied she hadn't paid more attention to her son or his impending accomplishment, but she was grateful she had people who'd help fill the gaps that she'd created by being so insufferably insufferable. She had a lot to make up for now.

Back at the cottage, Maddie said good night and withdrew to her bedroom. But between too much good food and tea, she had trouble falling asleep.

With only a sliver of moon leaking into the room, she knew it was time to get—and stay—focused on the future. And though she hoped it would include Rex, she needed to believe that their relationship would take care of itself, and that, no matter what, she and the baby would be fine. Because, with or without Rex, they would not be alone.

For now, she wanted to move forward; she decided to start with getting rid of those silly notes before someone found them and overreacted. So she sat up and turned on the nightstand lamp, then slid open the drawer and removed the envelopes. She would shred them all to bits.

But first, for no particular reason, she wanted to read the last one.

Determined to confront the pseudo-devil's anonymous work, she tore open a corner and extracted the sheet of white paper.

The lettering was done in the now-familiar black marker. The message, as with the others, was short:

WHAT PART OF GET OFF THE ISLAND DON'T YOU UNDERSTAND?

One day, a boy showed up at the cottage. He was not a little boy, but he was young. Around ten, I think. Cute as a button, with eyes that glittered like polished bronze.

"I can't find my dad," he said. He stood at the front door, holding on to the handlebars of his bike for dear life. At least he wasn't crying.

"Where'd you lose him?" I asked.

He shrugged his shoulders that were broad for his age. "He lives around here somewhere."

"Got a name?"

"His or mine?"

"Either. Both."

"He's Stan. I'm Reginald. But they call me Rex."

"You want a root beer, Rex?"

The boy scowled. "Thanks, but I can't take nothing from strangers."

"My name's Nancy. Now we're not strangers. Besides, you knocked on my door, not the other way around. So you want a pop or what?"

He shrugged again. "Okay. Sure."

I turned and went into the kitchen, where I'd been starting dinner, not that anyone would be there to eat with me. Anyway, it was hot out for October, so I figured the kid could use something cold.

"Thank you, Nancy," he said.

"You're welcome, Rex."

He took a big swig from the bottle as if he hadn't had a drink since the day before.

"You got kids?" he asked.

"I do! I have a brand-new baby granddaughter."

"Oh. Nobody bigger?"

"Sorry," I said, then asked, "Where do you suppose your dad is?"

"I've been up here lots of times with him, so I thought I knew the way."

"But you got messed up?"

"Yup," he said as if he were a cowboy, which he could have been cuz his skin was too pale to be Wampanoag. Then he took another swig.

"Do you know his phone number?"

"He doesn't have a phone up here. We only have the one at our house on Chappy."

I think my eyes got big then. "You rode your bike all the way up-island from Chappy?"

"Yes, ma'am. First time. It doesn't take as long when we're in his truck."

"Okay, if you tell me your last name, there's a good chance I can track down your dad."

He looked at me suspiciously again.

"My husband was a fisherman," I said. "He knows almost everybody around here." I didn't mention that I did, too.

The boy sighed, which seemed a funny thing for a kid to do. "Winsted," he said. "My dad's Stan Winsted."

And that was how—and how long ago—that I met Rex.

Now that it looks like Rex and Maddie—who was the brand-new baby way back when—might be getting together for real and forever, they need to know the truth about some things.

Stuff I tried so hard to forget.

And don't know how to tell them to their faces.

Chapter 23

Maddie's days were spent with bar charts and projections and too many hours of screen time, and—while juggling sharing her father's car—running a billion errands. In the evenings, she read some of the books they'd sell, so she'd be better able to recommend titles to customers, per her dad's suggestion.

In between the chaos, she'd tried to assess whether—once Stephen was gone and what with Rafe still in Amherst—she and Grandma were going to be safe in the cottage, especially now that Maddie's pregnancy was obvious. Would the note-writer see it as an opportunity for . . . what?

After reading the last note, she hadn't shredded them, though she still wanted to believe that three notes in five-and-a-half months hardly indicated an emergency. She did, however, vow that if one more showed up, she would call Brandon. Or the police before then, if she got scared. It would no longer matter if the effort seemed pointless.

She spoke to Rex again, twice. Because he'd been tired, the first call was brief; the second was longer, when—surprise!—he did most of the talking, mostly about how he could go outside in a wheelchair now and how beautiful it was up in the hills with views of the Pacific, and that a rich scent of bougainvillea filled the air because spring came early out there.

Neither conversation had provided an opportunity for her to drop the pregnancy bomb. Or maybe she was reticent for reasons she didn't want to analyze.

Suddenly, it was April first—the day before Maddie's appointment with Dr. Mason, and the day before Stephen would leave. She'd barely slept, but now, as slivers of dawn softened the night sky into morning, Maddie longed to go for a run. She needed some worthwhile exercise; a mile or two might clear her head.

She bundled up—bravo for stretchy yoga pants—then tiptoed to the kitchen, exchanged her slippers for her Nikes at the back door, and donned her down parka, wool scarf, hat, and mittens. Unfortunately, as soon as she stepped outside, she realized she'd dressed for the Berkshires. Though hardly Southern California, the Vineyard climate was more temperate than it was in Green Hills, except when the wind kicked in, of which there was none that morning.

So, she deposited her wool accessories on the back steps and made her way through the dunes and down to the beach where, to her surprise, it was high tide, which meant running would not be fun. It was too warm for her parka, anyway.

Standing on the sand, looking toward the horizon, she wilted. As busy as her life now was, the challenges had come too fast for a woman who was used to spending too much time with her head in a book.

She peeled off her parka, spread it on the beach, then sat on it and wished that some things could be different.

"I wish you were still here, Mommy," she whispered into a thin line of froth that edged an incoming wave. "Because I really need you now." She didn't often admit those things, but they were always there, beneath her surface.

Then another gentle wave rolled in, and with it, Maddie heard her mother speak: *A lot of good things are coming for you, my dear. And you deserve every bit and more.*

Which was what Maddie needed to hear. She closed her eyes and softly said, "Thank you."

After a pause, a low voice behind her said, "You're welcome."

She quickly turned. Instead of Hannah, she saw her father.

"Dad . . . ?"

"You sounded so sincere, I thought I should reply." He moved closer, then crouched beside her. "I thought you'd gone for a run."

"What gavc me away?"

"The sneakers by the back door were gone, but your slippers were there. And your hat and scarf were on the steps. I figured you changed your mind about wearing them."

"It's too hot. And the tide's in, so no running for me."

"And you were talking to . . . ?"

"My mother." She tried to sound matter-of-fact.

He mused a moment. "I still do that on occasion."

Though he'd never declared it, Maddie was not surprised. "Does it help?"

"Sometimes. Other times she ignores me." He laughed.

They sat quietly then, their eyes locked on the soothing motion of the water. Then his voice grew serious. "If you don't mind me asking, were you talking to Hannah about something I can help with?"

"I was looking for reassurance. For hours and sometimes for days I'm confident about my decisions. Then I get slammed with moments of awareness that I'm faking, that everything I'm doing is wrong." She didn't recall ever being that candid with her father. Maybe Hannah was there after all, with them in spirit, helping them help each other. Perhaps she always had been.

Stephen grew pensive as he chose his words carefully. "People who have the courage to question their decisions are usually the ones who are doing fine. It's the ones who think they're right all the time who have the most to learn."

Maddie smiled. "Did my mother teach you that?"

"No," he said. "My students did. So did you. Your mother only taught me to love you."

Which also was what she'd needed to hear.

Then Stephen took her hand and suggested they walk over to the shop and see how things were shaping up. They had, after all, been so buried in working on the logistics, they hadn't checked in for days.

Because it was still early, Maddie didn't expect they'd see anyone. But the front door was unlocked and the inside lights were on.

Sounds of loud, vibrating music greeted them inside. A man stood in the far corner, his back to them, his hammer thwacking to the beat.

"Hello?" Stephen shouted above the noise.

The man turned: he was older than Rafe, younger than Maddie, but looked vaguely familiar.

"Hey, Mr. Clarke." The hammering ceased first, followed by the music. "Sorry, I wasn't expecting visitors."

"No problem," her father said. "Have you met the boss?" He gestured to Maddie.

"I have. How are you, Ms. Clarke?" He had blond hair and dark eyes and cheerful, plump cheeks that looked as if they'd been glued onto his round face.

"Please, call me Maddie. And I'm sorry, I know I've met you, but I can't remember where."

"Dave worked on the cottage after the fire," her father said. "Carpentry and painting."

"Oh, right. You're responsible for the beautiful bedroom suite."

"Guilty." He smiled, then motioned to the bookcases he'd been hammering. "What do you think of these?"

"They look wonderful. I didn't know they'd be custom made."

Dave nodded. "I'm making them deeper than standard ones, so they can hold oversized books. You'll be able to slide them in, spine out, like regular books, so they'll have room to breathe. Which is important with the dampness around here."

Maddie was amazed at the things other people—except her, the bookshop owner—had accomplished while she'd been in a semi-daze.

"That's terrific, Dave. You must have been doing carpentry awhile."

"Not really. I was a fisherman like my dad—maybe you know him? Bud Erikson? Anyway, we were out in a storm right after Labor Day and the rough sea nailed me with a bad bout of vertigo; it took a long time for me to shake it once I was back on dry land. The doc said it might be triggered again if I go too far out, and he politely suggested that I find another career." He pouted, but only briefly. "Accidents sure can change your life in a flash."

Of course, that made Maddie think about Rex. "How awful for you," she said, again pushing down her thoughts. "But how lucky for us."

Dave grinned. "Kevin saved me, by giving me all kinds of jobs. Rex, too. Daria and I live in a house my dad owns, but we've got four kids, so whatever I get really helps."

"Good thing I'm still here and don't charge them rent." A husky voice made its way in from the front door.

"Hey, Bud," Stephen said. "Maddie, meet Bud Erikson."

Bud had a light complexion that looked like it had been

sunburned too many times; it highlighted Shar-Pei-looking wrinkles framed by a scruffy beard. He wore a stained yellow slicker and matching pants and sported a scent of fresh-caught halibut or something like that. Maddie figured that a photo of him should be on a package of frozen fish. Or on a poster for the movie *Jaws*.

Then she remembered that she'd seen him before: He was the grumpy guy at the potluck who'd been yakking about Arnie's Bait & Tackle, in the remains of which they now were standing. So, as unappealing as Bud was, Maddie reminded herself that without having overheard that conversation, she wouldn't have a bookshop in the making.

"Nice to meet you, Mr. Erikson," she said. "Dave's doing a great job."

"We should all be so lucky to be able to retire at age thirty-eight," he blabbed, as if Dave had had a choice. "I've been fishing nearly sixty years and I'd 'a killed for a break like that." He clucked as if he thought that was hilarious.

Maddie glanced back at Dave. "Please tell Kevin we dropped by. If he has a chance to run up to the cottage, we have a few things to go over with him. I'd call, but I don't like to bother him if he's working at the ferry." She turned to her dad. "Shall we get back to work?"

They said good-bye to the Eriksons and quickly left. When they were nearly up the hill, Maddie realized Bud Erikson had said he was "still here." It wasn't an uncommon saying, yet, coupled with the man's coarseness, it was like the second note: **WHY ARE YOU STILL HERE?**

Which could be a coincidence.

If Maddie believed in those.

Grandma got home from Joe's midafternoon, and at six thirty she roused from her afternoon nap and padded into the living room, where Maddie and her father had been immersed in their laptops since returning from Dave and Bud and the bookshop.

Setting fresh logs in the fireplace, Grandma announced, "I'm lighting these now." She struck a wooden match and tossed it into the fireplace. "Joe sent me home with a nice hunk of sea bass if either of you feel like cooking dinner. Or I suppose I can do it if you landlubbers don't know how."

Maddie glanced at her dad, who now wore a similar "I have no idea how to cook a hunk of fish" expression.

"Give it your best shot, Nancy," Stephen finally said.

"The trick is to soak it in milk before you fry it," Grandma said. "It takes away the stink."

"Ahhh," Stephen added, "a major plus."

Maddie smiled, reminded again, thanks in large part to her pregnancy, it was a miracle that her father and Grandma were getting along so well.

"You may laugh, Mr. Clarke," Grandma replied, "but I learned that little trick from my father, Isaac Walks-With-Thunder Thurston. I taught it to Joe, and I taught it to Rex when he was a kid. Darned if Rex doesn't cook it that way in his restaurant."

Rex, Maddie thought. *Tonight, I'll call him again.* And, come hell or high water (another of Grandma's favorite sayings), she'd tell him about the baby.

Forty-five minutes later, the trio was feasting on the sea bass with roasted potatoes (from the root cellar), and carrots and tender spinach that Grandma had grown and canned early last summer while she was concocting the scheme to lure Maddie to the island.

The food tasted great, until her father said he was packed and ready to leave in the morning. "I got a slot on the nine-thirty boat; I was told I was lucky there was space. I had no idea the ferries would be booked on the first of April."

Maddie set down her fork. "We still have lots to learn about this place." It was a useless comment, but helped fill the air while not revealing how much she'd miss him. The last thing she wanted was for him to feel guilty about going.

"As for the conference," Stephen added, "I hope you know I'd cancel if I didn't think you could handle things on your own now."

She helped herself to more fish. "Thanks, Dad. And I know you'll be a phone call away, but I promise not to abuse that."

"Well, if you need instant answers, you can always ask Evelyn."

Maddie smiled and thought, *Evelyn.* The attractive, supportive woman. If all was as it seemed.

"Good grief," Grandma said. "How hard can it be? It's not like you'll be competing with Barnes and Nople." She smirked, because she no doubt knew the chain store's name was Noble, not Nople.

"You're correct," Stephen said. "After all, we're on the Vineyard. So it's only a little bookshop by the harbor."

That time, both women rolled their eyes.

Then Maddie ate her last bite of dinner and said, "Speaking of phone calls, I hate to depart from this fascinating conversation, but I must excuse myself to call Rex." She didn't mention what she was going to say to him. Or that she had to do it right then while her spirits were high. And before she lost her nerve. Again.

With that, dinner was done.

"Here we go," she whispered to her belly once she was in her room with the door closed. "Time to talk to Daddy."

With phone in hand, she sat on the comfy rocking chair by the window and only allowed herself to take one long breath. Then she touched the "call" icon.

One ring. Two. Then . . .

"Hi! Maddie, is it you?"

She was startled that he sounded like his chipper, energetic self.

"I was going to call in a few minutes," he said.

It really was him. Sounding like himself. Acting like himself. Which threw her slightly off balance.

She stumbled over her words, struggling to remember how she'd planned to say what she needed to say before he had to hang up to eat, sleep, or have another round of PT.

"It's . . . you," was what spluttered out.

"In the flesh. How are you?"

"Me? How are *you*?"

He hemmed for a second; hawed for another. "Believe it or not, I'm doing really well. Which was one reason I wanted to call you tonight. I'm so much better that the doctor said I can have my walking papers."

His walking papers? Maddie hadn't realized that, in addition to breaking his neck, Rex hadn't been able to walk at all. She knew he'd been using a wheelchair but . . .

She stopped trying to think straight. Instead, she simply said, "That's . . . great." An image of him strolling around the bedroom, rocking their baby in his strong arms came to mind.

"Yeah, and there's more."

"Yes?" She had good news, too. But his voice sounded eager, so she wanted to let him tell her his news first. She wasn't, however, prepared for what he had to say.

"I'm coming home, Maddie," he said. "I'll be there tomorrow."

Chapter 24

After they hung up, Maddie shrieked. The next thing she heard were feet scuffling out in the hallway, followed by two sharp knocks on her door, which then burst open. Grandma and Stephen rushed in, no doubt expecting something awful had happened to her. Or to the baby.

She shared the news.

She shrieked again. "No! He can't come home tomorrow! I see Dr. Mason tomorrow!"

Stephen quieted her down, saying he doubted Rex would be on the red-eye, so chances were he wouldn't get to the island before her one o'clock appointment. Then he asked if he'd said what time he'd arrive in Boston, if he planned to fly into Logan, and if he wanted Maddie to pick him up at the boat or if Taylor would be there.

Maddie was dumbfounded. "I was too stunned to ask."

Stephen laughed.

Grandma rubbed her hands together and said this was more fun than *Jeopardy!*

Thinking quickly, Maddie said, "I'll text him later and find out when he'll land. Then I'll figure out the rest. If Taylor's there, that's fine. But I want to surprise him . . . and see his face to make sure it's really him, and that he's really okay." She didn't add that she'd stand there and wait for hours if that was what it took.

Then the image of that brought on another shriek. "What will I wear?" She practically sprinted toward her armoire.

Stephen looked at Grandma—his new best friend—and said, "You should have seen her the first time a boy asked her to the prom."

Maddie stopped, redirected her footsteps over to them, hugged Grandma first then Stephen, and shooed them from the room. "Go back to whatever you were doing. I have things to do."

Once the older duo was out of sight, she started prowling through her closet. Though she would have loved to don the beaded skirt, she decided it wouldn't fit over her belly now. She needed something less revealing. After all, Rex had been through a lot; she didn't want his homecoming to be about her. Not yet.

Two hours later, with clothes strewn all over the bedroom, she settled on a loose shirt—the same blue as her eyes—her stretchy pants, and a multicolored wool cape that should help mask the evidence.

She sucked in a breath and texted him.

WHAT TIIME WILL YOU GET INTO BOSTON? SO I CAN MAKE SURE THE PLANE LANDED SAFELY!

Happy and exhausted, she crawled into bed and promptly fell asleep before he replied.

Early the next morning, she pulled on her warm robe and slippers, then checked her phone. He'd returned her text after midnight, nine o'clock California time:

LANDING AT LOGAN AT 3:00.

Wonderful, she thought. That would allow plenty of time for her appointment. Maybe she'd have a quick lunch first in the hospital cafeteria—unless she was too excited to eat. She started to respond with a heart emoji, then changed her mind and sent a thumbs-up instead. She didn't want him to feel pressured by their relationship (whatever it was or would be) before he was on island ground.

After making her bed, she headed to the kitchen for tea. Which was when she realized she had no idea how she was going to get to Dr. Mason's, let alone the ferry terminal. It had been weeks since she'd totaled her car, but she—and her father—had been too busy with bookshop distractions to hunt for a replacement.

At eight o'clock that morning, Stephen was at the kitchen table, one hand holding a bagel with cream cheese, the other poised over his laptop, quietly scrolling through the news headlines before he headed to the boat.

Maddie had set her alarm so she'd be awake to say good-bye.

"What will you do about the car situation?" he asked. "I can't believe we got so wrapped up in working that I forgot about it."

She stared at him blankly; she couldn't believe that she'd forgotten, too. "So did I."

"I'm so sorry."

Forcing a laugh, she said, "Don't worry, Dad. If that's the only thing we've forgotten, it will be a miracle. I'll take care of it. I'll call Joe after you leave." But the pained look on his face told her that her father felt responsible. Of course he did. "Let's look on the bright side," she said, as she gave his shoulder a quick squeeze. "At least I can walk to work!"

Then she glanced at the clock. "Speaking of leaving, you'd better get going, Dad. They want you in queue an hour before departure, and it'll take you thirty minutes to get there." He sighed, closed his laptop, and gathered his things, while she nibbled on a bagel and drank half a cup of tea.

When he was ready, they hugged. "Safe travels, Dad. And, please, don't worry about me."

"Oddly, my daughter," he replied, "I rarely have."

Sad to see him go, but so glad that he'd been there, she hugged him once more, then headed for the shower as he headed out the door.

After showering and dressing she added a little makeup, not that it would last long, but it made her feel like she looked her best, which boosted her spirit, though Rex coming home was all the boost she needed. Then she put on the silver bracelet with the shiny oval of wampum that he'd given her for Christmas. The last thing she did was toss her makeup into her purse so she could reapply it before seeing him.

For a pregnant woman on the cusp of telling the baby's father that they were expecting, Maddie thought she was remarkably calm. Until she called Joe.

"You're where?" she asked.

"Hyannis."

"But that's on the Cape."

"Correct. Nancy was running low on a special kind of ash bark she uses for her baskets. So we came over to buy more at the woodworking shop."

"I thought she never left the island."

"She doesn't. She usually orders her supplies. But this time she refused to wait for a shipment."

Maddie told him about her transportation dilemma.

Joe pondered it for only a few seconds. "Can you get a ride up to my place?"

"Probably." If Kevin wasn't around, Dave might be at the bookshop. If not, she could always call a cab.

"Well," Joe said, "Orson's up there. Keys are in the kitchen on top of the fridge."

"She can't drive a stick shift," Grandma's voice squawked in the background.

There might have been another option, but Maddie didn't have the patience to think about it then. If it was either drive Orson or spend the day traipsing around with the meter of a taxi click-clicking, she'd pick Orson. How bad a stick-shift driver could she be?

"Tell Grandma I'll be fine. It's straight down State Road with only a couple of turns. I'll take good care of the old guy. And maybe tomorrow you'll have time to give me a thorough run-through? I'd like to use him until Rafe gets here."

Joe said it wouldn't be a problem because, with sweet Joe, not much ever was.

After hanging up, she grabbed her things and headed out the front door to try and get a ride to Joe's. But as she dashed out the door, something caught her eye. It was white. It was tucked partway under one of the granite steps. And **MADDIE** was printed on the front.

With her hand starting to shake, she grabbed the envelope, tore it open, and pulled out the expected sheet of paper. It didn't take long to read the message:

LAST CHANCE.

Her legs wobbly, her heart racing faster than it should have, Maddie shoved the note into her purse and briskly trekked down to the bookshop where, luckily, Dave was hard at work. Kevin wasn't there; Dave said he had "stuff going on today."

She didn't take the time to wonder if that meant he and

Taylor planned to greet Rex at the boat. It didn't matter; Maddie would be there, come hell or high water—as high as that which, on occasion, flooded Five Corners down by the ferry. With luck, an accident with Orson wouldn't stop her, either.

Dave said he'd be glad to take her to Joe's. On the way to Aquinnah, she asked if he would wait until she felt sure that she could safely drive the stick.

As expected, the back door to the house was unlocked; the key to Rafe's shiny red pickup was right where Joe said it would be. When she went back outside, Dave already sat on the passenger side of the pickup; he said he'd decided to review the gears with her.

Orson started up right away and hummed like a new top. Dave directed Maddie to go out to the road and up to the circle by the lighthouse; he said it would be good practice.

His idea turned out to be essential; she ground every gear, her stomach lurching in tandem with each misstep on the clutch. Or maybe the lurching was due to the new note in her purse.

After fifteen or twenty minutes, and Dave's patient instruction, the grinding eased; she made it around the loop from the lighthouse to the shops at the Gay Head Cliffs, around to the Aquinnah Cultural Center, and down to the restrooms in pretty good time without many mistakes. She repeated the trip a second, and third time. After the fourth, she drove back to Joe's with confidence.

And Dave said she'd do fine.

She thanked him for his impressive tutorial, said goodbye, and started off to the hospital, firmly expecting that Dr. Mason would say not only was Maddie too old, but also her blood pressure was too high to give birth to a healthy baby. And that she was sorry, but because she was pregnant there wasn't much she could do to stop Maddie's trembling.

Maddie hated that she seemed to need having something to worry about.

She drove so slowly—with only two or three missteps—that she didn't make it to the hospital until twelve fifteen. Plenty of time to call Brandon, because the time had come. She parked the truck and picked up her phone.

After two rings, his voicemail kicked in.

"This is Brandon Morgan. I am out of the country on business; I'll return the last week of April. If this is urgent, please contact my law partner, Heather Goodwink, at our regular office number. Otherwise, leave a message, and I'll try to get back to you in a day or two. Thanks for your patience."

Maddie disconnected; a sound like a *grrr* rose up from her toes. She would not leave a message. Brandon couldn't help if he was in Montreal.

Once inside the hospital, Maddie found Dr. Mason's office. It was only twelve thirty. Though she hadn't had lunch, she wasn't hungry. But once seated in the waiting room, she was able, oddly, to relax. Which wasn't easy, since two other patients there were both very much pregnant and might have been Maddie's age—if their years were added together. They no doubt presumed she was there for perimenopause pamphlets. After all, her once gleaming black hair now showed a strand or two of silver.

"Madelyn?" a woman's voice from across the room called.

Maddie stood and followed the woman down a hall and into a tiny examining room. After a few standard welcoming checks—BP, temp, pulse rate, et cetera—another woman appeared: She wore a white coat and a smile and didn't look much older than the duo in the waiting room. She introduced herself as Dr. Mason.

"So," the doctor said once the formalities were done, "you're expecting."

That's when Maddie bit her lip, lowered her chin, and no longer was relaxed.

What she wanted to say was: "I'm being threatened."

What she wanted to say was: "I'm opening a shop that I have no business opening."

What she wanted to say was: "I'm afraid Rex will hate me."

But all Maddie could say was: "Yes. And I'm too old to be having a baby." Then she started to cry.

Once her mini meltdown was over, Maddie felt composed again. And calm. Dr. Mason was nice. She spoke softly as she examined Maddie and reviewed her history. Then she said Maddie was in excellent health, that many women her age were having babies now, that knowledge of how to make things safer for both mother and baby was far greater than ever before.

Then, she asked if Maddie would like to see an ultrasound.

Surprising herself, Maddie said no. "I'd rather wait until the baby's father is here."

The woman nodded with understanding.

By the time Maddie left with reassurance that the prenatal vitamins she'd been taking were fine and with an appointment scheduled for the beginning of May, she was calm.

After leaving the office, feeling better, she walked to the café. Though the dining room was closed, they offered grab-and-go food until three o'clock. So she ducked inside and bought a ham and cheese sandwich, a root beer, and a big ginger cookie because she felt like celebrating. Then she carried her lunch to the hospital's comfortable vestibule, where sunshine reflected off the harbor and sparkled through the wide wall of windows, and where, at last, Maddie settled into the comfortable sofa, quieted herself, and ate and drank in peace.

Though she'd barely started eating, she stopped and checked her phone: almost three o'clock. She searched for flights from L.A. to Boston: One had just landed and was taxiing to the gate.

She stifled a gasp. It was real. Rex was almost home.

Though she knew it was a two-hour bus trip south to Woods Hole before Rex could hop on a ferry, Maddie quickly stood up, crinkled the wrappings around her half-eaten lunch, and dropped them and the equally half-empty root beer bottle in the proper recycling bins. Then she darted into the restroom, freshened up her makeup, and checked her cape to be certain it covered her secret. It had been three months since she'd seen him; she wanted to look and feel her best.

Once out of the hospital, she climbed back into Orson and was so nervous she shifted into first gear instead of reverse and nearly rammed into a car while backing out of the parking space. Finally, she made it; finally, she left the lot and took a left onto Beach Road, grateful it was still off-season so there was little traffic and the drawbridge wasn't raised. With angels no doubt at her back, she glided through Five Corners and into the Steamship Authority lot without even a tiny incident.

She parked Orson and checked her phone: three twenty-five. He could already be on a Peter Pan bus. So she sat and waited, her eyes drilled toward the jetty, and on the stretch of huge boulders behind it where the big white boat would soon curve into the port.

When the four-thirty arrived, she focused on every walk-off passenger who descended the gangplank; she didn't bother watching the vehicles that crawled out of the freight deck—after all, Rex had his "walking papers" now. She repeated the process with the five-forty-five. A few times she glanced around the parking lot, wondering if she'd see Taylor and Kevin. But she did not.

Soon the sun was low in the sky and the air had chilled. Afraid Orson would run out of gas if she continued to sit there running the heater, Maddie decided to go into the terminal.

As the seven o'clock boat pulled into its berth, she stepped closer to the door in order to peer outside: surely he'd be on this one. Her heart started to beat faster again.

At last, the boat docked; she stepped outside to wait and watch. There she had a full view of the wide white doors of the freight deck as they rolled open and the crew began to make ready for the vehicles to exit. Again, on the side of the boat, the gangplank was wheeled to the mid-level. But before the passengers started to disembark, vehicles began to exit. The first one off was an ambulance. And Maddie thought, *Thank God that's not for him. Or for me. Not for either of us this time.*

Standing close to the disembarking queue, Maddie glanced from the gangplank back to the ambulance as it inched toward her. The lettering on the side said it was a private one from Boston.

A disturbing feeling crept over her. As it moved slowly, about to pass where she was standing, she wished that she could see into the back. But all she saw was the passenger side of the vehicle, where a woman sat, staring straight ahead. She was an attractive woman, well-dressed from what Maddie could tell, wearing what looked like a chic wool coat and hat, and a cashmere scarf wrapped loosely around her neck. She did not appear to be in an EMT uniform, though Maddie realized she couldn't know that what with the winter coat and all.

The vehicles stopped for a moment to let the stream of walk-off passengers who'd exited from the gangplank cross over to the parking lot. Scrutinizing every male figure in the crowd, she did not see Rex.

Which made her think: *Is it possible that* he *is the patient in the ambulance?* She'd assumed that he could walk under his own steam, but had she been wrong? And had the woman in the passenger seat been an EMT . . . or someone else? Someone like . . . Annie Sutton?

Maddie stood, staring at the back of the ambulance as it pulled out onto the street, leaving her standing on the side-walk, just as a thin layer of fog started to roll in.

Chapter 25

After ditching a lame idea to stay at the terminal until the next boat arrived, Maddie returned to Orson, started him up, and cranked up the heat. She checked her phone to see if Rex—or anyone—had texted and she'd missed it. But no one had. As badly as she wanted to call Taylor or Kevin, she did not want to intrude. It was bad enough she'd thought it was her place to surprise Taylor's brother, especially since Maddie had no way of knowing how Taylor really felt about Maddie being pregnant. Just as she didn't know if Rex had been in the ambulance and if the front-seat passenger was Annie Sutton—or if Maddie's hormones, not her intuition, had surged again, determined to wreak havoc.

Maybe Google could help.

Without listening to her common sense again, she hastily entered Annie's name. Instantly, the screen lit up. Best-selling mystery author. Screenwriter. Nominated for an Academy Award last year. And there were many photos of a pretty woman with black hair and green eyes like her brother Kevin's. Which was no help, because Maddie hadn't seen the passenger on the front seat close enough to judge.

Numbness, disappointment, sorrow: The trio of emotions drifted through the fog and settled in her pores.

She wondered if she should text Rex. Ask if his flight had been delayed. She could have googled that, too, but she didn't know what flight he'd actually been on, other than it arrived at three o'clock. She supposed she could check every flight into Boston today. Instead, she sighed, and dropped her phone back into her purse.

Sooner or later, she'd hear something. If not from Rex, maybe from Kevin, who might be more inclined to be in touch than his wife.

Determined to relax, Maddie made it up the hill surprisingly smoothly, then she was struck by a bolt of inspiration. Yanking the steering wheel into Cronig's parking lot, she made a sharp U-turn. If she hurried, she might make it to the hospital in time to see the EMTs roll the gurney out of the ambulance.

Because it was off-season, and it wasn't far, Orson got her there in record time despite the misty air. She deftly steered under the portico for the Emergency Room, where it was empty. Because no ambulance was there.

She stopped, snapped off the ignition, and jumped out of the bright red pickup, not caring if her wool cape wasn't hiding her swollen belly.

The waiting area inside was empty, too, except for a lone man sitting behind an intake window, his eyes fixed on a computer screen. Maddie approached him.

"Did the Boston ambulance arrive?" She tried to sound as if she knew one had been en route.

He pulled his gaze from the screen. "From the boat?"

She forced a smile. "Yes. It got off the ferry ahead of me."

He glanced at the screen again, then back to her. "Sorry. No ER check-ins tonight from Boston or anywhere."

Her half-baked grin morphed into a scowl. "But I saw it drive off the freight deck . . ."

"Sorry," he repeated.

Staring at the floor, Maddie knew there was nothing left to do. So she turned and started to leave.

"Wait," the intake man said. "I can try Windemere for you."

Maddie said she thought that was a nursing home.

"They also have a wing for short-term recuperation for residents coming back from off-island hospitals and rehab. I was on my break and might have missed it; they turn around fast this time of night. Especially if they're worried about fog cancelling the last boat. Hold on . . ." He tapped something into his keyboard. Then, speaking into his headset, he asked if a new patient arrived in the past few minutes. He thanked the person on the line, then looked at Maddie.

"It was here." He told her how to get to the hospital annex and into Windemere.

Maddie's sneakers pumped down the hallway; she made it to the door at the same time Kevin and Taylor came in from a different direction.

"Maddie!" Kevin exclaimed as if surprised to see her. "He's back!" His words were hurried, as if he was a six-year-old at the Vineyard's renowned Ag Fair.

Taylor kept moving toward the entrance, while her husband stood next to Maddie.

"He texted me last night and said his plane would land at three, but not that he'd be in an ambulance."

Taylor entered a door; it closed behind her.

Kevin sighed. "Yeah, he still has to do rehab. But he's here, back in one piece. Almost." He smiled, then added in a whisper, "Have you told him?"

Maddie said no. "So please don't."

"My lips are sealed 'til you say otherwise."

She nodded thanks. Then she glanced to the door where Taylor had disappeared.

"Why don't you go in, Kevin," she said. "Rex must be exhausted from the trip, and you should be there with Taylor. I'll check on him tomorrow." She should receive an Oscar for acting so composed.

Kevin frowned. "But . . ."

Maddie hoisted her purse strap onto her shoulder and started to turn away. "It's fine. I have lots of time. Especially since now, as you said, he's back in one piece. And please don't tell him I was here. Just say I'll be in touch tomorrow."

With that, she made her way outside to Orson, who, in his snazzy red coat, looked much happier than Maddie felt. She climbed inside and sat, only a gentle hill up from the water, staring at the lampposts, where the misty fog now cloaked itself around the rays of light.

The only thing that might have made the past hours more upsetting would have been if Maddie got back to the cottage and found another note; thankfully, she did not. Instead, she was greeted by tantalizing aromas of Grandma's fresh-baked rosemary bread and chowder.

"Where've you been all day?" Grandma asked, while Maddie was hanging up her cape.

She told her Rex was back. "I tried to see him, but can't until tomorrow."

Grandma scurried closer as if they were in a castle and Maddie wouldn't hear her.

"Will you tell him about the baby when you see him?"

"Not unless it's the right time. First, I want to see how he is." She wove around Grandma and went to the stove, where she started scooping chowder into a bowl.

Grandma scurried again. "Well, you'd better hurry up, or he won't know until he meets you in the department of labor." The "department of labor" was Grandma's favorite term for the maternity section of the hospital.

Because she'd barely eaten that day, Maddie devoured her supper, for which the baby seemed pleased. Grandma suggested that she had a fisherman growing inside her.

Stephen would have laughed if he had been there. Maddie sighed, already missing her dad.

After they were done with supper, she wanted to be alone. "Time for me to go into my room and read another book my father ordered. I'm taking notes so I might be halfway helpful to our customers."

Grandma looked at her. "Don't forget to read kids' books, too."

"I won't. Thanks."

Thirty minutes later, she was curled up in bed, reading a little-known but gripping mystery. She became so entrenched in the story that when her phone rang, she nearly shot up off the bed, as if the villain from the novel had snuck into the cottage.

Then realizing the call might be from Rex, she grabbed the phone.

"Hi, Mom," said the happiest voice that Maddie knew. "Whatcha doing?"

And Maddie knew the time had come to tell her son about the "baby-and-Rex" news.

"Holy crap!" Rafe yowled.

Maddie laughed. "That's one way of putting it. Though you might want to change your college lexicon when he or she is here. At least until the teenage years."

"Sure, Mom. But wow. This is amazing."

Maddie agreed. "I hope Rex feels the same when I finally get to tell him." Then she filled Rafe in on Rex having been granted his "walking papers" and being back on the island though apparently he wasn't walking much, if at all.

"So he doesn't know yet?"

"Not yet. I hope to tell him tomorrow."

"Wow," her son said again.

Maddie laughed. "But enough about me. What about you? Has spring training started yet?"

"Tomorrow. It'll be fun. But the truth is, I'd rather be there helping Joe. And you, too, especially now."

"I'm fine, honey. I saw the doctor today, and she agreed. So please don't worry. What's important is that you enjoy these last weeks at Amherst. Not to mention that your team depends on you."

"We depend on every one of us. Speaking of which, I only had a chance to make four baskets for the bookshop. Sorry. I'll do better once I'm there."

"Don't worry about that, either. Grandma's working up a storm."

"Will she be able to come with you to graduation? Will Rex come, too?"

At least he hadn't asked if she wanted to marry Rex. Some things about his generation were far more sensible than those that came before.

"I don't know, honey. We'll have to see how things pan out." She made sure she was smiling when she said it because she'd always believed facial expressions could be interpreted over the phone. Then she had a grim thought.

"Your dad and his family will be there?"

"Are you kidding? Because he's a 'successful'—his word—alum, he's pissed he wasn't asked to be commencement speaker."

Yes. That sounded like Owen. Then Maddie realized that commencement would be toward the end of May. A lump swelled in her throat.

"Is graduation Memorial Day weekend?" she asked, wondering how the date had escaped her.

"Yup. It's that Sunday."

The weekend the bookshop was scheduled to open. The grand opening date not only for new businesses, but for the entire island to kick off summer. Why hadn't she thought of that earlier? *Because you've been a mess*, she thought. Even worse, she'd be heavily pregnant by then, and Owen was far more critical of unmarried mothers than Rafe's generation, or even theirs.

"And . . . when's the baby due?" her son teased.

"July twelfth." It was the first time she'd shared the date that Dr. Mason had "assigned."

With a hearty laugh, Rafe said, "Well, it'll add to the interest of the festivities, won't it?"

She gritted her teeth and hoped her theory about facial expressions was incorrect. "Don't be ridiculous, honey. We're adults. Well, not counting the twins. We'll all be there for *you*. No one or nothing else. Got it?"

"Yes, but Dad . . ."

Maddie refrained from saying, "Your dad's a jerk, Rafe." Instead, she lied and said, "Your dad will be fine, too. In fact, I'm sure he'll be thrilled that I finally have another life."

"You're too generous, Mom."

For a moment, Maddie suspected that Owen had said derogatory things to Rafe about her already. She'd never asked, and didn't care to know. Her son was smart enough to know the difference between reality and Owen being Owen.

Then Rafe said he had to get some sleep so he'd be prime for training in the morning.

After they hung up, Maddie tried to get back into reading, but she couldn't concentrate. All she could think about was Memorial Day weekend, when she'd be almost seven-and-a-half months pregnant and very noticeable. She'd also have to figure out how the bookshop could open when the owner was off-island. Changing the opening date probably wasn't an option—ads were already placed and paid for. The only answer would be if she could find someone she trusted who could fill in. Francine was the most likely, but she'd be busy with the Inn. Still, maybe she'd have a suggestion.

Pulling the comforter around her, Maddie turned off the lamp and prayed that sleep would come quickly and peacefully. But it did not.

At some point in the night, she heard a soft ding from the nightstand. A text alert. She didn't move, wondering if it had been her imagination. Or her note-writer, hoping that texting would have a stronger impact. After a few seconds, it dinged again.

She reached over and retrieved the phone. The red dot indicated that indeed there was a text, so that part was real.

Squinting, to avoid turning on the lamp again, she read: I MADE IT TO THE ISLAND. AT WINDEMERE REHAB. COME VISIT. It was signed with a smiling emoji.

She might have stopped breathing for a moment.

Then she did what a woman in love most likely would have done. She bounded out of bed as quickly as her baby-heavy body was able to bound.

Racing into the bathroom, she washed up, brushed her teeth, and flung on a little makeup: She looked tired, but happy; exhausted, but elated. Then she threw on the outfit she'd worn the day before because it was one less thing to have to think about.

Twelve minutes after the text arrived, she dashed off a

message for Grandma, flew out the back door, and raced up the hill where she'd parked Orson. Jumping into the pickup, she flicked on the ignition and barreled toward Menemsha Road, grinding the gears a couple of times but not caring, heading toward South Road that would take her to State and then to Martha's Vineyard Hospital where her baby's father had asked her to visit.

She hadn't noticed that it was only three o'clock in the morning.

Chapter 26

"You can't come in."

"Please," Maddie begged as respectfully as she could manage. "He just flew home last night." She stood outside the door where Taylor disappeared only hours earlier.

"I'm sorry, but he's sleeping," the man on the inside said, one hand on the door handle, prepared in case the visitor became unpleasantly insistent.

She shook her head. "No. He texted me a few minutes ago and begged me to come." She fumbled for her purse, ready to grab her phone to prove it.

"It doesn't matter. Visiting hours start at eleven, more than seven hours from now. I suggest you come back then."

In spite of her determination to not take no for an answer, Maddie's lower lip started to tremble. Maybe if she cried, he would change his mind.

"Please." She lowered her voice. "He was almost killed in an accident in California. He was in the hospital out there for three months."

Pause.

"He lives here, right?"

Maddie nodded. "In Edgartown. He was born here. And now he owns the Lord James restaurant."

The man sighed and paused again.

Then he asked, "Are you a family member?"

There it was: the glancing blow. Maddie felt her hope evaporate.

"I'm as close as family can get."

The majordomo shook his head. "Sorry," he said and began to shut the door.

"But . . ." Tears formed in her eyes though she hadn't even tried. She wondered if she should tell him she was pregnant, then shamelessly open her cape so he could see her rounded belly.

But she couldn't do it, because he might tell Rex.

He shook his head again and said, "We'll see you at eleven." He gave her a semi-sympathetic smile.

And then he closed the door, practically in her face.

As Maddie steered Orson through Five Corners and back onto State Road, the darkness was becoming wrapped in fog again, thicker than before. She remembered when she'd been four or five and Grandma told her a Wampanoag legend that the giant Moshup, Creator of the island, gave them the gift of fog, a soft blanket to protect his people from harm. The thought made Maddie smile now, even as she eased her foot up off the accelerator in case the gift turned into a nightmare.

With no cars in the area and, thanks to Moshup, only quiet, Maddie decided to enjoy the drive. To her, fog felt peaceful, much like the stillness of a heavy snowfall in Green Hills; both acted as cushions for the earth, nature's sound barriers that silenced humans, their voices and their vehicles.

She drove up the hill and passed Cronig's Market, where she'd made a U-turn the night before, and realized she felt calmer than when she'd left the hospital—now that she knew

Rex would be well cared for in the last leg of his rehab. As for her, she knew she needed to practice patience, which would also be a good exercise for after the baby came.

Not far past the market, she noticed the Black Dog Café up ahead. Its lights were on but murky, clouded by the fog; inside, the café workers must be getting ready to open. She wished they were open so she could get a breakfast sandwich or a muffin. But then her thoughts had to refocus as a blur of headlights approached her from behind. *Another damn fool on the road in the wee hours*, she thought.

Beyond the Black Dog, State Road dipped and curved; to the right was the overlook of Tashmoo Pond, where it became more difficult to see and more menacing to drive. She thought about turning into the parking lot and waiting out the worst of the visibility, but it might take a long time, and she'd most likely get cold, in spite of Orson's new heating system. Besides, she realized the gas gauge looked precariously low.

So Maddie kept driving, the headlights behind her creeping closer, glaring into her mirror like halogen ones did. That, and the fact that she was not alone on a desolate road in the pea soup, did not feel comforting but foreboding.

With maybe ten more miles to go if she veered off State at North Road, Maddie knew it would take longer if she stayed on State to South Road and turned onto Menemsha Road. But because the South Road route was more populated, she thought it might be safer if the fog became so thick she couldn't see.

After making that decision, she flicked her eyes to the rearview mirror and was nearly blinded; the headlights were now on high beams and drawing closer to Orson. An ominous feeling, a warning, a harbinger suddenly gripped her. And Maddie knew she had to stay the course—in case her stalker was the author of the notes.

The toughest part was restraining herself from stepping on

the gas in order to escape the eerie headlights nearly hugging Orson's rear bumper now. And though her pulse was racing, Maddie was getting tired.

Without closing her eyes (though she really, really wanted to), Maddie prayed to Moshup and to God and to her ancestors and her mother, and to anyone else who might be listening, that what she was feeling was not akin to Grandma's portentous sense of someone walking over her grave. Especially since the needle for the gas gauge had dropped another mark.

Carefully navigating the curve at the West Tisbury Village Cemetery, with now surprising precision, Maddie shifted again—grinding the gear that time—as, thankfully, Orson carried her safely down the small hill, then up the next one that led to Alley's and the library. But before she reached the top, something instantly changed. The blur of lights in the rearview mirror shifted– the vehicle took a sharp left turn onto Edgartown Road and disappeared into the fog.

Maddie needed to catch her breath. Pulling into an empty lot beyond Alley's, she brought Orson to a stop. Her arm muscles ached; her head hurt now, too. As for her brain, she berated herself for having been paranoid, because, realistically, no one would have known she was out before dawn, let alone someone who'd want to risk driving in the dangerous early hours without a better reason than to try to intimidate her. The one good thing was that the danger seemed to have passed; she decided it was now safe to keep driving to Menemsha.

As if in agreement, the baby gave her a swift kick.

Thanks to another miracle, there had been more than enough gas to get her to the cottage. Yet Maddie remained restless for what was left of the night, though by the time she was back in her bedroom it was almost five thirty, which hardly could be called night, despite that the sun didn't rise until nearly seven.

She went to bed, but at six fifteen, she pushed the covers off and gave up the struggle. Getting up, she showered and dressed—again—in the same clothes. If she did not see Rex today, she'd need to find another camouflaging outfit to put on.

Once she was mildly ready to face the day, she sat at the table, drinking caffeine-free tea, which did not help make her more alert. At least the baby had no trouble going back to sleep.

Inside the cottage, it was as quiet as it had been in the fog. Joe had an appointment down-island this morning, so Grandma had announced last night that she'd be "sleeping in." It was a good chance for Maddie to go back to reading: Maybe she'd be capable of tackling a few of the children's books.

But something else had to come first, if for nothing else than her peace of mind.

She left the cottage at eight o'clock, too early to visit Rex, but not too early to gas up Orson, then visit the Chilmark Police Station, which she knew covered Menemsha.

Once the tank was full, she pulled into the police station parking lot. Then, armed with the notes and a new resolve to stop being stressed by envelopes left under a rock, a breather phone call, or mystery cars creeping up on her at night, she marched into the building, holding her head up high.

"I think I'm being threatened," she said to a young officer at the front desk. She recognized him from . . . somewhere, but had no idea from where.

He stood up and raised his eyebrows. "Threatened by whom?"

Maddie smiled at his excellent grammar, then wondered if she'd ever be able to shed her college professor-ness.

"I don't know," she said. "I've never done anything to harm anyone. But I have proof . . ." She took the notes out from her purse.

"The chief's in today," the young man said. "He's the one you need to talk to."

Maddie thanked him and waited at the counter while he vanished down a hall. Then she remembered why she'd recognized him: He'd been the young officer at "the scene" of her accident. Hopefully, he would not hold that against her. Or mention that she'd come close to harming someone then.

In less than a minute, the officer returned and asked her to follow him.

The police chief stood and introduced himself as Ken Lawrence. He was tall and lean, with salt-and-pepper hair and broad shoulders. He looked nothing like the only police chief she'd ever met: Alan Delaney of Green Hills, who was old and had a rounded belly larger than hers was now.

After their introductions, Chief Lawrence sat behind his desk, and Maddie, across from him. The young man, whose name she learned was Officer Lindstrom, sat next to her. The men appeared to be the only two officers in the station at the time.

Without hesitation, Maddie gave a quick synopsis, then handed the chief the notes, one at a time, in chronological order.

GET OFF THE ISLAND. AND DON'T COME BACK.

WHY ARE YOU STILL HERE?

WHAT PART OF GET OFF THE ISLAND DON'T YOU UNDERSTAND?

And finally: **LAST CHANCE.**

"After the second note," she said, "there was a strange phone call that was only someone breathing. Maybe it wasn't related, but it was upsetting." Then she told them about the car following her vehicle too closely in the fog earlier that morning. "I come from a small town where the roads are dark at night, but up-island it's more remote, and, with fog . . . well, I guess I'm not used to that yet."

The chief opened a desk drawer, took out a pair of thin vinyl gloves, the kind people had worn in supermarkets during the first weeks and months of COVID. He examined the notes carefully.

"Has anyone touched these other than you?" he asked.

She shook her head. "Well, except for the third envelope. My father found that one. He handed it to me. But he didn't open it."

He slipped each note into a separate plastic baggie, sealed it, and labeled it with the date Maddie said she'd received it. Then he grilled her about who might have sent them or if she'd had an altercation, no matter how trivial—in a shop, on the street, anywhere with a stranger who might have found out who she was.

"Not that I can think of," Maddie replied. "But after the last note—and, even scarier, the vehicle following me last night—I'm afraid for my family's safety. And that whoever is doing this will try and sabotage my new business."

The chief nodded, as did Officer Lindstrom.

"Are you new to the island?" the chief asked.

Maddie gave him the rundown of when and why she'd come and that she now was there to stay.

"Wait," he said, his face breaking into a smile, "you're Nancy Clieg's granddaughter?"

"Yes."

"You're opening the bookshop on the harbor?"

She nodded, not surprised that the grapevine was so efficient.

"You stayed in Aquinnah after the fire, right? At Rex Winsted's place?"

Her hand flew to her stomach, thanks to a weird instinct. "Yes. I actually found the first note there. The rest came to Menemsha once we moved back to the cottage. Whoever delivered them clearly knew where I was."

He gestured to the notes. "Does Rex know about these?"

"I didn't tell him yet. He just got back from California . . ."

"Good. Yeah, I heard about his accident. Horrible. How's he doing?"

"He was well enough to fly home," Maddie said, then added that she planned to see him after she left the station. "I guess he'll be at Windemere a little while."

The chief glanced at his watch. "Visiting hours there don't start until eleven."

She wanted to roll her eyes, but held the impulse back. "Right. I learned that the hard way. Rex texted me during the night. I immediately went to see him, but they wouldn't let me in. He must not have known what time it was. Anyway, that's why I was out at that ungodly hour when the fog rolled in and the strange vehicle bizarrely followed me up State Road to the cut-off to Edgartown." *There*, she thought. *Now the police have the whole story. And maybe I can get some sleep.*

The chief nodded, as if putting the pieces together. "We'll do some digging around," he said. "Do you mind if we keep these?"

"Of course not," she said. "But will you make copies for me? In case I decide to show them to Rex? It might give him something to think about while he's in rehab."

"Good idea. He knows a lot about the Vineyard and the people."

Maddie nodded and the men stood up.

The chief handed the notes to Officer Lindstrom again. "Copy these, please. As for you, Ms. Clarke, I'm glad you brought this to our attention. But try not to worry. They've been so sporadic, after, what is it now, five months? Which suggests the sender probably isn't violent."

The word *violent* hadn't crossed her mind, and she wished he hadn't said it. But Maddie thanked him.

"Be sure to tell your grandmother that her favorite constable says hello," Chief Lawrence added with a smile. "She still thinks I'm twenty-one."

"Some days she still thinks *she's* twenty-one," Maddie replied and returned the smile. Then she left his office with the junior officer and waited while he made the copies.

In a few more minutes, she was back in Orson, heading toward Vineyard Haven, and wondering how she'd kill two more hours before she could see Rex.

Chapter 27

"Maddie."

She teared up. She'd spent the past hour and a half in the waiting room; it made her feel better to know he wasn't far from her. And now, she heard him say her name.

"Come closer. You look so beautiful."

His voice was no longer coarse. But he was pale and looked like he'd lost a lot of weight. He was half sitting up, half lying on his back.

She stepped closer. She'd expected that whatever hair he had would have grown, but someone had shaved his head to newly bald before sending him home. Maybe Annie had.

He reached up and took her hand. "I feel like I've been gone a year."

She nodded, struggling to convince herself that this time, he wasn't a dream.

His touch was warm.

"Cat got your tongue?" he asked.

Tears rolled down her cheeks. "Rex," was all she could manage.

He smiled, closed his eyes, and drew her hand to his chest. "I've missed you," he said.

"Me, too, you."

A nurse entered the room; Maddie remained standing, Rex's hand still on hers, his heart beating softly against her palm. The nurse checked the monitors and two tubes snaking into his arms. She asked if Maddie wanted to sit.

"Okay," she replied, determined to keep her hand where Rex had placed it.

Maddie watched as the nurse went over to a chair and removed a large item from it, which she placed atop a storage cabinet. The item looked like a neck brace. A very large one.

The nurse noticed Maddie staring at it. "We're weaning him off it now," she said. "He's been in it since the accident. Except, of course, during surgery." She slid the chair to Maddie, who had almost forgotten that Rex had surgery—two surgeries, she was told, though she supposed there could have been more. But, as last night's majordomo had reminded her, Maddie wasn't family.

She managed to sit while her hand kept contact with his chest.

The nurse made some entries on her iPad, then looked at Rex.

"PT at eleven thirty," she said. "They can't wait to see you. And, by the way, welcome home."

Rex lifted the hand that was not holding Maddie's. "Thanks, Ruth Ann. It's great to be back."

The nurse waved back and left.

"I was in school with her," he told Maddie. "All twelve years." He started to laugh, then abruptly stopped.

"Does it hurt to laugh?" Maddie asked.

"Nah. I'm a tough guy, remember?"

"I don't care if you're a total weakling. I only want you here. Well, not here in this bed, but here. Near me." She didn't know if it was okay to say that, but the words had tumbled out. "It's been a long haul for you."

He smiled. "You're wearing your bracelet."

She glanced at her wrist; she smiled back. Then she thought about Annie Sutton. But the idea of Annie being—or not being—there no longer mattered. What did matter was that Rex was there and seemed happy to see Maddie.

Glancing around the room, she asked, "How long do they think you'll be in here?"

"No idea. Days, hopefully. Weeks, maybe. It depends on if I cooperate."

She knew he'd dredged up his sense of humor to minimize the drama of his situation. If humor helped healing and recovery, Rex was sure to be raring to go in no time.

"But let's not talk about me, okay?" he said. "I want to know what's going on with you. Kevin said the bookshop's coming along, that your dad's been a big help, and that you're opening on Memorial Day weekend. That's kind of incredible."

"It sure is. Kevin was right. My dad put all the start-up systems in motion—financial stuff, inventory, even a marketing plan for Rafe to handle. But Dad left yesterday, and he'll be gone until . . ." She couldn't very well say, "Until the baby's born." She blinked and reassembled her words. "Until our grand opening."

"I can't wait to see it. Kudos to him for helping out."

"Kevin's been terrific, too. And his painter, Dave Erikson? You probably know him, too?"

Rex frowned. "I don't know Dave well, but I'm glad he's working out. I've known his father, Bud, since I was a kid. He's a miserable old salt. Not one of my favorite people." He snorted. "Then again, he might say the same about me."

Shifting on the chair, Maddie knew this wasn't the conversation she wanted to be having.

"So . . ." she said slowly, "you feel okay this morning?"

"Better than okay for seeing you. Probably not okay enough to dance, if that's what you have in mind."

She closed her eyes a second. "Well, dancing isn't on my calendar, either. But I do have some other news for you. But if you're tired or in pain, it can wait 'til later."

"No, I want to hear all the news that I've missed out on. And I want to hear it now. Don't make me drag it out of you. Wait. Let me guess." He pressed the fingers of his free hand to his lips and squinted as if pondering. His cinnamon eyes widened. Then he offered her a wide grin—the grin that she had missed so much. "I know!" he said. "You're pregnant!"

He was joking, of course. But if he'd come up with anything else, Maddie would have laughed and said, "Guess again." They might have had a few minutes of silly banter, the kind between two people who had good chemistry.

Instead, she sat, unmoving, not knowing what to say.

Then a dark-haired, mustached man came into the room. He wore a white uniform; an ID card dangled from a lanyard that he wore around his neck. Behind him was a young blond woman wearing white pants, a pink smock, and a similar ID.

"Rex Winsted? I'm Greg and this is Rosie with the ponytail. Hate to interrupt, but we're from PT, and it's time for us to see you strut your stuff!" He glanced at Maddie. "Your friend will be back in about an hour, give or take." Then the duo marched over to the bed and Greg started pushing levers and raising the bed rail on the side where Maddie sat, while Rosie tended to the IV poles that apparently would accompany Rex to wherever PT was. Then Rosie picked up the very big neck brace and assembled it around his neck.

Maddie tried not to look horrified.

"We'll make sure to bring him back safe and sound," Greg added. "If you plan to stick around, you might want to take advantage of our wonderful café. It's not exactly Michelin-starred, but we think that's only because the judges haven't been here yet."

With that, Rosie propped open the door and Greg

wheeled the bed away while Rosie then escorted the IV poles beside it.

Maddie caught a glimpse of Rex's hand as he held it up and waved good-bye.

Sitting in one of the small booths, picking at a Cobb salad, Maddie realized that Greg from PT was right: the café deserved a Michelin ranking. Maddie figured the food would taste even better if she had an appetite. Then the baby squirmed, so she knew she needed to keep feeding the poor little thing. But as she took another bite, she sensed someone standing by her table.

"Fancy seeing you here," a familiar voice said.

Maddie looked up and saw Francine. She laughed. "As I recall, it's not the first time both of us were here at the same time."

Francine sat across from Maddie and set her coffee cup on the table. "A nurse at Windemere said you might be here while our long-lost friend is in physical therapy."

"You came to see Rex, too?"

Francine nodded, her big, dark eyes shining. "I can't believe he's back. My kids are going to be so excited." She frowned. "Well, Bella will be. Reggie's still too young to understand much of anything beyond *Blue's Clues*."

"I take it that's a kids' TV show?" Maddie knew she had a lot to learn—so much had changed since Rafe was born.

"Yup. He loves it." She took a swig of coffee. "Have you seen Rex yet?"

Maddie had a bite of the French bread that came with the salad and nodded.

"How's he doing? Does he look different? Can he communicate okay, or do you have to do the talking?"

Looking perky and adorable as usual, with her twenty-something-year-old's optimism and the energy to make things happen, Francine once told Maddie she considered Rex her adoptive father. And right then, it took every bit of restraint that Maddie had not to blurt out the news she was about to tell him—if she ever got to see him long enough and uninterrupted.

"He looks great. A little thinner, maybe, but great."

Francine's eyebrows went up. "You're not prejudiced, right?"

"Maybe a little. But he does look great. Someone even shaved his head. Maybe it was Annie."

"Or Beth."

Thankfully, Maddie hadn't taken another bite or she might have choked on it.

"Beth?" As in the nurse Maddie had talked to?

"She's a caregiver who was with him at Annie's. She's nice. An older woman. She traveled with him from California. The doctor wouldn't approve of him making the trip without medical supervision. Anyway, Kevin and Taylor came to the hospital last night to be sure Rex was settled, then they brought Beth to the Inn, where she stayed last night. They picked her up before I left to come here; they were taking her to breakfast before putting her on the boat so she could get back to Logan and fly home."

So Beth, not Annie, was the woman in the ambulance last night. In spite of Maddie's resolution to ditch jealousy, her heart squeaked *Yippee*, as if she, not Francine, was a perky twenty-something-year-old girl.

Then Maddie had a thought.

"Speaking of Rex," she said, pausing to gather her composure, "when he's done with PT, can you give us a little time alone before you come into his room? I need to talk with him for fifteen or twenty minutes."

It was, after all, past due. For starters, Maddie didn't think she could hold back another second, and though she was eager to tell Francine about the baby, she also was determined that Rex would be the next person to know.

Francine's sly little smile indicated that she might already be aware why Maddie wanted alone time with him.

Maddie smiled back.

Hoping that some extra time would enable him to get resettled once PT was done, she sat with Francine until twelve thirty, then made a beeline for Windemere. But when she stepped into the room, Kevin and Taylor were there.

"Hey, Maddie." Kevin was the first to speak. "Nice to see you again." He sat in the chair where she'd sat earlier.

"Hello, Maddie," Taylor said from her post at the cabinet that held medical items she'd apparently been examining.

Rex smiled; his cervical collar was still in place, and he looked worn-out.

The avocado rumbled in Maddie's tummy. Could she stand to wait another minute? And, with Francine soon to be there, Rex's room would turn into party central and Maddie would never have a chance to tell him about the baby, maybe not for another day.

No! her insides cried.

So she cleared her throat and said, "Hi, everyone."

Kevin stood up and offered her the chair.

"Yes, thanks," she said. But before sitting down, she added, "And I think you'll both understand if I ask you to do something that's important to me."

Kevin pressed his lips together, no doubt so he wouldn't smile.

Taylor merely leaned against the cabinet, watching Maddie.

"Could you please give me a few minutes alone with Rex? I need to talk with him in private, and I've waited a long time." *There,* she thought. *I said it.*

Kevin was the first to speak. "Come on, Ms. T.," he said

in the way he often addressed his wife. "Let's leave these two alone." Guiding Taylor from the room, he turned and gave Maddie a salute. "Take your time," he said.

The door closed and Maddie was left, still standing, with Rex still reclining in the bed.

"Wow," he said. "I'm starting to think this is serious." His voice was steady. But if he was conjuring potentially bad scenarios, his calm expression didn't reveal it.

She dragged the chair close to the bed and sat down as she had earlier.

"It is," she said. "But it's a good serious. At least, I think it is." At that point her courage started to slide. Could she do this? Could she truly tell him? Should she wait . . .

And then . . .

"You were right," she blurted out, "I'm pregnant."

His face sagged a little; his chin started to quiver. "Oh?" was all he said.

She gave him a minute. Or maybe it was only five or ten seconds. "Oh?" she asked. "That's it?"

He closed his eyes.

Her heart plummeted to her toes.

"That must be exciting for you."

Exciting?

"What?" she asked.

His eyes opened again but they were on the bedsheets, not on her. "Hey, it's what I get for being gone so long." He ran a finger around the top rim of the giant collar as if it had become too tight. "I'm happy for you, Maddie. And I hope the guy you found is nice." He flashed a glance her way. "If he's not, he'll have me to answer to."

She blinked. "What the hell are you talking about?"

He looked straight at her that time. "I didn't want to rush things with you. I tried to let you know how I felt, but I guess I did a lousy job. My bad. But I've been away three months. It never occurred to me you might find someone else—or even want to. My bad again. I'm sorry. And I only said I'm happy for you because I figured it was what I was supposed to say." He closed his eyes again. "Thanks for stopping by to tell me. Now, would you mind asking my sister and Kevin to come back tomorrow? Say I'm tired and sore from PT and I need to sleep."

Maddie grabbed his hand, dropped her forehead onto the mattress, and let out a soft groan. Then she raised her head and said, "I love you to pieces, Rex Winsted. But sometimes you can be a dumb-ass." She didn't think she'd ever said that word before, and because she had, she found it rather amusing. "Don't worry. I'll clean up my language before our baby's born . . . which will be somewhere around July twelfth. About nine months from the day after Cranberry Day."

He stared at her. He didn't move, not that moving was something he was able to do very well right then, anyway.

"Maddie?" he asked with his gentle smile.

"Yes?"

"You're not kidding, are you?"

She let go of his hand and stood up. Then she opened her cape and cupped her hands around her belly. "If we weren't in a public place, I'd be happy to lower my pants and open my shirt so you can see firsthand."

"It's true? You and I? A baby?"

She nodded several times in rapid succession.

He put his hands to his face and the big lug started to cry. He reached out for her hand, and she took it in hers, and she sat down again, and they cried together.

Chapter 28

"So," Rex said as he rubbed his hand—the one not attached to the IV drip—over his bald head, "what do you think? Do you want to get married?"

She supposed the question was inevitable.

"What I want is to not rush into anything." Her voice stayed steady, her conviction strong. Because she was being truthful. "Especially now, with the baby coming, and with our even more immediate priority being for you to get well." She paused. "Okay?"

"Okay. But for the record, I think marrying you would be great."

She knew if she spoke then, her voice would waver. So she closed her eyes and rested her head on his hand. It wasn't the right time to tell him she'd already thought about it; it wasn't the right time to remind him that she was about to open a business, and that he would soon have to catch up with his. It wasn't the right time to talk about logistics, like where they should live. It wasn't the right time to talk about marriage. He needed to let the news sink in. Until then, he was home, and that was what mattered. For now.

"You're okay with waiting to decide?" she finally asked.

"I'm okay with whatever you're okay with. But beware . . . the patience I'm showing right now might only be the pain meds talking." He laughed and squeezed her hand. "I love you, Maddie Clarke."

She thought about the card she'd found in his chest of drawers; she gulped. "And I love you, Rex Winsted."

"And I love that we're having a baby together."

"Me, too. Very much."

Upon hearing that, he fell asleep, the corners of his mouth turned up in a smile.

"Your mother would be so happy," Grandma said, as she dished up their dinner—a thick stew made with locally raised chicken and a mix of root vegetables harvested last autumn that she and Maddie had canned. And more of Grandma's rosemary bread.

Maddie ate everything because it tasted so good, but, in truth, she was exhausted and would have preferred going straight to bed. She'd stayed at the hospital all day, dozing while Rex napped, only leaving his bedside in late afternoon to pick up an "on-the-go" sandwich at the Black Dog Bakery down the street because the hospital café had closed at two o'clock. She was tired then, too, and only had eaten half of the sandwich.

Her visit had been interrupted intermittently by nurses checking Rex's vitals while others brought IV fluids and the pain meds he'd referred to. Also, Francine stuck her head in quickly "just to make sure," she said, that he was in one piece; an aide stopped by with a message that Kevin and Taylor would return that evening.

In spite of the busyness of the place, the people closest to Rex had given them privacy, for which Maddie was grateful. She knew that would change once the news of the baby became public, because many others would want to join in their fun. Life would be hectic, but it would be wonderful, because their baby would come to know love before she (or he) was even born.

"Tomorrow, Joe's going to bring me to see Rex," Grandma announced now, her voice startling Maddie, who was so tired she'd been eating in silence. "And, by the way," Grandma went on, "I hope you don't mind, but I told Joe about the baby. I thought he should hear it from one of us rather than at the post office or the dump."

Maddie swallowed.

"Did you hear me?" Grandma asked.

"Sorry, Grandma. It was a long day. But, yes, I heard you. You're going to see Rex tomorrow. And Joe knows I'm pregnant. It's fine. I told Rex."

"And?"

Maddie set down her spoon. "And he's elated, Grandma. He really is."

"Good." She twittered a little and grinned a little, as if she was elated, too.

"I'm sure he'll be happy to see you. But can you wait until after lunch? Visiting hours start at eleven. I'll be there by then, but his physical therapy is at eleven thirty and takes an hour. He'll be tired after that, but you won't stay too long and wear him out, will you?"

"I'm ninety years old, Madelyn. I'm not stupid. I never stay long if someone is infirmed."

Maddie closed her eyes. "Sorry, Grandma. I'm afraid this day has done me in. Go whenever it works best for you and for Joe. It'll be fine. Rex will be fine. So will I."

"Apology accepted. But be careful not to take on the personality of your soon-to-be sister-in-law."

It took a few seconds for Maddie to realize Grandma was talking about Taylor. "She won't be my sister-in-law if Rex and I don't get married."

Grandma sat back and folded her hands in her lap. "Rex won't marry you?"

"We won't marry *each other*, Grandma. Not yet. We both have too much on our plates—especially him right now with his recuperation—to make such a major commitment too fast."

"But . . ."

Maddie took a deep breath. "Please, Grandma? We need you to give us some space on this, okay? And some time?"

Grandma sighed. "Oh, you kids. Well, all right. But I always suspected that's what happened to Taylor. Believe it or not, she was a happy little girl, a pretty one, too, with her big mane of red hair. The story goes that her boyfriend died in a boat accident right before she found out she was pregnant with Jonas. That could have been when she got so . . . strange. Standoffish. By now you know how she can be. Years later I wondered if it happened way before that." She shrugged. "Some things I can't remember."

Standoffish felt like the right word for Rex's sister. "If it's any consolation, I think my personality has already been formed, so I don't expect I'll turn into Taylor, whether or not Rex and I get married."

"All I know," Grandma continued, on a roll now, "is at some point, the girl totally changed, which was probably thanks to her mother, who never acted happy. Anyway, they lived on Chappy, so we didn't know each other very well. Except Rex, of course. Once his dad built the cabin—his getaway, he liked to call it, and who could blame him for wanting one?—well, his boy Rex was a fixture at Fuller's ice cream stand, like you were. Hey! Maybe you two met way back then but forgot! Maybe this baby has been karma all along. Oh! We'll have to tell Rafe about that. Speaking of your son, have you told him yet?"

"That I'm pregnant, yes. Like everyone else, he's thrilled.

But did I tell him that Rex and I won't be getting married? No. And you might be surprised, but he didn't ask. His generation knows that people should get married when and if they're ready. But they can't always have babies when they want."

"Times change." Her voice was sad now. "But you'll miss out on the fun I had when your mother was born. Your grandfather and I . . . well, I suppose part of it was because we were young."

Maddie smiled. "Rex and I aren't young, Grandma. We don't need to play house to be happy. And our baby will be fine because so many people are going to love her. Or him." She stood up. "And I'm sorry I haven't been a better dinner companion, but I'm really tired. The stew and the bread were terrific. Thank you. But I have to get some sleep. I'll clean up the kitchen in the morning."

Grandma said not to worry, that she'd clean up. Which indicated that, despite the lack of marriage protocol, she must really be happy. Maybe the baby would trigger some nice memories for her of when Hannah had been born.

After crawling into bed, Maddie quickly fell asleep, and sensed her mother beside her, cheering her on.

"I need to tell you something," Rex said shortly after Maddie arrived the next day. "But first, you need to know I had the strangest dream last night."

"Care to share?"

"Oh, yes. You were in it." He was sitting in a high-back chair, his neck unencumbered as part of the "weaning off" stage. "And though I'd love to tell you the details, you might think my concussion was worse than it appears."

She dragged the visitor's chair closer to him and set it away from the now only IV pole so she could face him. She took his hand. "So tell me! It's not nice to tease a pregnant lady."

"There. You see? I must still be dreaming. In my dream I heard you say you were going to have a baby. *Our* baby. So please, don't pinch me and make me wake up."

One of the many wonderful things about Rex that Maddie loved was how often he made her laugh. How he stripped away her serious side and gave her happiness for no concrete reason.

"I'd bat you over the head with your pillow if you weren't already physically vulnerable," she said.

He smirked, an expression of pure innocence sweeping across his face.

"Stop that," she said. "If you make this pregnant lady laugh too hard she'll have to pee, which is already an issue."

"Oh, great. Now you're going to have mood swings, right?"

"Be grateful. You pretty much missed those. And, anyway, now that you're here I'm too happy to be moody. So please tell me what you need to tell me. As long as it's not that you want to move to California."

"No way. If I never see a palm tree or an orange again it'll be too soon. No. It's something else. Kind of a secret." His voice grew somber, as if he'd shifted from his "fun Rex" persona to his all-business side. He paused another moment, then looked her in the eyes.

"Her name was Raejean," he said.

Maddie's heart flip-flopped a little.

He paused again. "It was back in Boston, when I had my restaurant there. She did the books. All the financials. And we lived together."

He waited for Maddie to digest that, as if she thought he was a man without a past. As if she was naïve and didn't know he was a human over fifty.

"I started to tell you this, when we had our picnic on the beach."

She remembered. Apparently, he was ready to share the rest of the story. She tried not to brace herself, but did so, anyway.

"I remember," she said with a soft smile of support because she sensed she needed to hear this.

"Okay. Here goes." He smiled back at her. "One day, the cops showed up at the restaurant and hung a sign on the front door: CLOSED UNTIL FURTHER NOTICE. I had no idea what was happening. Then they arrested me for a pile of crimes including writing bogus checks, embezzlement, tax evasion, and a few financial things I'd never heard of. It was a Friday. Our busiest night. I figured they'd realize their mistake, and I'd be back in time for the dinner rush."

Maddie was stunned. This was hardly another tale of when he'd been a boy on Chappy and was "arrested" for shooting squirrels.

"I had a great lawyer, a regular at the restaurant," he continued. "He put up bail for me and started digging around. Turned out, Raejean did it. All of it. In the process, she'd set up the books to make it look like I'd done it. Me. Not her." He rubbed his chin. "When I got home, she wasn't there and her stuff was gone. I remember sitting on the couch with no clue what to do. Raejean and I were together seven years. I trusted her, so I stayed out of the financial end of things. Stupid me."

It felt like something from a bad movie. With a lousy plot. And no way for a happy ending. Maddie kept listening.

"I tried calling her a million times. I left messages. Finally, she called me back. I asked her what the hell was going on."

He closed his eyes as if to regain his balance.

"She whined. She said she screwed up but hadn't meant to. She was going to go to the police and tell them everything, but decided not to. She said, 'I'm sorry, Rexy'—she called me that, which I detested—'but I couldn't do it.' I asked her why not. She said, 'Because I'm pregnant, Rexy. I'm going to have our baby.'"

In that moment, everything Maddie had thought was going to be her wonderful new life started to crumble. She'd been wrong to think that Rex was perfect. So wrong to think their relationship could work, that having a baby with him would be an amazing experience based on love and trust. The bottom line was that she didn't know him, after all.

He already has a child.

A small thing he'd failed to mention long before Maddie was pregnant.

She wanted to stand up, excuse herself, and leave the room. She wanted to go outside, climb into Orson, and try and figure out what in God's name she should do.

She got as far as standing up.

"No," he said. "Please don't go."

"I think I know the rest," she said. "You took the blame because you didn't want her to go to prison and have your baby born there."

"My feelings for her were gone. But I wanted the baby to be safe. I should have handled things differently. Instead, I had to be a macho man, a martyr for his kid."

Maddie headed for the door.

"No, don't . . ." was the last thing she heard him say.

Chapter 29

The worst thing for Maddie to handle was that Rex already had a child somewhere in the world. No, she thought, that was not the worst thing. The worst thing was she hadn't known. She wondered how many others did, people who hadn't told her because Rex was an islander, not a washashore like her. He was the one they'd known and loved since he'd been a little boy, Grandma Nancy included.

How many others could have mentioned it but didn't?

She started Orson and backed out of the parking lot without making a single driving error. Perhaps she was too tense about something more important than worrying about which gear she should be in.

Deciding that it was a perfect day to walk on the beach and think, she pulled out onto Beach Road and, instead of going up-island, she turned toward Oak Bluffs. With the sun glinting against the sky, and the air as pure and fresh as spring, she made sure to notice the flowers blooming along the roadside—happy purple crocuses and yellow daffodils that would soon be joined by rich colors of tulips. It was like that in Green Hills, though they would appear later. Nature in the Berkshires had a slower timetable; maybe Maddie did, too. Maybe everything had been happening too soon.

Should she go back to her old life, with a newborn in tow? At least she knew what to expect. She knew the people and the place and what and whom to trust and what and whom not to.

At least the bookshop wasn't open yet, so she'd save public humiliation if she quietly stepped aside. With luck the townspeople could find another tenant, so it wouldn't cost her every dime she had.

Driving past the center of Oak Bluffs, she soon came to the narrow strip of land that stretched between Nantucket Sound and Sengekontacket Pond. After the small Jaws Bridge (named for its edge-of-the-seat role in the 1970s movie), Maddie steered Orson into a parking space and got out. She walked along a sandy path bordered by thickets of beach roses that would unfold their pink and purple fragrant blossoms later in the season.

She reached the beach, where she looked down at the sand, where soft mounds were sculpted not by footprints, but by the morning breeze. She took off her shoes and socks, longing to feel the sand beneath her feet.

Then she moved slowly, her toes combing the myriad shells—quahog, scallops, razor clams. After only a short time, a hint of blue caught Maddie's gaze. Bending down, she scooped up a piece of sea glass, its color powdered by the dust of ocean salt that had taken many seasons in the water to create. It was large, about two inches high, and close to that across its widest part; it tapered to a point, thus shaping a heart. On a day when she thought hers might be breaking, it felt more than coincidental that she'd found it, as if it was waiting for her.

Her eyes teared; she slipped the treasure into her pocket. And that was when she knew what she must do next.

If she returned to Green Hills, she would raise the baby by

herself, and stop being dependent on others—specifically, her father. She'd find a way to get a place of her own with room for the baby and for Rafe when he was around.

If she stayed on the Vineyard, she'd remain with Grandma Nancy and fulfill her unspoken commitment to care for her. If the baby's constant presence would be too chaotic for Grandma, Maddie would reconsider how to rearrange the living quarters.

If Rex wanted to be a real father, that would be up to him.

Most of all, Maddie needed to feel in charge of her life as much as anyone could be. It was something she hadn't considered before coming back to the island. Until then, having been raised in a small, safe town, she'd been protected—overly, she knew—by her father, which was not his fault. After his wife died, his life must have been difficult. But because Maddie had been sheltered, her expectations for her own life had, like Green Hills, been small, with no room for expansion. That needed to change.

She'd start by tossing out her expectations of others—which would free herself and them. She would take care of herself, starting by returning to the hospital and listening to whatever else Rex had to say. Then she'd carve out a future that had room to keep growing and adapting along the way. She and Rex could co-parent. Or not. If nothing else, it would resolve the issue of where they would live.

Reaching into her pocket, rubbing her thumb over the surface of the sea glass made smooth by time and the tides, Maddie knew that love came in many forms, but real love needed an open dialogue. Truth was going to be important for her, for the baby, and for Rex, if he was so inclined. She could only hope that he wouldn't abandon this child, too.

He wasn't in his room.

Maddie glanced at her watch; it was past one o'clock.

Maybe Greg and Rosie were late getting him to PT. She half considered going to the café for lunch, but decided not to. Once Rex returned, she would not stay long. It would only take a few minutes to say she was sorry for walking out, sorry for having taken for granted that this baby would be his first child. She would, however, add that she was sorry he had not told her sooner. Then she'd tell him she could not have him as involved in her pregnancy as she had hoped, at least not now. She'd say, with honesty, that she and the baby would be fine. And then she'd leave.

With those decisions, she sat down to wait, and to hope that she remembered everything she wanted to say.

Ten minutes later the door opened: it wasn't Rex, but a young aide.

"Oh!" The girl stopped as if surprised to see someone. "Sorry. I'm here to . . ."

"Mr. Winsted is in physical therapy," Maddie said with a smile.

The girl grimaced. "I don't think so."

Looking at her watch again, Maddie said, "He should be. Usually, he's there from eleven thirty to twelve thirty, so he must have gone in late. I stepped out for a bit, so I'm not sure when they took him."

Tiny frown lines scattered across the girl's forehead. "No," she said, "they sent me in to get his things. He's been moved to the hospital. To ICU."

Maddie went rigid. "Intensive care?" The baby kicked.

"Yes. Second floor over there, too. But I don't know if he can have visitors."

Maddie bolted to her feet. "What happened? He was fine a little while ago . . ."

The girl's eyebrows went up, then down. "All I know is I have to get his things."

Grabbing her purse, Maddie brushed past the aide, rushed

out the door, and sprinted down the stairs and toward the main hospital in search of the nearest staircase because surely it would be faster than waiting for an elevator.

She found it.

With one hand on her belly, she whispered, "Hold on, okay?" Then she bounded up the steps, two at a time.

The doors into the ICU were shut. Locked.

She bit her lip. Her eyes darted in all directions. Then she spotted a small sign on the wall that read PUSH TO ENTER. Beneath it was a doorbell.

She pushed.

Nothing happened.

She pushed again.

The door opened. A man in blue scrubs and a white coat, his mouth donned with a blue mask, stood in the doorway, blocking her view of what lay within. He asked how he could help.

"Rex Winsted," she cried. "Is he okay? May I see him?"

"He's being treated and is in good hands," the masked man replied.

"Please," she said. "I must see him."

"No disturbances. Doctor's orders."

"But . . ."

"Are you a family member?"

"Yes. Well, I'm his fiancée." She pulled back her cape, her baby bump quite visible.

His brown eyes didn't reveal if he believed her. "Sorry. If you'd like to leave your phone number, we'll contact you when his doctor says you can see him."

"Any idea how long it will be?"

"No. Sorry."

She shoved her hand into her purse and whisked out a piece of paper and a pen. She quickly wrote her name and phone number on it and handed it over.

"I'll wait downstairs in the main entrance until I hear from someone. Please don't let it be too long."

"We'll do our best." He took a step back into the ICU; the door shut behind him and beeped twice, as if it had locked.

Maddie stared at it a moment, foolishly hoping it would open again. When it did not, she decided that she and the baby had had enough exercise for one day. So she walked toward the elevator.

She stepped inside and touched "L" for lobby. After an irritating pause, the door crawled to a close and started its unhurried descent. Maddie hugged her middle, her tears falling faster than the elevator.

Then, when Maddie thought this day couldn't get any more miserable, the elevator stopped, the door opened, and Grandma and Joe stood there.

"What the devil's going on?" Grandma barked, her voice bigger than her frail body.

"They told us he's in ICU?" Joe, the calmer of the half siblings, spoke softly yet with concern.

"Don't bother going up," Maddie said, wiping her tears. "I have no idea what happened, why they moved him so . . . suddenly . . . from Windemere. But they won't let you in. I already tried. We're not family."

"The hell we aren't," Grandma said and marched around Maddie, called for the elevator, and stepped right in. "Are you two coming or not?"

They rode to the second floor in silence.

"I'm Rex Winsted's grandmother, and I demand to know what's going on with my boy," Grandma Nancy snapped at the greeter—the same man who'd turned Maddie away.

The man held up a finger. "Wait here. I'll be right back."

The door shut. Followed by the two beeps.

And the three of them waited.

Maddie's back started to ache from standing on the concrete floor. Or from her sprint up the stairs. She put her hand on her belly again.

"Okay, Madelyn," Grandma said as they stood there, eyes drilled on the door. "Why don't you know what happened? Weren't you with him?"

She flicked her eyes to the floor. "No. They had to get him ready for physical therapy."

Grandma's eyes bored into her, as if she didn't believe her.

"Let her be, Nancy," Joe said. "She's as concerned as we are. Probably more. Don't forget she's pregnant." He looked at Maddie; their gazes met. "By the way, congratulations. I'm happy for everybody, even for me. It will be fun to have a little one around. We haven't had one in the family since . . . you."

Maddie relaxed a little and smiled. "Thanks, Joe. I'm glad you know now."

"Did you tell Rex yet?" Joe asked.

"I did. He's happy about it." Or at least he'd *said* he was happy about it, she thought, but did not add the rest. Instead, she shifted from one foot to the other.

Then the locked door opened again.

Expecting to see the same man in blue scrubs and the mask, Maddie took a step back.

The person standing there was Taylor.

"You must be the fiancée," Taylor said, her words laced with sarcasm. Then she looked at Grandma Nancy. "And you must be the grandmother." She shut her mouth and glared.

The muscles in Maddie's spine tightened; she leaned against the wall.

"You been here all along?" Grandma asked.

"No. But I am listed on my brother's paperwork as his next of kin. Luckily, I was in OB so I got here right away."

"And they know you, right?" Joe asked kindly, because that's how he was.

"As a matter of fact, they do. As you might recall, I'm an EMT."

How could we forget? Maddie wanted to say but "minded" her tongue, as her father liked to remind her when she was a child.

"Is Kevin here, too?" Joe asked nicely. At least one of them was remaining civil.

Taylor shook her head, her long hair swirling like a pinwheel of ginger. "He's working." She did not specify where.

Maddie thought that unlike Rex and her, Taylor and Kevin could be labeled "an unlikely couple." Yet somehow, they seemed bonded. Romance could be bewildering.

"Can you tell us what happened?" Maddie asked quietly, her heart weeping. "And if Rex is okay?"

"He had a blood pressure spike. Two-sixty over one-thirty. Not good. But it's good that he was here. The nurse saw it when checking his vitals before they took him to PT."

"It's serious then," Maddie said.

"You bet. This kind of thing often goes unnoticed. Which is why they call high blood pressure 'the silent killer.' But it's coming down now." Finally, she said something positive.

"Do they know why it happened?" Maddie asked.

Taylor shrugged. "When it happens like this, it's usually due to stress. You saw him this morning, right?"

A saber of guilt sliced through Maddie's heart. "I did."

"Did you upset him? Like did you tell him you're pregnant?"

Grandma went stiff with Taylor's caustic words; of course, she'd had no idea that the woman already knew.

As for Maddie, she wouldn't give Taylor the satisfaction that she might have flustered her.

"I did. And Rex is happy about it."

Taylor pursed her lips. "Okay. Well, if you all will excuse me, I should get back to him." She turned and knocked twice on the door. No doorbell needed. Not for her, the EMT. The next of kin.

"Will you call with any updates?" Maddie asked.

"Sure," she said, unconvincingly.

The door opened. Before entering the unit, Taylor reached into her pocket and turned back to Maddie. "And I guess this is yours," she said, and handed Maddie a piece of paper.

As the door closed behind Taylor, Maddie glanced down at the paper and saw the words: **GET OFF THE ISLAND. AND DON'T COME BACK.** She knew her name and phone number were on the other side, right where she'd hurriedly scrawled them for the ICU attendant.

Later in the evening, Maddie's phone rang. The caller was "Unknown." When Maddie answered, all she heard was breathing.

I never took a likin' to that girl, Taylor. Maybe she'd been sweet and cute with that mop of red hair when she was a kid, but she turned into a nasty adult.

Or maybe she was only that way with me. Maybe I have a way of doing that to people on account of all I went through way back when. Winnie Lathrop once told me I have a way of shutting people out. If that's true, and if Winnie really knew me, she wouldn't need to wonder why. But nobody knows me, not why I feel the way I feel or why I did the things I did.

Nobody knows those things, not even Joe.

I made sure of it.

Besides, doesn't having secrets make me just like other folks?

Chapter 30

May

Maddie spent the next several days drowning her anxiety by organizing the bookshop, worrying about Rex, and once in a while, feeling sorry for herself. She called the ICU every day to see how he was doing, and Kevin filled her in whenever he heard something. Taylor stayed at the hospital the whole time.

Just before the calendar turned to May, Rex was moved to a room in the main hospital until he was stable enough to return to rehab. Maddie breathed more easily. But any hope she had to visit him was quickly squashed.

"Unfortunately, setbacks, even small ones, can interfere with the progress he'd been making, in unrelated ways," Maddie had learned from a doctor—via Taylor, via Kevin.

So Maddie promised Taylor, via Kevin, that she wouldn't try to see Rex unless he asked for her. It was for the best; her guilt was more massive than she could have imagined, and she wouldn't blame him if he never wanted to see her again.

Meanwhile, her second appointment with Dr. Mason went well—the baby was growing nicely, and Maddie continued to be physically healthy. Again, however, she declined to know the baby's sex.

"Maybe next time," she said. She didn't add that it depended on if Rex was still interested.

With the bookshop's interior "paint and polish," as Kevin called it, finished and looking great, the time had come to start setting out the products. She planned to hold off on filling the bookshelves for another week or so when more books arrived; for now, she'd begin with the baskets.

Opening a box of the large- and medium-size baskets that Grandma had made, Maddie was awed by the blend of craftsmanship with simplicity that included decorative accents of hand-tooled dots that outlined the shapes of shells and butterflies. A few had strips of light, creamy ash; others were from hickory, a richer brown with golden hues. The results were breathtaking; that they'd been made by a woman over ninety, with severely arthritic hands, was astounding. Maddie was proud that that woman was her grandmother, her *wutt∞kummissin,* in their Native language.

Next came the two dozen small baskets that Rafe had shipped the week before: Of the same ash and hickory, they weren't as elaborate as Grandma's, but nonetheless were charming and should sell well. Best of all, Grandma had given him an A++ for the quality of his work.

Maddie was trying to determine how to arrange the different basket sizes and styles when the door to the shop opened.

"Sorry," she called, without looking up. "We're not open until Memorial Day weekend."

"I know that." The voice was familiar.

Setting down a basket, Maddie turned, and saw Taylor standing in the doorway.

"Oh," Maddie said, her throat tightening. "Is Rex . . . ?" She didn't know how to finish her sentence.

"He's fine. Got moved back to rehab this morning."

A million drops of relief flooded through Maddie. "That's wonderful." And it was. But then she doubted Taylor had driven all the way up-island to convey the rehab message. She could have called. Or texted. Or asked Kevin to pass it on.

Maddie gathered her wits and her patience as best she could.

Taylor tossed back her mane and spun it into a ponytail, snapping an elastic band around it. "I came to apologize," she said.

If she next said she'd stopped by to say King Charles would be there for the grand opening, Maddie would not have been as surprised. So she simply stood there, staring at Rex's sister.

"I was too harsh on you, for which I'm sorry," the auburn-haired curiosity continued. "But I wasn't ready to lose my brother. I'm not sure I ever will be." She looked at the floor.

"I was about to take a break," Maddie heard herself say. "Join me for tea?" She went to the "Tea and Scones Corner" area of the shop and plugged in the hot pot. "Our kitchen isn't set up yet, and Grandma hasn't yet packaged her teas, so right now we're dependent on the good people at Twinings. Is green tea okay? It's decaf."

"That's fine," Taylor said.

Maddie got to work as a proper hostess; when she turned around again, Taylor was sitting on a folding chair by the window that overlooked the harbor and the deck. She'd opened another chair for Maddie.

Yes, Maddie thought, Taylor, indeed, was a curiosity.

The water bubbled.

Maddie poured, brought the mugs to where they apparently were going to meet, and sat.

"It's nice of you to come," Maddie said, "but there was no need to apologize. Rex's ordeal must be horrible for you, Taylor."

"And a tiny bit for you?" she asked.

Maybe Kevin had slipped a bottle of "be nice to Maddie" pills into his wife's morning coffee. She almost sounded compassionate.

"I can't say it hasn't," Maddie said, "but you . . . you went out to California. And now these past weeks . . ."

Taylor raised her eyes up to the ceiling. "The hardest part was seeing him in the coma." Then Taylor did something completely out of character: She cried.

Maddie wasn't sure if she should acknowledge it or pretend she hadn't noticed.

"I'm sorry," Taylor apologized again, wiping her tears, and then taking a gulp of tea. "I've been kind of crazy lately."

"I know the feeling."

After a pause, she asked, "What about you? Have you been feeling okay? With the baby?"

"I feel great. I want to be on prenatal vitamins for the rest of my life."

Taylor laughed. Out loud. Which was another surprise. "I was sick as a dog with Jonas. Almost every day for nine stupid months."

Then they talked about the mysteries of being "with child," at one point commiserating, even laughing. It didn't seem that Taylor was accustomed to sharing her emotions with a friend; Maddie wasn't sure that the woman had many of those. But then Taylor became serious and shared her story that she'd been pregnant as a teen and had watched the father of her baby drown. He'd been a kid from a wealthy, summer family—her loss was magnified when she told her parents she was pregnant and her father shipped her off to Boston and told her to never return. She studied the floor again, the wavy old boards having been replaced by gleaming new ones.

Maddie didn't need the details to tell she must have suffered.

"Anyway," Taylor added, "I had Jonas and gave him to my boyfriend's parents to raise; I had no choice."

Maddie was appalled.

"I didn't meet my boy until he was out of college, when he came to his grandparents' summer home on Chappy—they'd raised him to think they were his mom and dad. They'd had no idea I was back on the island, taking care of my mother after my father died. The fact that Jonas and I are close today still amazes me."

Maddie had an urge to ask about Rex's child, if she knew how old the child was, or where he or she lived. But she quickly stopped herself. That information had to come from Rex, not his quirky sister.

After saying all she evidently wanted to, Taylor finished her tea and said, "But I've taken too much of your time. I only came to apologize and to ask a favor."

So . . . the woman has an ulterior motive. Which might explain why she'd been so nice. Maddie sat up straight. "Go ahead."

"Can you hold off seeing my brother until tomorrow? Another day will give him time to get resettled. He'll be in rehab at least another couple of weeks, so there'll be plenty of time for you . . ."

"Does he want to see me?"

Taylor nodded. "He's angry with me that I wouldn't let you come even when he was in ICU. I'm sorry for that, too, but it felt like the right decision at the time."

Maddie took solace in that: Rex had wanted to see her all along. "I know how that feels, but thanks for telling me. I'll go see him tomorrow. What's a good time?"

"He'll finish PT around the same time. So, one o'clock?"

"I'll be there."

Taylor nodded, stood up, and walked her mug over to the

sink. "By the way, this place looks great. You'll have a nice little business here."

After Taylor left, Maddie remained bewildered. But she also was grateful that, in spite of her "perils with Owen," as she liked to think of her former marriage, no one had ever tried to take her son from her. Maybe because her father had been there, protecting her.

So if her blowup with Rex had ultimately caused Taylor's transition, maybe a small blessing had come out of it. All she really knew was that instead of continuing to feel sorry for herself, she now felt sorry for Taylor. Because apparently, accidents weren't the only things that could change life in a flash.

That night, Maddie called Rafe.

"Hi, Mom," he said. "Your timing's great. I was looking for a good reason not to study for an economics exam."

"No! Don't tell me things like that. Would you rather I called tomorrow?"

"Nope. I know the stuff anyway."

Of course he did. Rafe was brilliant.

Maddie smiled.

"How's Rex?" he asked.

"Getting better every day." It wasn't a lie. "But I want to talk about you."

"Me? Boring subject, Mom. Worse than economics."

"Okay, then let's talk about graduation. Rex will be in the hospital another couple of weeks, so we'll have to rule him out. But Grandma wants to come. And Joe. Is that okay?"

"Absolutely awesome. My friends will love them, especially since I've spent my whole senior year talking about them. Don't tell Grandma, but I'm going to wear my great-great-grandfather Thurston's arrowhead outside my graduation garb so everyone will see how proud I am of being Wampanoag."

She couldn't speak.

"So will everything else be okay, Mom? Like, will you be okay with Dad?"

"Everything will be fabulous. As for your father, yes, I'll be fine. You haven't told him that I'm pregnant, have you?"

"Nope. My only disappointment is I'll be somewhere offstage when he sees your nice big belly. You do have a big belly now, don't you?"

She looked down. "I do. And it will be even bigger in another couple of weeks. And you're sure you won't be embarrassed?"

"Why would I be embarrassed? I'm not the old lady having a baby."

"Not funny."

He laughed. "I know. Sorry."

"Apology accepted. So you'll make room reservations for us?"

"Already done. I already figured Joe might want to come to help out in case Grandma gets out of hand, so you have three rooms, bought and paid for."

She paused. "By your father?"

"Yep. I figured it's the least he could do, Mom."

He didn't elaborate, and she didn't pry. Her son was an adult now, more than capable of making his own decisions. She supposed she'd need to remind herself of that more than oncc.

Nonetheless, after they said good-bye, Maddie's stomach felt queasy, despite the prenatal vitamins she wanted for the duration of her life. She guessed it was because the next day she'd face Rex, and the list of things she'd planned to say to him were now long gone from her mind. Maybe it would be better if she winged it, anyway.

* * *

Maddie bungled her way through the next morning by killing time weeding out closets and dresser drawers that did not need weeding out. Finally, she put on stretchy pants, a camisole, and a vibrant red tunic—a color that the clerk at The Green Room in Vineyard Haven said complemented the coppery shade of Maddie's skin. One thing was certain: Thanks to the weeks since she had seen him, Rex would be shocked to see how much bigger her belly was.

Once she made it to the hospital and parked Orson, she turned off the ignition and unhooked her seat belt. Then she rubbed her belly to calm the baby, which she hoped would calm her, too. After a few deep, rhythmic breaths, she got out, walked slowly across the asphalt, entered Windemere, and took the stairs up to his room, the same one where he'd been before.

He was awake. And alone.

"Hi," she said, stepping inside. He looked healthier than the last time she'd seen him.

He smiled, and her heart began to melt. "Hi back. I didn't know when, or if, I'd see you again. And, by the way, you look . . . beautiful."

"Rex . . ."

He held up his hand, palm first. "No need to explain. I'm glad you're here. And I'm sorry about the drama of the past few weeks."

Tears sprang to her eyes; her lower lip started to tremble before she could press her teeth down on it. She stepped closer to the bed. "I'm the one who's sorry. I'm the one who did that, who made your blood pressure spike. Which must have been so scary for you. And not that it matters, but it scared me, too."

He shook his head, reached out and took her hand. "Maddie, don't. First of all, it wasn't your fault. I was on a new med that my BP didn't like. It wasn't you. But I'm okay now. Honest."

She wanted to believe him.

"Please," he said. "Sit. We need to talk."

Her belly felt upset again, but she didn't want to rub it because she didn't want him to think there was a problem with the baby.

She began to move the chair next to the bed when she realized the big neck thing was gone. "Where's your neck brace?" she asked.

"Dumpster," he replied.

She smiled and pushed the chair close to the bed.

He took her hand.

Her anguish melted, truly melted, right there on the spot.

"I wasn't finished when you left," he said. "My fault again, not yours. I should have told you what happened from the end to the beginning, not the other way around."

Maddie didn't know what he was trying to say, but wished he'd hurry up.

"Raejean . . ."

Her insides cringed. After all, she already knew that though he hadn't been married, they'd lived together seven years, almost twice as long as she'd lived with Owen. She shifted on the chair.

"Wait. I started that wrong again. I should have said, 'It wasn't until I was in prison that I found out there wasn't, and never had been, a baby.'" He paused, letting that sink in.

It took a minute. Maybe more.

"Raejean was never pregnant. My attorney ran into her a few months after I was arrested, and told me 'in no way' did she look pregnant, when by then she should have been bulging. When he questioned her, she laughed and took off. Bottom line was she didn't want to take the blame for her shenanigans, so she tricked me into it. And then she disappeared."

The only sound in the room was the gentle hum of a couple of machines that Rex was still hooked up to.

"You're serious," Maddie finally said.

"Yup."

"Couldn't you have fought the conviction?"

"My attorney and I talked about it. But I couldn't prove she lied to me—it was a 'he said/she said' kind of thing without a drop of proof. By then I was mentally and physically exhausted, anyway. So I kept my mouth shut and did my time. Which helped me get out in three years instead of five to seven. Unfortunately, I'm still considered an ex-con. I should have told you all this when we first started seeing each other. But things with us happened fast . . . and it's not exactly the kind of thing you want to mention on a first date. Or even on a second. Plus, we always seemed to have people around us. Then I went to California, and . . ."

Maddie's hand felt safe and warm in his, as if it had always belonged there. "It wouldn't have mattered to me, Rex. You had me hooked from the beginning." Saying that made her realize it was true. "I only wish you'd told me sooner. When you finally did, I wondered if there were other things you'd been holding from me. And that maybe I shouldn't have been so quick to trust you after all." There. She'd said everything that mattered the most to her. "On top of that I thought there was a child out there in the world who you had abandoned."

Resting his head back on the pillow, he shut his eyes. "I can't believe I did that to you. I'm so sorry, Maddie." Then he looked at her again. "When Taylor said you'd be here today, I planned a whole speech that went something like, 'If you want to bail on me now, I understand. I'll support the baby, I'll sign my life away to you—and her, or him. But please, let me be in the baby's life.'" He tightened his grip. "Corny, huh?"

And in that moment, Maddie knew she'd never, ever,

want another man but Rex for a life partner, however they wound up figuring that part out.

"I love it when you're corny," she said.

"And I love you that you do. And I promise never to keep a secret from you again. Okay?"

She nodded. "And I'll keep none from you."

"And we won't keep any from our baby."

"Well," she said, "not unless it's for his or her good."

"Her," Rex said. "I really don't care if it's a boy or girl, but for now, let's think of our baby as a her. And that she'll be as sweet and amazing as her mother. And make no doubt about it, she will be my one and only. Unless you think we should have more."

Maddie was about to burst out laughing, when another thought leaped into her mind. "Hey!" She sat up straight, her eyes grew wide. "Do you want to hear her heartbeat? Do you want to see her dancing inside me?"

Rex jerked back a little, which made both of them wince.

"Ouch!" she said.

After a short pause, he grimaced but said, "Are you talking about an ultrasound?"

She grinned and nodded simultaneously. "The doctor asked me, but I said I wanted to wait until the baby's father could be with me. Only if you want, of course."

"Can we do it today? Like *now*?"

Maddie laughed again, which felt so good she hardly heard the knock on the door. Then it opened a few inches.

"Rex? Are you in there?"

It was a man, who sounded casual—more like a friend than a medical professional.

"Yeah? Come on in, whoever you are."

He was a tall man like Rex; he looked sort of familiar in

his blue shirt and navy tie, dark pants, and . . . *Oh, no!* Maddie thought. It was Ken Lawrence, Chilmark's police chief, aka constable.

Chief Lawrence, of course, was only one of four people—including Brandon, Officer Lindstrom, and, naturally, Maddie—who knew about the notes. *Five* people, if Taylor had put two and two together when she'd handed back the note Maddie had given the guy in the ICU. *Six*, including the despicable person responsible for having written them.

Thankfully, the chief was looking at Rex and not at her.

"Hey, man, how're you doing?"

"Geez, Ken, haven't seen you for a while. What's happening?"

"Not as much with me as I guess with you." At that point he looked at Maddie and smiled a pleasant smile, but didn't seem as if he recognized her. "I brought someone to the ER and thought I'd stop in and say hi. And make sure they're treating you right."

"Everyone here's terrific, no complaints," Rex said as he nodded. "It's been a long haul, but I'm through the worst. The best medicine is that I'm home."

Chief Lawrence nodded. "Happy to hear that." Then he turned to Maddie again.

She sucked in her breath.

"And it's good to see you, Maddie. How's the bookstore coming along?"

She nodded, because everyone else had. Then she said, "It's good. Opening in a few weeks."

"No more threatening notes?"

The temperature in the room felt like it plummeted. She was looking at Chief Lawrence, but could feel Rex's eyes suddenly bore into her.

She shook her head. "Nope," she said. "All is well." Even she wouldn't have believed her, thanks to the way her voice was quaking.

After some uncomfortable seconds, Rex broke the proverbial ice and said, "Hey, Ken. Pull up a chair. This sounds like something I should know about."

Chapter 31

The Chief stayed nearly half an hour, until a nurse came in and said it was time for Rex to get up and walk, and that she needed to supervise him doing it. Before Maddie knew it, she was alone in the room, and extremely grateful that Ken hadn't shared details of the notes with Rex.

"We're pretty sure it was just some prank stuff," he'd replied. "Remember what it was like to be bored as a kid in winter?" He no doubt was experienced at reading people's expressions, and the look of horror that must have appeared on Maddie's face must have helped shift the conversation.

She was also grateful for the nurse, because Ken took her interruption as the time to leave; he said good-bye to Maddie and followed the nurse and Rex out into the hall.

As Maddie sat, alone, she craved a glass of chardonnay. A big glass—even though she rarely drank alcohol, and certainly couldn't now, what with the baby. She only wished the topic of the notes hadn't come up right after she'd agreed with Rex that they would not have secrets from each other.

Thankfully, she was saved from her frustration because Francine arrived with three-year-old Reggie in tow.

"Hey," Maddie said, "you're a welcome surprise."

"Where's the patient? Every time I stop by, he's unavailable." She tossed her oversized bag on the floor. "I'm starting to feel like he's avoiding me. I even brought this little guy so Rex could see his namesake."

"Hi, Reggie," Maddie said and rose to greet them.

The "little guy" lowered his head, then bashfully raised his big, dark eyes to Maddie.

"You are the sweetest boy," Maddie said. Reggie was a wonderful reminder of how children can easily direct one's perspective to joy. She touched her belly and smiled.

"He hopes your baby is a boy," Francine said as she took a play mat from her oversized bag, unfolded it, and spread it on the floor, then placed three dinosaur-shaped trucks, a coloring book, and a small container of crayons on top. Reggie sat down on the mat and started to play without being prodded. "He says if Rex has a boy then he'll have someone to play with who won't boss him around the way our Bella does."

Maddie laughed. At least Rafe was old enough to know better than to "boss around" a sibling. *Rafe!* she thought. She'd forgotten to ask Francine about someone to run the bookshop on Rafe's graduation day.

"I need a favor," Maddie said. "I stupidly scheduled the bookshop opening for Memorial Day weekend—and Rafe's graduation is that Sunday. I know you'll be busy with the Inn, but do you know anyone who could fill in for me for the day?"

Francine thought for a moment, then said, "As it happens, I do. How about me? Lucy will be home on the island for the summer, and she's already excited to be back working at the Inn. So she can cover for me there. I can ask Charlie to cover for me at the Lord James, and I'll cover for you. Sound good?"

"Sounds great." Especially when Maddie remembered that "Charlie" was the name of Rex's sous chef.

"But you're going to go only for Sunday?" Francine asked. "Not for the whole weekend?"

"No. We'll leave Saturday after I close the shop, and have enough time to catch the late boat back on Sunday night. A whole weekend there might knock me out, anyway. Especially since my ex will be there. Yuck."

Francine laughed. "So, let's see. By then you'll be, what, more than seven months pregnant? And you don't think that doing a round trip to and from Amherst in twenty-four hours won't do more than knock you out? Have you forgotten how exhausting the last couple of pregnant months can be? Like how every hour seems like a month?"

Maddie slumped in her chair. "Yes, I had forgotten."

"Never mind. I shouldn't have said all that. But yes, I'll be happy to babysit your new shop. And if you need me for Monday, I can arrange that, too."

"You're an angel, Francine. I wish everything wasn't happening at the same time, but once gradation's behind us, my father will be here, too, and he can take over if I fall asleep between the bookshelves the next day."

Smiling as she watched her son line his dinosaur trucks up for a race, Francine said, "You're going to be a busy lady."

"In summer, isn't everybody on this island busy?"

"Good point. The traffic coming through Edgartown is already a nightmare." Francine's comment was benign, but made Maddie think of something—or rather, someone—else.

"Hey," she said, "I have a question about something Rex mentioned."

"Shoot."

"It's about Annie Sutton. Is she going to move back here?"

"Heck, no, she's not moving back. She loves her work, and there's a guy she's been seeing for a while. Phil, his name is. Anyway, no. Why? Does Rex think she is?"

"I don't know. Which was why I was wondering."

Francine narrowed her dark eyes and squinted at Maddie. "Please tell me you don't think there's something between Rex and Annie, because there isn't."

"No?"

"No. She's like a sister to him. Or was, when she lived here. So please. Don't let it cross your mind again."

Maddie smiled. "I won't. And thanks." *The end*, she told her leftover teenage brain.

Then the sound of creaking wheelchair tires announced the arrival of the room's occupant.

"Wow!" Rex exclaimed as he rolled in and spotted Reggie. "My favorite pal is here!"

The boy gave him a toothy grin and held up one of the trucks. "T-Rex," he said. "Like you!"

"That's me, all right. A dinosaur."

The caregiver behind him asked if they'd please leave for a few minutes so she could situate her patient in his bed. "He had quite a workout today."

Francine scooped up Reggie. "We'll be in the waiting room. Let us know when the coast is clear." With that she waved and, toting her son on one of her narrow hips, swept out of the room.

Then Maddie stood up. "Actually, I think I'll take off. Francine has hardly seen you, and, as she reminded me, sometimes pregnant ladies get tired." She leaned down and kissed him. It was wonderful to feel her lips on his again. "I'll see you tomorrow. Kevin or Taylor or both of them will probably be here tonight. Sleep well, and don't let anyone wear you out." She kissed him again and headed for the door.

"Wait," he called after her. "When you come back tomorrow, bring the notes, okay? When Ken followed me out into the hall, he suggested that I take a look."

Maddie was reluctant; Rex needed to get well, not take

on her little drama. But she also knew that, sooner or later, he'd pry them out of her, if only to protect her. Which, she supposed, was a good enough reason.

She smiled. "For now, please, concentrate on getting well. It's almost summer. You don't want Francine to have to be responsible for both the Inn and the Lord James, do you?"

In the morning, Maddie didn't rouse until ten thirty. At first she panicked—she had so much to do. Then she remembered that was a Green Hills attitude. As a pregnant old lady living on the Vineyard, she could allow herself to sleep in if she wanted. So she closed her eyes, slept another half an hour, and didn't make it to the hospital until after one o'clock.

"What took you so long?" Rex joked when she sauntered into the room. "You have more important things to do, like work?"

"No, you incorrigible man. Nothing's more important than seeing you. But I wanted you to rest after PT." He looked good; he had "color in his cheeks," as Grandma would say.

"It's Sunday. No PT today. And I'm greedy because I was without you all damn winter."

She pulled the chair next to the bed. "And I was without you, too. It's a miracle we both survived." She was half joking, half serious. Hopefully, he'd never learn how weirdly she had acted in those first few weeks.

"Which brings me to another topic," he said. "Furniture."

She sat down. "Of course it does. Furniture is so important to life's essentials."

"You're laughing at me!" he teased. "But have you thought about baby furniture yet?"

She paused only a few seconds. "I've thought about lots of baby things." In truth, rather than furniture, she'd thought about clothes and a car seat—which she'd need if she ever got a car—and diapers and a breast pump.

"Like a crib?" he asked. "And a changing table? And a jumpy seat?"

"A jumpy seat?"

"Don't laugh! I only want you to have everything you'll need. And to be sure you know that living on an island means that planning ahead is usually essential. Like now."

"Okay. So, do you have a plan?"

He reached over to the nightstand, pulled out a drawer, and extracted a small notebook. That's when Maddie noticed that his IVs were gone; he must have been taken off the heavy-duty meds.

"Yes, I have a plan. Taylor brought me this. And I have my phone, so I've been surfing the internet—do they still say that?—and making lists. Other than sleeping, eating, and PT, I have little else to do."

She listened patiently as he read the options and the items he preferred and why. Needless to say, she was impressed. Especially because the baby's daddy was taking charge.

"You're amazing," she said when he was done.

"Well, I figured since I'm not the one who'll be doing the 'giving birth' part, I could at least do this. If you don't mind."

"Absolutely, I don't mind. I guess I figured I'd have time after the shop opens."

He shook his head and said, "All you'll need to do is bless my choices and pick out the color."

"Please don't say 'pink or blue.'"

He smiled. "Only if we find out when we can see the ultrasound."

Before Maddie had a chance to answer, a woman dressed in green scrubs came into the room. She was carrying an iPad.

"Mr. Winsted? I'm Dr. Page. I'm a resident working with your doctor. I'd like to go over your discharge papers, okay?"

Rex looked from her over to Maddie, as if she must have known this was going to happen, but she had not.

Dr. Page continued. "Your doctor has agreed to let your sister sign you out. He has, however, noted that because of your occasional bouts of vertigo and the need to continue strengthening your leg muscles, you should be situated on a first floor. He understands you live on a second floor, so he talked with your sister and her husband and they want you to live with them on Chappaquiddick, where she can supervise the balance of your recuperation. You're scheduled for a follow-up appointment a week from Friday. Meanwhile, if you pass your 'final exams,' as we like to call them, we should have you out of here by Wednesday."

Life moved quickly after that.

Before leaving the hospital that day, Maddie stopped at Dr. Mason's office and explained Rex's situation, and that they'd like to have the ultrasound before he was discharged.

But the scheduling department couldn't find an opening until after Memorial Day. "The obstetric sonographer is only on the island Thursdays," a young woman said.

"Oh," Maddie replied. "A nurse can't do it?"

"Only one who's had the proper training."

"After Memorial Day" would, of course, be when Rex was living on Chappy in the house where he'd been born and raised, and when Maddie would—hopefully—be juggling customers at the bookshop.

She made the appointment anyway, and decided to figure out later how they'd get there.

The hours and days started to close in on her as she hurried to put finishing touches on the bookshop while trying not to neglect Rex, which became more challenging after he passed his "final exams," was discharged from Windemere, and went to Chappy.

She waited two whole days before going to see him.

Kevin greeted her and led her to the outside deck where Rex was already ensconced. The house was an old, gray-shingled Cape, which Kevin said he'd "reconstructed" inside. It had a large bedroom on the ground floor and two bedrooms upstairs; though Kevin and Taylor used the large one, they'd moved upstairs for "the duration of our houseguest," he said, then added, "I'm pretending we're on an exotic vacation in somebody else's house."

Then he excused himself and left them to take in the sun that was warm for May. A scent of flowers filled the air; Rex noted that they weren't exactly bougainvillea, but they were nice.

Though Maddie had considered asking Grandma if he could finish his recuperation at the cottage, she knew that Chappy was a better option for him. Taylor would be there, and Kevin could be if she could not, as had happened that day. Also, as an EMT, Taylor would know if Rex got into trouble and she could get him to the hospital much faster, because Chappy was closer to it than Menemsha was. So as badly as Maddie wanted him with her, he was safer there.

Besides, if he'd been at the cottage, he might have found the newest note that had arrived the day he was discharged. She'd shoved it into her purse with the copies of the others, and assured herself she'd deal with it, either by bringing it to Chief Lawrence or ripping the damn things up, every one of them, once and for all.

There was no such drama on Chappy, where they now sat drinking Grandma's lavender-based iced tea concoction that Maddie brought. Though Rex seemed to enjoy it, he said he would have preferred beer.

She shook her head and closed her eyes, luxuriating in the sun, and listening to the melodies of birds who flitted in and out of the beech trees and scrub oaks around the yard. Silence and peace, she knew, would be gone in two weeks when the bookshop opened and Rafe would graduate.

"So," Rex said, stirring her from tranquility. He set down his glass, folded his arms, and looked at her squarely. "Any more threats?"

She wished he hadn't asked; the bigger her belly grew, the harder it had become to dodge his questions. So she simply shook her head and said, "No threats."

It wasn't exactly true. But, unlike the times before, when she'd opened the last envelope that was addressed to Maddie, the sheet of paper inside was blank; not a single word had been printed on it. Then she noticed that something else was in the envelope. Turning it upside down, she shook a small black-and-white photo into her palm. It looked like a yearbook photo. Martha's Vineyard High School. Class of 1972. The picture was of Hannah, Maddie's mother.

On the back someone had printed: SHE WOULD NOT WANT YOU HERE.

Again, ambiguous. Again, unsigned.

Despite the sunshine now, Maddie shivered at the memory, at how the image of her mother had numbed her, as if she'd been injected with a quart of Novocain.

"I still want to see what you have." Rex sounded insistent.

"Later," she said again and looked away.

"Maddie, stop it," he said firmly. "Didn't we agree on no more secrets?"

His rebuke startled her. Did she really want to argue with him over something so trivial?

Trivial? Were the notes really trivial? Or the phone call? Or the stupid vehicle behind her on that foggy, Stephen-King-kind-of-night?

Rex is right, she felt her mother whisper. *Stop it.*

Maddie lowered her head.

"I love you," she said. "And I'm excited about everything ahead of us. The known and the unknown." She patted her belly. "But I expect that down the road we'll both have things we'll need—or want—to do on our own, right? Problems that we might not need to bother each other with?"

He shrugged. "I guess."

She reached over and took his hand. "But if we get stuck, or if we need to talk something out, we'll have each other. But I don't want to drag you into all my bumps and scrapes. We'll both have businesses to run; together we'll have a child to raise. But we'll still be individuals, won't we?"

"Sure. But I have no idea what that has to do with threatening notes."

"They weren't really threats, Rex. They were simple suggestions that maybe I don't belong here. I'm probably not the only washashore who's received them. Or something like them."

He laughed, lifted her hand, and kissed it. "If you want to handle this yourself, Maddie, that's fine. I don't like it, but I won't get in your way. You took it to Ken, so I guess I need to let him do his job."

"Thank you," she said, though she didn't really believe that the subject was closed for him.

"I do have another question, though," he said. "Are you still determined not to marry me?"

Rex was remarkably good at tossing important stuff out of left field.

"I'm not determined about anything. But I want to wait. Let's see how we are as a couple first, so we won't wake up a year or two or ten from now feeling like we rushed into anything because of the baby."

He sighed. "How will I know when you're ready?"

"Oh," she said with a smile, "don't worry. I'll tell you."

"Okay. As the mother of my only child, you're a smart woman. But, once in a while, can I be your knight in shining armor? I am a man, you know."

Maddie rolled her eyes and laughed.

The best part was that Rex laughed, too.

Chapter 32

It was done. The bookshop was ready for business, awaiting the grand opening on Friday—the day after tomorrow. Rafe's graduation would be Sunday—the all-terrain bike Maddie had ordered as his gift arrived that morning. If Maddie had forgotten anything, so be it. She was no longer a student, fearful of being graded as a shopkeeper or as a mom.

After scanning the shop for the one-hundredth time, she was pleased. Rafe had sent the sign—Kevin and Dave had already hung it over the front door, near where Arnie's Bait & Tackle once had been. It looked terrific.

Somehow, everything had found its place and looked inviting, from the merchandise to the layout to the shades of sea glass on the walls, which were warm, not overpowering, enabling the multitude of books to be the stars. And stars they were, with their colorful spines promising entertainment, information, and everything in between. Maddie especially loved the children's section upstairs that included fanciful play mats featuring characters from popular kids' books. She'd gotten the idea when she'd seen the one Francine had for Reggie.

The tiered shelving for "Grandma's Merch," as Rafe had

branded the crafts, filled a corner and looked inviting. Later, tins of Grandma's herbal teas would join them—Rafe was in charge of acquiring the needed permits so they could be sold.

Having given Francine a crash course in checkout procedures the day before, Maddie had also talked with Evelyn, who'd offered to deliver fresh flowers from her gardens every few days—"They'll speak to the beauty of the Vineyard far better than store-bought ones," she said.

So, everything was ready. And Maddie had nothing left to do that day except drive to Chappy to pick up the giant batch of scones that she'd asked Rex to make, because when your baby's father is a chef and master baker, why settle for less? He'd welcomed the task, saying it would help him feel like a real person—instead of a patient—again.

With a last glance around the shop, she went outside and locked up. Then, eager to waddle—which was how she now walked—to the lot where Orson waited, she turned and almost crashed into Chief Lawrence.

"Oh!" she exclaimed. "Hello."

"Sorry," he said. "I'm here unannounced."

"The police don't have to announce themselves. At least, not where I come from." She felt silly for having said that, as if she'd had a slew of encounters with the Green Hills Police instead of none.

"I happened to be in the neighborhood, and decided to stop by and say I'm sorry, but I have nothing to report. Whoever wrote your notes didn't write in cursive—not many people still do that—and it's tough to track someone who's good at printing block letters. And today most people own a Sharpie."

Of course, Chief Lawrence didn't know about the last message on the back of her mother's yearbook photo. Under other circumstances, she might have told him then, but she'd been on her feet too long already that day, and she wanted to get to Chappy and back before the traffic started swelling with tourists who were arriving early.

"The fact that the paper and envelopes are garden-variety probably doesn't help," she suggested, trying to be polite.

"No kidding," he said. "We checked Granite, the Paper Store, and daRosa's—they all have similar types. But I did want to find out if you've had any more, let's call them 'events'? Like when the vehicle followed you? Or the phone call?"

She shook her head. And suddenly she had to pee. Which, unlike threats, could not be ignored.

"Thanks for the update," she said, "but I'm in kind of a hurry. The shop opens on Friday, and I'm crunched for time today."

He tipped his cap. "No problem. Let us know if anything else happens, though. I'd like to say we'll keep digging, but starting this weekend . . ."

"I know. The season starts."

"Right. We have extra hands, but . . ."

"No problem. Oh, and I just remembered something I forgot inside. Happy Memorial Day, and thanks again." With that she gave him a small wave, unlocked the door, and hurried to the restroom before her baby girl or boy caused her to splatter the new floor.

The scones looked fabulous, of course. Rex had made five dozen—a dozen each of cinnamon, cranberry, and poppy seed, and two dozen blueberry, which he said would sell more because he'd spread a light glaze on top. "And who doesn't like sugar?" he added.

Then he packed them up and told Maddie to be on her way, saying he was sorry he couldn't deliver them up-island, but his sister had hidden the car keys.

Maddie kissed him and promised that once Taylor let him return to public places, she'd hand the bookshop over to her father for a day, and they could go to the Cape and buy baby things—and maybe a car for her. She told him to start making a list, the thought of which seemed to make him happy.

On the way back to Menemsha she was grateful to Taylor for keeping Rex from distracting her in these chaotic days. Which was exactly what Joe had been doing with Grandma, though they hadn't needed to exchange any words about it.

Then, also thanks to Joe, who'd included WiFi in Orson's retrofit for a new generation, Maddie's phone rang. She touched a button on the steering wheel and there was Rafe, as if he were sitting next to her on the freshly upholstered bench seat.

"Hi, honey," she said.

"Hey, Mom. Sounds like you're on the road."

"Breaking Orson in for you has been a dream. I'll miss him when I have to drive a brand-new something-or-other. But I don't think I'll opt for a stick shift. It's kind of fun, but annoying to have to keep thinking about."

"Aww . . . sorry. But, hey, wouldn't it be cool if you drove him here for graduation?"

"It would, but, sorry to say, all of us wouldn't fit. Especially because I'm now a blimp."

"Good point. And I really only called to make sure you're still set for Sunday."

"You bet I am. I'll close the shop early on Saturday, and we have reservations on the six-fifteen, so we should be in Amherst by ten o'clock. At least we shouldn't have to deal with much traffic at that time of night."

"But you'll miss the sunset crowd at the beach," he said.

"We'll have lots of sunsets ahead . . . but only one Amherst College, summa cum laude graduation."

He laughed, because Rafe wasn't one to brag.

"Not to change the subject, but I forgot to tell you that our yearbooks arrived. Or, as we've been saying around here, 'the *Olio* hath landed.'"

When Owen first showed Maddie his Amherst yearbook from 2002, the year he'd graduated, he explained that the word *olio* was from the seventeenth-century word that meant "a variety of things." He added that his fellow students said the yearbook was more like a hodgepodge than a variety, designed so they could look back at a blast of memories instead of stuffy formal portraits shot in a studio.

The word *yearbook* sparked another thought. As far as Maddie knew, her mother's was intact, along with other mementoes Hannah had treasured and Grandma had boxed up. Maddie remembered that it had been among the cartons in Grandma's airport storage unit and was in Maddie's bedroom now. Unless someone had sneaked into the cottage, found it, clipped out Hannah's photo, and then trashed the book.

The thought chilled her.

"Mom?" Rafe said. "Did you hear me?"

"Yes. Sorry. I was distracted by a sheep trying to cross the road." It wasn't a total lie; a sheep was peering at her from a pasture, as if searching for a break in traffic. It was, however, surrounded by a fence and a gate that looked like it was locked.

"I'm not going to laugh," Rafe said. "Instead, I'll say good-bye so you can pay attention."

"Good idea." She told him she loved him and that she'd see him Sunday.

It then took every ounce of patience she had bottled up inside her not to stomp on the gas pedal. Fortunately (or not) the swell of summer traffic had begun; more vehicles were on the road now than in January, some of which might be police cars in speed traps. More important, bearing her baby in mind, she did not put Orson to the test.

When she finally reached the little lot behind the cottage, she grabbed the bags of scones, hurried down the slope, and in the back door. Carefully setting the bags on the counter, she took a deep breath, then quickly went into her bedroom, found the carton of her mother's memories, and riffled through them until . . .

She found it: *Martha's Vineyard High School Class of 1972.*

She flipped through the pages until she reached the senior photos: A, B, C. And there was Hannah Clieg, so young and pretty, her black hair thick and shining, her dark eyes sparkling, her whole face smiling, her image at eighteen forever captured in a formal studio photo that was anything but stuffy. Best of all, it was perfectly intact.

But as Maddie started to close the book, a photo on the page below her mother's caught her eye: a blond girl with high cheekbones. She wore a tailored blouse and a single strand of pearls. Under the photo was the name: Evelyn Davis. *Evelyn*, as in Brandon's mother; as in her mother's childhood friend. Who, no doubt, had the same yearbook.

She forced herself to eat Grandma's herb-roasted chicken, not because she didn't like it—typically, it was delicious—but because Maddie had no appetite. However, the baby probably did. So she ate. At least with Grandma chattering about the upcoming trip to graduation, Maddie didn't have to talk. Or try to camouflage the impact of having seen her mother's photo. She only needed to stop thinking about it and erase the possibility now in her mind that, for some unknown reason, Evelyn might have sent the notes.

Dinner took forever to finish.

"When one cooks, the other cleans," was a routine Maddie had learned while living with her father. As she stood at the sink, looking out at dusk, she supposed if she and Rex ever wound up living together, she'd have to resign to a permanent role of washing, rinsing, drying, because she'd never dare cook for him.

Rex.

Why hadn't she shown him the notes? Was she honestly still trying to protect him from getting upset while he was recuperating? But he was doing so much better. In fact, if he could find a way around his sister, he'd surely wrap up in a blanket and hide in Orson's bed in order to be at Rafe's graduation.

After drying the roasting pan, Maddie said sweet dreams to Grandma, who was toddling off to bed, and waited until she heard the bedroom door close. Then she dug the notes—and her phone—out of her purse, sat on the couch, and called Rex.

When he answered, she simply said, "I'm so sorry."

"Oh, good," he said. "I love it when someone other than me thinks they've done something they have to apologize for." He always had a way of calming her, of restoring whatever peace she might have rattled. "So, what brought this on?"

"My mother's picture."

"Okay. Can you begin at the beginning?"

She pulled out all the notes. "The notes. I got another one, which makes five. They're all written in block letters using a felt-tip marker." She read them to him, in the order in which she had received them. She told him when each one had arrived and under which rock. The only time he let out a sigh of frustration was when she added that the first one was left at his cabin, and the second at Grandma's cottage on the day he left for California. "The others came to the cottage, too."

He asked her to read them again. So she did.

Then she told him about the creepy phone call and about the night that he'd come home, how she was at the boat, hoping to see him, but hadn't expected that he'd be in an ambulance, so when he texted her at 3:00 a.m., she'd rushed to the rehab center, but they wouldn't let her in. Then came the part about the vehicle that followed her up State Road, after which she told him about the second, breathing call the night he went into the ICU.

Finally, she told him about the day he'd been discharged, when she received the picture of her mother from the yearbook. She couldn't bring herself to say that Evelyn might be involved.

"Jesus," Rex said when she was done.

"The worst part was I thought someone had come into the cottage, found her yearbook, and cut her picture out. Thankfully, that didn't happen." She would have cried again, but talking to him helped her start to feel better.

"What did Ken say about that one?"

"He doesn't know. It arrived after I'd given him the other notes; you were getting situated at Kevin and Taylor's, and my mind was in a million directions."

"Oh, Maddie," he said softly.

They didn't speak again for half a minute, maybe more.

Then he asked, "What year did your mother graduate?"

"1972." She paused. "Why?"

"I'm wondering if someone in her class has a grudge. Maybe a guy she'd dated and was pissed when your dad came along."

Maddie was stumped. "I have no idea." But she knew it could be possible. "Should I tell Chief Lawrence?"

"Hold off on that. I'd like to see the yearbook first and hunt for a clue or two myself."

"I don't know when I can get it to you, what with the opening . . ."

"No need. There must be one stashed around here somewhere. My father was on the school committee for years; I'm sure there's a bunch of yearbooks stashed somewhere in this house. At least it's a place to start. Maybe I'll find a prom picture of her with our note-writing guy."

She smiled. "Mr. Winsted, I learn something new about you every day."

"I know. I lead a fascinating life, don't I?"

"More than mine!"

"Next thing I'll tell you is that my father was on the school committee because my mother gave music lessons to the kids at school. Did you know that before she married Dad, she played flute at the Metropolitan Opera in New York City? No one ever figured out how he lured her to the Vineyard, though everyone agrees she was not happy here."

She frowned. "You're serious, aren't you?"

"Yes. Believe it or not, sometimes I'm capable of it."

"And sometimes I think I'm going to have my hands full if our baby takes after you."

"You absolutely will. Good thing I'll be looking out for both of you."

"Yup," she replied. "Good thing."

Chapter 33

With less than a day until the opening, Maddie planned a quiet afternoon. Instead of futzing around the shop, tweaking this and that, or driving to Chappy to see Rex again, she decided to rest and store up her energy for the days to come: the grand opening of the bookshop and the whirlwind trip back and forth to Amherst. Sometimes, it was still difficult to believe that the unsettling days of winter were behind her and that only good things lay ahead.

Sitting at a tea table on the back deck of the bookshop, she knew the island was ready. The air felt electrified. Pulsating. Ready for fun. The sun was warmer; the sky, clearer; the water, bluer. The season was poised to begin, waiting only for the starting gate to open.

With a soft smile, Maddie closed her eyes and listened to the gentle splashes as small motor boats were launched, one after another, into the harbor. All week, she'd heard the music of summer preparation and its rituals of energy. Even as she now heard footsteps clomping on the narrow walkway that joined the backs of the shops and boathouses, she wasn't disturbed by it. Until she heard a man's voice.

"Afternoon, Miss Clarke." The tone was gruff, grating, and oddly familiar.

Maddie winced. She opened her eyes to the unwelcome sight of curmudgeonly Bud Erikson.

"Mind if I join you?" he rasped.

More than anything, Maddie wanted to say, "Yes, I mind. Now go away." Instead, as the new shopkeeper on the harbor, she smiled and said, "Please do. Would you like a cup of herb tea? We're not officially open until tomorrow, but I could make one—hot or iced—for you."

He frowned, his thick eyebrows meeting head-on at the bridge of his wide nose. "Not much of a tea man. But thanks for the offer."

How on earth did he have a son as nice as Dave? Shaking off her distaste, Maddie sat up straight and tried to look halfway pleasant. Then she remembered his comment when he'd stopped by the shop before: "I'm still here," the grumpy man had said. The same words that appeared on the second note on New Year's Day.

She folded her hands in her lap and tightened her grip of her fingers.

Bud's eyes were busy scanning the glass doors that served as the rear entrance to the bookshop. "Did my son do a respectable job inside?"

"He sure did."

"He used to be a fisherman like me."

"Yes, you mentioned that before. It's nice that he found something else that he's good at." She couldn't believe how calm and controlled her voice sounded when inside she was quivering.

The man guffawed. "I didn't say he was a good fisherman."

"Well, he's a good painter. And he helps Kevin with other things, which are very much appreciated." For some ridiculous reason she felt she should sing Dave's praises to his father.

"You're the one who cleared the tables at the potluck, right? On Cranberry Day?"

She felt her eyes open wide as she said yes, surprised he'd paid her any notice, what with him having been deep in conversation with a Wampanoag man about Arnie's Bait & Tackle.

"I've been wonderin' something. Did you hear what we were saying about Arnie's? Is that how you wound up with this place?"

Maddie wasn't sure how to respond. "Let's say it gave me the idea." She forced a smile, unsure what he was trying to get at, if anything.

"Well, I'll be." He scratched his bristly chin, then skimmed his gaze across the back of the shop again. "I wish you all the best. God knows you've done wonders with the place. For starters, it smells better now. And though I'm not much of a reader, summer folks will lap it up. Up-islanders will, too."

It was difficult to tell whether he was being nice or wanted something. Not that she cared. She only wanted him to leave.

"Your grandmother's Nancy Clieg, right?"

Has he stopped by just to grill me? And if so, why? Maybe he wanted to make her nervous the day before the shop opened, though why on earth would he do that?

The baby did a somersault inside her. Maddie stiffened.

"Yes," she said, "Nancy's my grandmother. She's made some of her traditional baskets that we're going to sell at the shop."

Like herbal tea and reading, baskets did not appear to interest him.

"So, Hannah was your mother, right? You going to sell any of her paintings?"

Maddie grew cautious. "No," she said.

"Huh," Bud continued, once again scratching at his stubble. "Damn good artist, she was."

"You knew my mother." It came out as a statement, not a question. She started to perspire.

"Sure. Everybody knew everybody back then. I was a couple of years ahead of her in school. A right pretty girl, that Hannah Clieg."

And then things seemed to make sense. The notes. The yearbook. Was Bud Erikson the mystery man who, as Rex suggested, might have had a "thing" for her mother? Had they dated? Had Hannah dumped him for Stephen Clarke, the washashore who'd whisked her off to America? All these years, Bud might have harbored a grudge. Seeing Hannah's daughter might have dredged up his old pain, might have made him want Maddie to *Get off the island. And don't come back.*

"It's you," she said.

He flinched. "Huh?"

"You're the one. It's why you came here today. You sent me the notes. And you cut the picture of my mother out of her high school yearbook." The baby was blessedly still, as if waiting for Maddie to say her piece. "You don't want me here."

Bud harrumphed, the way he had at the potluck. "Lady, I have no idea what you're talking about. I don't do herbal tea or books, and I sure as hell don't write notes to anybody."

"I don't believe you." She reached for her phone to call Chief Lawrence.

Then Bud stood up and adjusted the collar of his flannel shirt that must have seen better days a few decades earlier.

"I'll say it again," he said. "I have no idea what you're talking about. I only stopped by to extend my good wishes to you. And to ask you how it feels to have Rex Winsted as the father of your baby. Seeing as how his father killed your mother. And got away with it."

With that, Bud marched off, disappearing among the other shops along the harbor.

And Maddie's world came crashing down.

Several minutes passed before she could think clearly. When she did, she reasoned that Erikson's announcement was a lie. A twisted fabrication by a man who'd been dumped by his teenage crush.

Unless . . . was he telling the truth?

Even worse . . . did Rex know?

His father killed your mother. And got away with it. Could it be true?

And . . . had Rex known all along? Rex . . . the man who was so intent on them not having secrets?

Surely others would have known. The accident was forty years ago, but, as Maddie was so often reminded, the Vineyard was an island. She doubted that the grapevine was any less effective then, before the internet. Secrets had a way of spilling over and spreading, the way the tidal water seemed to like flooding Five Corners.

Finally she stood up, looked out over the harbor, and held her baby belly while crying silent, aching tears. How could she pretend to live a snow-globe kind of life if her baby's grandfather had killed her grandmother?

It was unimaginable.

Unless it was a lie.

Please, God, let it be a lie.

She had to learn the truth. But she couldn't ask Rex. Not yet. Not until she knew more.

Which meant she'd have to confront the one person who might know more than she'd ever let on to Maddie. After all, Grandma Nancy had been in the cottage, only steps away from where Hannah was killed by the nameless, faceless hit-

and-run driver . . . only steps from where, in just a few hours, Maddie would open her little bookshop.

Or not.

"Who killed my mother?" Too antsy to sit on the sofa, Maddie was standing by the fireplace, leaning against the mantel that held Hannah's painting of Maddie and Grandma walking the beach at sunset, the tiny pottery bowl with the daisy painted by a four-year-old Maddie, and the cracked, ragged quahog shell—one of many that had spilled from Hannah's tin bucket on impact, the lone shell Grandma had salvaged from the street corner on the harbor where her daughter had died.

Grandma sat facing her, staring into the fireplace, her eyes glossy but vacant as she squared her shoulders and postured defiance.

"How would I know? It was a hit-and-run. And why are you asking me this now?"

Maddie's cheeks flared. "Was Rex's father driving the truck? Did he kill her? Has everyone on this bloody island covered up the truth?" She had stopped trembling while she'd racewalked from the bookshop up to the cottage. Even her voice wasn't shaking. It was as if her determination had overridden her emotions.

But Grandma seemed equally determined. Leaping to her feet uncharacteristically fast and, surprisingly, without faltering, she barked, "It was a *tourist*, Maddie. You know that. Whoever it was got on the boat and slithered like a snake back to the mainland, back to who-knows-where. Nobody knew his name. But everyone agreed he must have thought his life was more important than a poor Wampanoag girl's. If you don't believe me, go down to the *Gazette*. It's all there in the newspaper files."

Grandma began to pace on her toothpick legs. "I thought you were a smart woman, Madelyn. But why are you accusing me of knowing something different, like I'm some kind of criminal? I'm an old lady whose daughter was killed decades before her time. Did you for one minute think about how reminding me of the worst night of my life would make me feel? I'm ashamed of you, Madelyn. Your mother would be, too, if she'd lived long enough to see you doing this to me."

Then Grandma stomped off to her bedroom and slammed the door, leaving Maddie standing numb, weighted with unanswered questions and now also with guilt.

And then there was a knock on the back door.

"I know who sent the notes." Rex stood on the steps.

Maddie had moved into the kitchen and stood at the back door, glaring at him.

"Can I come in?" His voice was somber.

"No." It occurred to her that maybe later she'd wonder if the way that they were standing—Rex on the bottom step, Maddie inside and elevated half-a-foot higher so they were nearly eye-to-eye—gave her the courage to feel like she was the one in charge.

He gave her a bewildered frown. "Is something wrong? Are you okay?"

She wondered how he'd gotten up-island. Had he driven for the first time in months for something he could have told her over the phone? Something she'd already figured out? Unless he intended to lie?

She closed the door and flipped the lock. Then she shut her eyes, only one thought swirling in her mind: *Had he known? All this time, had he known?*

He knocked again. "Please, Maddie. I know who sent the notes and why."

"Go away."

She left the kitchen, went back into the living room, sat

on the sofa, and stared at her mother's painting on the mantel, at the small pottery bowl with the daisy Maddie had painted, at the quahog shell, one of the last things Hannah had touched before Rex's father killed her.

She shivered.

And felt sick to her stomach.

Pressing her hands against her belly, she leaned over, stared at the floor.

"My poor baby," she said softly. "I don't know what to do."

Suddenly, fists pounded on the front door. "Maddie! For God's sake, open the damn door. When did your grandmother start locking doors, anyway?"

She wanted to scream. She wanted to shout that he should go back to Chappaquiddick. Or, even better, that he should go to hell. She did not want to see his face. Ever. Again.

Oh, God, she thought, as she started to rock back and forth, *what if my baby is a boy and looks just like him?* She wanted to cry.

Then there was . . . silence.

Maddie retreated to the sofa, where she stayed for a long while. It could have been minutes or hours or days—she'd lost all concept of time. At some point, the baby alerted her that using the bathroom was essential. On the way down the hall, Maddie noticed that Grandma's bedroom door remained closed. She thought she might have heard crying coming from within.

But Maddie kept walking.

Once situated in her bedroom, she wanted to crawl under the comforter and never get up again. Instead, she sat in the rocker by the window and stared out into nothingness. It wasn't long before daylight passed into sunset, and the traditional applause and cheers of happy people rose up from the beach.

The weekend—the season—had begun an evening early. And Maddie knew there was only one thing left for her to do. She pulled out her phone, stared at it a moment, and called the only person she could trust who might know the truth.

"Maddie?" her father asked when he answered. "Is everything okay?" Sounds of highway traffic hummed in the background.

"You're driving," she said.

"I am!" he said with a laugh. "I'm almost to Amherst. Believe it or not, Owen called earlier today and invited me to the parents' brunch tomorrow morning."

Maddie flinched. *Owen? A parents' brunch?*

"Tomorrow's Friday. Graduation isn't until Sunday."

"Right. But some of the parents decided to make a weekend of it, starting with the brunch thing. Rafe told his dad you couldn't make it until Sunday, so Owen invited me. We'll be busy while the graduates are with their friends. We're going to visit the Emily Dickinson house and the college art museum and take a tour of Quabbin Reservoir—Did you know that in 1938 the state flooded four small towns to create the reservoir because Boston was running out of good water? Anyway, I hope you don't mind being left out. I would have checked first, except it was a last-minute thing. But I don't suppose that's why you've called. Tell me. Is something wrong?"

Her body had gone numb again; her father's nattering hadn't helped.

"I'm fine," she said. "So is the baby. But I learned something today . . ." Without warning, she started to cry.

"Maddie?" Stephen asked. "Hold on a second . . ."

She cried and held on.

"Okay," he said a minute later. The traffic sounds were no longer audible. "I pulled into the service plaza. Now tell me what's going on."

She cleared her throat. "I . . . I learned something today . . ." she repeated.

"What?" His voice was a combination of gentle strength and comfort and was coming from the perfect father that she knew.

The only way Maddie could do this was to get the words out fast. So she took a deep breath, then spit out the question: "Did Rex's father kill my mother?" She stared at the wall, waiting for an answer.

"Who the hell told you that?" Strength and comfort gave way to anger.

"An old fisherman."

"What's his name?"

"Bud Erikson."

Stephen paused. "Dave's father."

She cried again. "Yes. What should I do about Rex, Dad?"

"Do you think it's true?"

"I don't know. I thought maybe you did."

"No, honey, I don't. Does Rex know?"

"I haven't asked him."

"Maybe you should start there. It could be a lie. Maybe this Bud character wants to stir up trouble where no trouble is warranted."

Yes, Maddie thought. *Maybe Bud had had a crush on Hannah that he never got over. Or maybe he had a different reason to lie*. Her crying stopped. She started to feel hopeful that this could be cleared up.

"He's a strange man, Dad. I asked if he'd been sending me the notes, but he claimed he didn't know what I was talking about."

Stephen paused. "What notes?"

Maddie gulped. Her father didn't know about them because she hadn't told him. So she gave him a quick rundown and hoped he'd forgive her for not telling him sooner. "I first thought they might be from a woman who was jealous of Rex and me being together. Or someone who didn't want me to open the bookshop. Now I'm not sure. Rex came here to tell me who sent them, but Erikson had just told me about Rex's father, so right now I don't want to talk to Rex, never mind have to look at him."

Stephen paused again, then sighed. "From the small amount of time I've spent with Rex, it's obvious he cares about you a lot. And, like it or not, he is the father of your unborn child." He let that sink in before reiterating, "You need to talk with him, Maddie."

"But how, Dad? Where do I start?"

"You start at the beginning. You start by hanging up the phone and calling him. Before you let more time elapse. It isn't worth putting this stress on yourself or your baby when the story might be a sham."

He was right and she knew it. She also knew she could not do it with a phone call.

Chapter 34

It was fully dark when Maddie left the cottage and started walking up the hill toward where she'd left Orson. The night air was chilly for the end of May; when she'd taken a flashlight out of the hall closet, she should have also grabbed a jacket. But if she turned back to get one now, she might lose her nerve to drive to Chappy; her tunic would have to do. Besides, Orson had that new heater.

So Maddie kept walking, swinging the flashlight from side to side. Which was how, as the lot came into view, she noticed that a pickup was parked next to Orson. It was Rex's.

She stopped. If he was inside, he no doubt had seen the beam from her flashlight. But she couldn't see anyone in there. At least, no one who was moving.

She stepped closer.

Still nothing.

Then, tipping the beam toward the ground, she moved up to the driver's window. And saw Rex's silhouette behind the wheel.

And he wasn't moving.

Either he was asleep . . . or he was . . .

Maddie wouldn't let herself think the next word.

With her heart racing, she held the flashlight just below the window; with her free hand, she tapped twice on the glass. Then three times.

He stirred.

She sighed.

She reached for the handle and whipped the door open.

"What are you doing?" she whispered into the night. "You scared me half to death."

He sat up, his eyes quickly scanning the pickup's interior as if he'd forgotten where he was. And why. Then he looked at Maddie.

"Oh," he said. "Hi." He rubbed his palms over his face.

"Get out," Maddie said. "We need to talk."

"Or you could get in here, where it's more comfortable."

She almost said no to him again. But her dad was right. She needed to hear him out. So she crossed around to the passenger side, climbed in, and closed the door.

"Who sent me the notes?" It seemed a good place to start, seeing as how he'd announced that he'd found the culprit.

Without hesitating, he said, "My sister."

Maddie froze. "Taylor?"

"Yup. The only sister I have."

"Seriously?" Her thoughts flared in what felt like hundreds of directions. "I don't understand."

"She wanted to explain it to you herself, but I thought it would be easier if you heard it from me."

"Are you sure she did it? But why . . . ?"

"It was partly my fault. And Kevin's. She overheard us talking about your idea for the bookshop, and it freaked her out. She decided to try and stop you."

"But why . . . ?" Maddie repeated, but Rex hushed her.

"First, you need to know how I figured it out. I thought about how you said the notes were printed in felt-tip black markers; Taylor uses those to track what she does at the properties she takes care of. And, unless a signature's required, she prints. Block letters. The non-cursive stuff. With that bit of deduction, I looked for my father's yearbooks."

"And you found them," Maddie said. And then she knew he must be right. "And the picture of my mother wasn't there."

"Class of 1972. Yup, Hannah's photo was clipped out."

She closed her eyes, grateful, at least, that the culprit who'd sent her the notes didn't turn out to be anyone else, especially Evelyn, since Stephen now seemed to enjoy the woman's company.

"But Rex," Maddie said, "I don't understand. Taylor was always standoffish with me, but I thought she just didn't like me. Then, when you were at Windemere, she came to see me. She said she wanted to apologize for shutting me out. It was clear she was afraid she might lose you. She even told me Jonas's history. Anyway, I thought she wanted to be friends. But another note came after that. This makes no sense."

He toyed with the steering wheel. "Did you tell your grandmother about Bud?"

Maddie blinked. "I did. She thought I was accusing her of being a conspirator in my mother's death. Then she stormed out of the room and went to bed. It was bizarre."

He nodded and gestured toward the cottage. "Come on. Let's find her. She needs to tell us her side of the story, because it's all connected. But before that, I need to say something important." He shifted on the seat, reached over and lifted her chin. "I love you, Maddie Clarke. And I had absolutely no knowledge of any of this until now. I need you to believe that, if you can."

Grandma was awake and in the kitchen making a grilled cheese sandwich. She probably waited to leave her bedroom until she thought Maddie had left. But she looked at them without surprise.

"I figured that someday you'd find out, Rex. For what it's worth, I never knew your father told your sister."

Maddie struggled not to interrupt.

"Let's sit," Rex said.

They sat at the table. Grandma brought a mug of tea along with her sandwich as if she was ready for a friendly evening chat.

"It was an accident," she began. "It was dark. Back then, the corner by the water was narrower than it is now. And it wasn't well lit. After it happened, Stan wasn't sure if he should cover up the truth or come clean. I was in shock. So I said telling anyone wouldn't bring Hannah back. My family was ruined. But, Rex, if people learned the truth, it would have ruined your family, too."

Maddie watched while Grandma took a bite of the sandwich and chewed.

"Because of your affair," Rex interjected.

Maddie's jaw went slack.

Grandma closed her eyes, then swallowed. "It wasn't an affair. Stan and I looked after one other for many years. And, yes, we loved each other. No offense to your mother, Rex, but she never adapted to life on the island. She was a city girl. If it hadn't been for you and Taylor, she would have left Stan long before my Hannah died."

She looked out the window, almost wistfully, as painful memories no doubt drifted back. "You were only a boy when I first got to know you. My husband had been dead a long time by then, but from the start, you were like the son I never had. You were kind and sweet and a good kid, and you were a whole lot like your father; he and I had already been together half a dozen years. When you got older and started getting into scrapes, I used to wonder if it was because you found out about him and me."

Rex lowered his head and shook it. "Nope. That was just

me, acting out because my mother was . . . distant . . . to Taylor and me." He glanced at Maddie. "I figured that part out when I was in jail and didn't have much else to do."

Maddie reached over, took his hand in hers, and stroked it with her thumb.

"So what happened the night my mother died?" she managed to ask.

Grandma stared at her plate. "Stan thought you and your mother had already headed home to Green Hills—he knew you were supposed to have left that day. He didn't know you'd stayed an extra day so I could take you to the fair. Hannah didn't come with us because she had a headache, but later, when she felt better, she went clamming so she could make chowder. She always liked to make chowder to bring home to Stephen." She paused and pushed the plate away with more than half the sandwich still on it.

Maddie remembered that. At the end of each season, it was her job to set the container that held a pot of chowder with ice packed around it between her feet on the floor of their car and keep it steady all the way home. She closed her eyes for a moment now, then opened them when Grandma continued.

"Stan had been at his cabin," she said. "He decided to surprise me by coming over to spend the night before he went back to Chappy. But when he came around the curve on West Basin Road, well, that's when it happened. He wound up hiding out in Menemsha Hills all night."

She paused and sipped her tea. "He waited in the hills until the next night, then he left his truck there and walked here by way of the beach. I was still in shock. I had a houseful, what with Stephen arriving, the cops coming and going, and what felt like the whole tribe convening here. I went outside to see him; he told me what happened. He said someone had seen him and called the cops . . . but Stan talked with him before the cops arrived. As for his truck, Deke took care of it—it probably wasn't the first time the auto body guy helped out an old chum. So the cops decided a summer visitor had done it. They checked the boat schedules and other stuff, but came up empty. They had nothing to go on."

Rex and Maddie watched her, waiting for more.

Grandma shrugged. "We decided to leave it be. It not only would have hurt too many people to learn the truth, especially if a trial dragged it out with publicity and reporters and everything. 'Fisherman on Martha's Vineyard Kills His Lover's Daughter,' the headlines would have read. What made it worse was that Ted Kennedy was still a senator, and there were rumblings about him running for president, so the press had been bringing up all the Chappaquiddick stuff again. The Vineyard didn't need more bad publicity."

She frowned, then continued. "As for me, well, after Stan told me what happened, I never saw him again. How could I? I still loved him, I always have. But . . ."

She stopped, wiped her eyes, then said, "As time went by, I heard he was drinking and was no good to anyone. But it wasn't my problem or my fault. I'd lost my baby girl. And in a different way I lost my beautiful granddaughter, too. Until last summer when she came back."

The three of them sat quietly.

"Was Bud Erikson the guy who found her?" Maddie asked.

Grandma Nancy sighed heavily. "For years, I didn't know who it was. But right before Stan died, he wrote me a letter saying he didn't have long to live. He wanted me to know that Bud—who wasn't much older than Hannah—had been at the pier working on his dad's fishing boat. He saw Stan driving too fast down West Basin. He heard the crash. He rushed over and saw Stan standing there, crying. That's when Stan asked Bud to call the cops, and to say it was a hit-and-run. Which is what Bud did. He told the cops a woman was lying dead in the road."

Maddie winced.

"Bud's a talker," Rex interrupted. "It's hard to believe he's kept quiet all these years."

"Turns out that to keep his mouth shut, your father gave him a piece of land he owned over in Aquinnah; he did it to keep Bud's mouth shut. Other than Bud, I'm the only one who knew that. The land is near one of the properties Stan gave me, and it's where Bud still lives with Dave and Dave's wife and kids. Stan bought a few parcels back in the sixties when they were cheap. I never sold the ones he gave me. I've said I want to give them back to the tribe because the land was theirs in the first place. But the truth is, I never wanted it in the first place because I hate why he gave them to me—like they were his offering, his amends, for killing my Hannah."

They sat, none of them moving; none of them speaking.

"Even though Taylor told me," Rex said, "I can't believe that my father . . ." He didn't finish his thought.

Then Grandma's voice dropped. "I've been afraid you would find out. I've been afraid I'd lose the both of you, now that you're together."

Maddie glanced at Rex then back to Grandma. "That won't happen, Grandma," she said. "It wasn't your fault."

After a while, Rex made Maddie and him sandwiches, which they ate quietly, drained of energy and emotion. Rex mentioned that his neck was hurting; Maddie didn't want him to travel back to Chappy, especially in pain. So she asked him to stay the night.

As they went to bed, Maddie turned off the nightstand lamp and pulled the covers up to her chin.

"Rex?" she whispered in the darkness.

"Yes?"

"I love you very much. And what's more, I'm ready now."

He didn't need to ask her to elaborate.

At three o'clock the next morning, nestled against the man she loved, Maddie woke up with a cramp. She remembered the feeling. She was in labor.

Maddie knocked on my bedroom door a few minutes ago.

"Grandma?" she whispered. "We're going to the hospital. I think the baby's coming."

I nearly jumped out of my skin.

Then she asked if I wanted to go with them.

I thought about it for half a minute, then declined. I'd have plenty of time to see the baby. This time was for them.

But it was nice to know that, in spite of everything, they still love me. And that they forgave me.

Come to think of it, forgiveness might be one of the most important things in life. I wish I'd learned that sooner.

Epilogue

Liliana Fawn Clarke-Winsted was born at four o'clock Friday afternoon. Maddie and Rex named her Liliana, because they both liked the name, and Fawn—in honor of Maddie's great-grandmother, Spotted Fawn—so their daughter would carry a piece of her Wampanoag heritage with her forever. Mostly, they'd probably call her Lily.

Grandma wasted no time scampering down the hill and hanging a sign on the bookshop door: GRAND OPENING POSTPONED DUE TO BIRTH IN THE FAMILY.

Weighing five pounds, Lily was healthy for a baby who was seven weeks premature, and she was beautiful.

Grandma said she had her Hannah's perfectly shaped nose and mouth.

Stephen said she had Maddie's pretty eyes.

Taylor said she had Rex's mischievous smile and looked a little bit like him, too, except that Lily had beautiful, coppery-burnished skin, and, more important, she had hair.

At one point, when Maddie was alone with Taylor, Taylor thanked her for her forgiveness. She also admitted that her life had been scarred from bearing the guilt that her father killed a woman—a secret she'd never told anyone, not her brother, not her mother. She was not even sure that her father remembered that she knew—the night he told her, Taylor was only ten, and he was quite drunk as he often was in those days; she found him in the backyard, behind the shed, bawling his eyes out like he was a kid. That's when he blubbered out the hideous story, and young Taylor withdrew into a *hush, hush* world.

She also told Maddie that the day she'd gone to the cottage to see her, she'd planned to tell her that she'd sent the notes because she'd been afraid that, with Maddie becoming an island presence, the story would somehow come out, and people would wind up being hurt after all, and angry over all the lies they'd believed.

Once the word spread from up-island to down, questions arose as to whether Grandma, Taylor, and, of course, Bud should be arrested for their parts in the cover-up. But with Grandma nearly ninety-one, and Taylor having been so young when Stan told her the truth, Chief Lawrence suggested that, after forty years, there had been enough suffering and that few islanders, if any, would be inclined to want to see Grandma or Taylor incarcerated. Especially when Taylor admitted she'd become an EMT so she could help islanders in trouble—a small way that she hoped would help make up for what her father had done.

As for Bud, his son revealed that his father was dying. "Stage four melanoma," Dave said, and handed over the medical records that indicated he had only a few months to live. Bud said he told Maddie because he wanted a clear conscience before he died, and it seemed like the time to do it. Chief Lawrence, however, still needed to follow protocol and arrest him. It went without saying that Bud would most likely be released on bail, and probably be dead before his trial.

As for Maddie, she'd known for years that life didn't always go the way you wanted. It was, however, hard to accept that Liliana's arrival time prevented Maddie from going to Rafe's graduation. But, baby or not, Grandma and Joe made the trip off-island, to America.

Unknown to Maddie, Rex had arranged for Maddie to stay at the hospital through Sunday—where the internet was always dependable, unlike up-island. As graduation began, Owen—of all people—FaceTimed Maddie so she did not miss a moment of the Amherst College ceremonies. *Maybe*, she thought as she watched Rafe accept his summa cum laude diploma—his Wampanoag ancestor's wampum arrowhead proudly around his neck—*maybe Owen isn't all bad, after all.*

Then she warned herself to stop being a Pollyanna, that she had a little girl to raise now in a very different world from the one that even Rafe had been born into.

Later that evening, when Maddie and Rex were alone in the maternity room except for Liliana, who was sleeping peacefully in Maddie's arms, Rex handed her an envelope.

"A little thanks for giving me our family," he said.

Inside the envelope was the card she'd seen in his sock drawer: On the front were the stick figures of the boy and the girl, their hearts connected. Inside he had written: *I love you so damn much.*

Maddie was speechless.

"I was going to give you the card at Christmas with your bracelet, but I was afraid you'd think I was moving too fast."

They laughed.

"And there's more," he added as he handed her his phone.

She glanced at it and saw a photo of a room filled with lovely baby furniture. Then she realized the room was her bedroom at the cottage.

"If you hate any of it," Rex said, "I'll send it back. I ordered it all online Friday night; Kevin and Dave went to Hyannis yesterday and picked it up. Oh, yeah, and the dresser has clothes in it for Lily, and there's a stash of diapers and other stuff in the bathroom, because I didn't know where else to tell them to put everything. Taylor helped me figure out what you and Lily would need."

"Stop talking," Maddie said. "And kiss me."

And so he did.

Then he said, "One more thing . . ."

She playfully rolled her eyes.

"Remember the 'investor' I mentioned who was interested in helping out with the bookshop?"

Maddie had no idea what he next had up his sleeve.

"It's time for full disclosure: The investor was me. So now you know I've always got your back, if you turn away from me or not."

So, Maddie thought, Annie Sutton was definitely not on the horizon.

"And can you stand another thing?" he asked.

She laughed again. "Try me."

He reached into the pocket of his jeans and pulled out a small box. "I hope I didn't misread you, but the other night, when you said you were ready . . ." He opened the box, and Maddie simply whispered, "Yes."

In her mother's arms, baby Liliana made tiny little noises that sounded as if she agreed.

Later that night, Maddie suggested that Rex move into Grandma's cottage with them at least for the summer. Lucy was back and could manage the Inn; maybe Francine could run the Lord James until Labor Day. Rex would then have plenty of time to finish recuperating, and, even better, to spend the summer with his new family.

Rex agreed—then he broached an idea for Rafe and Stephen to use his cabin for the season, so they'd all have room to breathe. Come September, they'd figure how to make things work moving forward. Meanwhile, they'd be happy just being happy.

The little family finally left the hospital Monday morning. When they got to the cottage, Grandma and Joe greeted them, having already arrived safely from Amherst along with Rafe and Stephen, who followed them in case Joe missed the exit off the Mass. Pike. To welcome Liliana, the three men and Grandma had hung pink(!) balloons around the doorframes at the cottage and the bookshop.

"We decided everyone should know that my sister is here," Rafe announced.

By then, Maddie figured pretty much every islander knew.

Best of all, when Maddie, Rex, and their beautiful daughter went inside, Grandma presented them with a large parcel wrapped in pink tissue paper.

"For my great-granddaughter," she said, and Maddie was pleased that Grandma had her genealogy right.

Inside the pink paper was a breathtakingly stunning handwoven basket of thick hickory strips—a basket that was big enough to cradle Lily for many months. The thick lining was soft, and the intricate, hand-tooled dots formed outlines of butterflies to which Grandma had added tiny drops of pink and blue and green nontoxic paint.

Maddie cried, her tears of joy feeling nonstop these days.

Stephen and Rafe settled into Rex's cabin; on Tuesday, Stephen opened the bookshop, and Rex and Rafe went over to the Cape and bought a new SUV for Maddie, one with a boatload of safety measures.

Neighbor Lisa offered to help Stephen in the shop on weekends during the summer so Maddie could have a proper maternity leave; Maddie decided that Lisa's jumpers and bandannas would appeal to the laidback summer crowd and provide a nice contrast to Stephen's white shirts, dress pants, and leather slip-ons. In addition, as a native islander, Lisa would be great at conversing with customers and sharing all kinds of Vineyard stories that they'd surely like.

In mid-July, Liliana Fawn was baptized at the beach at sunset, the same beach where her Wampanoag ancestors had fished and swum and gone clamming for more than ten thousand years. Maddie's heart was warmed by the knowledge that her mother had been one of them.

Their growing group of close friends and family had gathered: Stephen and Rafe, of course, and Grandma and Joe; Francine and Jonas; Lisa and her husband, Mickey, and their two young kids; Dave Erikson, his wife, and their four kids. (Dave's father, Bud, had not been invited.) Brandon and Jeremy were there, too, and Evelyn, whom Stephen had picked up and brought (making Maddie wonder if there might be more to their story). Many tribal friends also attended, including Winnie Lathrop, who had fired the small clay pot that still rested on the mantel in the cottage.

Taylor and Kevin were there, honored to be Lily's godparents. They held her now, this precious gift from the Creator, this perfect little girl with her lovely scent of new life and the untold possibilities that lay ahead.

As the ritual progressed, Maddie stood watching, holding hands with Rex, knowing that, no matter what, she had found the place where she belonged, with her sweet, healthy baby, and the man she loved so much.

When the baptism was finished, Taylor and Kevin moved to the side with Lily, and the pastor asked if Grandma Nancy and Stephen Clarke would please step forward. No one but Maddie and Rex—and the pastor—knew what was coming next. After a moment, Maddie moved to Grandma's right side; Rex moved to Stephen's left. As the couple stood side-by-side, Rex took Maddie's hand again.

"Ladies and gentlemen," the pastor began, "as an added bonus, we are also gathered here today in the presence of God and friends and loved ones, to celebrate the marriage of Madelyn Hannah Clarke and Reginald Stanley Winsted . . ."

At that point, Maddie felt her father's eyes on her; she turned and saw his tears form. Next to her, Grandma sniffled. In the background, Lily gurgled.

Then Rex squeezed Maddie's hand, and they looked into each other's eyes and smiled, their joy needing no more words because their hearts were full.

Acknowledgments

When an author is halfway finished with a manuscript and breaks her right arm (and of course is right-handed), the world kind of stops for a while.

There is not enough gratitude to sufficiently thank my amazing family and friends who came in shifts from near and far and cooked and cleaned and shopped and let me sleep and made me laugh when I needed it most. Linda, Jay and Linda, Cindy, Marcia, Steven, Paul, Jim, Mike and Jane, Jaimie . . . you are the very best.

Also, many thanks to my neighbors who got me to appointments and brought my mail and checked on my well-being, and to other treasured friends and readers who sent cards and texts and good wishes and coaxed me back to my desk.

And to my agent, Loretta Fidel; my editor, Wendy McCurdy; and, of course, to my readers, thank you for your patience. The Little Bookshop thanks you, too.